Praise for
# THE BAD LUCK BRIDE

"With its beautifully defined, exceptionally appealing protagonists, intriguing secondary characters, and graceful writing deftly leavened with wry wit, this classic romantic story line becomes something marvelously fresh and new, thus making MacGregor's stellar debut a must-read."
—*Booklist* (starred review)

"An enjoyably complex treat." —*Kirkus Reviews*

"Sparkling. The book's promise of a delicious story is well realized, building anticipation for future installments."
—*Publisher's Weekly*

"MacGregor delivers a well-paced, powerfully plotted debut. MacGregor's characters are carefully drawn, their emotions realistic and their passions palpable. Watch for MacGregor to make her mark on the genre."
—*RT Book Reviews*

"*The Bad Luck Bride* is a deftly woven Regency romance, interspersed with plots and plans and passion. Ms. MacGregor is now at the top of my automatic buy list."
—*Night Owl Reviews* (Top Pick!)

"Readers, rejoice! We have a new writer to celebrate. Janna MacGregor writes with intelligence and heart. Smart, smart romance."
—*New York Times* bestselling author Cathy Maxwell

"Delightful! Janna MacGregor bewitched me with her captivating characters and a romance that sizzles off the page. I'm already a huge fan!"
　　—*New York Times* bestselling author Eloisa James

"*The Bad Luck Bride* is a stroke of good luck for readers—the intricate plot, arresting characters, and rich emotional resonance will leave you swooning."
　　—*New York Times* bestselling author Sabrina Jeffries

"Janna MacGregor's *The Bad Luck Bride* is a seductive tale filled with suspense and unforgettable characters. A must-buy for historical romance readers."
　　—*USA Today* bestselling author Alexandra Hawkins

Praise for
**THE BRIDE WHO GOT LUCKY**

"MacGregor once again demonstrates her remarkable gift for effortlessly elegant writing, richly nuanced characterization, and lushly sensual love scenes in the second brilliant installment in her new Cavensham Heiresses series, following *The Bad Luck Bride*."
　　—*Booklist* (Starred Review)

"MacGregor has a real talent for developing every facet of a romance."　　—*Kirkus Reviews*

"A heady mix of action, wit, and sexual tension. Readers will eagerly turn the pages to see how this intense story concludes."　　—*Publishers Weekly*

"MacGregor is well on her way to becoming a fan favorite."　　—*RT Book Reviews*

"Deliciously provocative in historical detail . . . there is everything in this novel and more. This is definitely a keeper! *The Bride Who Got Lucky* is absolutely brilliant!"
—*Romance Junkies (5 stars)*

"This book is truly enchanting."
—*Bookriot*

**Also By Janna MacGregor**

THE BAD LUCK BRIDE
THE BRIDE WHO GOT LUCKY

# *The* LUCK OF THE *B*RIDE

## JANNA MACGREGOR

St. Martin's Paperbacks

THE LUCK OF THE BRIDE

Copyright © 2018 by JLWR, LLC.

All rights reserved.

For information address St. Martin's Press, 175 Fifth Avenue, New York, NY 10010.

ISBN: 9781250116161

Our books may be purchased in bulk for promotional, educational, or business use. Please contact your local bookseller or the Macmillan Corporate and Premium Sales Department at 1-800-221-7945, ext. 5442, or by e-mail at MacmillanSpecialMarkets@macmillan.com.

Printed in the United States of America

St. Martin's Paperbacks edition /May 2018

St. Martin's Paperbacks are published by St. Martin's Press, 175 Fifth Avenue, New York, NY 10010.

10  9  8  7  6  5  4  3  2  1

*To my darling Rachel*

# Acknowledgments

❦

As always, my editor, Holly Ingraham, has my eternal gratitude. Thank you for your talent, insight, and direction. You always have the best suggestions. Jennie Conway, Marissa Sangiacomo, and Meghan Harrington— you all are priceless. Thank you to Lesley Worrell, Jon Paul, and the fantastic art department at St. Martin's Press. My covers are simply divine. To everyone at SMP who had a hand in March and McCalpin's story, I'm so grateful for your support.

Pam Ahearn, I'm simply in awe of you. Thank you for everything. Kim Rozzell, you make everything so easy for me.

Corinne DeMaagd, Charlotte Russell, and Christy Carlyle—your friendship is truly a gift.

Greg, thank you for putting up with me when I hole away for hours to write. You are my dream.

Finally, the most important thank you goes to you, my readers. You mean the world to me.

# Prologue

*Leyton, just outside of London, 1805*
*Lawson Court*

Accustomed to the hustle and bustle of a busy household, March Lawson sat completely numb while the longcase clock marked the passage of time second by *everlasting* second. The rhythmic movement of the pendulum failed to interrupt the stony silence that entombed her in the study, her father's domain. Since they'd returned, she spent most of her time here as the familiar smells of leather and ink provided some comfort with sweet memories of her father. His journal lay open on the desk as if waiting for him to return and finish the estate bookkeeping.

One week shy of her seventeenth birthday, March had calculated she'd spent two hundred and three months on this earth. One out of two hundred and three wouldn't normally garner much attention, but that infinitesimal fraction of time had allowed chaos to steal everything.

Dark misery pounded through her with the strength of a rough surf in a gale storm. She and her three siblings had only been gone a month, twenty-seven days to be exact. Now, she was the head of her family, one that consisted of a one-year-old baby brother and two sisters, ages eleven and ten. Under siege by a grappling confusion, her mind reeled. Her siblings hadn't a clue the devastation that had awaited them on their return from Brighton.

She didn't possess such luck. She'd known for the last two weeks. A letter had arrived by special courier to inform her and Hart Pennington, the family's escort, that her parents had succumbed to influenza. Wise or not, she'd waited until the return trip to share the tragic news.

Thank God she'd had Hart or she would not have survived the journey home. Kind and gentle, he'd taken great care to distract her siblings during the carriage ride so March could consider their future and her new duties as head of the family.

Thirty years older than March, Hart Pennington had been in her father's employment for over ten years serving as personal assistant and secretary. He was the one her father had chosen to rush them out of Leyton to avoid the influenza outbreak. When it was safe to return to Lawson Court, Hart had escorted them to their parents' graves and gave comfort as the place markers were set into the ground. From that day forward, he was Uncle Hart and as much a part of their family as she was. Unfortunately, he wasn't currently there to help, as a close friend had needed him to visit.

It made little difference whether Hart was there or not—this was her responsibility.

The house had grown eerily quiet. The pendulum of the longcase clock had suddenly stopped as if afraid any noise or movement would draw the attention of Death back to their doorstep.

*The rotter.*

The great thief had stolen the most vibrant and vivacious individuals of their small community into its cold embrace—including her parents. When her mother had fallen violently ill, her father had sent March and her siblings away in hopes they'd escape the illness while he stayed to nurse his wife. After two days, her mother had died. Her father had lasted less than a week. Knowing the love her father had for her mother, March doubted he expired from the assault of the disease's high fever.

He'd died of a broken heart.

"March?" A small voice cracked, exposing the inability to withstand any more tears. Juggling their brother Bennett in her small arms, ten-year-old Julia struggled with the weight of the healthy baby as she closed the distance to stand by March's side.

She pasted on the best smile she could muster. Once again, her youngest sister needed comfort. "What is it, my love?"

"Who will take care of us now?" Like the gentle beating of an angel's wings, her sister's whispered words floated like wisps of air toward her.

"I will." March leaned forward and brushed her forefinger against Julia's pink cheeks.

"What about Faith?" Julia's thin voice grew ragged as if ready to burst into hysterics again. "Where is she?"

Julia, her youngest sister, had been practically inconsolable when she'd discovered their parents were gone and the secure home they'd all taken for granted had changed forever. Since then, Julia needed an immediate accounting if she couldn't find her siblings.

"Faith went to bed early," March answered. "She's exhausted."

"Who's going to take care of Faith?"

"Sweetheart, we've discussed this." March had tried her best to reassure her sister over the last two days, bestowing all the extra attention she could to alleviate Julia's haunting fears. She'd spent hours holding Julia as her sweet innocence had been destroyed by each tear that stained her cheeks. No matter what comfort she offered her sister, it didn't seem to help. In the lonely hours of the night, Julia nightmares tore open every one of March's newly closed wounds of worry.

Her sister had every right to be terrified.

*She* was terrified. She swallowed, hoping it would hide her own fear and weepiness. Otherwise, Julia's despair would erupt again.

Out of nowhere, Bennett whimpered, a sure sign he was miserable in Julia's arms. Attempting to quiet his fussiness, the tiny girl bounced him up and down. The erratic motion infuriated the infant, and he let loose a bloodcurdling scream of outrage sure to make a banshee grimace.

"I just changed him, so he's not wet." Julia carefully passed the baby to March. "I suppose he's hungry."

March held the bundle close to her chest and walked a narrow path to and fro, all the while patting his back.

"March?" Julia whispered. "Who'll take care of him?"

"I will." The incessant use of her name grated her already thin hold on sanity, but her sister must feel the need to repeat it—over and over—as if it were a sacred prayer and would keep her safe.

Julia nodded just as though she understood a great maxim. "He's your baby now, and you're his mother."

The innocent declaration tore the remaining shreds of March's world asunder with the truth she couldn't deny. This was her new life. She'd never escape this massive responsibility, not until her brother grew old enough to manage Lawson Court.

March took a deep breath to calm the anxiety that had

wrapped itself tight around her heart. There was no earthly way she could manage the estate on her own. She'd already written her father's London solicitor asking for help. Her father had established trusts and guardianships for all of them in the remote chance something like this would happen. Lord Burns, a friend of her late grandfather, would be appointed guardian for the family and the estate with the added responsibility of trustee for the Lawson children's personal trusts.

To survive her own grief, March clung to the belief Lord Burns would act quickly, and all would be well.

Julia's lips began to quiver. "M-March, I'm scared."

"I know, Jules." She nodded as tears burned her eyes. "Me, too. Nevertheless, we're still a family. Whatever I have to do, we'll stay together. I promise."

"I believe you." Her sister turned to leave, then pivoted on one small foot. "I'm sorry you don't get to dance."

"What?" Still pacing while comforting the infant with rhythmic pats, March allowed her full attention to fall on her sister. Over the last two days, her sister's fitful musings ran the gamut from disabling grief to unhealthy giddiness. This sudden change was yet another example. Such extremes made it difficult for March to understand the little girl's mood.

"Your spring." Julia's brow bunched into neat lines.

"My spring? I don't understand."

"Like summer, winter, and autumn." The little girl wiped her nose on her sleeve, the remnants of her latest tears. "Momma told me all about it."

*The upcoming Season.* "You mean my introduction into society?"

Her little sister nodded. "I'm sorry you won't get to wear your pretty gown and slippers. Momma showed them to me the last time we were in London. The embroidered stockings were soft. They reminded me of our lambs' wool."

"Don't worry about that. There are other things much more important." She gently tapped Julia on her button nose while keeping the baby tucked close. "Like you."

"If I get a spring, March, I'm giving it to you," Julia declared.

"Thank you, Jules. That's very generous." Her sister was a dear—a very small and very scared dear soul.

March's life had taken a different route, one she had no clue how to navigate or where to turn. Selfishly, she couldn't deny her disappointment. She'd looked forward to the upcoming Season.

Over the last year, she'd dreamed about meeting other young women and men who would become her lifelong friends as they started their path to adulthood together. With her mother's guidance, she would have learned how to become a proper young lady and a productive member of society. More importantly, she'd find a husband, one who would cherish and protect her just like her father had done for her mother.

A cold knot twisted in her stomach. What if she never married or found the happiness she had always considered her due?

She shook her head. She was worrying for nothing. Once Lord Burns contacted her, life would resume to a new normal. He'd come and see to their needs. He'd help replace the household staff who either had succumbed to the influenza or had quit after her parents' death. Only Mrs. Oliver, the housekeeper, remained, and she was still recovering from her bout with the disease.

March would have her Season next year.

Such a thought didn't bring much comfort. There was no use denying what she really wanted was for her parents to walk through the door and end their ordeal. Her mother would comfort the baby, and her father would lift Julia in the air and make her laugh. Faith would join them with her ever-present book in hand. They'd all be a happy family once again. If there were a merciful God, he would find a way to turn back the clock two months.

She prayed for something that was inconceivable, and her heart shifted inside her chest in a poor attempt to escape the despair.

"So, you won't leave us?" Julia's reedy voice thinned and broke March's reverie.

"No, sweets. I'm where I want to be. I want you to be here, too."

"March?" Fear, stark and vivid, glittered in Julia's beautiful doe eyes.

The uncertainty in her sister's voice impaled her, and she feared her chest would split wide open.

"Who'll take care of *you*?" Julia whispered. Her sister had asked these same questions every day, and the answer to this one was always the same.

*No one.*

She bit her lower lip hard enough to draw blood. Bitterness was a useless emotion. The quicker she accepted the circumstances, the less misery she'd face. "Papa has provided for us. We'll all take care of each other. That's the way it should be."

The baby bawled at the top of his lungs. Tears welled in her eyes once more. So lost in her own grief, she'd forgotten to go to the village today for supplies. What a wretched mess.

Her brother's cries turned into heart-stopping screams. They had no food in the house, but at least there was a little milk. It was past ten o'clock at night, much too late to go to the village for supplies. Tomorrow, she'd replenish the pantry. Within a week, she'd hear from the solicitor. All would be well.

"Sweetheart, would you heat the rest of the milk for your brother?"

Julia dipped her head, but it didn't hide the tremble of her lips. "I'm sorry, March. Please don't be angry. I drank the last of it."

The baby's breath hitched as he struggled for enough air to scream again. A panic, one she'd fought every waking hour since her return to Lawson Court, welled within her. She gasped in a desperate attempt for control.

"March, I—I'm sorry. I was hungry." Julia's tears started to race down her reddened cheeks. "Are you going to leave me, too?"

# Chapter One

*Eighty years later*

"M iss Lawson, you're relieved of your duties as housekeeper." The viscount squinted and lifted his chin. The attempt resembled the sour face he always made when he drank an unsweetened glass of lemonade. "Immediately."

*This was simply rich.* March summoned thoughts of dirty laundry to keep the hilarity of his pronouncement from overtaking her in a bout of laughter. If only his words were true, she might get a much-needed rest. An image loomed before her of lazing in bed with a tower of the latest gothic novels on the nightstand, but she pushed it aside. There was no use to wish for things that won't happen.

Her responsibilities were endless today. This morning, she'd already taken inventory of the pantry, planned the meals for the week, paid the butcher, and balanced the weekly housekeeping ledger. She still had to assess the damage from the newest leak in the roof. Where those funds would come from was anyone's guess.

The viscount steepled his fingers on the desk, then

regarded her with an attempt to lift one haughty eyebrow skyward. The effort failed miserably when both
eyebrows shot up and delivered what could only be described as a look of surprise.

March pretended to cough. Otherwise, a bubble of
laughter would burst from her chest. The viscount could
always lighten the moment. She leaned back in her chair
and decided to enjoy the interview as best she could since
the afternoon promised to be even more hectic than the
morning. She had to go through the attic and sort through
the old clothes. The dressmaker planned to stop by tomorrow to determine if any of the gowns were fit for altera-
tion. Since Parliament had convened early this year, the
start of the London Season was only several weeks
away. She needed to see Mr. Willingham about a delivery of wood and coal. They'd already run through the
budgeted allotment for the next six months.

"My lord, I can leave at the end of the week, but I expect my full weekly pay and fare for transportation back
to London." Her even, dulcet tone was quite remarkable
considering he was discharging her from her duties.
"May I ask the reason for my dismissal?"

With a tug of his neckcloth, the viscount met her gaze.
The shock on his face better resembled a wide-eyed trout
flapping on a riverbank seeking an escape back into the
water. He schooled his expression quickly, but an odd
hint of something, perhaps disappointment, replaced his
look of surprise.

"Very well. You're entitled to an explanation." When
he swallowed his discomfort, the tiniest hint of an Adam's apple bobbed up and down. "I've repeatedly asked
that the weekly menu not include ham and beans."

"My dismissal is over ham and beans?" March almost
choked on the words. She bit her tongue in order to keep

from guffawing. Her effort to hide her humor failed miserably. Stains of scarlet mottled the viscount's face.

"Last night made the third time this month it's been the main course for dinner. I despise the lumps and the congealed mess. Why isn't there any sweets on the menu, I ask you? Your replacement, Miss Faith, has agreed to take your position with the assurance I'll have more desserts. You may finish the week as you train her."

March let out a sigh. Her heart squeezed at the pain of her failure. "Bennett, first, it's 'why *aren't* there any sweets on the menu' instead of 'isn't.' Second, this is the best I can manage under the circumstances. Third, picking Faith as my replacement? What about her—"

"Her injured leg has no impact on her ability to do the work. You've repeatedly told us that she's capable of anything and can do what she wants," her nine-year-old brother challenged. The young viscount drew a deep breath and blew his unruly black locks out of his face. The startling green of his eyes was a welcome sight. His face appeared to change daily with hints of the man he would become. Every day he favored their father more and more.

"Sweetheart, that's very kind of you to say. I'm sure if Faith heard it, she'd be pleased, too. However, dearest, please don't kick the desk. It'll mark the wood," March gently chided.

With a huff of disgruntlement, Bennett turned and stared out the window. It had to be difficult growing up as the only brother to three older sisters. He had no older male to emulate or teach him how to be a proper young lord, much less what his responsibilities would entail when he reached adulthood. He needed a proper tutor, and an education befitting a viscount.

"I'll try my best to serve more sweets. That's all I can promise." She'd bruised his pride. It wasn't the first time and wouldn't be the last. Not that she wanted to, but they had to face realities in the viscount's household. There weren't any extra funds for sweets.

Abruptly, he faced her, and his voice held a rasp of challenge. "March, how many times must I ask? Please address me as 'my lord' when I'm in my study. Besides, it's my desk, and if I want to kick it, I will." Suddenly, a charming lopsided grin broke across his young face. "Are you willing to change the menu? You really will try to have more sweets?"

"I'll see what I can do, but no promises." The eagerness in her brother's face provided another reason to fix what was wrong with their household. She desperately wanted to grant his wishes, but the steady gnaw of guilt weakened whatever resolve she called forth. She would have to do the unthinkable again if they were to survive the next couple of weeks and make it to London.

For over the past year, their family had struggled financially without any household or estate allowance. The year before, the amounts were so minuscule, they would not have purchased enough grain and hay for the two horses they owned. Lord Burns never answered her letters or explained why he cut off the estate's allowance.

Thankfully, she had prepared for a rainy day and set aside funds in case of emergency. The roof repair last autumn had consumed most of the money—and it still leaked. To say their life was a soggy state of affairs was an understatement. There was never enough. Now, she was down to their last five pounds. Their tight-fisted guardian, Lord Burns, had disappeared without a word where to reach him. That had been over a year ago. There'd been no explanation from anyone that he'd died.

To make matters worse, her father's solicitor had retired with no one to take his place. There was no replacement guardian. However, there was a successor trustee, who managed the money set aside for the Lawson sisters.

March had been the one to contact the Marquess of McCalpin, the successor trustee. He'd sent a lovely letter of introduction and had informed her that his personal solicitor would lend assistance in his successor trustee responsibilities. That had been over two months ago. To date, neither the marquess nor his solicitors had deemed her requests for money worthy of much attention.

She'd been horrified to discover the marquess was the brother of her banker, Lady Emma Somerton, who was a dear friend.

Tired of scrimping and saving, March wanted her money, the funds her parents had set aside for her wellbeing. Desperate times called for desperate action. Somehow, she'd find the money they needed.

"Lord Lawson, I'll try my best."

After everyone had retired, March sat at her brother's desk and smoothed the expensive sheet of vellum for the fifth time, the movement a nervous habit. With a slight hand, she dipped the quill in the inkwell. The simple movement caused a tremor to run through her limbs, and the effect was severe enough she had to replace the writing instrument in its stand. She leaned back in the chair.

The effort to write the money request caused her stomach to roil in defiance. This was what she'd become over the last several months—a forger, an embezzler, a thief, and a liar of the worse sort. Her family and Hart had no idea she was stealing. She swallowed her apprehension and picked up the quill again.

Circumstances required bold moves. If she must suffer remorse, let it be for something big. She was tired of

shuffling and scurrying around the bills that demanded
her attention daily. She had little choice if she wanted to
stop her siblings' hellish existence.

There was no advantage to waiting. Once the letter
was finished, the funds would become available within
five days. Over the last several weeks, she had mastered
the simple process. With a deft hand, she would sign the
directive as the Marquess of McCalpin.

Not once had anyone questioned the marquess's signature, or more accurately, *her* signature. The marquess's
solicitor had completely ignored her previous letters
seeking additional funds and help, which obviously
meant the marquess didn't care what she did.

With the marquess's signature, the funds would be deposited in her account at E. Cavensham Commerce. The
bank was the creation of the Countess of Somerton, the
marquess's sister. The institution, a bank for women by
women, was a wildly successful enterprise in operation
for less than year. Lady Somerton had personally sent
March an invitation to bank with her. For March, it had
been a godsend. She had little funds invested there, but
used the institution for small loans when the need arose.

The stopgap measure had ceased to meet her family's
needs over the last several months when their remaining
tenant had suffered devastating damages during a horrid
winter storm. March had nothing else for collateral to
offer E. Cavensham Commerce. The only real valuables
she owned outright were a pair of her late mother's earrings, and they currently resided in Lady Somerton's
bank vault. How ironic that March's most trusted financial advisor was the sister of a man who apparently didn't
have time for her family.

If she lost the tenant, the entire estate would be in
bankruptcy by year's end. Forced to take greater action,

March did the unimaginable. Her family's position of weakness had left her no choice but to embezzle from her own dowry, aka her trust fund.

Like an imaginary box full of pencils, her trust was full, but instead of pencils, it contained money. Until the marquess signed it over to her, the money belonged to the trust or the pencil box as she liked to think about it. Though it was for her benefit, only the marquess had the power to release money to see to her needs.

The marquess had ignored her polite but insistent request for the release of funds. Her money still sat in that *pencil box*.

She and her two sisters each had a twenty-five-thousand-pound trust, a handsome amount specifically intended for their dowries. However, once a sister married, or as in March's case, once a sister reached the age of twenty-five, the trust would cease with the monies distributed to either the sister's husband upon marriage or the unmarried sister at the age of twenty-five.

March straightened in her chair and cleared her throat. She had no other options if she wanted to protect her family. Her trust should have ended with the money under her authority. She should be able to spend the funds on anything including sweets for her little brother without anyone else's approval.

The crucial time had come to take her sisters and brother to London. The need had turned dire when their only cousin from their father's side, Rupert Lawson, had started to drop in unannounced. His sly purpose was to pursue Julia's hand in marriage.

Though he spouted how advantageous such a union would be for Julia and the rest of the family, March knew the truth. He only wanted Julia as a way to gain control of their fortunes.

    March's embezzling proved she would do anything to
keep Julia, Faith, and Bennett safe from their cousin.
They were too vulnerable at Lawson Court. A move to
London was their safest option.

    To afford the move, March had to take money from
her account. Ever pragmatic, she had kept the marquess's
single letter stating that he'd prefer if she directed all requests to his personal solicitor. She'd followed the marquess's directions. However, when little resulted from her
requests for money, she took matters into her own hands.
It had been relatively simple to write the withdrawals and
sign the marquess's name.

    So far, no one had noticed the withdrawals. If by her
actions, she faced charges for embezzlement, her only
hope was that the magistrate would understand her quandary. The funds were rightfully hers and her withdrawals had been relatively minor until now.

    The quill scratched noisily against the paper. When
she considered the requested amount, she lifted the writing tip from the vellum. As the local vicar, Mr. Nivan,
had proclaimed from the pulpit last Sunday, whether you
steal an apple to satisfy your hunger or a diamond necklace you covet makes little difference. In God's eyes, it's
the same sin with the same result, a fiery banishment to
Hell.

    With a bold flourish, she finished the amount of one
thousand pounds and signed the missive. If it made little
difference whether it was a penny or a pound, she might
as well make the trip to Hell worth her while. She folded
the letter and lit the candle. Carefully, she melted the wax
over the letter, then set the marquess's seal, the one she'd
secretly commissioned a retired engraver to make. The
engraver, a longtime family friend, had insisted he not
take any payment for his deed.

She dismissed her remaining disquiet. Tomorrow, the Marquess of McCalpin would direct a deposit of one thousand pounds from Miss March Lawson's trust into her account at E. Cavensham Commerce for immediate withdrawal.

The fireplace suddenly hissed and snapped with a new vigor. She sat back in Bennett's chair and stared at the theatrics offered by the flames. Lucifer must be personally preparing the fires for her arrival.

She summoned the energy and stood. It was time to go to the kitchen and prepare the old slipper tub. With everyone asleep, the kitchen offered her privacy for a long soak. She needed it tonight.

Every time she wrote one of those letters, her actions dirtied every inch of her soul.

Even if she bathed until morning, she'd never feel clean again.

# Chapter Two

❧

McCalpin House
London

A dozen penguins, perhaps two dozen, stood as Michael Cavensham, the Marquess of McCalpin and the heir to the Duke of Langham, entered. The supposedly docile creatures possessed an aggressive bite. The ones in front of McCalpin could tear him into shreds if he wasn't careful.

*Christ, it was always the same.*

He had absolutely no idea how many men sat before him, but they all looked like formally dressed flightless birds. Black breeches, black waistcoats, black morning coats, and white shirts with matching neckcloths.

Oh, he'd be able to figure out their number if he had ten minutes. However, the sharp minds in front of him would recognize something was amiss after a couple of moments. Particularly if he had to use his fingers to count. They'd be horrified if the calculation required he take off his boots so his toes could lend assistance.

McCalpin stiffened his body and allowed a slight sneer to tip one corner of his mouth. In some perverse way, he relished the challenge to guard his secret. He was a master at it. The years at Eton had taught him that he could do no wrong. He'd never been questioned why he was always ill when a mathematics exam was scheduled.

No one expected much effort from a ducal heir anyway. The fact he'd made high marks in his other subjects thrilled the provost, but more importantly, had appeased his father's desire that McCalpin perform well in his studies.

Indeed, he'd learned his lessons and flaunted his success in other subjects to his advantage.

One audacious penguin actually sighed and checked his pocket watch.

By McCalpin's own rudimentary calculations, he was only a half-hour late today. Not a single soul would question why he never made an appointment on time. Everyone presumed a ducal heir to be haughty, vain, and seasoned with a healthy dose of an inflated view of one's importance. He made certain the group of men before him were never disappointed in their expectations.

They'd be shocked if they knew that a clock was an instrument of torture for the Marquess of McCalpin. Calculating the precise minutes he had before attending a meeting with his staff took a Herculean effort on his part. One he had decided long ago wasn't worth the effort. If he was ten minutes or two hours tardy, they'd wait for him.

Simply because he was the powerful Duke of Langham's heir and needed their assistance to keep his estate running smoothly and profitably.

"Sit, gentlemen," he called out as he sat at his massive burl maple desk. Before him, papers, journals, and record books were stacked in perfect order as if offerings on an altar. The inkwell was uncapped and the quills sharpened. His seal and the accompanying wax were to his right, ready for his use when he'd sign the documents that required his attention.

His trusted and younger brother by a year, Lord William Cavensham, sat beside him. The duchy's auditor, Mr. Wilburton, a man in his late forties with gray hair, sat in front of his desk. On either side of Wilburton, the duchy's two stewards, Mr. Severin and Mr. Merritt, waited to give their monthly reports.

In his mid-thirties, Mr. Severin managed McCalpin's estate, McCalpin Manor, nestled in the beautiful hills of Hertforshire. McCalpin trusted the quiet but resolute man completely. Mr. Severin had served as under-steward to Mr. Merritt. In his early sixties, Merritt had managed the ducal ancestral seat, Falmont, for the last thirty years. Falmont was more like its own city and ran with an efficiency that London proper should envy. A testament that Merritt was a genius.

Mr. Merrit's job required he keep Mr. Severin informed of the financial status of the mighty estate, but more importantly, Merritt continuously trained Severin for the day when he'd become the steward of the duchy when McCalpin became duke.

McCalpin's personal solicitor, Mr. Russell, sat on the chair just outside the circle of trusted advisors with his portable writing desk open. He sharpened a quill in preparation to take notes. The rest of the penguins sat in a semicircle around the room. McCalpin always focused on the five men who surrounded him unless someone else needed to give a report to the group.

With such an efficient staff, they quickly finished their monthly business. Once again, both estates had made a profit. McCalpin signed the documents in front of him as needed and stood, signaling the meeting at an end.

"Lord McCalpin, there's a personal matter that needs your attention." The bright sunshine reflected off Mr. Russell's dark red hair in a manner that reminded McCalpin of autumn apples fresh from the harvest.

He nodded and lowered himself to his leather chair behind the desk. Because of his height, he'd had the piece custom-built to accommodate his long legs. "The rest of you may leave."

The various advisors, stewards, under-stewards, agents, junior solicitors, and bookkeepers left, leaving Russell and another man in attendance. William stood to leave also, but McCalpin cleared his throat, the sign for his brother to stay for the last matter. William played a vital role as McCalpin's personal advisor. No one except for William knew the true extent of his failings, his idiocy, but his brother didn't judge him. He helped and protected his interests, but more importantly, he protected McCalpin's secret.

Mr. Russell waited until the study door closed before he began. "My lord, allow me to introduce Mr. Jameson, my firm's new bookkeeper assigned to your estate."

"Lord McCalpin, it's an honor to serve you." The stranger stood and sketched an elegant bow. Handsome, with a pleasant voice and countenance to match, Jameson exuded confidence, and his eyes flashed with a keen intelligence.

"Mr. Jameson, a pleasure," he answered. A bookkeeper could easily discover his subterfuge. With a swallow, McCalpin tried to tame the fresh attack of nausea. Unfortunately, like a buoy, his trepidation would not sink. It bobbed and floated in his gut constantly.

"In reviewing the Lawson sisters' trusts, Mr. Jameson was the first to discover the odd requests for disbursements from one of the trusts. It appears you've approved them, but we wanted to ensure that it's your signature." Russell approached the desk and placed the documents in front of McCalpin.

McCalpin didn't spare a glance. "In what way are they irregular?"

"The requests don't appear to come from McCalpin House. A street urchin delivers them. Plus, the requests are increasing in amount and frequency," Jameson offered. "At first, it was five pounds requested per week. Then, it increased to fifteen pounds. This week, two requests in the amount of thirty pounds each have crossed my desk."

McCalpin leaned back in his chair and lifted a brow. "That is unusual as I haven't approved any disbursements."

"All are withdrawals from Miss March Lawson's trust. Nothing from the other children's trusts," Russell answered. "Since they come to my office signed by you, I assumed Miss Lawson had contacted you directly."

McCalpin didn't comment as he skimmed the documents, never focusing on the amounts. However, a disturbing sight caught his attention. The handwriting on the page was his, but it wasn't the way he signed his name. Perfectly centered on the bottom of the last sheet of vellum was his signature.

He always signed his name at the bottom right of any document.

"No, she hasn't seen me. I assumed *you* were the one managing the accounts and approving the amounts." McCalpin smiled, but there was no humor—just a warning, like a dog growling while its tail slowly wagged.

William leaned forward slightly. "That's not your signature?"

McCalpin shook his head.

Russell's brow wrinkled into neat lines reminiscent of McCalpin Manor's furrowed fields. "My lord, Miss Lawson recently sent several more requests to our office directly, and I have those here for your review also."

McCalpin took the letters. He quickly read the first letter until his eyes stumbled across the amount of one hundred pounds. It was substantial, and her explanation stated that the estate needed it for repairs due to a particularly violent winter storm. He let out a sigh in resignation. One more distraction that needed his attention.

"Why doesn't her brother, the viscount, ask for these amounts himself?"

"Lord Lawson is nine years old, my lord," Russell gently reminded him. "There is no successor guardian named for the children or the viscount's estate, just your appointment as the successor trustee for the sisters' trusts. If you're not approving these irregular requests, and I'm not approving them, then who is?"

"Are you're suggesting someone is embezzling from Miss Lawson's trust fund?" William asked.

"That's my conclusion," answered Mr. Jameson. His serious frown twisted his visage into something that looked like a gnarled tree trunk. The sight would scare a baby to tears.

"Shall I visit Miss Lawson at Lawson Court, my lord?" Russell asked.

"Don't bother. I'll request she come to London instead and meet with me directly." McCalpin shook his head. "I still don't understand why I was appointed to manage the daughters' money. I don't even know these people."

"In my opinion, the previous Lord Lawson employed

rather shoddy solicitors. Errors are rampant through their legal work. The prior trustee of the three daughters' trusts and guardian of the children and the viscountcy was Lord Burns. The title of the Marquess of McCalpin is the named successor trustee responsible for the daughters' trusts. Your late uncle, who previously held the title, was friends with the late viscount. There isn't anyone else named as successor guardian in the documents." As if that explained everything, Russell packed up his portable desk. "I'm sending Mr. Jameson to review McCalpin Manor's records. Severin wants someone else to audit the books before we present the quarterly review to Wilburton."

McCalpin nodded. "One more thing. Send me a record of all the withdrawals from the sisters' trust funds. That'll be all." After the others left, he stood and faced William. "I should have done something about this before now. Our darling sister gave me quite a tongue-lashing over Miss Lawson. She banks with Emma."

"Emma took umbrage with you? The stars must be out of alignment. She normally saves her rants for me." William poured himself another cup of coffee and brought one to McCalpin. "I'll be more than happy to look into Miss Lawson's affairs. Once you get the report, send word to me over at Langham Hall."

Once again, his aversion to numbers had caused more work for himself. "No, this is my mess. I failed to give a proper review of the documents when they first crossed my desk. I thought it was another administrative task Russell's firm could handle. Obviously, it requires my attention."

"I'm at your disposal, McCalpin."

"Thank you." The laugh started deep within his chest.

Whether it was relief from the fact that the monthly meeting was over or the debacle with the Lawson family made little difference.

William raised an eyebrow. "What is it?"

McCalpin laughed at the absurdity that *he* was responsible for yet more money. Finally, when he got his humor under control, he answered, "Whoever is embezzling those funds signs my name better than I do."

"Good morning, Faith," March called out to her sister. "You're up late this morning." She turned her attention back to the mirror. The village seamstress hissed under her breath, scolding her to stand still.

March wrinkled her nose. Unfortunately, the woman's misplaced rebukes held no sway. The seamstress' efforts were better directed at the monstrous piece of fabric covering March from the neck down. The puce gown was revolting. It had been one of her grandmother's formal dresses, but without the lace trim or the coordinating iridescent black gauze overlay, the gown's color closely resembled grass after the first autumn frost. Why ever had she picked this color and, for goodness' sake, this style? It made her look like a plump Amazon warrioress.

Faith walked stiffly into March's bedroom dragging her left leg. "Today I feel as if I'm ninety instead of nineteen. There must be a storm brewing. I can barely move. Mrs. Oliver brought warm compresses to my room along with breakfast. That's why I'm late." Her sister turned to the seamstress. "Good morning, Mrs. Burton."

With a mouthful of pins, the seamstress grunted a greeting. "You're next." The woman pricked March with a pin when she took the final waist adjustment, payment for March's inability to stand still. "I believe I'm finished."

The woman had a flair for communicating her ideas while balancing at least twenty straight pins between her lips. Indeed, if her talent for sewing was as accomplished, maybe March would look like something other than a sack of feed.

"Mrs. Burton, if it wouldn't be too much of an inconvenience, perhaps I can come to the village later?" Faith asked softly. "I'm not certain I can stand long enough for a proper fitting."

"Just send a note when you're feeling better." The seamstress nodded and gathered her belongings. "Miss March, I'll see you tomorrow for the bookkeeping?"

March nodded. "Shouldn't take much more than a half hour."

Mrs. Burton scowled at the hem of the puce gown. "You add and subtract those numbers in your head. The first time you came to the shop you finished so quickly I didn't believe you could've balanced a single column of figures. When I checked the calculations, there wasn't a single mistake. You have a quick mind and a remarkable talent for mathematics."

"Thank you, Mrs. Burton." *If only she was as quick with her sewing.* March presented a pleasant smile while taming her errant thoughts. Mrs. Burton had been kind to Faith and Julia, her other sister. That was all that mattered. Her sisters needed the gowns before the Season. If she pressed the seamstress, they might have them before the end of the month. What else could she do? She was trading her bookkeeping skills for dresses. She released a pained breath. Beggars couldn't complain or be choosers when desperate for morning gowns.

Mrs. Oliver, their housekeeper and only servant, escorted Mrs. Burton to the door all the while chatting about the upcoming foxhunt. Alone with Faith, March changed into her day dress, a sturdy, muslin frock the shade of mud. It matched March's hair color perfectly.

"Dearest, let me help you pick out the colors for your new dresses," Faith gently suggested as she gazed at March's attire. "With your beautiful dark hair and coloring, brighter colors such as jewel tones would favor you more than those muted colors you prefer."

"Nothing would help me. I'm a simple sheep farmer, but if you want to accept the challenge, then by all means, you have my permission," March said.

Her sister's offer to help with the impossible task was a true testament to her patience. Faith was all things lovely with a sweet disposition to match. Her hair glowed with a color best described as warm sunshine, and she possessed velvety-blue eyes. Faith caught the attention of every young man in the area, until she walked. None chose to call upon her in any serious fashion. Faith never said a word, but March knew it hurt deeply.

Faith grimaced as she rested against the bed. Some days her limp was slight, and March could forget that her middle sister had suffered an injury as a young toddler. Today, the cold dampness haunted her sister.

Memories of the accident were permanently seared in March's mind—all the blood, the shouts, and her father rushing forward to scoop Faith into his arms after she'd been trampled by a horse. Her sister's recuperation took six months. From that day forward, she was always at the forefront of March's thoughts and deeds.

Faith's lack of suitors would soon change. March intended to open the viscount's London townhouse for the sole purpose of giving Faith and Julia a Season. The city offered the opportunity to seek out the best medical treatment from experts who might relieve Faith's suffering. As important, Bennett needed a proper education, one that would prepare the young viscount for his entrance to Eton.

The bedroom door burst open with a *whoosh,* and Julia rushed in waving a note in her hand. "My word, I've never seen such a sight! The most handsome liveried footman brought this note to *me*," she squealed. "And asked if I would see it delivered to *you*."

"And good morning to you, too!" March chided as Julia handed the note to her.

Julia stopped and blinked hard. "Oh my, I didn't see you, Faith. I apologize for my haste." Then she gave a quick wink. "Good morning, my dear sisters." She gave a grin and looked to March for approval. "Better?"

March narrowed her eyes then returned the grin. "Better. Next time, call us 'my dearest and most superior sisters.' "

Julia raised an eyebrow in protest. Her eighteen-year-old body was burgeoning into full womanhood. Julia favored Faith and was as much a beauty as her sister. Young men waited for March's littlest sister after Sunday services and the community gatherings always under the pretense to chat. While their efforts were entirely innocent, March kept a watchful eye. One could never be too careful, particularly when their cousin Rupert had started to take an interest in Julia.

"This is no time for games, March. The footman is waiting," scolded Julia.

"Who's it from?" Faith asked.

"The wax bares the seal of the Marquess of McCalpin." Her heartbeat accelerated in a staccato rhythm. "I wonder what he wants with me." She suspected his summons related to the rash of small withdrawals she'd made within the last several weeks. She swallowed the panic that started to rise. Whatever happened, she'd explain her actions and hope for the best.

March used her finger to lift the seal. With a quick scan of the missive, her suspicions grew stronger. "The Marquess of McCalpin has summoned me to London. He wants to meet this afternoon."

"That doesn't give you much time to get ready," Faith said.

"Oh, March! He's finally taken notice. Maybe we can move to London sooner." Julia's smile could have lit a ballroom for hours. "We'll finally be able to hire a proper tutor for Bennett."

March simply nodded without paying much heed as her thoughts were spinning. Indeed, it was entirely possible the marquess was ending the trust and she would have control of her fortune. She bit her lip and forced the flutters of anxiety away. Perhaps he didn't know that she'd embezzled funds using his signature and seal.

Julia jumped to Faith and gathered their hands together. "We're going to have a Season. Just imagine you and me dancing with the handsomest men in London." Julia presented Faith with a mock bow. "My lady, may I have the honor of tonight's midnight waltz?"

Faith giggled and inclined her head. "Indeed, kind sir. It would be my pleasure."

March's newfound hopes slammed to a halt much like a cantankerous horse refusing a jump at a hunt. "Please, we must be ready for disappointment. We're not acquainted with this man. He may be worse than Lord Burns, who completely ignored us."

Julia's brows grew together in puzzlement. "Do you think that's possible?"

"Of course," March retorted. She clenched the missive in her hand as the familiar ire over their poverty rushed through her. Perhaps it was fear for her future. It made little difference at this point. "No one has taken the responsibility for our welfare seriously. None of my letters were ever answered."

March paced the length of her bedroom. There was no use delaying the inevitable. She'd face her fate with her head held high. She had a right to her own money. She'd pledged to protect her family, and she'd keep that promise. "I'm leaving for London. Hart will accompany me. I'll inform Mrs. Oliver of my plans."

A fleeting glimpse of worry stole across Faith's face, then her blue eyes narrowed as she tilted her head. "You're concerned. Nay, frightened. What is it?"

Her sister was too observant by half. March tugged at the sleeves on her dress. A nervous gasp escaped on her next breath. If her sisters had any idea how low her morals had sunk, they'd understand the foreboding sense of doom that haunted her.

"Nothing. I have much on my mind." Her lips tightened into a faint smile for her sisters. "There's no cause to fret."

*At least not yet.*

She needed to calm down. There was no possibility he could have discovered her one-thousand-pound withdrawal, and if he gave her access to the funds today, then he'd never learn of her deception.

Once again, she took command and proceeded with an assurance a trained Shakespearean actor would admire. "If I leave now, I'll be in London within the hour."

"I'm going with you." A hint of steel tempered Faith's gentle voice.

March shook her head. "There's no need."

Faith carefully made her way to block March's pacing. "You can't arrive at the marquess's home with only Hart and no chaperone. If I travel with you, you're least likely to garner unwanted attention."

She didn't trust her voice, so she nodded. Truthfully, having her sister for support would help her face whatever the marquess deemed important enough to demand her presence. He must be an arrogant man since he hadn't even considered how she'd travel to town.

"I'll come, too," Julia enthused. The girl was still twirling in circles with her imaginary dance partner.

"No." The clipped word caused Julia to stop midstride.

"Are you angry with me?" Julia's voice quavered and her eyes grew wide.

How could she have she snapped at her little sister? No matter how many times she'd reassured her, Julia was still sensitive about March leaving.

She rushed to her side and tugged her sister into her arms. "Sweetheart, I didn't mean to growl at you. It's been a hectic day already."

Julia nodded, but the previous brilliant light in her eyes had dimmed.

"Forgive me?" March whispered. For the world, she wouldn't hurt Julia and felt absolutely abysmal now.

Julia nodded and swept a sweet kiss across her cheek. "Always."

March returned the kiss. "I need you to stay with Bennett and help him with his history lesson."

Julia rolled her eyes. "I'd rather memorize ten deportment lessons."

March considered how much of a deportment lesson she could learn during the short ride to London. What was a proper introduction when meeting the man you were impersonating? What do you say when he discovers you write his name better than he does?

# Chapter Three

March picked up the heavy iron knocker shaped in a lion's head, and banged it against the massive mahogany door. "Thank you both for coming with me."

Standing beside her, Uncle Hart studied March with a frank, assessing gaze. Such a look coming from him was akin to a thousand spiders dancing across her back. Slim, fair of face with light brown hair streaked with gray and blue eyes, he stood a little over six feet. Even though he was her father's age, the years had been kind to him.

Faith took her hand and squeezed. "We'll get through this. Your forbearance has kept our family safe and sound. You've done everything in your power to protect us. Don't worry."

Her sister's face reflected a steadfast and serene peace. March swallowed that strength as if feasting after a weeklong fast. She couldn't crumble into a mass of doubts, not yet.

"This is a side of you I've never seen before. Nothing to be frightened of, my miss," Hart whispered. "The marquess has most likely summoned you to discuss you and your siblings."

"Of course." The words failed to calm the icy fear that slowly twisted and twined inside her chest. A nervous gasp escaped on her next breath of air. The door swept open, revealing a footman dressed in a navy-blue velvet double-breasted coat, matching pantaloons, and a perfectly fitted powdered wig. In silence, March stood with Hart and Faith on either side and waited for the invitation to enter the Marquess of McCalpin's home.

Almost as if the handsome servant saw through her ruse, a slight grin crossed the man's face then disappeared. "May I help you?"

"I'm Miss Lawson and this is . . . is Miss Faith Lawson and Mr. Hart. We're here on a business matter to see the marquess." March resisted the urge to turn and run back to the cart. She held out the summons as proof they were invited. She forced her feet to stay planted and waited for what seemed liked hours. "He requested my presence."

The footman motioned them forward, and March followed him into the vestibule. Her breath caught in her throat at her first glimpse of the home. Tiles of alternating black and white marble lined the floor of the large entry. A massive mahogany table stood in the center with a flower arrangement of more than three-dozen red roses surrounded by other exotic flowers that March didn't recognize. She inhaled the scent and immediately thought of summer. The marquess must have a greenhouse on the premises. Only the wealthy could afford such extravagances during the cold winter months.

To her right, an expansive circular staircase led to the second floor. Her eyes swept the length of the stairs but stopped at the sight of the most handsome human to have graced the earth with his presence.

On the stairs and dressed in a moss-green riding jacket and buckskin breeches covered in mud, he had turned when they'd entered. March's gaze collided with his, and her heart stumbled as if missing a dance step. From the distance, there was no doubt his blue eyes matched the brightest feathers of a kingfisher. His chestnut hair sported wet curls, most likely from the exertion of an afternoon ride. Time stood still as she studied his face. Radiant sunshine from a window next to him caressed his check and surrounded him in a ring of light. He could have been the model for Michelangelo's *David*. She'd never seen such perfection in a real man before.

Obviously, this vision was not as impressed with her as she was with him. Without acknowledgment, he continued his way upstairs, leaving her and his halo behind. March's breathing relaxed, but regret gathered like a gray haze over her.

How fitting that a luminous light courted him while nimbus clouds seemed to be her bosom companion. She could have stared at *David* for hours and still not grown tired of the vision. He couldn't be the marquess, since her banker, Lady Somerton, bore little resemblance to this man. Whoever he was, his bearing exuded strength and a graceful confidence that demanded attention.

The footman gave a slight nod to another servant, presumably the butler, who came forward.

"Miss?" The butler tilted his head slightly and waited for her response.

"Miss March Lawson, Miss Faith Lawson, and Mr. Victor Hart. Lord McCalpin requested I call upon him . . . on a matter of importance." March delivered a slight smile and clenched the missive demanding her visit.

"Please accompany me. You may wait in the salon while I inform his lordship you've arrived." Without waiting for a response, the butler executed a precise turn and walked away. March followed with Hart and Faith close behind.

After they took their seats, the butler left the three of them alone. Hart was the first to break the silence. "Would you like for me to speak on your behalf?"

"No, thank you. Our family's happiness and security are my responsibility." March straightened her back as she adjusted her well-worn gloves. They were her Sunday best.

The butler reappeared with an army of maids and a footman with a formal tea service. Cakes, tarts, and candied nuts towered over a triple-plated serving dish. Bennett would have been enthralled with such treats.

"Miss Lawson, I had refreshments prepared in case you might be famished after your travel from Leyton." The butler smiled reassuringly. "Shall I serve?"

March jumped to her feet. "That's very kind, but I'll pour. I'm sure you have better things to do than wait on us."

The butler's mouth tilted down as he considered her comment. "Of course. A lady such as you would want to do the honors. We don't have many guests—" As if he misspoke, he changed the subject. "Lord McCalpin is regrettably detained. I hope you don't mind waiting."

"Not at all." God, she sounded desperate. *No, she was desperate.* The summons had to change her family's fortune. "Thank you, Mr. . . . ?"

"I'm Buxton, his lordship's butler. Is there anything else I can get for you?"

March smiled at his kindness, a wonderful omen for her upcoming meeting. An ogre wouldn't employ a nice staff. "No, thank you, Mr. Buxton."

The butler nodded and left. With her stomach dancing a jig, she could only manage one tart. Faith and Hart ate everything except one lone pastry. Faith eyed it with an ardent yearning, but left it. Buxton returned within a half hour and escorted them into the marquess's study. By then, March wasn't at all certain this visit was such a good idea. Her palms were slowly turning into water pots, making her kidskin gloves rather sticky.

Perhaps she should have taken the time to respond to the marquess's demand by writing a letter. What would she have written?

*My dear marquess, please excuse my embezzling.*

McCalpin pushed his fingers through his wet hair in an attempt to tame the renegade locks. After his quick bath, he'd found a fresh change of clothes laid out for him in his dressing room. William strolled into the room with several documents. "Thank God you're late for your audience with Miss Lawson. You should see this. You've made another withdrawal request from Miss Lawson's trust. This time in the amount of one thousand pounds."

McCalpin finished buttoning the gray waistcoat and took the papers. "Same as before?"

William nodded.

McCalpin quickly read the document. When he reached the numbers, his mind stumbled to comprehend, but his eyes couldn't decipher the amounts. His heartbeat started to race, and he forced himself to breathe deeply. Why did those little symbols cause him such agony? "It looks like my signature, but I didn't instruct anyone to do this."

Will's brow creased as he considered the documents in his brother's hand. "That's why I knew it was forged. I instructed Mr. Russell to discover where they're coming from."

What would he do if William wasn't by his side? McCalpin adjusted his neckcloth. His entire life would be in an uproar. "And? Don't keep me in suspense."

"The directives are coming from Lawson Court in Leyton."

"Are you suggesting that a nine-year-old boy is forging my name to steal from his sister? That's preposterous. How could he master my signature? How did he get my seal?"

Will plopped his large frame on an upholstered stool beside the looking glass that McCalpin stood before.

"I don't know," Will answered running his hands through his hair in frustration. The blue of his eyes resembled McCalpin's own, but his hair was a shade darker. The color always reminded McCalpin of sable. "But someone from Lawson Court is forging your name. By the penmanship, I'd say it's one of his sisters."

"What kind of a family would steal from one another? How old are the siblings, again?" McCalpin adjusted his cravat then slipped on his morning coat.

"According to the birthdates in the trusts, the oldest daughter is twenty-four, the middle sister is nineteen, and the youngest is eighteen. I've written their birthdates and ages on a piece of paper next to the trust for your ease. Apparently, their parents died during an influenza outbreak years ago." William rested his ankle on his other leg. "The eldest daughter has repeatedly written to Russell and claims she's twenty-five. Usually women claim they're younger, not older." He shook his head and laughed. "Congratulations, McCalpin. You're responsible for not only the trusts, but a Lawson daughter who lies about her age, and an embezzler as well."

It boggled the mind to think he was entrusted to protect the funds for the Lawson sisters. He couldn't even keep simple household accounts straight. "I don't even know these people."

William lifted a brow. "You have quite the mystery on your hands."

"My lord?" Buxton had entered the dressing room. "I apologize, but Miss Lawson, her sister, and a Mr. Hart are in your study. I had tea served." He cleared his throat as if suddenly uncomfortable. "The eldest Miss Lawson appears nervous. She has a death grip on the letter you sent."

William shot out of the chair. "Oh, you must let me join your cozy little chat. We might be able to have some fun with this."

"Perhaps the eldest is stealing her own funds." McCalpin lifted one brow. "I wouldn't dream of keeping you away from the festivities. How shall we spring the net?"

March sat across from Faith and Hart in a small sitting area in front of a large window that overlooked the street below.

"March, shall we leave?" Hart's deep gravelly voice broke the eerie silence.

Twisting and untwisting her fingers into knots must have been the first visible clue she wasn't at all confident in her purpose. As if on cue, the study door swung open and her *David* walked in accompanied by another equally handsome man. Resplendent in a black coat, gray waistcoat, and tan breeches, *David* surveyed the three of them for a moment. The large fire in the hearth crackled, almost as if calling out in greeting. He made his way to stand in front of them. A blast of heat hit March's cheek. Her purpose today dictated she succeed in getting her funds released, not moon over a man.

The simple truth? He was a man, nothing more and nothing less. Such a thought should lessen his effect on her concentration.

Unfortunately, it didn't.

"Miss Lawson." Her *David* took her hand in his and sketched a perfect bow. "I'm Lord McCalpin."

She stood and dipped a curtsy. Ripples of heat radiated up her arm from where his hand held hers. The warmth he created with a mere touch could melt the sea ice in the Arctic Ocean.

With an elegant turn, the marquess extended the same greeting to Faith, who did her best to curtsey. To his credit, he didn't bat an eye at her sister's difficulty mastering the movement.

"Mr. Victor Hart." Her old friend stood tall and didn't shy away from the formidable ducal heir in front of them.

"I'm McCalpin." The marquess shook Hart's hand in greeting. "Allow me to introduce my brother, Lord William Cavensham."

Lord William greeted everyone. The smile he extended to Faith was simply spectacular, but Faith pulled her hand away as if wary of the gentleman before her.

She'd do well to follow Faith's lead. These two men were stunningly handsome and could steal every argument she possessed. She released a silent sigh.

"Thank you for coming on such short notice." The smile on Lord McCalpin's face transformed him from a handsome mortal to a breathtaking Greek god. "I think we're long overdue for an introduction."

"Indeed." March cleared the bevy of bullfrogs that had decided to take up residence in her throat.

The marquess quirked an eyebrow, then smiled warmly. "Follow me."

Her stomach slipped to her knees along with the delicate cherry tart she'd eaten. Her perfect man was the new trustee, and she needed his help. That was the only reason she was there. If she kept up that mantra, she'd survive this interview. With a hefty dose of apprehension, she followed him to the far end of the room.

Beside his massive desk, the marquess turned and faced her direction. He extended his arm toward her with his palm face up. Without thought, March clasped his large hand tightly in hers. He would quickly deduce her desperation if she didn't comport herself with a little more dignity. His hand contained an inherent warmth and strength that caused a slight tremble to erupt from her toes to her head.

"I thought we'd already introduced ourselves," he whispered with a wink. "But if you'd like me to do the honors again, I'd be happy to."

After a slight bow, he released her hand and again, motioned toward a chair in front of his desk. The impish smile on his face could've charmed a roomful of sour dowagers.

She pressed her eyes closed in an attempt to settle the butterflies that flittered in her chest. He was simply pointing what seat she was to sit in, and she had thought he wanted to take her hand again.

*He must think I'm an artless fool. Good God, could this be any more mortifying?*

Faith and Hart settled on a lush sofa toward the entrance of the room, but March felt the comforting heat of her sister's gaze on her back. She took a deep breath to gain some order over her scattered senses. Her family's welfare depended upon her surviving this conversation and convincing the marquess to release her money. His brother settled in the chair next to her.

Once seated behind his desk, Lord McCalpin leaned forward to close the distance between them. "Miss Lawson, tell me about you and your family," he commanded in a low, composed voice.

March answered quickly over the cacophony of her beating heart. "I seek the money my father left me."

He tilted his head and lifted an eyebrow.

Her cheeks flamed, but she continued to blather on without answering his request. "In truth, I turned twenty-five over three months ago. I'm not certain why you haven't released my funds. Whatever the reason, I just want to clear up this misunderstanding and get my money."

*There was no question. She was an absolute utter buffoon.*

The way she'd bumbled her presentation proved it. She stared at her clasped hands so she'd not have to witness his inevitable disdain. There was no turning back now.

Normally, men didn't have any impact on her. She was not a woman whose looks lent any type of persuasive power to an argument with the opposite sex. She'd always prided herself on her wits and ability to negotiate the highest sale prices for the estate's wool. It was more productive than a coy smile or a dramatic bat of the eyelashes, neither of which she had mastered effectively. Nevertheless, what little talent or intelligence she possessed had completely deserted her.

"Humor me before we discuss money," McCalpin drawled. "In reviewing your family's situation, I've discovered there's not a guardian for your siblings or the estate named in your father's documents. After Lord Burns' death, no one has helped you, I take it? How have you managed?"

"I live with my two sisters and our brother, Bennett. I've been running the estate for the past eight years." She delivered a slight smile. "I plan to retain a solicitor. I . . . we need a guardian appointed for the estate. I'm perfectly capable of looking after my family."

His mouth dipped into a frown and, for a moment, his eyes studied her with a curious intensity. "Miss Lawson, you have my sincerest apologies for not contacting you sooner after Lord Burns died. We're both aware that you're not of age to receive your trust money. I had my solicitor review the documents to insure I was correct, which he verified. You may not receive your inheritance until next year."

With a slight shake of her head, she struggled to comprehend. If the man had jumped on his desk and danced a jig naked, she wouldn't have been more shocked. "Sir, does my trust not end when I'm twenty-five? I was born in 1788, making me, indeed, of age."

McCalpin reviewed the parchment on his desk then returned his gaze to hers. "The trust states you were born on the twenty-third of November, 1789."

She bit her lip and clenched her hands into fists. He stared at her mouth before his eyes narrowed. She might steal from her own trust, but she wasn't a liar.

Completely out of her realm, she wasn't prepared for this meeting. She should have written a response requesting the reason for the interview. He had already grown suspicious of her, and he held her future and her family's happiness in his hands. Not to mention, he held her teetering career as an embezzler on the precarious edge of ruin.

"Rest assured I will do everything in my power to perform the duties as dictated by your father's request. Perhaps it's best if I have my solicitor inquire about your brother's estate."

"This is pure madness," she blurted.

"Perhaps on your part, Miss Lawson, but I can assure you that I'm quite sane." A grimace crossed his perfect mouth. The effort prominently displayed a full lower lip that deserved a firm bite in retaliation. The sliver of emotion in the marquess's cool eyes warned her things were going from bad to disastrous. "Surely, the estate is flush with funds? It pays for itself, I assume?"

She tapped her foot to keep from stomping it in anger. "Sir, flush? We've received nothing. There hasn't been any allowance for the estate's operation all year."

"Miss Lawson, I don't manage the viscountcy estate. Just your trusts." He leaned back in his chair and delivered the coldest stare she'd ever received in her life. It could have turned a summer shower into a blizzard. She lifted her chin in response. His attention suddenly snapped to Hart. "Could you explain who Mr. Hart is?"

Immediately, she regretted her snappish tone. She pushed aside an unwelcome wave of embarrassment. Ever mindful of her cause, a logical argument was always more persuasive than raw emotion. "May we continue to discuss my trust? My father's solicitors must have copied the birth date wrong, or perhaps poor penmanship causes the eighty-eight to appear as an eighty-nine in my birth year. That has to be the explanation."

Lord McCalpin assessed her with a wary intelligence. "Excellent theories, Miss Lawson." He glanced at the trust document before him, then pushed it toward her. "Unfortunately, the gentleman who wrote this document had a hand that was neat and precise." He turned his attention to the front of the room. "Mr. Hart, it appears Miss Lawson refuses to comment on your relationship to the family—"

"Mr. Hart was employed by my late father when he

served under the Envoy Extraordinary and Minister Plenipotentiary to the United States. He was my father's aide de camp and stayed with my family after we lost our parents." She drew a breath and prayed for control and patience.

"Mr. Hart, are you related to the family?" The marquess's sinfully dark voice floated over her as if tasting her. She shook her head at such thoughts in a desperate attempt to gather her wayward senses.

Without a hint of emotion, Hart answered, "No, my lord."

McCalpin propped both elbows on his desk. "Miss Lawson, tell me more about your living arrangements."

She clenched her fists once more. What more did the man want from her? "We have one servant, Mrs. Oliver, who helps me run the house. She's been with us since I was a baby."

"Do you have any other family?" He straightened the papers in front of him.

For some odd reason, it reminded her of Bennett's recent attempt to fire her as his housekeeper. "We have one cousin, but he lives in his own home close to Leyton."

"Is there perchance a suitable chaperone who lives with you and your family?"

"No. At my age, I'm a perfectly acceptable chaperone for my sisters." She squared her shoulders and refused to turn away from his direct gaze.

"It's hard to fathom that the solicitors bungled your birthdate. However, if you are twenty-five as you claim"— his gaze pierced hers—"I will gladly give you your money with the proviso you present me proof. I will not shirk my responsibilities as trustee."

This man dared to keep her property under his control, when by all rights it should be in her possession. March struggled to remain calm. She lost the battle as her temper rose, and that never boded well for anyone, particularly her.

In a flash, she stood with her well-worn brown muslin dress rustling in protest against her movements. "You've shirked your responsibility to us before. Why hasn't your solicitor answered my correspondence? You can't withhold those funds. I'm twenty-five. That's my money. You've never even visited Lawson Court," she challenged.

"Is that an invitation, Miss Lawson? If so, then I readily accept." Matching her movements, McCalpin stood and leaned over the desk to bring his eyes level with hers. "I have a duty to protect your money, and I plan to carry out that responsibility. Even if it means protecting it from you. Remember, I can and I will keep those funds." A light flashed in his dark blue eyes that indicated his anger matched hers. "Do you have proof of your birthdate? A letter from a clergyman verifying it perhaps?"

March swallowed, then leaned in closer. In a crisp dictation, she answered, "Such records are usually kept in the family bible. The one recording my birth was lost when my parents left New York to return to England. You'll have to accept my word."

"That's not enough," he said tersely, tightening his stance.

March remained standing. To sit would mean she was giving up her claim. "There are repairs that must be made to the tenant's home, and our home was damaged in a winter storm. Some of the roof damage has been repaired, but the estate still owes money to some local businesses that have kindly extended credit."

"You would use your own funds for these repairs and debts?" He narrowed his eyes.

"Lord Burns didn't provide any monies last year. When he died, there was no one to give me money for the estate management. I have no other choice than to pay for it myself until I can choose a guardian for the estate." She clasped her fingers together in a desperate attempt to gain control over her anger. "As there is no guardian to say otherwise, I'm opening our family townhouse this spring and will move my sisters and brother to London for the Season. My sisters are of such an age they should take their rightful place in society. Bennett, my little brother, inherited my father's title and should experience the educational offerings only London can provide. Since you, sir, are in charge of my sisters' monies also, I hope they aren't prey to the same sort of mistakes rampant through my documents."

A brief scowl shadowed Lord McCalpin's face, and his lips thinned in displeasure. "If what you say is true, then I readily agree your situation warrants immediate attention. Allow me the opportunity of seeing the estate for myself. Is that too much to ask?"

He ran a hand down the length of his face. The effort seemed to eliminate some of his anger.

"Let me evaluate your requests for tenant repairs and the estate's debts. The idea of bringing your family to London isn't to be taken lightly. It's a massive undertaking. That's all I can promise today."

"Sir, I'm not asking you to take over the estate. I'm asking for—"

Lord William placed several letters on the desk. March's heart stopped mid-beat when she saw her forged requests for funds. Bile scourged her throat as her face heated with humiliation.

She could face anything except for the marquess's beratement in front of Faith and Hart. For her shame to be made public to her family was a burden she didn't think she could bear. McCalpin reached for the letters. Without a second thought, she placed her hand over his, a completely inappropriate gesture hidden from Faith and Hart. It made little difference at this point. He would ruin her if she didn't stop him.

"Please, not in front of them," she whispered, the words so faint she wasn't certain she'd said them.

He continued to pull the documents toward him, but regarded her. It had to have been her imagination, but his eyes seemed to soften. She almost missed the slight dip of his chin in acknowledgment. His gaze went to his brother. Silently, they communicated with one another, and Lord William stood and walked to her sister and Hart.

"Miss Faith, there's a lovely portrait of my late uncle, the previous Duke of Langham. When he was the Marquess of McCalpin, I understand he became a close friend of your father's. May I show it to you? He was a handsome fellow. People say I favor him, and I'd like your opinion."

Faith reluctantly nodded, and Hart rose to join them. Protective, he wouldn't allow Faith to wander off with the young aristocrat without his presence. The trio left the room, and she found herself alone with the marquess. She sat back down in the chair and waited for her sentence.

"Do you know what these documents are?" McCalpin asked. By the absolute defeated expression on Miss Lawson's face, he had his answer.

She cleared her throat. "Yes."

"Did you forge my signature?"

She nodded gently, and a thick wave of dark brown—almost black—hair escaped from her simple chignon.

He regarded her carefully. Their earlier conversation had grown quite heated. What type of woman would dare impersonate him? One who must have spent hours practicing his signature. She had used his identity and his standing in society for her own purposes. Impersonating a noble was a high crime, and she'd done it anyway.

She wasn't a classic English beauty by any means. She was more exotic in her looks. Her brown eyes sparkled with intelligence. Before he'd shown her the forged withdrawals, he'd found her stalwart confidence intriguing. He'd even found her earlier awkwardness over their second greeting charming.

Through it all, his title or wealth didn't faze her. She only saw him as a stumbling block. Truth be told, he enjoyed going toe-to-toe with her. The rapier-quick retorts and bold challenges were refreshing.

"How did you get my seal?" he gently asked.

"My father kept all of your uncle's letters. I found an intact wax seal of the Marquess of McCalpin and took it to a family friend who's a retired engraver, and he made it for me." She stared at her clasped hands and refused to look at him. "I kept your first letter of introduction as our new trustee. I used it to practice your signature."

Her face had turned scarlet red. She was mortified. Instead of pleased that he'd received her confession, McCalpin hated that he made her feel such embarrassment. However, it was his responsibility to protect the family's funds.

"Have you used it for anything besides withdrawals from your trust?" he asked.

She stiffened at the question, but managed to stare into

his eyes. She shook her head. "Never. I would never harm you or my family. I only did it for my . . ."

What could his little embezzler possibly say to justify her behavior?

"We needed new shears, or I couldn't finish shearing the sheep. I need to sell that wool to cover our household expenses." His lips trembled for a moment before she continued. "The estate isn't profitable."

He gazed at her in disbelief. "You shear the sheep on the estate?"

"Yes. Hart helps if he's at Lawson Court, but he travels frequently. Besides, I'm faster than he is and can shear two sheep to his one." When she swallowed, the movement emphasized her long neck.

He collapsed in his chair and stared at the woman. It was inconceivable what she was claiming. She was the daughter of a well-respected member of the nobility.

"I understand how trite this must sound, but I'm truly sorry I used your identity." Her eyes dipped to her lap. Whatever she studied must have given her courage since she soon met his gaze. "Lord Burns had control over Lawson Court and was never generous." She drew a deep breath. "For the past several years, he didn't see fit to give us much money. When I learned he'd passed, I wrote to you as the successor—"

Buxton entered the room. "I beg your pardon, my lord. Lord and Lady Pembrooke have arrived."

After a slight nod to the butler, McCalpin's attention returned to the woman seated in front of him. "Miss Lawson, the hour grows late, and I have other duties that demand my attention. I'll visit Lawson Court as soon as possible. I trust we're in agreement that you're not to write any more requests using my *seal*."

"But—"

He wouldn't let her have a word edgewise. "Immediately, I think it best that you have someone deliver your copy of my seal to me. You'll find I'm generous to a fault, but I won't tolerate foolishness or any more of your shenanigans. If you or your family needs something, I invite you to come and seek my advice. I won't turn down any reasonable requests."

"Is it possible I could have some money now?" She exhaled as if the weight of the world had been set on her shoulders. "You see I need—"

"From what I've learned today, I think it best if any disbursements wait until I have the opportunity to review the estate and learn more about you and your family." He lowered his voice. "Wouldn't you agree?"

Her eyes glistened with tears.

*Oh God, he'd done it. He'd made her cry.*

"Miss Lawson, there's no harm done," he said quietly. "The amounts you took were miniscule. When I visit, I'll see what repairs are required. That's all I can offer at this point. You shouldn't spend your money on the estate. Your father wanted you or your husband to have it."

She nodded once, then stood. Without any farewell, she turned and left the room.

In his twenty-nine years, he'd accumulated his fair share of experiences with women of all ages and personalities. Never once did he ever remember bringing one to tears.

It was something he hoped never to experience again.

He felt lower than the mud in a carriage rut.

Lord McCalpin had issued his dismissal, and March couldn't wait to escape. Tears welled in her eyes at his denial of her request. She should have argued more but her pride had stopped her. They were in desperate need

of wood and food at Lawson Court. Now, she had no way
to get any funds. To wait another year felt like a lifetime.
Decorum wouldn't feed her family, but it kept her from
falling into a ball and weeping for the rest of the day.
Even that selfish luxury was out of her reach. She still
had to muck the barn and repair the plow horses' tack.

She spun toward the exit, determined to gather Faith
and Hart as quickly as possible. She walked with as much
dignity as she could muster as she left the marquess's
presence. When she entered the vestibule, a handsome
couple looked her way.

The auburn-haired woman held a bundled baby close
to her chest, and her beautiful face glowed with happiness. She reached up on tiptoes to whisper something to
her equally handsome husband. He laughed and wrapped
an arm about her waist to pull her close. His finger traced
a gentle line down the baby's cheek.

March's humiliation slightly melted at the sight of two
people so obviously in love and delighted with their infant. She had always envisioned such a life for herself—a
loving husband and a family of her own. Now, that dream
was what she wanted for Faith and Julia—a love, strong
and true.

The woman smiled as if she and March were dear
friends. Suddenly, the woman started toward her as if she
wanted to address her, so March stopped and waited.

The woman's happiness seemed to light her from
within and grew in vibrancy the closer she got. With no
warning, she rushed passed without a second look in
March's direction and called, "McCalpin, you're home!"

Heat flamed her cheeks again. She'd mistaken the
friendly gesture for herself. Trying not to draw attention,
she watched the group's exchange.

The marquess greeted the couple with a warm embrace to the woman and a handshake to her husband. "What mischief did you and Pembrooke bring me today?" McCalpin's voice echoed with true affection as he peeked at the baby and smiled. "William is roaming the halls somewhere. He'll be delighted to see you, too."

Aware that she was rudely staring, March turned her attention to Faith and Hart, who had joined her to watch the happy reunion. "I'm ready," she whispered.

"Lord and Lady Pembrooke, may I introduce Miss March Lawson, Miss Faith Lawson, and Mr. Victor Hart." Lord McCalpin's voice was matter-of-fact.

March turned and greeted the couple.

"It's a pleasure to meet one of McCalpin's elusive friends," Lady Pembrooke said.

March lost the ability to speak for a moment. No one could ever mistake her as his friend. "My lady, I've never met Lord McCalpin before today."

"Fortune smiles on all of us then." Lady Pembrooke didn't hide the merriment from her eyes. "Do you live in London?"

"Miss Lawson is here on a business matter. She resides in Leyton. Her younger brother is the young viscount, Lord Lawson." McCalpin stealthy sidled next to March and addressed Lord and Lady Pembrooke. "Will you wait for me in my study? I'll only be a moment."

With her husband by her side, Lady Pembrooke ignored the marquess and stood closer to March. "I have friends in Leyton. Mr. Roger Jordon and his niece Miss Lucy Porter? Do you know them?"

March nodded. "Mr. Jordon is kindly teaching my brother chess."

A dazzling smile lit Lady Pembrooke's face. "I visit them quite often. The next time I'm in town, perhaps you'd join us for tea. You must bring Miss Faith also."

"Thank you, my lady. We'd be delighted," she answered.

Lord William joined them and held out his hands. "There's my namesake. The rascal is growing more handsome every day." It became apparent he had little experience with babies as he took the infant in a fumbling embrace.

Without thinking, March rushed forward and placed her hand under the baby's head. "You must cradle him close." She kept her voice soft as the infant was sleeping. "He doesn't have the strength yet to support his own head."

The group turned and stared at her as if she'd grown horns on her head. She swallowed, hoping to stave off another round of mortifying flushes. "I . . . I apologize for my forwardness."

"No need to apologize, Miss Lawson." Lady Pembrooke shook her head. "Liam does need the support. I was about to take him from William's clumsy hands."

"You wound me, cousin." Lord William cradled the baby close to his body and hummed something in a deep tenor.

"Have you had much experience with infants, Miss Lawson?" McCalpin peered intently at her.

"I've been responsible for my brother since he was one," she whispered, always mindful of a sleeping infant. She glanced at Lady Pembrooke. "I won't keep you any longer, my lady. Good day, Lord Pembrooke."

The Marquess of McCalpin turned toward her, but she didn't bother to extend her hand or wait for a good-bye greeting. She nodded at Faith, and the trio exited the hall for the entry.

The faster she could leave, the less chance she'd say

something she'd regret. How in the world had she ever looked upon him as Michelangelo's *David*?

He was more like the devil with donkey ears.

McCalpin escorted the Lawson sisters and Mr. Hart to the front door. March refused to look in his direction as she took her leave while Miss Faith just nodded her farewell.

As he watched the trio make their way to the street, McCalpin's gaze narrowed on March's back. When he'd asked her about the forgery, her humiliation had caused her cheeks to darken to a deep pink. He'd immediately recognized her as a kindred spirit, since he understood her embarrassment.

He experienced paralyzing shame every time he believed someone would uncover his utter stupidity when it came to numbers. Always on the verge, he felt it every waking hour—always speculating if today would be his downfall, the day he failed in his duty.

McCalpin exhaled a painful sigh. If he'd been more diligent, perhaps he'd have caught her forgeries immediately and saved them all the extra effort and heartache. Now, he had to put more work on William's shoulders with the Lawson family affairs.

Miss Lawson's dismissal without a word made him grin. The young woman was obviously uncomfortable around him. However, no one would ever describe her as missish with the intent to get her way through flattery. Tall with beautiful dark brown hair and matching coppery brown eyes that flashed like molten gold when challenged, she would do very well in society. Men would no doubt flock around her.

He chuckled at her claim she could shear a sheep. He'd

pay money to behold such a sight. More importantly, her audacity to come into his house and demand money intrigued him. For some absurd reason, he wanted to find out more about the woman. Unlike others, she didn't seem impressed with him or his title, a refreshing rare event these days.

Buxton silently stood beside him. He lifted his eyebrows and watched the guests leave. "My lord, I had the kitchen prepare one of my famous tea services, much like the one you and Lord William can never finish. Your guests ate every bite. Very unusual for ladies to indulge so freely."

"Perhaps the hour-long trip from Leyton gave them a ravenous hunger," McCalpin answered.

Buxton clasped his hands in front of him and continued his watch as the trio climbed into a pony cart. "Indeed. I'd hate to think they hadn't had a proper meal before arriving."

# Chapter Four

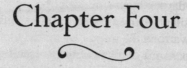

After the Pembroke family left, McCalpin and his brother returned to work. Several hours later, they'd finished a review of the estates' monthly budgets, and McCalpin had approved the plans for a renovation of the gardens at McCalpin Manor.

"Seems Lady Miranda has her sights on becoming your duchess." William sat in the chair in front of McCalpin's desk and took a sip of brandy as he stretched out his legs. "Clever how her father is constantly inviting you to dinner."

"A lot of good it will do. She can stand in line behind the others." A wave of distaste rippled into a grimace. McCalpin hated society chits whose only thoughts centered on luring him into matrimony. He wanted to be the one to pursue his mate and future wife, not the other way around.

He had very specific criteria for a wife. He wanted someone who would support his political work, perform marvelously as a hostess, and be someone well respected by the *ton*. However, the lady in question must have a strong aptitude and interest in the management of his estate and the future duchy. He didn't want just anyone prying into his business, but a wife, a life-long partner, whose values and talents would make his life all the easier.

"What did your little embezzler have to say for herself when you confronted her over the thousand-pound directive she'd forged?"

McCalpin took a swallow of the warmed spirit and let the liquor bathe his throat in a welcome relief that eliminated some of his weariness. Even with a fine glass of brandy, he dreaded to answer. "I didn't ask her. It would have been unspeakably cruel since she practically melted into her chair with embarrassment when I offered proof of her other withdrawals."

William took a deep breath and released an audible sigh. "Did Miss Lawson explain the smaller sums?"

McCalpin closed his eyes. All he could picture was March leaning over his desk with fire in her eyes insisting she was twenty-five. "Perhaps the smaller amounts were a test to see if I'd notice what was happening with the money. She claims the estate isn't profitable. When you took Mr. Hart and Miss Faith Lawson on the tour of the house, did you discover anything?"

"Nothing of importance. Miss Faith is a starch defender of her sister. She did share that Miss March has been supervising the estate since she was sixteen." He took another swallow of brandy. "I had a devil of a time keeping her with me. She insisted she return to her sister's side." Will rested his elbows on his knees and regarded him. "She seemed to think you would be rather harsh with her sister. What exactly did you do?"

"Nothing, really. I asked her how she got my seal. She told me she had one made from a letter our uncle had sent

to her father years ago. Pretty ingenious if truth be told."
He took another sip of brandy. "I told her to send me the
seal. I instructed her not to use it again." He remembered
the expression of utter defeat that had made her normal
peach tones turn almost pasty in color. "She looked devastated."

Will shook his head. "Whatever they're spending the
money on, it's not fashions. Miss Faith's dress was thread-
bare and several seasons out of fashion." He hesitated a
moment, then continued. "On our way back to rejoin you
in the study, Miss Faith asked if I minded if she took the
last tart from the tea service for her brother."

He pressed his eyes shut. To think they didn't have
enough food made him want to pound a wall. He should
have done more for the Lawson family when he first discovered he was responsible for the trusts.

"Do you think your little embezzler is spending it on
herself?" Baffled, William stared at him.

"Not likely. Her clothes were in worse shape than her
sister's was. There were several spots on the elbows that
appeared to have been patched from underneath." He released a breath of frustration. "Perhaps their circumstances are as dire as their clothing appears to be."

"There's only one way to find out. You or I could take
a trip to Leyton and see exactly what the situation is at
Lawson Court," William suggested.

"I better make the effort as I'm responsible for the
Lawson sisters' dowries. I'll visit tomorrow." McCalpin
released a breath he had not been aware he was holding.
"Miss Lawson said she used part of the money to buy a
new shearing tool."

"Your little embezzler shears sheep? My, my, a woman
of hidden talents. I imagine she probably possesses a
depth of farming knowledge that would make an ingénue

call for the smelling salts. If you change your mind and want company, just send word to Langham Hall. I'm going out tonight with Mother and Father to some dinner. Are you coming?" Will stood to take his leave.

"No. Nevertheless, do pay attention. You know how father is. He'll want to discuss everything in detail the next time we all gather to have dinner. The man thrives on politics."

William propelled himself away from the blue velvet chair and swept a hand through his hair. "McCalpin, I hate listening to political dribble. You're the one who enjoys it and gets everyone to listen to your arguments. Your talent for finding common ground between your adversaries is becoming renowned."

He enjoyed politics as much as his father did. However, he walked a fine line in such discussions. Any talk that spiraled into conversations about revenues, taxes, or money made his head spin.

"At next week's family dinner, Father is going to discuss you taking a seat in the House of Commons." Will eyed him warily. "You're forewarned, brother. Your reward for the way you handle people. 'A natural-born politician' is what father calls you."

McCalpin's indignant arched eyebrow melted, and he loudly exhaled. His so-called talent was simply a ruse to keep his weaknesses hidden.

"I'll do anything to help you. You know that," William offered.

His brother's simple words conjured up a long-ago memory that never ceased to haunt McCalpin.

He would steal away into the nursery and laboriously work on his numbers. Sitting for hours, he tried to win the battle of learning to add and subtract correctly. One day, William had completed an assignment within a half-hour, and his reward was an extended riding lesson.

Finding the task almost impossible, McCalpin had refused to cry in front of anyone. After several hours alone, he let the tears slip free. The hot splashes fell to the paper, causing the ink to run like black rivers and ruining his work. He'd worked all morning and had only completed half of the assignment.

His governess Mrs. Ivers hated him for his inability to do the calculations. When she found him staring at a page of incomprehensible scribblings, she'd taken a ruler to his knuckles.

"Your father would be better served if you were locked away in some remote tower on one of his lesser estates." Her haughty voice paralyzed him, and he couldn't move or protest. "I should tell His Grace that his precious heir is nothing more than a dullard incapable of counting his monthly allowance."

She'd broken the skin of his knuckles, and pain seared a path across his hand. However, he vowed not to flinch— he'd not give her the satisfaction.

She struck him again and sneered. "If you can't master these simple tasks, you'll never learn your multiplication tables much less how to manage the duchy. You'll be the Duke of Langham in name only. Someone else will be pulling your strings and running the duchy."

She raised the ruler once again. He closed his eyes hoping it would lessen the stinging torment. The familiar whiz of air hissed as the ruler flew through the air, and he tightened his gut in readiness.

But the piercing pain never occurred.

A small wee hand covered his.

When he opened his eyes, William stood between them.

"That is the last time you hit my brother." The quiet determination on William's face made him appear years older than seven. "When I tell our father you've struck the marquess, I have little doubt you'll be looking for a new position this afternoon."

Incredulous, Mrs. Ivers' mouth gaped open. Without another word, she spun on her heel and ran from the room.

As if nothing evil had happened, William placed an orange before him. "Riding lessons aren't any fun if you're not there."

McCalpin laid his head on his arms to hide the tears that now streamed down his face. Once under control, he wiped his eyes. There was nothing to hide as they both knew he couldn't do his assignments. "You shouldn't have done that. What if she turns her ire on you?"

"She won't be here." William had peeled the orange and had placed the fruit before McCalpin. "I'll never let you suffer like that again. From now on, I'll always be by your side."

The memory of his brother's staunch defense that day still had the power to make McCalpin's throat tighten.

"You're not going to like what I have to say, but"—William's deep tenor brought him out of his reverie—"perhaps you should think about marrying someone with enough intelligence and interest in politics that she could help you."

"A wife?" McCalpin clenched the brandy, but thankfully the leaded glass didn't shatter. "And how shall I go about finding this paragon? Take out an ad in *The Midnight Cryer*? 'Ducal heir who can't add two numbers seeks a diamond of the first water with implicit deportment, political savvy, and the analytical skills of an advanced mathematician as his future duchess.'"

William strode to the settee in front of the fireplace and sat with a dejected plop. "I'm not trying to start a fight."

"Are you tiring of our arrangement, Will?" A knot rose in McCalpin's throat.

"Absolutely not. I'll always help you." William rose to face him. "A wife would be a helpmate with all the trappings that comes with being the Marchioness of McCalpin." He lowered his voice to a whisper. "One day you'll be the Duke of Langham. The perfect duchess would make your life not only more pleasant, but she could help you shoulder the responsibility."

William had always been McCalpin's best friend and greatest champion. Whatever was of interest to McCalpin always became a shared interest with William. When they were growing up, his younger brother always followed him around, mimicking his movements. William had made their childhood a fond memory. Time after time, they shared adventures with the accompanying scrapes and bruises.

William had never displayed or hinted that he envied it was McCalpin and not him who was their father's heir. Their travails in the classroom under the tutelage of Mr. Maxwell were only bearable because of William. He always helped McCalpin in his assignments and never tormented him over his difficulties.

Neither did Mr. Maxwell. When reports were required of the boys' and Emma's progress, the tutor had focused on the areas where McCalpin excelled—languages, literature, and logic.

The kind tutor had been one of the most influential people in McCalpin's early life. When he'd struggled with a lesson, Mr. Maxwell had patiently sat and broken the problem into several tasks that made it easier for him to understand. They'd practiced the more difficult ones repeatedly. The tutor had once confided his younger sister found reading as difficult as McCalpin's constant struggles with numbers. The learning strategies he'd developed for her were ones he applied to McCalpin, and it resulted in one of the few times in McCalpin's life he didn't feel as if he needed to hide his shortcomings.

What he wouldn't give to find that type of peace again.

With a steadying breath, McCalpin made the only decision a loyal brother could reach. "Thank you for your advice. I always thought I'd marry someday, but perhaps I should give it more consideration."

William's audible sigh of relief filled the room. "That's wise. Father told me that Aunt Stella is leaving me her estate in Northumberland. Our parents think I should start to spend some time with her." William shifted in his seat as if uncomfortable, then stood. "Let me know about Leyton, will you?"

"Will"—McCalpin lowered his voice—"a moment, please."

William nodded, but a new uncertainty had crept into his expression.

"I know you're sacrificing your own happiness by helping me. I'll not forget it. All my personal investments are to go to you. Russell has drawn up the documents, and Somerton knows my wishes also."

"God, I hate it when you talk like this. I'm your brother, and I love you. It's not a job. It's what family does for one another." William's familiar lopsided grin made an impromptu appearance. "I'm curious. What are you going to do with Miss Lawson's one-thousand-pound withdrawal?"

McCalpin hesitated. Like a thief, disquiet stole into his thoughts. "Give it to her, but no more. When I see her,

I'll tell her it's the last monies she'll receive without my personal approval first."

Will nodded.

Immediately, his thoughts retuned to the lovely Miss Lawson and her penchant to consider her trust as nothing more than her own personal bank. No matter what, he'd not let anyone take advantage of him and his weakness.

# Chapter Five

March leaned back in her chair and stretched. The stiffness in her neck was a painful reminder she had failed to move in over two hours as she balanced the household accounts. How could they spend so much money while everything was falling apart around them? Regardless, she needed the accounts to be in perfect shape when the marquess wanted to review the estate and its financials. She clung to the belief he'd help them; otherwise, she didn't think she could survive another year of such dire circumstances.

Julia squeezed through the crack in the open door. "Cousin Rupert is here and demands to see you."

Her sister's evasive action didn't stop the man from barging into the study. Rupert Lawson examined the contents of the room, taking particular notice of a valuable small painting above the desk behind her, the crystal inkwell that had been a gift of some foreign dignitary, and the sterling silver tea set on the desk. By the arrogant smirk, he must have been pleased with his accounting.

Rupert still smarted over the fact that her brother, Bennett, was Lord Lawson while he remained a simple "mister." However, as Rupert's father was the younger brother of her father, March tolerated his visits.

A pallid ghost of a smile lined Rupert's face. "March, bad form to keep me waiting. Why is that lovely creature Julia answering the door? You should invest in a footman."

The man's voice could clear vultures from a fresh kill.

"Julia, thank you. Will you see if Bennett needs help with his lessons?" She didn't want her sister within ten feet of him. She already knew the gist the conversation would take this afternoon. March would fend off an offer for Julia's hand while Rupert belittled her and the rest of her family.

He fought to remove the leather gloves from his pudgy hands. His body had grown corpulent over the years, including his swollen head. Granted, he had once been handsome, but his taste for spirits and extravagant dinners had taken a toll on his features, and his waist had thickened.

"Cousin, where are your manners? Oh, the thought escaped me. You don't have any. Your parents spent too much time in New York." Using an ebony cane for support, he squeezed his hefty body into the chair beside the desk. "I'll take a glass of brandy. The wind is quite wicked this morning."

Her cousin's appearance would make doing the household ledger appealing, but the best course of action was to finish this interview. "I could offer you tea."

A triumphant smile spread across his mouth that caused his red cheeks to congeal in round circles. His eyes squeezed shut much like a rat with a delectable morsel. "Times that bad, eh? Do yourself and your family a favor. Let me take care of you."

March rose from the desk and walked to the fireplace. It would take little effort to kick his chair over and watch as his arms and legs flailed like a beetle trying to turn over when it had landed on its back. Pleasure at such an image allowed her to answer his question with an even temper.

"That's not necessary. We have everything we need." She tilted her head and forced a smile, though he deserved a sneer.

His cane wobbled as he rose from the chair. "I've observed your spending habits in the village. You have no money." With a deep sigh, he placed his beaver hat upon his head.

March thanked the merciful heavens for small miracles. He was leaving. She kept her hands busy and tended the small fire. "Thank you for your visit." She didn't dare turn, for fear he'd stay longer.

"You really have no other alternatives. No one wants you or your crippled sister. Now Julia"—he fought to take a deep breath and wheezed—"would make a fine match with a local farmer or perhaps a younger son of a local gentry's family. However, being foremost a good man and head of this family, I intend to marry her. I'll not let you and Faith starve. Bennett needs a man's influence. The boy must learn how to carry himself."

"How kind of you to offer," she demurred. "But we've gone over this before. There's no use in rehashing old arguments. My sisters shall have a Season in London before they marry."

"What nonsense! You're just wasting money you don't possess. Let me marry Julia, and I'll see you and your sisters are welcomed into society with open arms." He walked to the door and turned. "I'll come to dinner on Sunday. We can discuss it in more detail then. Oh, by the way, I'm running the hounds over Lawson Court's acreage in next week's hunt. In exchange for the courtesy, I'll present the foxtail to Faith after church. It'd be a high honor."

"Pompous, cruel arse," March whispered. White-hot anger lit a fire through her veins. Her cousin's only purpose was to humiliate Faith publicly with his cruel deed. Just another attack in his war to win Julia's hand. No doubt, the Marquess of McCalpin's signature and wax seal might come into use when she dealt with the odious Rupert Lawson.

Tonight, she'd write a letter forbidding Rupert from trespassing at Lawson Court. It would be her last act with the marquess's seal before she sent it to him. Even if the marquess wasn't currently responsible for the estate, he had a vested interest in her family. He'd not allow Rupert to hunt on the property.

Without waiting for her response, he continued, "Did I mention that the north pasture wall has fallen? Your sheep looked to be escaping."

"Why didn't you tell me?" March dropped the fire iron and whirled to face him, but he'd left the room. For such a large man, he moved incredibly fast. "Because, no doubt, you probably caused the damage," she whispered to no one.

She pushed a stray lock of hair from her face as she raced to the entry of the house. They couldn't afford to lose a single sheep. She had counted on that wool this spring to pay for part of the estate expenses.

She struggled to free her cloak, hat, and gloves from the hook by the front door. "Bennett, come quickly."

Book in hand, her brother bounded down the steps. "What is it?"

"The sheep are free in the north pasture. I need your help bringing them back. Do you know where Hart is?"

Bennett shook his head. "He left early this morning."

Without waiting for her brother, she flew down the drive. Bennett would follow immediately. When they reached the pasture, the scene before them was utter chaos. Sheep streamed through the fallen rocks of the wall as if invited by the Prince Regent himself to an outing. Some of the animals stood within feet of the opening chewing grass, while the more adventuresome had roamed into the furrowed field beside the north pasture.

Both she and Bennett made quick work of herding the animals back into their own pasture. Their sheepdog performed marvelously as he nipped the hind legs of the most rebellious rams and ewes, forcing them farther back into the field away from the fallen rock.

With Bennett's help, she stacked enough stone back into place so that the sheep would have to jump if they wanted to escape again. It wasn't a permanent fix to the problem, but that would have to make do.

"Let's see if we can move this one." March waited for her brother to heft one side of a particularly large rock. "If we can manage this one, it'll keep the opening closed until Hart can repair it properly."

Bennett nodded and took a deep breath. His arms surrounded one end of the rock, and she took the other side. On the count of three, they hoisted the limestone mass. He stumbled under the weight, and the stone shifted toward March. She managed to step away before the rock smashed her boots, but a sharp edge ripped through the glove on her left hand.

"March, I'm sorry. . . ." Bennett's eyes widened, and his lower lipped trembled.

She glanced at all the red that bubbled through the rip in her glove. Once through, the blood flowed fast like a raging river in a flood. Time stood still, and she was unable to think of anything else as she waited for the pain to catch up with her thoughts. The throbbing sensation finally slammed through her hand. "Go get help," she whispered.

Her brother took a step toward her, then pivoted on a foot and broke into a frantic run.

With every beat of her pulse, pain thumped throughout her hand and spread up her arm as if laying siege to her body. Instinctively, she raised her hand above her heart and pressed the wound close. The sticky liquid seeped through her clothing, and a heady metallic smell wafted through the air. She turned from the smell and took a deep breath, hoping it would calm her thundering heartbeat. She wobbled on her feet. The sight of her own blood always made her feel faint. It was ironic, really. She was a farmer and never bothered by it when she hunted or dressed a fowl for dinner. Nor did it bother her to take care of Bennett's many scrapes and bruises.

However, when she saw a drop of her own blood, her mind reeled with images of poor Faith lying on the field with her broken leg covered in blood.

She shifted her feet apart to steady her stance.

"Miss Lawson?" A deep voice hovered above as if an angel called her forward. It reminded her of brandy— smooth, dark, rich. "I was on my way to the house when I saw you and the boy."

She shook her head to clear the miasma that blanketed her. With a stumble, she squared her shoulders.

"Miss Lawson, are you unwell?" The warm voice was one she now recognized and came from over her shoulder.

This was no angel. If she fainted on the spot, she would count it as a blessing. She'd not have to deal with *him*.

"Miss—"

"My lord." She swallowed to clear the thickness that clogged her throat. She turned her head to glance behind her. The movement caused her to sway, but she willed herself to remain standing. "No. I'm injured. That was my brother you saw."

The whirl of a black greatcoat swept by her. Suddenly, the Marquess of McCalpin stood before her. His eyes widened when he caught sight of the hand she held close to her body.

"Stop." Her whispery plea sounded weak to her own ears. Her body took control at that moment, trying to rid itself of the shock by shivering uncontrollably. "Please. I'll—I'll faint if you come closer."

He ignored her command and took the forbidden step forward. A response so typical of a male—always charging ahead when the most prudent action required one to analyze the situation. The vision of him swam before her eyes. Her shivers intensified, and her whole body shook.

"Will you allow me to examine your hand?" He reached for her, and she pitched forward.

Her vision grew dark, and the ringing in her ears increased. Abruptly, the world tilted sideways as she fell. When he caught her, warmth enveloped her and arms of banded steel held her close. She closed her eyes and breathed deep. The scent of pine and leather layered with something male chased away the iron scent that had invaded her nose. For a moment, all was well in the world. Unfortunately, her relief was short-lived. No doubt, her blood was staining his clothing. She tried to pull away, but his arms held her tight.

"I'll ruin your coat," she whispered.

"Shh." He studied her face. "I'm going to lean you against the wall and get something from my mount." He didn't wait for her acknowledgment as he lowered her into a sitting position.

She sat still and observed his movements. He stepped to his horse, a big dappled gray, and opened a bag tied to the saddle. It took too much effort to watch anymore. She rested her head against the rock wall. A slight breeze caused her hair to dance about her face. She lost track of time. It was difficult to concentrate. Somehow, he'd reached her side and knelt before her. The blade of a knife caught the light with a flash of silver.

"A knife?" Her voice echoed inside her brain as if she were talking inside a barrel.

He took her injured hand in his, the gentle touch reassuring.

"I can't look down or I'll faint." She closed her eyes. The effort kept her from swooning and hid the sight of her blood.

"You don't need to watch. I'm just cutting the glove away from your hand. I can't see how badly you're injured unless I examine the wound." The low rumble of words buzzed around her like a giant honeybee. "Will you allow me to do that?"

She shook her head and tried to pull her hand away. These were her last pair of work gloves, and she didn't have any extra money to replace them.

"Please, don't." Her family's humiliating circumstances caused her face to heat. Why couldn't the flush have settled in her body instead of her face? At least she'd have some much-needed warmth. She took a deep breath to salvage some dignity. "They're my last pair."

The strength in his grasp kept her from successfully removing her hand from his.

"Trust me," he whispered, "they're ruined. May I cut it off?"

With no other choice, March reluctantly nodded her assent. A few tugs, and her fingers were free. "What do you see?"

The heat of his hand beneath hers was a startling contrast to the coolness of her palm. He must have taken his glove off. The comfort of his touch settled her shakes until they diminished into slight tremors.

"It's a nasty cut that will require a few stitches. I need to wrap your hand until I get you to the house."

"I didn't know you were arriving today." She had no idea if she was speaking aloud. The blood had robbed her of her senses.

"Our last meeting left me curious. I decided to visit sooner rather than later, and hoped you could answer my questions." The gentleness in his voice matched the compassionate touch of his hand.

She dared to open her eyes, and he was staring at her. The blue in his eyes was deeper than any sapphire. Her *David* was back—not some arrogant goat who sauntered about the world as if it owed him everything. Today, he would slay any foe that threatened his world.

"Oh." *What a moronic thing to utter.*

She clenched her eyes tight and tried to think of something witty. When she opened her eyes, he had untied his neckcloth and was wrapping it around her hand. She couldn't look down so she concentrated on the sun-kissed skin of his neck, layered and corded with tendons and muscles that peeked from the opening of his shirt. Good heavens, could the man's beauty not bother her for any length of time?

When he rested on his haunches above her, she dared not steal a glimpse of his muscled legs. Either a view of his legs or the sight of her blood would be the death of her.

"Stay here and I'll fetch Donar." His hand still rested under hers. He pressed her hand against her chest and caused another wave of lightheadedness. "Keep your hand elevated."

He left her side, then brought his horse around.

"I'll help you stand." Without waiting for her acquiescence, he pulled her up. When she weaved unsteadily, he brought her against his chest. "I'm going to pick you up and lift you onto the saddle."

She stiffened in his arms. "You can't. I'm too . . . too large. You'll hurt yourself."

"Are you calling me weak? You insult me after I've taken great care of you?" His gaze captured hers, and the tiny lines around his eyes hinted at his amusement. "Are you ready?"

Before she could protest, he lifted her onto the horse's back. "Grab his mane with your right hand and hold tight."

She did as instructed. At this point, she didn't have the wherewithal to argue. Her vise-like grip had to be painful for the horse, but it was the only way she could ensure she'd not fall off the other side.

Gracefully, McCalpin lifted himself into the saddle and settled behind her. He reached around her and gently took the reins draped to the side. "Easy now. Lie back against me, and I'll get you home."

He reeled Donar in the direction of the house. Across the field, Hart raced toward them on one of the draught horses the estate owned. He came to a sudden stop. Donar danced back several steps as if displeased with the intrusion of the workhorse.

McCalpin patted the dappled gray and murmured something that immediately calmed its skittishness.

"I just returned from the village, and Bennett told me

what happened. He's coming with the cart." Hart didn't spare a glance at McCalpin. His eyes widened when he saw the bloodstains. "How bad is it?"

McCalpin pulled her tight against him. His warmth embraced her, and the shock of the accident had suddenly made her very tired. Everything, including the conversation, moved slowly.

"She'll need it sewn up, but the cut was straight." The scent of pine joined the heady experience of his arms enveloping her. If she had perished, then this was surely heaven.

"I'll inform Mrs. Oliver. She's the best with cuts that require stitches." Hart reeled the draught horse around, then galloped away.

McCalpin bent his head toward hers. If she wasn't mistaken, his chin had just brushed against her ear as if imparting a great secret. "There's no cause to hurry. It appears the bleeding has stopped."

With a voice as smooth as thick velvet, she could listen to him for hours, maybe days, even if he were reciting the ledger from her household accounts. All she could manage was a nod.

It made little difference if they ever made it back to the house. Heaven with her *David* was quite nice.

Completely ignoring her protests, McCalpin swept March from Donar and carried her inside to the kitchen. An older woman, the presumed Mrs. Oliver, waited for them by the table with everything required to mend the cut already prepared. There was even a small glass of brandy poured.

"Miss March, let me have a look," Mrs. Oliver clucked. She didn't spare a glance at McCalpin. With a surprisingly quick flourish for an old lady, Mrs. Oliver had his neckcloth free from March's hand and thrown into a heap on the floor by his side. "That cloth is ruined."

When the old lady twisted her hand gently to investigate the depth of the gash, March winced and grew paler than when he had first found her.

"Mrs. Oliver, this is the Marquess of McCalpin." The foreign wispiness in March's voice betrayed her suffering.

She bore little resemblance to the woman who had challenged him in London. When she'd parried his constant questions that day she sat in his study, she had a brightness and self-assuredness about her that drew his respect. Not someone easily dismissed as he'd discovered.

Now, her skin resembled newly fallen snow, and her mouth had tightened in a line. All her shimmering defiance had deserted her. She refused to show any hint she suffered, but her pain was evident if the creases around her eyes were any indication.

"This will sting, but we need to clean your hand." Mrs. Oliver brought a pan of water to the table. She was extremely gentle with her as if many times before, she'd experienced March's reaction to blood.

March stiffened in response. Without second-guessing himself, McCalpin grabbed her other hand in his. The water beneath a frozen pond had to be warmer than her skin. He placed his other hand over the top of her hand and gently rubbed the circulation back. Mrs. Oliver nodded her approval. As soon as March's hand hit the water, she flinched.

He leaned forward and whispered in her ear, "Squeeze my hand. Think of how angry you were when you came to see me."

"What she ought to do is think of who caused all this.

Rupert Lawson." The old woman practically spit her disgust across the room. "Nothing good ever comes—"

"Mrs. Oliver, please . . ." March's voice trailed to nothing.

The old lady narrowed her eyes. "Only reason you're hurt, my miss."

McCalpin's gaze darted from the old lady to March. "Who's Rupert Lawson?"

"My cousin," March offered weakly. "How am I going to shear this week?"

"I shouldn't have brought *it* up." Mrs. Oliver gently took March's hand out of the water and dried it. She trickled a little brandy over the wound, eliciting a hiss from March.

"It'll keep it from festering when I sew it up." Mrs. Oliver directed this tidbit to McCalpin.

He nodded absently and took what remained of the brandy and held it to her lips. She shook her head and turned away.

"Drink it," he ordered.

Her gaze darted to his. Fear clouded her eyes. Again, he held the glass to her mouth. This time she took a sip and immediately coughed.

"Four or five quick stitches ought to do the trick," Mrs. Oliver announced. She gently placed March's outstretched hand on the table, then turned her back in such a manner that it hid her movements from both of them.

He glanced around the neat, but barren kitchen. The house would once have been quite a handsome establishment. The architectural details included intricately carved moldings and two large crystal chandeliers. The previous viscounts had quite a fine taste for all things. The spacious kitchen had the facilities to accommodate a large staff. The oven and massive fireplace rivaled the ones in his father's London home. Though it was the dead of winter, the fire consisted of only a couple of logs. Just one small roasting pot sat nearby.

Mrs. Oliver turned briefly and gave McCalpin a nod to signal she was about to sew up the wound. She resumed her position with her back to them. Silence descended, and March tightened her hold on his hand as she waited.

The lines around her pursed mouth reminded him of pure agony. A woman should never suffer like this.

"If I have forty-three sheep that all need to be groomed before shearing, how will I get the work done?" March muttered to herself. "If I get on average of a half-pound per fleece . . . no, now that they've gotten into the mud, I'll be lucky to get a quarter of a pound. What's that amount?"

Her grip was surprisingly strong. When he'd examined her out in the field, the coldness of her hand, heightened by her roughened skin, indicated she was accustomed to physical work.

She jerked slightly and pressed her eyes closed as Mrs. Oliver sewed the first stitch. "Help me with the figures." Her voice thinned to a suffocating whisper as she pleaded with her eyes for his help. "I need to know how much we'll have."

His heartbeat raced as he realized what she wanted. He had no earthly clue how to calculate such a number.

Not here, not without chalk. Not without a board. Not in front of her.

"*Miss March,* leave your damnable sheep worries be. You have more important things to concentrate on at this moment." The affection in the servant's voice was unmistakable. "Those animals will be your downfall. Try to think of something pleasant while I work." Without a glance, she addressed McCalpin. "Perhaps, my lord, you could get her mind off those wool bags."

There was only one thing to do to keep March preoccupied. Gently, so as not to scare her, he brushed the back of his fingers against her cheek and brought his mouth close to hers. Her eyes flew to his.

"Think of this," he whispered before he brushed his lips against hers. It was the perfect way to take her mind off the needle, but more important, off her calculations.

March exhaled and opened her eyes. Her gaze darted to his once again, and the pulse in her lovely neck throbbed in answer. The copper color of her irises was stunning, and flecks of brown and gold accented it. He'd never considered brown eyes particularly attractive, but hers were rich and sweet like warmed brandy. The dullness gone, and in its place was surprise.

March's servant was completely absorbed in her work. He took advantage of the opportunity and lowered his mouth to hers again. Shocked at his own eager response to her taste, he wanted to explore her luscious mouth at leisure. He drew his tongue against the seam of her lips.

She flinched.

*What was he thinking to have stolen a kiss?*

"I apologize," he whispered and drew back. "I'd hoped the distraction—"

"Mrs. Oliver," she whispered in return, "another stitch." Her pale complexion had warmed to a hue that reminded him of the spring's first roses.

"That didn't take too long, now did it? I'm proud of you, Miss March," the old woman chortled with her back still turned. Gathering the necessary wraps to protect the stitches, she stepped away from the table, then stilled. With a wry smile, she winked at him. "I'm grateful for the comfort you offered too, whether she realizes it or not."

Completely oblivious to the old woman's teasing, March lifted her hand and examined the wound.

"My pleasure, madam." He devoted his attention to March. "May I?"

Her gaze drifted from her hand to his eyes. He focused on the brilliant pink of her cheeks and her red swollen lips. She took deep breaths, as if she'd run across the estate. She held her hand, palm up, for his inspection. Sewn in even neat stitches, the wound was pink, but there was little sign of bleeding.

"An admirable job, Mrs. Oliver," he offered while smiling at March. Her eyes widened in answer.

The old woman nodded as she stepped close with clean white strips of linen. "I've done my fair share of tending wounds over the years. You have to be quick with the needle and not dillydally."

As she wrapped March's hand, a young lad stepped into the kitchen. "Are you all right?"

For the first time, McCalpin saw March smile, one that bespoke true affection. It was one of those rare smiles that he'd remember his entire life. She was breathtakingly beautiful.

"I'm fine, Bennett."

"I'm sorry . . ."

"It was an accident, sweetheart. Let's not mention it again." Her normal refined brightness finally replaced her earlier flat tone. "Let me introduce you to Lord McCalpin."

The boy, who favored his sister in both features and

coloring except for his startling green eyes, stepped forward and regarded McCalpin. Without any prompting from his sister, he held out his hand. "I'm Lord Bennett Lawson."

With a nod, McCalpin shook his small hand. "It's a pleasure."

Bennett grinned. "Call me Lawson. That's how men address each other."

"Only if you call me McCalpin." He glanced at March. She directed her attention to her brother. Without pain and shock marring her features, she was striking. Her fondness for her brother made her radiant.

She extended her hand out for her brother's inspection.

"May I see the stitches this evening?" Bennett asked. Before she could answer, March's brother turned his attention to McCalpin. "Did you get the chance to examine it? How many stitches?" His gaze met McCalpin's as if it was completely normal to ask such questions of a marquess.

"Five." As a boy, he'd been fascinated by cuts and wounds also. "Straight cut but will leave a scar, unfortunately."

"A badge of honor. I wish I could have seen it." Bennett grimaced. As was typical of youth, his focus quickly turned to other matters. "As a thank you for rescuing my sister, I'd like to invite you to stay for dinner."

"Bennett—" Before March could finish her protest, McCalpin took her uninjured hand and gently squeezed.

"Stay for dinner, McCalpin," the boy cajoled.

"Bennett, I'm sure Lord McCalpin—" The color was starting to deepen on March's face, the perfect pink replaced by the most enticing scarlet.

"How lovely. Thank you, Lawson." He'd finally see

exactly what their circumstances were and why she was forging his name to embezzle those funds.

March discretely nodded to Mrs. Oliver. The old woman's eyebrows shot skyward.

# Chapter Six

The set table was reminiscent of Christmastide dinner. The delicate china that bore the viscountcy's seal, the polished silver serving pieces, cutlery, and even the massive centerpiece of evergreens and a few apples and walnuts brought an unabashed elegance to the formal dining room. Only the buckets strategically located to capture the rain that leaked from the roof marred the scene in front of her family and Lord McCalpin.

March pressed her eyes closed at the humiliation of their current circumstances. Yet, McCalpin needed to see how they were living and change things for the better. She just prayed that the modest feast splayed before him would be enough to keep his attention throughout dinner.

The roasted pheasant was supposed to have lasted for two days, but with the marquess accepting Bennett's invitation, they were lucky to have it on hand. March wouldn't take any so there would be plenty. Besides, her hand had started to pound with throbbing pain. She'd never be able to cut the meat.

She chanced a glance at Bennett, who sat enthralled with McCalpin's discussion of London's museums. Serving the fowl this evening meant Bennett would suffer through ham and beans for two days this week. Would he have invited the marquess to join them if he knew the result of such an invitation?

How inhospitable of her to even think such thoughts. The look on her brother's face was pure rapture. So starved for an adult male's companionship outside of Hart, he'd probably subject himself to a week's worth of the meager offerings.

Bennett insisted he sit at the head of the table. The large chair seemed to swallow his small body. McCalpin sat to his right. She sat at Bennett's left. Loyal Faith sat next to her, and Julia sat next to their guest.

Faith leaned close. "I don't know how you did it, but the table looks magnificent."

"Miss Lawson." The sinfully dark voice commanded her attention. "I agree with Miss Faith. Everything is simply delicious."

"Thank you, my lord." She tried to smile, but the pain had increased to the point that such an effort only resulted in a grimace. Her voice sounded as dull as a rusty ax. "We don't have the opportunity to entertain much at Lawson Court. We're delighted to have your company."

His eyes narrowed as if he doubted the truth of her words. The blue of his eyes pierced hers. Her *David* was back in his full glory. For a moment, she couldn't breathe as she gazed upon his perfection. This close to him, she could make out a faint scar that marred his square chin. It was the only imperfection in his features. To call him handsome was like calling Michelangelo someone who played with rocks and painted as a hobby.

"You're not feeling well," he whispered.

Bennett tilted his head in her direction at the marquess's question. "March, are you all right?"

A sudden flush washed over her face when everyone's gaze settled on her. "I'm fine." She took a sip of wine. The crisp taste washed away the irksome bile that had taken refuge in her throat. She only hoped she'd make it through the evening without dying of embarrassment or falling off her chair in pain.

"My lord, tell us of the entertainments you enjoy in London." Julia's simple question hinted at her desperation to escape their paltry existence.

McCalpin grinned as he played with the stem of his wine glass. His large fingers dwarfed the fragile crystal, but there was an inherent gentleness in his hands. He'd treated her with the same care out in the field. Even though she couldn't remember much of their interaction, she'd felt safe and protected.

She relived the kiss he bestowed upon her in the kitchen. Her lips still burned from the touch. Another example of his kindness, but one that didn't mean anything more than what it represented. She was a sheep farmer, and he had simply tried to relieve her pain and squelch her fear with a harmless flirtation.

"Miss Julia, that question begs a thousand answers. During the day, I take an early morning ride in town for exercise. Then I return to work on the business of my father's estates. It's only in the evenings that I have cause to enjoy all the wonders of London's offerings. . . ."

His words trailed to silence as Maximus, Bennett's monstrous black cat, stopped all conversation as he strolled into the room, making a grand entrance. Bigger than a lapdog and most felines, his size and speed served him well. He was the best mouser they had. With raised eyebrows, McCalpin regarded the cat as it promenaded through the dining room. He gently placed his napkin beside his plate and devoted his full attention to the spectacle taking place.

With a saunter that any London dandy would envy and his tail straight in the air, the cat regally paraded through the room as he made his way to Bennett and their guest. A small animal—*a very dead small animal*—dangled from his jaws. With an elegant pause worthy of a king, Maximus regarded McCalpin with his startling golden eyes. The black cat must have found him worthy of his offering. With great fanfare that would rival a volley of trumpets announcing the Prince Regent, Maximus dropped the small rabbit to the ground, then blinked.

Bennett's eyes grew round, and a laugh escaped. "Lud! Maximus! What a catch!" Her brother's gaze shot to the marquess. "We'll eat well tomorrow, McCalpin. Rabbit stew for dinner. Would you care to join us?"

"Bennett, no!" March didn't hide the strong rebuke.

"Why? We have food for tomorrow. Why shouldn't we share our good fortune?" Completely oblivious of the awkwardness he and his cat had created, Bennett left his chair, then petted his charge. "Nice work, boy."

"We'll discuss this later," March bit out as she directed her gaze to Julia in a signal for her sister to remove the poor rabbit.

The cat had the audacity to purr loud enough that his low rumblings echoed through the room. One giant paw shot out and tapped the carcass twice as if tempting it to move so he could pounce again and repeat his performance.

Julia jumped away from the table, upsetting her chair. "*Eww,* that's disgusting."

Without glancing at anyone, Faith got up from the table and picked up the rabbit with her napkin. With halting steps, she left the room and turned left. There was little doubt she was delivering the rabbit to Mrs. Oliver for a determination if they could dine on it tomorrow.

Heat assaulted March once again as she couldn't deny the truth. Indeed, if Mrs. Oliver declared it eatable, tomorrow, they would dine on rabbit stew and be thankful for Maximus's hunting prowess.

McCalpin's gaze locked with hers. She tried to swallow her mortification.

Of all the days for that feline, who believed they all served him instead of the other way around, to present his latest kill, today was not the day. Then, for Bennett practically to announce their poverty?

This was an unmitigated disaster of epic proportions.

"Miss Lawson—" The steel in McCalpin's voice cut her to the bone.

"Shall we continue our discussion in Bennett's study?" If he started to lecture her in front of her family, she'd fall to pieces. Her family hadn't a clue the true level of their destitution. After everything that had happened today, she'd not withstand a withering diatribe about her family's circumstances. She already felt like a failure, one who couldn't provide for her loved ones. Today made Rupert's words all the more bitter. If she didn't do something soon, Julia would be married to that fiend and they'd all be under his thumb. Her sweet little sister would make such a sacrifice if she believed it would help the family.

An involuntary shudder passed through March. Under no circumstances would she allow Julia to marry Rupert. It was a vow she intended to keep.

"I'll join you," Bennett said.

"No, Lawson. Allow me a private conference with

your sister," the marquess announced in a voice that would brook no argument.

"But it's my study," Bennett grumbled still petting the cat.

March held her hand above her heart to lessen the throbbing pain stealing her breath. The strong scent of spirits wafted toward her. McCalpin held a flask to her.

"Take a sip, Miss Lawson." The sharp edge in McCalpin's voice warned he'd not abide any argument from her. "You're as pale as a ghost in November."

March blew out a breath and took the silver flask. The fumes burned her nose, but she took a drink and immediately started to cough. The heat of the liquid burned her throat as she swallowed. McCalpin nodded his head, encouraging her to take another swallow. Without arguing, she complied.

McCalpin took the Louis XV chair across from her. His mammoth size dwarfed the frame, and the chair creaked in protest at his invasion. He regarded her with a calm expression as if it was completely natural to share a flask of brandy with her after dinner.

"Thank you," she whispered. The searing pain in her hand started to ease. "I must apologize—"

"Will you eat the hare tomorrow as your brother indicated?" The sound of his voice echoed like the retort of a pistol.

"If Mrs. Oliver believes it's not spoiled." She forced herself to hold his gaze. It was mortifying to acknowledge the extent of their destitution. Her father, the previous viscount, had been a well-respected member of the government's foreign office and had served England unselfishly in his tenuous work with the United States. More importantly, he'd been a loving, doting father. He'd have been horrified if he knew his children's fate. Reason rallied as it always did when the circumstances of their poverty confronted her. As trustee, the marquess only had to sign a piece of paper resulting in their situation immediately rectified on the morrow. There was no use hiding the truth from him.

She dismissed the shame that had strolled into her conscience and was currently holding court with her thoughts. "What we ate tonight . . . should have lasted all week." She brought her injured hand down to rest in her lap. "If we don't eat the rabbit, I'll have to . . ."

"Christ," he muttered under his breath. "How long have you been living like this?"

"When my parents died, I took over the estate and the bookkeeping. I was sixteen, almost seventeen. So, to answer your question, eight years." She stole a glance at McCalpin's face and immediately thought of an etching of Mount Etna her father had once shown her as a little girl. Immobile, the marquess possessed a look of impassiveness tinted with an unpredictability that could erupt at any moment.

"We had a reserve of funds available but not enough to last through the year. I've managed to keep everyone fed and clothed, but this year"—she took a deep breath and held it for a second—"the roof was damaged during a winter storm. I had no recourse but to have it repaired, but it still needs additional work. If it wasn't for your sister's bank, I'm not certain what we would have done."

His gaze bore into hers with a dispassionate expression she couldn't decipher. If it was disgust, she couldn't— no—wouldn't allow herself to care. She'd done everything she could think of to protect Lawson Court and her family. Only when circumstances turned so dire had she started "borrowing" her own dowry funds using his signature. She tipped her chin up an inch.

He lifted one perfect eyebrow. The gesture made him look more handsome than any man had a right to be. "You bank with my sister, Lady Somerton." The words more of a statement than a question.

She nodded. "The countess has been my salvation over the last four months. She offered me employment at her bank, but I had to decline as our circumstances turned quite drastic."

His eyes narrowed as he considered her. "Did you write Lord Burns? Tell him of your circumstance?"

She nodded slightly. "Over the years, he ignored my requests for help. He never once visited after my parents died." She straightened in her chair. There was no use hiding the insidious predicament her family faced. "My cousin, Rupert Lawson, has taken an interest in Julia. I'm not in favor of his attentions toward my sister. He wants to become the family's guardian. It'll allow him unlimited access to our funds. I'm not certain there would be any left when they come of age."

"The next in line to inherit your brother's title wants to be his guardian and manage the estate? No court would ever agree to such an appointment." The incredulous look on his face would have been comical, but the truth was far from funny.

"Be that as it may, my siblings don't have a guardian and no one has responsibility for Lawson Court, so he could easily petition the court." By now, small tinges of pain had taken up residence in her fingers. It wouldn't be long before her hand started to throb once again. "The solicitors that my father employed for his legal work were incompetent, to say the least. The inferior work is rife throughout all his directives for our care. You only have to review my trust document for proof."

He pursed his lips at that innuendo.

"Rupert views Faith and me as tainted goods. Faith because of her injury, and me because I work the fields and care for the estate. Rupert's interested in Julia is the best means to acquire our monies. There's nothing to keep him from kidnapping her and taking her to Scotland. She's a loyal girl, and if Rupert could make her believe it would be the best scenario for the family, she'd sacrifice herself for us."

She swallowed but refused to turn away from his direct gaze. By the time he left, he'd know every one of her secrets. "The money I've tried to take from my trust will be used to launch Faith and Julia in society. They deserve the opportunity to make a match that will provide them with security and an escape from the hellish existence that we've lived under for the last eight years."

He nodded and rewarded her with a gentle smile that transformed him from handsome to heart stopping. She rose gently and attended the fire with her right hand. The simple task would distract her from his overwhelming presence.

Never before had such masculine perfection graced their home. With broad shoulders and a chest that narrowed to slim hips, he reclined in a manner that reminded her of a deadly panther relaxed but with a hidden strength that could strike in an instant. She'd seen that look countless times when Maximus would relax in the sun, soaking up its warmth. However, the slight twitch of his tail warned that he was always hunting as he had lazed about—just like the slow tapping of the marquess's finger against the arm of the chair.

She licked her lips at that thought. The marquess was the most virile creature she'd ever seen in her life—and he'd kissed her this morning. It'd been nothing more than a deterrent to her pain. Nevertheless, it was still the most delightful kiss she'd ever received in her life. She touched her fingers to her lips recalling the stroke of his tongue there. A glance in his direction caused her breath to catch. His gaze, hot and fiery, had settled on her mouth. His lips tilted upward in a slight grin that made her believe he could read her thoughts.

"And what about *your* hopes for a match, March?" The low gruffness in his voice soothed, but his words startled her like a lick of Maximus's rough tongue.

"I have none." She'd always dreamed of a match, but she'd quickly dashed such hopes when the weight of the estate fell upon her shoulders. She tilted her chin and regarded the marquess. "My only concern is for my family's welfare. I'll see my sisters married, and Bennett raised before I think of myself."

He stood and sauntered over to her. With an easy insouciance, he towered over her. Normally, she was the one who peered down into the faces of other men, but McCalpin stood a good six inches taller. Somehow he made her feel petite, a rare feat since she was tall—only four inches short of six feet.

"No thoughts of a husband or children in your near future? That's hard to fathom." He slowly reached out with his hand. The instant his finger touched her skin she gasped. He ignored her outcry and caressed her cheek with the back of his forefinger. "Such softness," he whispered.

"What are you doing?" Her voice trembled. She wanted to blame it on the throbbing pain, but she knew better. His touch could sooth a cobra. The heat of his hand coaxed her closer. Instead, she forced herself to step back.

"I'm trying to decide what to do with you, March." The sound of her name on his lips sounded like music, a soft serenade to lower her defenses. "And decide what type of woman stands before me."

He closed the distance between them and lowered his mouth to her ear. Without touching, the warmth of his breath caused her to shiver in a way completely different from this morning. Indeed, he could easily be her downfall.

"*La mia truffatrice*," he whispered. "*Mon beau voleur.*"

She didn't understand the Italian, but there was no mistaking his French. *Beautiful thief.* "I didn't steal," she protested.

"Until you turn twenty-five, the money belongs to the trust." He chuckled at her outrage. "When I first saw your forged requests for funds, I was completely amazed. The *M*'s were undeniably mine." He tut-tutted as if she were a contrary child who needed discipline. "How do you think I should punish you?"

"It's my money," she hissed.

"The kitten has claws." His pupils had dilated to a point where only a sliver of blue was visible. He tilted his head and regarded her. A gentle smile broke across his handsome face. "You'd like my punishment. It'd be similar to the kiss I bestowed upon your sweet lips earlier to dissuade you of thinking of your stitches. But I'd take more from you than just a gentle press of lips against lips."

"I'm not a kitten." She inhaled deeply. "Nor am I yours to play with."

He laughed, and the rich sound filled the study. "Indeed. Neither is my signature. Your little act must cease. I've instructed my solicitor to allow your one-thousand-pound request and have it deposited into your account. Do whatever you want with it. I'll start putting the estate back into profitable working order. However, I want a full accounting on what you've spent so far. Understood?"

She had no choice but to nod in agreement. Today, she had teetered as if on a precipice with no one to catch her. Why should now be any different? Life always dealt her a hand where she struggled daily while not having a clue about the future. Her pulse galloped at the realization he knew everything she'd done. She concentrated on the exotic wood crown molding that surrounded the study's ceiling. Every foot of wood contained a carved pattern of the Parthenon. Normally when she studied the columns, she found a familiar comfort, but not tonight.

"I don't want to see any more documents with my forged signature come across my desk." His voice softened. "I'll not be pleased."

She pursed her lips. This time she didn't nod her acquiescence.

"How's your pain?" he asked in a quiet voice that rumbled with some emotion she couldn't identify.

"Worse than when I came in here."

"Take this and drink half of it tonight." He extended the flask in an obvious gesture that she should accept. "Tomorrow, drink the other half before bed. The day after you shouldn't need it. If there's any sign of infection, send word to me. We'll have a doctor attend you."

The hum of his voice required she respond. With a brisk nod, she accepted the brandy.

His gaze caught hers. "Thank you for dinner. Your family was gracious to welcome me."

"It was our pleasure," she whispered. Her heart still hadn't settled after the revelation that *he was fully aware* that she'd tried to embezzle the astronomical amount of a thousand pounds from her own trust fund and forged his name.

He nodded and turned toward the door. He faced her once again with his brow crinkled in neat worry lines. "March, things will change for the better. You'll not have to carry this burden alone for much longer, I promise."

Without waiting for an answer, he strolled out of the room.

She pressed her eyes closed and waited for the pain to consume her again. What exactly was he promising?

# Chapter Seven

M cCalpin waited in his father's study after the summons had arrived earlier in the day. As a boy, then as a young man, he'd often heeded his father's call and waited in the spacious, masculine domain of the Duke of Langham for discussions, reprimands, and even celebrations. Every time he walked into the house, a familiar energy resonated deep within its walls, but for the first time ever, he could not ignore the innate silence that had descended. Only his brother remained living at Langham Hall with his parents. The rest of the family had moved on and started their own families.

Several years ago, his older cousin, Claire, who grew up with him, married Alexander Hallworth, the Marquess of Pembroke. Then his younger sister, Emma, married Nicholas St. Mauer, the Earl of Somerton and heir to the Duke of Renton. Claire was raising a family, and Emma was expecting her first. The family he had always cherished was changing and adding new generations.

A powerful sense of restlessness coursed through his

veins. He had always known he must marry and produce an heir for the duchy, but he'd pushed such a thought into the future. Not anymore. The time had come for a serious consideration of a wife.

"McCalpin?" William stood before him. "You're daydreaming."

"I've got several things on my mind." McCalpin exhaled. "I'm glad you're here. When I visited the Lawson family earlier in the week, I could only come to one conclusion. I've petitioned the Court of Chancery for guardianship over Lord Lawson and his family."

"Your little embezzler?" A smile broke across his brother's face as he took the seat next to McCalpin.

His lips twitched as his gaze settled on the wide expanse of Langham Park before him. The carefully manicured lawns, exotic plants, and magnificent trees didn't hold his focus. A tall, lushly curved, dark-haired farmer had taken command of his thoughts. He could still taste her delicious mouth that hinted of fresh peppermint. Her soft skin rivaled the most luxurious cashmere. He closed his eyes, remembering the silent "O" she'd made with that luscious mouth when he'd called her kitten.

He shook his head to leash his wandering musings. "Will you help me?"

"If you'll wipe that foolish grin from your face, then absolutely." William winged an eyebrow. "Same type of help?"

McCalpin nodded. "I'll need to present a full accounting on the state of the viscountcy."

The Duke of Langham strolled in with his wife on his arm. Each was a powerful presence on their own, but when combined as a united front, they were a force even the Prince Regent could not dissuade. Both he and William stood when they entered.

Obviously, he had misconstrued the summons. He believed this was nothing more than a call to go over their respective schedules for the next couple of months. His father had insisted he start to take a more active role in the duchy. With his mother present, the summons wasn't as innocuous as he first had believed.

"You're looking well." The Duchess of Langham smiled fondly and took his hands before she kissed his cheek.

"Duchess, you are as beautiful as always." He returned her kiss.

"We understand you've assumed financial responsibility for the young Viscount Lawson and his sisters?" she queried.

"Yes. When the old trustee died, the documents named the Marquess of McCalpin as successor. Obviously, they must have meant Uncle Michael and not me. However, the family is in serious straights. I petitioned the Court of Chancery for the guardianship for the young viscount and his sisters. Do you know the family?"

The duchess gracefully sat in the chair next to McCalpin. His father sat at his desk and waved a hand for William to join them. "Lord Lawson's father was the unofficial envoy to the new United States. He came home after Grenville, who served as foreign secretary to the Crown, appointed George Hammond." He furrowed his brows. "He was a friend of my brother from university, and his father, the old viscount, was a friend of my father. Do you know who was named their guardian?"

McCalpin sat in one of the chairs in front of the duke's mahogany desk and extended one leg. "I had Russell research their situation. Apparently, after Lord Burns passed, no one came forward to take the responsibility."

A grin broke across the duke's face. "Well, it's a huge responsibility, but one that needs to be addressed. I'm glad you realize what's required and are ready to make the commitment to their family."

With a tilt of her head, he became his mother's sole focus, which was never a good sign. It meant she'd taken a personal interest in the development. "It's a shame there aren't any family members who would step forward. What are their ages?"

Ah, well, if he was going to follow through on his promise, he needed to make the full commitment. "The viscount is nine, and his middle and youngest sisters are nineteen and eighteen. I'm not really certain the age of the eldest sister. She said she's twenty-five and demanded I release her money immediately. She claimed she was a year older than the documents state."

"What did you do?" The duke looked through a pile of correspondence on his desk. When he looked up, his gaze cut to McCalpin's as if this was a test, and he wanted the right answer.

McCalpin leaned back in his chair. He'd been through this so many times before that it made little difference how he answered. The duke would somehow turn his words into an opportunity for a lecture on responsibility and duty. "I refused. She wants to introduce her sisters into society and bring the young viscount to London."

The duchess stole a glance at her husband before addressing McCalpin. "How do you know she wasn't telling the truth? Her desire to establish her sisters in society and bring her brother to town seems that she's taken the responsibility for their welfare to heart."

The fact the Lawson family suffered caused him a

deep shame. Even though they'd suffered for years before he became involved was little comfort. He should have personally seen to their welfare earlier instead of sending March to his solicitor.

However, last night had been a turning point. March's quandary that her family would eat the remains from their cat's latest kill made him angry with Lord Burns and truthfully with himself for his own lack of action. Today, he would change the Lawson's fortunes for the better.

He shrugged his shoulders. Neither of his parents would leave the matter be unless they knew the specifics. He would satisfy their curiosity without telling them how the young woman had forged his name to acquire funds. "She claimed the trust documents were written in error. I believe it was just too convenient of an excuse. I explained that she had to deliver proof before I'd release the monies."

"As the future Duke of Langham, it's expected that you will take over the responsibility." The duke looked to his duchess. "Lord Burns never left his estate. A complete recluse. Rumors were he was insane." He shook his head. "At the end, the poor man didn't recognize any of his staff and couldn't remember anything, not even what he'd eaten at his last meal."

The duchess patted McCalpin's hand. "That poor family probably hasn't had any attention in years."

The duke leaned back in his chair, and his blue eyes twinkled in delight. "Seems you'll have to participate in the upcoming social Season with the sisters. Perhaps you'll find a wife this year."

At the mention of "wife," McCalpin stood. "All in good time, Father. Besides, I've not been appointed guardian yet."

The duchess delivered one of her brightest smiles. "It's not a question of if you become their guardian but when." She looked to her husband with pure delight. "Could any of your friends help make McCalpin's appointment come sooner? We'll help introduce the young ladies into society. I'll contact Lady Jersey for vouchers to Almack's."

"Madame, please don't—"

"Son, you know your mother. Once she makes a plan, there's no stopping her." The duke gazed upon his wife with a roguish smile. "Where will the family stay when they arrive in town?"

McCalpin furrowed his brow and shot a look to Will. His brother shrugged his shoulders.

"I hadn't really considered the situation. Perhaps I'll hire a chaperone since the oldest daughter, Miss March Lawson, wants to open the family townhouse."

"That won't due. She's a friend of Emma's." His mother straightened in her chair and glanced at her husband. "They should reside here. It'd be a pleasure to introduce them to society."

Within the span of a minute, everything started to spiral out of his control. "Wait! What, Mother—"

"Excellent idea, Ginny," his father added. He stole a glance at McCalpin and smiled. "An efficient way of killing two birds with one stone, as they say. You can escort your young charges and help me court some of the naysayers to my child labor law petition."

*More like killing two hares with one swipe of a paw.*

His parents had completely outmaneuvered him. There was one thing he hated almost as much as numbers—dances and balls and other frivolous entertainments designed to make it easy for husband-hunting misses to prey upon the bachelors of society. Unfortunately, he was one of those bachelors. With his parents in support of March's plan, he would soon be forced into the lion's den—the *ton* and all its horrid splendor.

"The guardianship comes at the perfect time." His father's steely gaze foretold that things were going to get more complicated than they already were. The air thickened with tension, reminding him of the days when he'd come into this room for a lecture on the proper behavior expected of the ducal heir.

Will finally spoke after being uncharacteristically quiet. "Father, I mentioned to McCalpin your plans for dinner next week."

His father narrowed his eyes. Obviously, he wanted to approach McCalpin without any forewarning. "I'll expect you to have dinner here practically every day since your wards will be staying here."

"I have no objection to taking whatever steps necessary to help the Lawson family, but I have no expectations you and Mother should be involved in this responsibility."

His mother smiled sweetly. "It's no bother, McCalpin. I'll enjoy having a full house again."

His father nodded in agreement. "Plus, you and I can work after dinner most nights before we attend the formal functions. It's my opinion you should take a seat in the House of Commons. Such an opportunity would be perfect preparation for the House of Lords. By the way, Severin found several discrepancies in the McCalpin Manor accounts. You need to have a conversation about that. I'm sure it's just a bookkeeping error, but it's best not to let these things fester."

McCalpin made a silent bow and left his father's study.

Will followed. "I'll look at the books this week."

"Thank you."

"When are you sending for the family?" William's tone indicated he treaded carefully with his question.

"I sent a note and a carriage filled with food and necessities to Lawson Court this morning. I informed March I'd be in contact next week about the specific date. They'll need dresses, shoes"—he shrugged his shoulders—"all the assorted and necessary fripperies."

He should have gone to McCalpin Manor for the winter. Only there could he enjoy some semblance of peace.

All of this was Miss March Lawson's fault. If she didn't have such kissable lips or deep-chocolate eyes, he could have escaped his parents' demands. Now, captured like that hare in Maximus's jaws, he would spend the next several months in town.

Perhaps luck would favor him, and the ladies would find matches relatively quickly. Then he could pass the guardianship to one of their husbands. When he mounted his horse, an image of March dancing with a faceless eligible bachelor popped into his thoughts, and unease crowded his thoughts.

It was beyond foolish to become jealous. He had strict requirements for a wife, and a known embezzler did not fit the bill.

No matter how delightful her kisses.

Mrs. Oliver quickly cut the stitches, and for the first time in days, March could actually clasp her hand in a fist. She released her breath and smiled at the kind servant. "Thank you. I have quite a bit of work that won't wait any longer."

Bennett rushed into the kitchen. "Come quick, March. One of McCalpin's fancy footmen is in the entry with a carriage full of food and a note for you."

She hadn't heard from the marquess since his visit several days ago and had thought he'd forgotten they existed. It wouldn't have been the first time, but once again, he'd surprised her. She followed Bennett and accepted the note from the footman.

Written in his distinctive hand, the marquess simply directed they pack and prepare for his further instructions. He would send a carriage to retrieve them within the week. The food and other necessities were for their convenience until they found themselves settled in town. He'd signed it with a simple *M,* and the parting words that she *could fill in the rest of the letters for him.* Her signature was better than his was.

Her heart beat faster at his kindness and blatant teasing. She could almost hear the deep rumble in his voice, the one that reached deep inside and caused every particle of her body to stand at attention. With a sigh, she carefully placed the letter in her pocket.

With two coachmen and the footman working efficiently, a generous mountain of food, exotic teas, and bottles of wine soon crowded every available space within the kitchen. Mrs. Oliver and Bennett carefully inspected the goods. Their respective "oohs" and "ahhs" added to the excitement. It was difficult to determine whose face was brighter. Both Mrs. Oliver and Bennett glowed with pure joy at the cornucopia of culinary riches. Indeed, they'd all dine well tonight.

After they finished a fine dinner of delicious smoked ham, beetroots, peas, and roasted potatoes, a magnificent dessert sat before them. To Bennett's absolute delight, he had two servings of the vanilla blancmange covered in crushed almonds.

At the end of the meal, March relaxed and smiled for the first time in ages. Her family's sighs of contentment joined together like voices in a church choir. After they cleaned the remnants of the feast, she retired to her room.

As she prepared a thorough list of what would be required to move to London, her thoughts returned to McCalpin. She couldn't wait to thank him properly for all he'd done. Without his assistance, she'd still be wrestling with how to manage the move, keep her family fed, and stave off Rupert's attention from their dire circumstances.

A soft knock brought her out of her musings. Faith and Julia popped their heads around the door. Their faces were alight with joy.

"Are we interrupting?" Julia asked.

March shook her head and slipped the marquess's note into her reticule. "Join me. I didn't know I could eat that much at one meal."

Faith widened her eyes. "Did you see the roasted pheasant for tomorrow? It made the ones on the estate look like miniature partridges."

"I think our luck has finally changed for the better, don't you, March?" Julia inquired.

"Indeed. Sit down, both of you. I want to tell you my plans." Her two sisters sat on the edge of her bed. "I need you both to stay close to the house and watch Bennett tomorrow. Though Lord McCalpin said he'd send for us, I don't want to wait. Hart is going to take me to the townhouse where I'll prepare for your arrival. As soon as Hart drops me off, he'll return and stay with you. I'll send a note to the marquess informing him that I've arrived. Once preparations are finished, you all will join me. I've made arrangements with Mr. and Mrs. Garwyn to attend the sheep while we're away." The blacksmith and his wife had been their friends for years and always helped when they could. "As payment, we'll share our profits from the sale of wool."

Faith nodded in agreement. Though she couldn't contribute as much, she shared March's interest in the estate. As ragtag as it was, it was their heritage. "That's a sound idea."

"What do we do if Rupert visits before Hart returns?" The slight tremor in Julia's voice caused March's heart to skip a beat.

"Perhaps it's better for all of us if you stay with Mr. and Mrs. Garwyn." She reached over and grasped Julia's hand. "You'll be safe until Hart returns. Agreed?"

Julia sighed in relief. "Agreed. I'll be glad when we can all be together again."

"Me too," Faith shared.

"Me three," March chimed in.

Deep inside, a faint flame of hope ignited. She'd be thrilled to see her *David*, too. The quicker she could open the townhouse, the faster they all could be together again.

# Chapter Eight

It took every ounce of restraint McCalpin possessed not to bellow to the rafters. Instead, he called for his carriage then reread the barely legible note from Lord Lawson.

> *McCalpin,*
>
> *I'm delighted to inform you that March is opening ~~the family's~~ my London townhouse at this very moment. My family and I will ~~arrive in London as soon as possible~~ follow shortly.*

It was the next sentence that sent McCalpin's blood boiling.

> *~~We~~ My sisters and I ~~hide~~ hid at the smithy's home until Hart returned from delivering March. I feared our cousin Rupert might descend upon Lawson Court and devour our new surplus of food. Thankfully, he stayed away. Once Hart*

*arrived, we all felt safe again. When March has
everything in order, she'll send for us.*

*In case ~~your~~ you are wondering, Maximus will
stay at Lawson Court with Mrs. Oliver. He
throws a fit when forced to travel in our cart. He
~~catched~~ caught another hare. This time we did
not eat it. Thank you for the food.*

*In closing, I'd like to extend an invitation to
dine with me again. I can't wait to see March,
and I look forward to seeing you at your earliest
~~convenience conveneince~~ convenience.*

*Yours,
Lawson*

*P.S. I guess I spelled convenience correctly the
first time.*

McCalpin fumed as he shared the young viscount's
exact sentiments. He *couldn't* wait to find the viscount's
oldest sister. Once he found her safe and sound, he would
wring her pretty little neck, then he'd give her a lecture
she wouldn't soon forget.

Only he couldn't shake the deep-seated worry that
twined like a spiky vine in his chest. Who was keeping
March safe?

No one, since she was alone in London.

When he stepped out of the carriage, darkness had descended on London. The cold winter night had swallowed the last hints of the sunset. The star-filled sky was
clear with a crisp bite as a gentle wind whipped his fur-
lined cloak around his boots.

Somehow, with March, he seemed to take greater note
of the passage of time. Only a quarter of an hour had
passed since he'd received Bennett's letter. Leaving his

footman to close the carriage door, McCalpin stormed
across the street toward the Lawson townhouse that
straddled the Mayfair and St. James areas of London.

As he approached the modest but elegant home, he
slowed his gait. Simple plain lines with minimal trim
gave the abode a rather regal air about it. The bright red
door welcomed visitors and was in striking contrast to
the white stone façade that lined the front.

It didn't appear anyone was home as the house sat eerily silent and dark, but the attached knocker indicated
the family would receive visitors. His gaze swept upward,
then stopped when he caught the unmistakable glow of
candlelight from a third-floor window. Someone was
there, and he'd lay odds it was his little embezzler.

After a brisk knock, he waited a few moments then
opened the door. She'd failed to take the necessary pre-
cautions of locking the entrance. Another item to address
in her lecture.

Darkness eerily shrouded the entry, but the moon
illuminated the staircase to his right. With quick steps,
he proceeded to the second floor. On a small side table
lay a candle and tinderbox. He made quick work of
catching a flame, then proceeded to the third floor.

A thick carpet covered the hallway and muffled his
footsteps. He paused when he came to the open door
from where light spilled into the hallway. At first glance,
it appeared that pandemonium had taken up residence
within the room. Fabric and outdated evening gowns
covered every inch of available space. Shoes, fans, ret-
icles, and gloves lay sorted into various piles. An ornate
cheval mirror, a massive piece of black lacquered wood
with gold-foiled trim, stood in one corner of the room.

Amidst all the disarray, March gazed at her reflection
while holding a faded ivory satin court dress to her body.

She closed her eyes and tilted her head to one side. Swaying slightly, she held one arm around her waist and the other wrapped around the bodice of the dress. Lost in her dance, March hummed gently under her breath. Her fingers lightly stroked the embroidery pattern of pale-pink and green flowers that decorated the overskirt. The sensual picture she presented mesmerized him.

Her dulcet alto warmed the room with sounds that called him forward. She was so entranced in her thoughts she didn't hear him approach. Slowly, she stopped her swaying as if her dance with her imaginary partner had ended. Her eyes fluttered open, and the gentle candlelight kissed her cheeks. At her serene expression accompanied by a slight blush, he took a deep breath. All thought escaped except for the vision before him.

At that moment, all he desired was to change places with the gown she clenched tightly to her body. The crushing need to sweep her into his arms pushed aside all reason. The urge to feast upon the sweet pout of her lips made him want to lose himself in her embrace. My God, she was a seductress without even knowing it. His little embezzler was temptation incarnate.

Her focus returned to the mirror. The moment she recognized him, her hands dropped to her sides, and the gown slowly fell with an elegant *swoosh* to the floor like a supplicant who worshipped her.

A vision of him taking the dress's place and kneeling before her made his entire body tighten. In a desperate attempt to shake the image from his thoughts, he swallowed. His gaze held hers in the mirror for a moment, then his perfidious eyes followed the sensual picture the mirror presented him. The buttons on the front of her plain brown dress were undone to her waist, and she didn't wear stays. The thin fabric of her plain chemise was a brilliant white in the candlelight. A beacon, it called him closer, enticing him to touch the creamy softness of her skin. The luscious expanse of her chest caused his breath to hitch. As a gentleman, he shouldn't spare a glance. Yet his mind and body revolted when his traitorous eyes lingered on the gentle swell of her breasts. As much as tried, he couldn't help but lower his gaze to her darkened nipples that gently pushed against the thin fabric, demanding his full attention.

She was a banquet of sensual delights, and he was a starving man.

"David," she whispered like a siren calling him nearer. The bronze and gold in her eyes shimmered in bewilderment.

At the sound of another man's name on her lips, he crashed into a massive proverbial rock much like those ill-fated mariners when they heard the sweet songs of the mythological sirens. Momentarily stunned, he stared at her. She blushed and covered herself. He prowled toward her until he stood not more than a hand's width behind her. Her heat called him closer, but he resisted her allure this time. His gaze captured hers in the mirror.

"David?" He ground his teeth to keep from roaring. No doubt, some nefarious farmer who would dare touch her and spoil her beauty.

Again, she blushed a beautiful pink then dipped her head. He placed his hand on her shoulder and trailed his fingers around the front of her neck. Her pulse pounded against his hand. With his thumb and forefinger, he gently clasped her chin and made her meet his gaze.

"You are." She swallowed, and the muscles on her throat rippled underneath his fingers. "The first time I saw you . . ." Her words faded to nothing, but she didn't shy away this time. The warmth of her gaze melted his trepidation.

"Tell me." He reached to cup her left cheek. With a light touch, he encouraged her to turn and face him.

Graceful in her movement, she pivoted and stood before him. She raised her head slightly to look into his eyes. "I walked through the door of your home, and you were standing on the steps after a ride. I'd never seen anyone so perfect and handsome in my life. The tilt of your head as you glanced at me reminded me of a sketch my father acquired in Florence during one of his journeys. It was Michelangelo's *David*. Then your kindness when I was injured and the food you sent. You're as fierce a protector as David was."

In her eyes, he saw what the honesty of that confession had cost her. Vulnerable with sharing her secret, March's chest rose and fell as if waiting for some pronouncement from him.

For a moment, he allowed himself to believe she did perceive him as perfection. Never before in his life had he ever felt perfect—far from it. Flawed and defective in so many simple ways, he'd dismissed any hint of adoration from females. If anyone knew what a simpleton he was with the simplest of figures, they'd laugh at his weakness. Once a woman understood his failing, they'd have him at their mercy. They'd only desire him as a means to a title of duchess, and a very prestigious and powerful one at that—the Duchess of Langham.

Yet the light from her eyes was heavenly, and he let himself bask in her confession as his heart pounded loudly. Without waiting for reality to intrude upon their moment, he closed what little distance there was between them. He cupped her cheeks, and his thumbs rubbed the high fragile cheekbones of her face. Her soft skin captivated him, coaxing him closer. He stared into her gaze, then slowly lowered his lips to hers.

At the first touch of his lips against hers, desire ran like a raging river through him, and his cock swelled as if flooded with her beauty. Her soft whimper escaped, and the need to pull her into the safety of his arms increased to the point of pain.

Reality interrupted his pleasure and he forced himself to pull away. This was wrong. She was his responsibility, not a woman he should seduce. He closed his eyes as his mind and cock warred against each other.

"March," he whispered. "God, you're lovely, but we mustn't." As he struggled to bring his desire under control, he traced her jaw with a finger and inhaled. As if under a spell, he couldn't quit touching her.

Finally, she must have realized how risky their behavior was and took a wobbly step back. She was as affected as he was.

"What are you doing here?" He scooped her hand in his and raised it to his lips, not letting her increase the distance too much.

"I thought to see if any of these old dresses could be remade into gowns for my sisters." She'd lost her skittishness, but her voice was still tremulous with passion from the brief firestorm they'd created together.

Still holding her hand, he bent down and picked up the ivory gown she'd held close to her when he'd entered. "You like this one?"

She nodded, and the radiance of her smile made him feel as if he'd just been crowned king. "My mother had it made for my first Season." She took a deep breath and released it.

Suddenly, he understood the significance of what she

was saying. "Your parents died." His eyes searched hers. He wanted to know everything she'd lost and struggled with through those years she'd cared for her family.

She wrinkled her pert but exquisite nose. It was a desperate attempt to conceal her disappointment, but pain flashed in her eyes and ruined the effect. "It doesn't make any difference. All that matters now is that Faith and Julia have the opportunity to make their introductions into society. Our family isn't as grand as many of the *ton* families, but we come from a long line of viscounts that have given unselfishly to the crown. Anyone who makes a match with either of my sisters will be lucky."

The power of her conviction pleased him. She was pragmatic, but well aware of the importance of family and the need to make respectable marriages for her sisters.

"It's not too late for you to be introduced into society either."

"Please." Her eyes grew hooded, and she raised her fingers to his lips, the touch intimate. "Don't spoil this moment for me."

"You'll not get an argument from me." He grinned, and she joined him.

In a flash, she must have realized the state of her dishabille and pulled her gown together. She turned around and faced the mirror. Her fingers fumbled over the buttons as she started to fasten her dress. He turned his back to her.

The brush of her hands and fingers against the muslin gown broke the silence. "You may turn around now," she announced.

Her smile could have melted a five-inch layer of ice on a winter's day. It was the perfect segue to determine why she was here in London alone and at this empty house. "I received a letter from Bennett. He was quite chatty and shared that you hid the family at the local smithy's so they were safe from your cousin."

"Well, you see—"

He waved a hand through the air. "If my recollection serves me, didn't I give detailed instructions? I told you that I'd send word and a coach when all was ready for the family to travel." He took a quick glance around the room. There was no fire in the fireplace, and undoubtedly, she suffered from the drafty cold. He held out his hand. "Come, let's go downstairs. Do you have a fire in any of the rooms?"

She nodded and accepted his hand. "In the kitchen. Are you hungry? I have cheese, bread, ham, and wine."

"Sounds delightful."

He escorted her out of the room. They walked side by side and descended the two staircases until they arrived on the lower floor. Down the darkened main hallway, she led him into the kitchen. A robust blazing fire had been well-tended and showed no signs of letting up.

As March busied herself finding plates and laying out the cuts of cheese and meat, he surveyed the domestic scene before him. An image of March heavy with child flashed before him. Shocked where his thoughts were going, McCalpin shook his head, then took a sip of the wine. He waited for her to sit before he partook of the offerings she'd served.

After he swallowed his first bite, he turned his full attention to her. She munched a sliver of ham and placed a piece of soft Camembert cheese on a slice of bread. When she finally noticed he was looking at her, she placed the food down on the plate and clasped her hands in her lap. "What would you like to discuss? Our kiss?"

"Kiss?" Her question was not the response he'd expected. Her face was impassive, but her lovely eyes darted everywhere but to his.

"Rest assured I won't think any less of you," she announced. "It was a magical moment for me. It's so rare that I . . ."

"What?" A prickly unease replaced his earlier calm.

"Have a man look at me," she whispered.

"As if desirable?" he asked. Immediately, he wanted to grab her hand and confess all the things he'd wanted to do with her in that attic. Anything to take the forlorn look from her face.

"Yes—no." She shook her head as if dazed. "As if he wanted to kiss me." She played with the bread on her plate, tearing it into little pieces.

He took a sip of the excellent full-bodied wine, perfect for a cold night like this. The fact that a lovely lady sat across from him made the drink that much richer.

"But I did. What if I wanted more than just a kiss?" he teased. She'd be magnificent in his bed stretched across him. Immediately, he tensed and wanted to recall the words. He'd wanted a kiss, a very sweet kiss. That was all.

Nothing more.

"Now, you're making fun of me," she retorted. "I don't want anything to jeopardize our friendship. I'm so thankful you've helped my family. I'd hate it if things became uncomfortable between us and you not visit at your leisure."

His gaze captured hers. "March, you misunderstand. We're not friends."

"Pardon me?"

"I went to the Court of Chancery and had myself

appointed guardian for your siblings and the viscount's estate. From now on, all decisions for the welfare of your family lie in my hands."

He'd expected her undying gratitude. Instead, he got a look sharper than a rapier, one designed to make him bleed.

"Over my dead body," she announced.

March held her temper in check by the most meager of threads. Magnificently fit and relaxed, the marquess leaned against the back of the chair and poured more wine into his glass. He raised a brow and regarded her, almost as if he was ready to laugh at her challenge.

With two sentences, he'd changed her entire world. The power he held over her was immense. He held not only her money, but also her family's happiness and welfare—not to mention their position in society—in the palm of his hand. They were at his mercy to do with what he wanted. This was the exact position she'd avoided with Rupert. The question for her was whether she trusted his actions—whether she trusted him.

"My lord, did you ever think to discuss this with me before you made decisions that impacted my family, not to mention me?" She tried to stay civil, but her ire had started to rise. She should be grateful. The burden she'd carried on her shoulders for her family's well-being wasn't hers alone anymore. Yet, somehow, she felt as if he'd betrayed her by going behind her back and making the decision without her input. "I should have been invited to the proceedings and asked my opinion on such an appointment."

He reached forward and took her hands in his. "After I left you at Lawson Court, I couldn't get the vision of you and your family having to eat rabbit stew out of my mind. I had to do something quickly. You shouldn't have to live in such dire circumstances. Nor should you constantly have to fear what Rupert Lawson might do to Julia. I couldn't see another option."

Sincerity brightened his startling blue eyes. The warmth of his touch provided a comfort, one she rarely enjoyed.

"I apologize for my abruptness." She gently squeezed his hands in appreciation. "It's just, well, you took me by surprise. I've been the one responsible for their welfare for so long."

"Let me share it with you. I promise I won't make any more decisions without your counsel." Without letting go of her hands, he stared deeply into her eyes as if he could see every struggle, every tear she had shed, every sleepless night she'd suffered since her parents had died. "Trust me."

He smiled, and the fire suddenly blazed as if he had the power to sweep all the darkness out of her life with just a look or a grin. To think such thoughts was too dangerous. She was setting herself up for a disappointment that would make a rogue wave appear like a ripple in a wading pool. He was a friend and nothing more—whether he thought so or not.

She tugged her hands free of his and stood to clean up the remnants of their meal. She was looking forward to falling into bed and actually sleeping late in the morning. Everything was ready for her family to arrive tomorrow. "All right."

"Excellent. I knew you were logical." His eyes widened with mischief as he waited for her response.

Even though she delighted in his teasing and exceedingly handsome company, exhaustion consumed her. "I should retire. I have an eventful day tomorrow."

Dismay darkened his face. "You're not staying here."

"Where else would I stay?" She took a deep breath for fortitude. All she wanted was to rest and not argue. "This is my family's home. I've worked all day preparing the residence for their arrival. Now, I'm sure you have better things to do than entertain me. Thank you for your interest and your visit."

"You're my responsibility also. Sometimes I seriously question your decisions. You failed to lock the door, and I walked right in without anyone to stop me." He took another sip of wine and immediately slipped into the confident lord who had his every wish and order obeyed. "My carriage is waiting outside. I'll take you to Langham Hall since that's where you and your family will be staying while you're in London."

"Did you consider my opinion in the matter?" she challenged.

"Don't be quarrelsome. Come, the duchess is waiting." He held out his arm and waited for her to accompany him.

She stole one last look around the room. The fire and the dirty dishes demanded attention before they left. "What about—"

"One of the footmen will tidy up and lock the house. Come," he commanded.

So much for asking her counsel on decisions that affected her and her family.

# Chapter Nine

∽◦∽

Over the last several weeks, March had reluctantly settled into the Duke and Duchess of Langham's home. Faith loved spending time in the library while Julia roamed the halls of the massive house memorizing the family history and cataloging the various rooms. She'd found a willing accomplice to her investigations—Pitts, the Langham family's butler, loved to regale Julia with the history of the family. Even Bennett was enjoying his stay since the duke good-naturedly spent time with him. Whether playing chess or discussing sheep farming, the two seemed to enjoy each other's company. However, the glue that kept everyone and everything organized was the Duchess of Langham.

A beautiful woman in her mid-fifties, the duchess had that magical charm that drew others to her. Not only kind and generous, but underneath, her fortitude kept the large household running smoothly while controlling the exhaustive social calendar both she and the duke seemed to relish. Hardly ever a night passed when the powerful couple didn't attend some social event, ball, or a dinner party at a political crony's house.

However, through it all, the Cavensham family came together at least once a week to share a meal. March and her siblings attended those gatherings. She was struck speechless at the duke and duchess's generosity and realized how blessed she and her siblings were to be treated as part of such a strong family that supported one another through disagreements and celebrations.

She closed her eyes and said a little prayer. Finally, her family was safe. If fate was kind to both Julia and Faith, and both were lucky enough to make matches this Season, then March would consider their sojourn to London an unqualified success.

Even March never lacked for company. Emma, the Countess of Somerton, visited quite frequently with her husband, Lord Somerton. As Emma was her friend and her banker, March found herself growing more and more comfortable in Langham Hall. She'd even developed a friendship with McCalpin's beautiful cousin Claire, the Marchioness of Pembrooke.

After their sweet kiss, it was hard to think of Michael as McCalpin anymore. He visited frequently, but spent most of his time with his father and William behind closed doors. The brief glimpses she enjoyed of his presence always made her day a little more joyous.

To think anything of the time she'd shared with Michael that night at the family townhouse was beyond foolish. She schooled herself to forget such nonsense. It was pleasant to be around such a lovely family, and that was all.

Moreover, one thing March was certain of, she was never foolish.

Over the past several weeks, the duchess had declared

March and her sisters needed new wardrobes. Like an army general commanding the troops, the duchess would take the trio of sisters to the best clothing and haberdashery establishments in town. Today March left on her own for a few items from Mademoiselle Mignon, the duchess's favorite dressmaker in all of London.

Once inside the shop, March idly stroked the blush-colored velvet. The slightest hint of pink immediately brought to mind Julia's perfect complexion. For her sister to wear in public a gown made from the striking fabric would cause a near riot in any London ballroom. Whatever it took, Julia would own such an ensemble before the month was out.

As was habit, March kept careful records of everything spent on their family. The vast wardrobes for Julia and Faith were no exception. She, on the other hand, had declined any new dresses. Yet, the duchess had insisted. Finally, March had agreed to a new morning gown for social calls and an evening gown for the duchess's ball. She'd politely refused any other purchases. There was no cause for such extravagance. When her sisters eventually settled with a husband and their own home, March planned to move back to Lawson Court until Bennett was grown and ready to assume his responsibilities.

What she would do after was still under consideration. She feared she'd be too old for matrimony and a hindrance to Bennett once he married and started to raise a family.

She pushed aside such worries. Other things demanded her attention, such as ways to enhance the gowns she'd made from her grandmother's old dresses. She took the lace, braided cord, ribbons, and other trims she had selected to the front of Mademoiselle Mignon's shop, the most exclusive dressmaker in all of England. Her reputation was legendary since her mother had helped dress Marie Antoinette.

March patiently waited for assistance. Since there wasn't much call for a sheep farmer's skills in the city of London, she'd hoped to offer her bookkeeping services in exchange for the trim or a least a discount. Money was always a worry, and she'd do everything possible to protect her family's fortune.

The modiste attended two elegantly dressed young women and an older woman who probably was their mother if her dress was any indication. The woman wore a dark peacock pelisse while the girls were dressed in sturdy but fashionable lilac-colored broadcloth cloaks. A polite argument about a lower neckline on one of the young ladies' gowns had erupted between the three women. Mademoiselle Mignon excused herself.

Dressed in a magnificent purple velvet with yards of black lace as an overskirt, the seamstress approached. "How may I help you today, miss?"

The modiste's warm dulcet tone enhanced her French accent, and her sharp gaze made March pay attention. As Mademoiselle Mignon evaluated her, March made her own quick calculation and came to the conclusion she could negotiate with this woman. Her own experience haggling over prices of wool throughout the years had given her a keen sense of a person's bargaining capability, and the seamstress had an abundance of it. No wonder her shop was so successful.

March carefully laid the bolts of trim on the table. "I would like to purchase ten yards of each."

The shop owner nodded her head and took the bolts to her cutting area.

March's gaze swept the shop. There must be hundreds of items that required a precise inventory in a shop this size along with careful records of the junior seamstresses' time and wages. "Mademoiselle, I wonder if you would consider some type of exchange for the trims I'd like to purchase. I have experience bookkeeping for establishments such as yours, and—"

The shopkeeper gently laid her scissors on the table. "Miss, if you don't have the money for the trim."

A deadly quiet settled as the three customers immediately stopped their argument to overhear her private conversation with the proprietress.

March bit her lower lip in an attempt to harness the familiar emptiness in her stomach. It always occurred when she discussed her lack of funds. However, she had the one thousand pounds that Michael had given her. It was more than enough to pay for her purchases.

Why she felt humiliation at all was puzzling. Perhaps the trim pieces represented nothing more than an extravagance. Deep down, she couldn't deny the real cause. The women overhearing the conversation would understand her circumstances and recognize her as the outlier she was—a person that had no place in their rarified society. "I have the funds. I bank at E. Cavensham Commerce."

The door chimes rang, warning another society paragon would witness her humiliation.

The young lady identified as Lady Miranda by the shopkeeper scoffed aloud, "She's one of *those women*. Pitiful souls who dredge their ugly business before everyone in London."

"Miranda, hush," her mother scolded.

The young woman drew her attention to her mother. "Why? You think the same thing."

Her sister reached out and placed her hand on Miranda's arm. "Listen to Mother, Mandy," she hissed.

Lady Miranda narrowed her gaze. "What is the matter with both of—"

"March, darling, there you are." The Duchess of Langham stood beside her and surveyed the group.

As if in an awkward dance, all four ladies, including the seamstress, curtseyed deeply. Murmurs of "Your Grace" rang through the shop. When they raised their heads, the women's cheeks bore a scarlet color as if subjected to a sweltering summer day.

The duchess nodded her head slightly, then turned her full attention to Mignon. "Wrap those up for me. Have them delivered to Langham Hall within the hour. Miss Lawson and I are late for tea with the duke."

The duchess wrapped March's arm around hers and escorted her from the shop.

A chorus of "Your Grace" followed them both outside, but the duchess didn't spare a look back. Outside the shop, a Langham footman stood beside the black-lacquered carriage. He opened the door at first sight of the duchess. With an innate grace, she took the forward-facing seat, and March sat opposite.

"As soon as Pitts informed me you had gone on a little shopping excursion, I raced to find you." The duchess made short work of taking off her gloves. She reached across the narrow space between and took March's hands in her own. "Darling, only the ugliest society vultures shop at this hour. Next time, just inform me you wish to purchase a new dress, and we'll have Mignon come to you for anything you need."

A fierce heat burned her cheeks, and she gently shook her head. "I wasn't shopping for a dress, just some trim. I have a few old gowns I'm altering for myself. With the upcoming ball, you and the duke have graciously offered to host for us, I can't ask for more from you. I can't tell you how much your generosity means to me and my family."

The duchess's brow wrinkled in consternation. "Darling, didn't you order more gowns when Mignon came to the house last week?"

March shook her head slightly. "There's no need. I'll make do with my grandmother's old gowns. My mother's dresses are too short and quite snug for my figure." She quickly gazed outside the window. This was almost worse than having to face Michael in his study and beg him not to embarrass her in front of Faith and Hart. To say the discussion was uncomfortable was a mild understatement. What little money March possessed, she needed to save every shilling for the estate and the upcoming year.

The burning sensation of tears demanded every ounce of her concentration. Would she ever be free from this constant worry over money?

The duchess squeezed her hands. "Didn't McCalpin tell you that I was sponsoring you and your sisters this season? That means I'm paying for your new wardrobes."

March shook her head. She didn't trust her voice as unruly shame threatened to overtake her.

"You have nothing to worry about. I'll take care of everything." The duchess patted her arm, then leaned back against the velvet squab. With a tilt of her head, she studied March. "Darling, I think we should consider a primrose or gold for a couple of your gowns. With your coloring, you'd look magnificent."

The duchess smiled in such a sweet, sincere manner it reminded March of her own mother when they had gone shopping for her gown to make her entrance into society. It was one of her happiest memories and permanently engraved on March's heart. Today, it brought little comfort.

"Thank you, Your Grace." She swallowed the pain those sweet memories inevitably brought. "Perhaps you should concentrate your efforts on my sisters. My needs are simple—"

The duchess narrowed her eyes in apparent confusion. "This is my gift to you and your sisters. The duke and I want to do this for your family. Your father and my husband's brother were great friends. It's our honor to help you." Her voice gentled as her gaze fell to March's face. "McCalpin is taking care of everything else, but the duke and I wanted to show you how much we enjoy you and your family."

March pressed her eyes shut to stop the flood of tears with little success.

"Your family's guardian has done a poor job of informing you what was happening," the duchess chided with a smile. She pressed a crisp handkerchief into March's hand.

"No, he's been everything gracious to my family ever since he first came to visit us at Lawson Court." March studied the elegant cloth, which was too fine to ruin. She quickly swiped the tears from her eyes with her own gloves. "You see, I was injured and without any concern for himself, he brought me back to the house and stayed with me when our housekeeper cleaned and stitched my wound."

She was rambling, but didn't care. Michael's mother needed to know what her son had done for her and her family.

"He didn't even care that I bled all over his coat. And then, when he discovered we didn't have any food . . ." She cleared her throat and straightened her shoulders in an attempt to get her unruly emotions under control. "No, Your Grace. Lord McCalpin is one of the most generous and honorable men I've ever had the pleasure of meeting."

The duchess lifted one finely arched brow, and another smile graced her lips. March couldn't quite identify what the duchess's expression meant, but it reminded her of a similar one that Maximus would bestow on his lowly humans when he'd finished the last drop of cream in the cup and was quite satisfied with himself.

"I see." The duchess chuckled. "How wonderful."

A breathtaking display of energy infused the family dining room at Langham Hall. The likes of which March had never seen. Tomorrow night, the Duchess of Langham was hosting a ball to introduce Faith and Julia into London society, and guests from the highest echelons of the *ton* and government would attend. Of course, the duchess included March's name on the invitations, but they both knew the ball was the hallmark for her sisters' introduction to society.

The duke sat at the head of the table and the duchess at the other end. March sat next to her. With a dip of her spoon, March sipped the excellent white veal soup. Flavored with port, the veal stock and cream were the perfect antidote to the cold winter night outdoors. A gloriously handsome footman refilled her wine glass without her requesting it. She'd never seen so many servants, all in perfectly fitted livery. With Pitts supervising the tableau, it seemed every person had their own personal footman attending them.

Light snow, a sign nature wasn't quite ready to release her hold on winter, blanketed the windows. If they were lucky, the frost would continue tomorrow. Any thaw would make the guests entrance into Langham Hall a muddy mess.

The conversation continued to grow in volume and merriment. The entire Langham family attended tonight. Emma and her husband, Nick, sat to the right of the duke. Claire and her husband, Alex, sat to the duke's left. Lady Daphne Hallworth, Alex's sister, sat next to her brother.

March's siblings sat at the middle of the table. Tonight, Bennett attended and joined the family in celebration since tomorrow promised to be an extraordinary day for the entire family.

"Your Grace," Bennett announced as he looked at the duchess. "Thank you for instructing Milton to show me how to use the bell pulls in my suites and the nursery." His eyes widened in amazement. "The footman shared that anything is at my fingertips. It makes the task of acquiring food, particularly sweets, so convenient."

"You're welcome, Bennett." The mirth in the duchess's voice was unmistakable, but she flawlessly kept a straight face. "Perhaps that will curtail the duke's habit of escorting you to the kitchen in the middle of the night. It disrupts the entire household."

"No." The duke's growl softened into a rough purr. "Just you, my little spoilsport." His eyes twinkled as he gazed at the duchess. "In our defense, Ginny, the boy and I have a sweet tooth."

After the laughter died down, Emma surveyed the table. "Will London be ready for the Lawson family when you take the town by storm?"

Julia gently laid her spoon aside and beamed. "Indeed, Lady Somerton. Your family has made all our dreams come true. I only hope that my sisters and I make you all proud."

"I hope we all survive the night." Faith played with

her serviette in a poor attempt to hide her nervousness. It was no secret to anyone at the table that March's sister was terrified at the thought of dancing. She could dance, but feared no one would ask her because of her limp.

Claire reached over and patted Faith's hand in a show of solidarity. "Just wait, Faith. You'll be the belle of the ball. No one will be able to resist your beauty, but more importantly, your generous spirit." She glanced at her husband, and a slight smirk adorned her lips. "If I was allowed, I'd ensure you had a dance partner for every set."

Her husband scooped up her hand and pressed a kiss. "Don't push me, Claire. I acquiesced to your demand we attend for an hour. Remember what Dr. Camden said. You have to start getting more rest. Liam is up at all hours of the night."

"I know," Claire offered. "Still two hours wouldn't hurt—"

"I agree with Pembrooke," Lord Somerton announced. "We won't stay much longer than an hour ourselves."

Emma shot a smile at her husband.

"We'll see how you feel tomorrow evening." To appease you, I won't mingle with the guests, and I'll observe the proceedings from the mezzanine.

With startling turquoise eyes and blond hair, the earl had to be the most handsome man in London. When he favored his pregnant wife with a blinding smile, it took every female's breath away. With a collective sigh around the table, everyone seemed to acknowledge the love between the couple. The earl and Emma's friendship had transformed into a love story even the bard from Avon would find inspiring.

March leaned back in her chair to enjoy the moment. Memories from long ago rushed forward. Her parents had shared similar evenings like this with her and her siblings. A contentment that had escaped her for years slowly took command of her mood. She was truly happy the Langham family had welcomed hers with open arms, but tonight was a simple remembrance of all they'd lost, too—the security and love her parents would have showered on their own children.

"Lady Somerton, I too am looking forward to tomorrow night's ball," Bennett announced.

Emma laughed, the rich sound brightening the room. "I do hope you'll save me the first dance, Lord Lawson."

Somerton placed his hand possessively over his wife's fingers. "Lawson, you're treading on thin ice if you think I won't fight for her."

Bennett delivered his best roguish smile. Truthfully, it closely resembled a charming lopsided grin. "Well, Lord Somerton"—Bennett leaned back in his chair and regarded the earl—"your wife did ask me for the dance first."

Laughter rang out throughout the room.

Somerton's eyes crinkled in amusement. "You make an excellent point. I shall have to try harder to win my lady wife's affections and keep young rogues like you from pushing me away."

Faith caught March's gaze and smiled, then dipped her head in acknowledgment. Their brother was transforming into a man before their eyes.

A flurry of activity from the attending footmen brought everyone's attention to the entrance of the dining room. Lord William and Michael entered with a flourish. Tiny crystals of snow clung to their shoulders and caught the light of the chandelier's candles, giving the men the appearance of magical creatures.

March's body vibrated like a tuning fork when she caught her first glimpse of him. An image of Michael sweeping her away from the room and bestowing a kiss crowded out all thoughts and created a smoldering heat in her belly. To have a private moment with him would turn the wonderful evening into something enchanting.

She released a pent-up sigh. It was ridiculous to entertain such thoughts. She couldn't expect more and had to prepare herself for the sight of him dancing and flirting with women who were elegant, sophisticated, and beautiful—everything she was not.

To settle her runaway thoughts, March bent her head and concentrated on the perfectly roasted fowl on her plate. Someone slipped into the seat beside her. When she turned to greet Lord William, it was Michael who bestowed a grin on her, once more transforming him into her *David*. Her heart beat frantically as if trying to break free.

"Good . evening, March," he whispered. Without waiting for a reply, he turned and greeted his family. "I apologize that William and I are late. Every fool in London must be out shopping at the last minute for Mother's ball. I've never seen such traffic."

The duke smiled warmly at his sons. "As long as you both are safe and sound, no one minds."

"He's just making excuses," William taunted. "I'm late because he's *always* late."

"A nasty habit you need to cure yourself of," the duke gently admonished.

"Did you have a productive day?" the duchess asked.

Michael directed his brilliant gaze at his mother. The Cavensham men's sapphire-blue eyes were legendary throughout England. Claire and Emma had emerald-green eyes that fascinated everyone. Yet to March, Michael's surpassed them all in their devastating beauty.

"Indeed. I worked on estate matters for McCalpin Manor all day. I'm pleased to say we accomplished quite a lot." Michael speared a piece of fowl.

He leaned slightly toward March as he addressed his mother. The heat of his body radiated toward her, and as if drawn by the force of his presence, she drew near. Who could resist such perfection? She shook her head slightly and tried to settle once again. This was dangerous. For her own well-being, she needed to be cautious and keep a respectable distance.

William had taken the seat across the table from her. Since the rules of etiquette were relaxed when the family dined together, March addressed him. "Lord William, did you enjoy your day?"

He squirmed slightly in his chair. If she hadn't been watching him closely, she might have missed it. Immediately, Michael stiffened beside her. Obviously, she'd struck a nerve somehow.

"Hmm, yes. I worked on estate matters also." He devoted his attention to the piece of beef on his plate. "Delicious meal. I'm famished."

"Where is your estate, Lord William?" Julia asked.

"I don't have one, Miss Julia." William turned to Pembrooke and Somerton. "What time will you arrive tomorrow? Perhaps we might have some time to chat before the guests arrive?"

"The duchess commands we arrive no later than two hours before the ball." Pembrooke nodded at Somerton. "So, we'll plan on it."

Somerton addressed Daphne. "How are you managing work at the bank? I want Emma to start taking more time away."

"Truthfully, I could use a little help." Daphne sighed, then grinned. "This afternoon, I was bombarded by no less than ten customers and several of them had to wait. Do you know anyone who has a talent for numbers?"

Somerton's intense gaze settled on March, and she immediately straightened in her seat as if being called to attention by the whistle of a British Navy Admiral. The earl then lavished one of his dazzling smiles. "Miss Lawson, would you have any interest in working at the bank? When Emma approached you before, you were too busy at Lawson Court. Since you're in London, perhaps your schedule might allow you to help."

The duchess smiled sweetly in her direction. That sign of affection was March's undoing. "I'd love to, my lord. Only if it's acceptable to your wife."

Emma scoffed. "Please, March. You know how long I've wanted you to work there. With your business experience, you'll help make the bank even more successful."

Somerton protectively placed his arm around his wife's chair. "Then it's settled. How about if you come to the bank the day after the ball?"

"Yes, I'd like that very much." The inclusive Langham family once again had taken her under their wings. "Thank you."

Emma smiled and nodded. "Excellent."

The duke turned his attention to Pembrooke, and the two men started a conversation about the upcoming week in the House of Lords.

"March?" Michael whispered.

As if called by a sorcerer, March slid her gaze to his.

"Are you happy?" he asked. With a stretch of his long legs brushing against her, he relaxed beside her.

The simple question along with his touch made her feel almost silly with giddiness. With an overwhelming lightness she hadn't felt in years, not since her parents had died, she managed a slight nod.

"I'm delighted." His whisper reminded her of a caress, the kind where a gentle finger ran across the skin of her face.

The tenderness in his gaze startled her. She'd imagined he touched her, hadn't she? Her gaze swept across the table. Hopefully, no one noticed the effect he had on her. Unfortunately, William stared at her as if she were some unique creature from the ocean bottom.

When Michael turned his attention to his mother, William leaned across the table. "What have you done with my brother, Miss Lawson?" he whispered. "Cast a magical spell on him?" Totally at ease, he slowly reclined and regarded her with a wary smile.

She took a sip of wine. Something was going on between the two brothers, and she had no idea what it was. They spent an inordinate amount of time together. When Julia had asked William about his estate work, he'd been quick to change the subject.

She had to acknowledge the truth. If she had the opportunity like him to spend her days in Michael's company, the sheep at Lawson Court might have to fend for themselves.

# Chapter Ten

❦

The family dinner ended, and everyone rose from the table. With tomorrow a busy day, no one lingered over tea or port. McCalpin exchanged good-byes with the family members who were leaving for their own homes. A sudden wave of discontent bit with enough force that he stopped before taking his own leave. The cause couldn't be that he tired of his lonely existence. He'd never experienced such an emotion in his life. Yet, seeing Claire and Emma leave with their husbands left him on edge for some reason.

He dismissed the irritation. It was little more than a reminder he needed to discuss what happened at the modiste's shop with March and explain she had no cause to worry over money anymore.

He briefly wished William a good night, then turned to March. "Would you have a few moments this evening? I'd like to show you something."

"Of course." She dipped her head, and a slight pink tinted her cheeks.

Every time he drew near, she seemed to blush. Really,

it was completely charming. Without a word, he leisurely led her through a stroll of the various halls of the massive home until they reached the family's portrait gallery, a lovely room that showcased the many generations of the Dukes of Langham and their families from the first duke, William, who had served King William and Queen Mary to the current duke, McCalpin's father. Floor-to-ceiling windows surrounded one wall and gave a spectacular view of the increasing snowfall.

Standing elegantly tall, she surveyed the scene outside before turning to him. Her face had softened, making her even more beautiful.

"It's so peaceful with the snow." She turned her attention back to the view of Langham Park. Her straight profile was like a lightning rod that forced a jolt of desire to charge through his body. He took a deep breath. He wanted to ease her concerns about money, not seduce her. However, it was becoming bloody near impossible to ignore her and the effect she had on him.

"It's a magnificent sight," he agreed, not tearing his gaze from her person. He cleared his throat and took a step forward. "March, let's sit."

He waited for her to take the settee that faced the window before he joined her. His leg pressed against hers, and he frowned. He hadn't done that deliberately, but he relished the heat of their contact.

She frowned in return. "Have I done something to displease you?"

"No, just lost in my thoughts." He smiled, hoping she'd relax.

She adjusted her bottom until they touched from hip to knee. She seemed completely unaware of his discomfort as she studied the softly falling snow.

"My mother shared what happened at the dress shop

yesterday." He studied her profile. When she swallowed gently, the movement emphasized the elegance of her long neck. God, he was tempted to place his lips there to see if she tasted as sweet as she appeared. A wild need to feel the throbbing of her pulse against his mouth coursed through him.

She turned, and a gentle smile favored her lips. "I'm afraid I made a fool of myself at Her Grace's favorite shop—"

He touched her lips with his forefinger to halt her words. "No. I apologize. I should have had this conversation with you earlier. I just assumed you were aware I'd take care of the expenses for all the preparations for the Season. Mother, of course, wanted to pay for your new wardrobes."

"Why would you do that?" she asked with incredulity. Her brow creased as she contemplated him as if he were a puzzle. "That's not proper."

"It's what a guardian does." He took a deep breath and continued. "My uncle was a close friend to your father's. My family is extremely loyal to friends, and I wouldn't have it any other way. By giving assistance, I know that the effort would please my namesake if he were here today."

She clasped her hands together and stared at them. "Thank you. That's very kind. Please don't worry about me. I'll take care of my own needs. My sisters"—she cleared throat—"and I appreciate all you and your family have done for us. For the first time in years, my family is safe and genuinely happy."

Much like he'd touch a skittish filly, he gently tilted her chin with one hand and forced her to look at him. "I want to afford you the same courtesy. I understand you only ordered two dresses. You'll need additional gowns with the busy social schedule Mother has planned. You're not still intent on altering your grandmother's gowns, are you?"

She shrugged her shoulders. "There's no need to worry. Faith and Julia offered to help me. They won't allow me to dress in anything that would be embarrassing to you or your family, I promise."

"You'd never embarrass me." Her stubbornness bordered on foolishness. Her dress, an elegant ivory satin trimmed with crimson ribbon, proved his point. He considered whether this was a silly game, but dismissed it. March was always straightforward even when he confronted her about embezzling the trust money. "Still, I insist you let me help. I want this to be special for you, too."

Her face was as still as the newly fallen snow. Finally, she smiled, and the cold drafts that swirled around them seemed to calm. "I appreciate the sentiment. But I need to save money—"

"March." He released a frustrated sigh. The blasted woman insisted on this nonsensical idea of finances. He had the money to help her and her family. He and William had gone through a generous budget that would have little impact on his investments or finances. They'd even sought their mother's council on it, and she'd been stunned at his generosity. "Why are you so adamant about this?"

She seemed somewhat sheepish. "I worry about the future for Bennett and me. I need to be certain that there will be enough so his estate doesn't suffer. You've never had to experience the distress of looking at accounts and bills and wondering—"

"It's not your worry anymore." If anything was more

certain than the sun rising, it was his complete wonderment at how to make sense of bills and accounts.

She smiled as if to appease him. "Thank you, Michael."

The sound of his name from her lips made his stomach twist into endless somersaults. Surprisingly, the effect was quite pleasant. Still, he wasn't convinced she really believed him or even trusted him.

"You're welcome. May I escort you to the family quarters? I need to go home before Donar decides he's had enough of the snow for the evening."

As they walked, he slowed his pace to have as much time in her company as possible without being too obvious. At the bottom of the steps to the family quarter, she studied his face with the most delightful smile. "Isn't Donar the name of the Norse god of storms?"

McCalpin leaned close enough that he caught her sweet lilac fragrance. His senses went on alert as every particle of his being became aware of her as a woman—one his body wanted.

"He doesn't like to get wet," he offered with a lift of one eyebrow.

She laughed, and the rich throaty sound was something he could easily grow accustomed to—every night.

"Good night, Michael." She turned and headed up the stairs.

"Good night, March," he whispered. God only knew how he would survive this guardianship.

And her.

March entered her bedchamber where a warm fire blazed in the fireplace. She marveled at the extravagances bestowed upon her and her family. The amount of wood in the fireplace would have kept Lawson Court's kitchen warm for three days.

She kicked off her slippers and looked with longing toward the bed. All hints of sleepiness disappeared when she saw four large boxes tied together with an exquisite black satin ribbon.

She approached the bed gingerly, then chided herself. A ribbon with an attached card from Mademoiselle Mignon's shop hung from the top box. A footman had obviously made a delivery mistake. The packages must belong to one of her sisters. She reached to remove the boxes from her bed when the card stole her breath.

Addressed on the folded piece of vellum was her name. The signature unmistakably Michael's. She should know as she'd practiced it for nearly a week before she'd summoned enough courage to write her first embezzling letter to his solicitor.

Carefully, she broke Mademoiselle Mignon's seal, then read the note.

*Dear March,*

*I couldn't resist when I saw this beautiful fabric. The other items were hand selected by the duchess. Trust me, she has excellent taste. I want you to feel as if tomorrow night is the introduction to society that you missed so long ago.*

*I'll be looking for that lovely girl. Your undeniable beauty will enhance the splendor of the fabric.*

*Don't.*

*I can hear you denying it now. Please for both of our sakes, let yourself dream of more than your sheep. Tomorrow night, set yourself free.*

*I want to dance with you in this dress. My only condition is that I pick the time.*

*Yours,*
*M*

March carefully untied the ribbon and folded it neatly. When she opened the first box, she inhaled sharply. Inside, a silk chemise and the faintest pair of pink clocked stockings lay nestled in exquisite rose-scented paper. Accompanying the stockings were the softest silken ties she'd ever seen.

She was almost afraid to touch the delicate fabric since her rough hands would undoubtedly mar the weave if it caught on her callouses. There was only one solution—when she prepared for tomorrow night's ball, she'd ask for assistance when she dressed. The duchess had kindly assigned two lady's maids to her and her sisters during their stay.

The next box was slightly larger. It contained an elegantly embroidered pair of stays that perfectly matched the chemise. Since this was a studier garment, she allowed herself to pet the soft fabric and caress the intricate pale pink and green flowers. The pattern was reminiscent of her old court dress, but much more intricately detailed. She took a deep breath and sighed. He must have told his mother about her dress.

With her lips tugging upward, she opened the third box. Inside the white paper, a pale-pink pair of dancing slippers decorated with seed pearls scattered throughout the silk begged to be touched. Reverently, she removed them from the box and discovered they were a perfect fit.

Finally, she opened the last box, the biggest of the four. When she uncovered the wrappings, her heart pounded, and she pressed her eyes shut. She carefully pulled out the most exquisite gown she'd ever laid eyes on. Made from the same blush-colored velvet she'd admired in Mademoiselle Mignon's shop, the gown was the height of fashion. Cap sleeves met with a décolletage that dipped low. The lowered waist would emphasize her flat stomach while the slightly fuller skirt would hide her generous hips. It was daring and bold but with a hint of innocence that she loved.

Wearing such a dream ensemble would make her feel feminine for the first time in her life. A matching velvet wrap was included in the box with another note from Michael. *Just in case we stroll outside* were the only words on the card.

Unable to contain her joy, she burst into laughter. In her entire life, she'd never received such an elegant gift. For a moment, the thought that she shouldn't accept the dress and the accompaniments stole her happiness—a joy she was starting to recognize regularly came from Michael.

Quickly, her common sense came to the forefront and pushed the hint of impropriety away. If the duchess had helped Michael shop for the magnificent clothing before her, who was she to refuse?

She held the dress to her body and stood before the floor-to-ceiling mirror that faced the wardrobe. Instinctively, she swayed as she hummed a little ditty her mother had taught her.

It was a shame society's strictures dictated she could share only two dances with Michael. If any more, *The Midnight Cryer*, the biggest gossip rag in all of England, would declare them married the next morning.

However, in her heart, a hope refused to grow quiet. She had truly started to care for the lovely man.

Indeed, he was a friend. But could she dare to hope for more?

She climbed into bed and refused to allow the lovely evening be ruined by her doubts. For the first time in her life, she allowed herself to imagine and enjoy the dream of a husband and marriage.

She closed her eyes and imagined her husband lowering his lips to hers for a kiss. Before the generous curve of his mouth touched hers, she glanced in his face.

It was her *David*.

# Chapter Eleven

The somewhat daunting and endless parade of guests finally trickled to a few dozen who stood in line to greet March and her sisters. The Duke of Langham stood between Bennett and March followed by Faith, Julia, and the Duchess of Langham. Though children weren't normally allowed at such events, the duke had insisted Bennett stand in the receiving line to meet the members of parliament who attended. The duke considered such introductions part of Bennett's education as to how to be a productive member of the House of Lords. Lord William had joined the receiving line midway through the introductions.

March had never seen so many people in her entire life. Everyone who was anyone had attended the duchess's ball for the Lawson sisters. However, the most heartwarming were the men who had remembered her father and his service to the Crown. Bennett and her sisters were enchanted with the stories about their parents. She'd been struck by how generous the duke and duchess had been in the introductions, effusing how remarkable the Lawson sisters were and how much they enjoyed having them at Langham Hall.

Lady Pembrooke's personal physician, Dr. Wade Camden, received a warm welcome from the duke and duchess. Tall with tawny-colored hair, the doctor was the epitome of grace and kindness.

When his attention turned to March, he didn't hesitate in his introduction of his friend. "Miss Lawson, may I introduce Dr. Mark Kennett? He's a colleague of mine from the University of Edinburgh," the handsome doctor offered.

"It's a pleasure to meet you, Miss Lawson," said Dr. Kennett.

March extended her hand, and the doctor sketched a bow. With dark red hair and a Scottish burr, the man exuded confidence and a sense of ease.

"Are you newly arrived in town, Dr. Kennett?" Faith asked. She leaned slightly, the movement a cause for concern. Faith had little tolerance for standing long periods of time.

"No, Miss Faith. I have a fellowship at the Royal Academy of Physicians."

"Kennett's caught a case of modesty, I'm afraid," Dr. Camden offered. "He recently presented to his distinguished peers a paper about the importance of exercise and manipulation of muscles as a way to increase one's ambulatory abilities, and it was wildly praised."

Dr. Kennett's ruddy complexion turned redder as he flushed briefly. His gaze fell to Faith's cane. "May I have one of your dances this evening?"

Faith stood a little straighter at the doctor's request. The smile on his face was genuine, and March held her breath to hear her sister's response.

Faith dipped her head but refused to meet his gaze.

"That would be lovely. I may not manage to last long on the dance floor."

He nodded in response, and the two handsome men moved down the line to greet Julia and Lord William.

"He seemed to be a nice gentleman," Faith whispered. "Do you think he could help me?"

The hope in her sister's voice hit March square in the chest. Her sister's suffering was always present, and she couldn't help but wilt a little at the desperation she'd heard in Faith's voice. "I don't know, sweetheart. I'll find out," March offered.

Faith nodded then turned her attention to the next guest who waited to meet her.

March took the opportunity and studied the ballroom. Glowing like a jewel, the room was magnificent. Streams of silver and gold silk hung from the massive windows. The refreshment tables sparkled with silver serving pieces polished to perfection. Gold candles littered the silver chandeliers and transformed the room into another world, almost as if the heavens had descended to entertain the guests this evening.

She glanced at the crowd of people hoping to catch a glimpse of Michael. He was nowhere in sight. The duchess had decided that the duke would dance with March, Michael with Faith, and William with Julia for the first dance.

For a moment, her confidence deserted her as she gazed at all the handsome men and beautiful women who crowded the outer edges of the ballroom floor. Suddenly, the truth slammed into every corner of her being. She was ill equipped to meet the expectations society would place upon her, namely a well-bred lady who was accustomed to such events.

The musicians had already started tuning their instruments. Boisterous laughs and the buzz of conversations floated toward them. The ball was officially set to begin.

The duke took the duchess's arm. "Shall we, my love?"

The duchess stretched up on her tiptoes and brushed her lips against his cheek. "As long as you save every dance after the first for me."

He colored slightly. "You never have to ask," he gruffly answered.

After they entered through the doorway, the duke and duchess stood aside so March and her sisters could enter. Side by side, the trio strolled into the brightly lit room. Suddenly, Faith stumbled. March grabbed her arm to keep her from falling. Absolute silence descended, and the entire gathering gawked as if they were some type of carnival act.

"I'm so nervous. Please forgive me," Faith whispered.

March cursed under her breath. She straightened her shoulders and pasted her best smile on her face. The sea of faces before them was transfixed on Faith.

With a sideways glance, March stole a peek at her poor sister. Her earlier rosy glow had paled. The pain of Faith's embarrassment stabbed March's heart, and she wanted to cry out at the unfairness of it all. How could this have happened now? Resplendent in the light orchard silk the duchess had Mademoiselle Mignon design, her beautiful sister appeared ready to burst into tears.

"Nonsense, my love. There's nothing to forgive." March took her hand and squeezed, hoping Faith would take every piece of strength and courage she could offer. "They're all entranced by you and your beauty. Take my place and dance the first set with the duke. That will set everything to rights."

Out of the corner of her eye, the duke started forward, but he was too late.

A man brushed against her, and March felt a caress of his hand on her lower back. "Softer than I could have dared imagine," he whispered in her ear. "Tsk, tsk, March. You shouldn't be trying to rearrange the dance cards just yet. I have the honor of the first dance with Faith."

A towering Michael emblazoned with a smile, one brighter than the light from the room's largest chandelier, hurried past and stood before Faith. His black evening coat and breeches emphasized his athletic build, and the ivory waistcoat, shirt, and neckcloth were perfection against his olive skin. When he leaned toward Faith and whispered, the ruby pin in the center of his neckcloth caught the light and glimmered as if it were a living creature.

Whatever he had said made her sister laugh. The beautiful sound rang through the silent ballroom. He extended his gloved hand in a commanding movement. Tentatively, Faith took it. Briefly, he turned back toward March and winked with a translucent smile only for her.

She couldn't stop, couldn't rein in the hope, and couldn't help but return a smile that mirrored his. Michael's breath visibly caught, and his smile grew even bigger. His eyes followed the line of her dress before returning to her face. For a moment, his gaze caressed hers, and her heart joyfully danced in reply. In the next split second, all sound shushed as the crowd waited.

That was when it happened. Between the opening first three notes of the waltz and the three fast beats of her heart, she fell—tumbled—then finally plummeted hopelessly and irretrievably in love.

With the Marquess of McCalpin, a powerful enigma of a man, who with his simple gesture of wrapping his strong and resolute arms about Faith's waist, proclaimed to the world that he, and only he, would have the first dance with Miss Faith Lawson.

Her *David* in his splendor had captured her heart, and March didn't even fight back or try to protect the pounding organ in her chest. Determined not to think too logically about what had just happened, she happily resigned herself to witness the magnificent moment her sister danced for the first time in public.

William escorted Julia to the floor, and March's tears threatened to spill at the sight. All she'd wanted for the last year had come to fruition tonight. Her lovely, beautiful sisters made their grand entrance into society because of Michael and his family's graciousness and charity.

The duke stood beside her, then bowed before her. "March, by the look on your face, I'd say the evening is a smashing success?"

March curtsied in response. "Indeed, Your Grace. I don't think I've ever been this happy in my life. Thank you and your lovely family for"—she waved her hand toward the dance floor in a tiny half circle, offering proof of the magic of the night—"all of this."

"You're welcome," the duke whispered.

The smile on his face robbed her of her breath. It resembled Michael's smile, the one that left little doubt there was genuine affection for the recipient.

"May I have this dance, my dear?" he asked.

Without a second of hesitation, March nodded.

The last five minutes of her life burrowed into a place deep inside her and took root. She'd recall this evening whenever she found herself lonely or unhappy. Forever engraved on her heart, it would provide hope in times of darkness.

Though she couldn't deny how lovely it would be if the night never ended.

After March had danced five sets, she found herself at the perimeter of the ballroom with the Duke of Langham. Needing a respite from the uncomfortably hot and loud crowd on the dance floor, she welcomed his company.

"Miss Lawson, I'd like you to meet Lord Fletcher. He and his family just arrived." The duke waved his hand at The Earl of Fletcher, who politely took her hand and bowed.

"It's a pleasure, Miss Lawson. I understand you and your sisters are newly arrived from Leyton." The silver-gray of his hair caught the candlelight from the chandeliers above their heads. A little older than the duke, Lord Fletcher's bearing indicated a man quite comfortable in the opulent surroundings of Langham Hall. "London is all the richer for your company."

Immediately, Michael joined their group, and in welcome, the candlelight seemed a bit brighter in his presence. Her pulse quickened as she, too, felt the heat of his nearness. Everything about the night was better than perfect. To call it extraordinary was like comparing a tiger to a striped barn cat. With all her senses heightened, she waited for his invitation for a dance. Perhaps, with the heat in the ballroom, he wanted to take a stroll outside. To have a few minutes alone with him would make the rest of the evening pale in comparison.

The duke nodded to his son, then addressed her. "Lord Fletcher has an estate in Suffolk where he's imported about one hundred Merino sheep from Spain."

The duke's comment with his sly smile made March

immediately take notice. Merino wool was highly valued by the wealthy, but the sheep didn't care for the cold wet climate of England. They prospered in the dry mountainous areas of Spain. Either Lord Fletcher was a dreamer who believed he could raise the creatures in England and succeed where other more-experienced sheep farmers hadn't, or he was a fool. Either way, his sheep-raising methods would undoubtedly fail.

"At my family's estate, we also raise sheep for their wool, though ours isn't as fine as a Merino fleece. But we've managed to constantly produce wool of the highest quality."

The duke smiled as if he approved of her comments. "Fletcher and I will soon *ram* heads in the House of Lords. He wants to impose a tax on all wool sold in England with the exception, of course, of Merino."

March tilted her head in answer. The duke's comment proved her theory. Fletcher was a fool. "My lord, wouldn't that seriously threaten the sheep farming in our great country? The selling price of wool is already too low, and to put any additional financial burden on the farmers would result in dire consequences. In addition, wouldn't it harm the growing woolen mills in areas such as Leeds? How much of a tax are you thinking of proposing?"

"A quarter or half a shilling per pound, Miss Lawson," Lord Fletcher answered.

She stole a quick glance at Michael to gage his reaction. His normal visage had turned pale, and his brow glistened with sweat.

As the duke questioned the earl, she leaned slightly toward Michael. "Lord McCalpin, are you all right?"

He nodded, but she couldn't inquire any further as the

duke caught her attention. "What kind of an impact would a quarter of a shilling per pound have on your estate, Miss Lawson?"

"An immense impact, Your Grace. I'd be bankrupt."

Before she could offer more, Michael whispered, "May I have the next dance?"

This was the dance he'd promised. Pure unfettered bliss pulsed through her veins. She could almost feel his arms around her. With a slight turn, she delivered her best smile. "That would be—"

"Of course, my lord." A typical English beauty with a slight build and blond hair dipped her head and answered Michael at the same time.

"Perhaps a glass of lemonade before the start would be refreshing." He held out his arm to the perfect English rose.

The young woman turned to Lord Fletcher, and immediately March's stomach twisted into a knot. It was Lady Miranda from Mademoiselle Mignon's modiste's shop. Heat blazed through her. She slightly turned away from the couple to hide her embarrassment.

People weren't interested in her. Certainly not Michael, and why would he? With her height and her muscular frame from farming, she was anything but what eligible men considered beautiful.

If she could fall through the floor, it would be the quickest escape. At her inept error, tears stung, but she refused to let them fall.

"Father, I'll return shortly," Lady Miranda offered.

"Take your time. Enjoy yourself." The encouragement in Lord Fletcher's tone was unmistakable as the handsome couple proceeded to the dance floor. He turned to the duke and whispered, "They'd make a fine match."

Without answering Lord Fletcher, the duke regarded

her. The gentle empathy in his eyes bore straight through her. "Would you care to dance, Miss Lawson?"

The offer caused another stinging heat to flame her cheeks. The duke must have seen her mistake.

"No, thank you, Your Grace," she whispered, "I'm finding it extremely warm."

With a sympathetic smile, he nodded. "Take the exit behind me. It leads to a mezzanine balcony," he whispered. "You'll be able to catch your breath there."

She bowed her head and cleared her throat. The effort did little to tame her humiliation.

Without another word, she quietly took her leave and quickly found the hidden staircase leading to the mezzanine above the dance floor. It was a perfect place to view the crowd below.

Shortly, Bennett stood beside her.

"You aren't in bed?" she asked.

Bennett's handsome face split into a merry grin, and like a tonic, she drank in the happy sight. "I haven't claimed my dance with Lady Somerton yet."

The earnest statement caused her to laugh. How could she deny him the magical evening? He had every right to enjoy this as much as she did. "I'll let you stay up for fifteen minutes, then to bed."

"Indeed," Emma said. Somehow, March's pregnant friend had sidled up beside her without making a sound. "I can't go to bed without my dance either." Dressed in a satin crimson gown that was daring and bold, the beautiful blond looked up at her and winked. "Besides, I don't get many chances to escape from Somerton."

March nodded and glanced down at the ballroom. Dr. Kennett was escorting Faith to the refreshment room. The good doctor must have noticed her sister's pinched mouth, a clear sign she was growing weary.

Julia danced with the newly titled young Earl of Queensgrace, a representative peer from Scotland sitting for the first time in the House of Lords. By all appearances, the two were enjoying each other immensely.

March's gaze swept across the ballroom, awash in all colors of the rainbow. She tapped her toes in time to the music, then stopped suddenly. Her traitorous eyes had found Michael dancing with Lady Miranda Fletcher. Enjoying some quip, Michael threw back his head and laughed. It had to be March's imagination, but his deep mellifluous baritone had traveled all the way up into the mezzanine and wrapped itself around her in a suffocating weight. The joyful sound knocked the breath out of her as if she'd fallen out of a tree.

Desperate to hide her distress, she stared into the distance, willing herself not to steal another peek at the perfection the couple presented to the crowd. Gripping the railing tightly, she didn't know if she could let go without falling into a heap of velvet, one completely emptied since her soul had withered to nothing. She gasped, not realizing she'd been holding her breath.

Emma's hand covered hers. "It means nothing. Father wanted him to dance with her as *he's* courting Lady Miranda's father for support in next week's vote in the House of Lords."

She didn't say a word as she continued to stare at the whirling couples below. Finally, she swallowed and found her voice in a shaky tone that betrayed her disquiet. "It's none of my concern."

*Liar*, her mind screamed, but she dismissed the warning. It was too late, as her heart lay pummeled on the ground.

"March." Emma's voice softened to a whisper. "Believe me, it's nothing."

The orchestra began the second waltz of the evening, and the notes brought forth shimmering memories of the sweet card she'd found enclosed with the dress she wore this evening. Absently, she rubbed her hands down the soft velvet, upsetting the nap. It was exactly how she felt—out of place and out of sorts. She didn't need a reminder of Michael's promise of a dance. There was only one more waltz, and that was the supper waltz. She'd already promised it to William and planned to retire shortly afterward.

She'd been a fool to even wish for anything more. He was the Duke of Langham's heir, and she was nothing more than a shepherdess. For heaven's sake, she had the scars from the work on her hands, wrists, and arms to prove she wasn't a lady. How could he ever see a life with her?

She pressed her eyes closed to stop tears from forming. Michael was a good man who treated her fairly after all she'd done. This ball and this night were his world, not hers. She'd do well to remember that piece of wisdom. It'd keep her heart from shattering into smaller and smaller pieces.

She pasted a smile on her lips and turned to Emma and Bennett. "I'd like to see that waltz now, if you please. In minutes, my brother might turn into a rat if he doesn't go to bed."

Emma stared at her with a crinkled her brow as if not believing the change of mood.

Bennett approached and then in a bow that would have made the fussiest dance master proud, asked, "My lady, may I have this dance?"

Emma turned her attention to the young lord and granted him a proper curtsy. "It would be an honor, my lord."

Bennett's happy face shot to March's, and he waggled his eyebrows. That simple expression garnered a real smile. She'd not let her disappointment over Michael rob her of this precious moment—her brother's first dance with a lady, even if the chosen lady was pregnant.

When the couple started to dance, March didn't try to tame her glee. Bennett's arm could barely reach around Emma's waist. Somehow, Emma adjusted their stance, and they stepped with relative ease and grace into the waltz movements.

As her laughter subsided into uncontrollable giggles, March clung to the beauty before her. Silly as it was, Emma with her brother was exactly the type of frivolity she needed at this despicable moment. There was kindness and friendship all around if she would just forget her sorrows and focus on the goodness. Her sweet brother's first waltz was a perfect example of all the happiness that awaited her. She'd not let her petty wishes for another life rob her of this special moment in time.

Emerging from the small hallway leading to the family quarters, Lord Somerton observed the proceedings. With a breathtaking smile that clearly showed his love for his wife, he sauntered forward and tapped Bennett on the shoulder. "Lord Lawson, may I have my wife now?"

Graciously, Bennett nodded and stepped out of the way. Lord Somerton took his beautiful wife in his arms and instead of leading them away, he swept Emma into the full waltz pattern.

Never in her life had March witnessed anything as breathtakingly beautiful as the couple before her—one full of life and love, dancing and cherishing each other. She brought her hand to her mouth in awe.

A familiar scent of pine wafted toward her, but she ignored it. Earlier, when she thought Michael had asked her to dance, she'd allowed her imagination free rein. Now, she'd not be tricked again. She was trying desperately to survive the rest of the evening without thinking of him with Lady Miranda. She wanted now, this perfect moment, to be the memory that wrested away her unhappiness.

"They are a sight to behold, aren't they?" Michael whispered.

She couldn't allow herself to look at him or she'd burst into sobs. All she could manage was a nod.

Bennett wrinkled his nose and directed his attention to the marquess. "Sometimes when March sees something that makes her happy, she cries. You should see her when she helps a ewe lambing. Like a spring shower if you know what I mean, McCalpin."

She tried to escape by stepping closer to the exit toward the family quarters. Michael stopped her, standing in her path with a gaze that reached deep inside and twisted her resolve. All the control she'd managed to summon within the last several minutes, he crushed into tiny shards.

Fearful he'd see what was in her heart, she turned back to Emma and Somerton's waltz. She'd never recover if Michael discerned her pathetic disappointment over his dance with Lady Miranda.

"Dance with me," he demanded.

Surprised, she blinked and tore her attention from the couple.

"Please," he said. The blue of his eyes captured hers, and she couldn't pull away.

She didn't want to. It was pure folly. No, a better

description was pure torture, but her heart demanded she agree. It might be her only chance. She called forth every piece of strength she had and smiled.

His warm hand possessed hers, and he squeezed her fingers as he led her close to Emma and Somerton. With an elegant turn, he took her in his arms. It felt like heaven. He led her in the sweeping pattern, and with no resistance, she closed her eyes, concentrating on his touch and the movement that threatened to make her dizzy.

"You are the most beautiful woman here tonight," he whispered close to her ear.

His warm breath teased her skin. Lost in the moment, she didn't respond. The need to relish every sensation he gave her this evening took precedence.

"I imagined how utterly right you'd feel in my arms, but the reality of perfection isn't an adequate comparison. The softness of the velvet to the silkiness of your skin—"

"Stop," she whispered. "There's no need to pretend this is anything other than what it is."

He seemed confused. "Which is?"

"A dance."

She chanced a glance at Emma and a besotted Somerton. Their happiness was almost tangible, and it caused a crushing emptiness inside her. She refused to let it overtake her. Not here, not in front of him. "You're the guardian of my family, and I'm an additional responsibility. You don't have to pretend anything else."

Bennett studied them as if trying to divine what was occurring between her and Michael. She didn't need her brother quizzing her in the morning in front of her sisters. How could she explain it if she didn't understand it herself?

How can someone fall in love and experience the most

euphoric moment of their life, her family finally taking their rightful place in society, then in the same evening feel as if a pack of wolves had shredded her heart?

She bit her lip and sighed. Michael narrowed his eyes and stared at her lips. He swept her in a perfect circle. Thankfully, the waltz finally ended and they came to a slow stop.

Emma covered her mouth with her elegant silk-gloved hand and yawned. "Come, Bennett. Lord Somerton and I will escort you to the nursery. I'll show you some of McCalpin's favorite hiding places when he was your age. Sometime you may need an escape from your lovely sisters. Tomorrow, I'll show you mine. In exchange, perhaps you'll share with Somerton that move you used to turn us. I quite enjoyed that."

Somerton drew her close and kissed her on the cheek. "Minx," he whispered, but it was still loud enough they all heard it.

With Bennett chatting away to Somerton, the couple took their leave heading to the family quarters.

Without letting go, Michael drew her into the shadows of a curtained alcove. Foolish as it was, March followed without any resistance.

Not saying a word, McCalpin waited until March finished her thorough examination of the floor. Thinly disguised, the effort kept her from looking at him. Finally, her gaze met his. Her beautiful eyes glistened with sadness, making his heart clench. Her hurt, mistrust, and longing combined into a maelstrom that nearly brought him to his knees.

Without thought of the decorum or propriety of meeting a woman alone in the middle of a ball, McCalpin trailed the back of his hand against her cheek. He cursed as his glove kept him from touching the silkiness of her skin. He ripped the offending piece off his hand, then returned to his ministrations.

She closed her eyes as if his touch soothed.

"Tell me what's happened?" he coaxed.

Her eyes fluttered open. She searched his with an intensity that surely exposed every flaw he'd so desperately tried to hide.

"Nothing." She shook her head. "Nothing important."

Her whisper caressed him in return. For the entire night, he'd wanted to take her in his arms. However, when she'd stood beside him and started to discuss wool prices and taxes, he had to escape. If he'd stayed any longer, someone might have asked him a question he would not have been able to answer. His inability to perform his duties laid bare for all to see.

His only solution had led him to ask Lady Miranda to dance. When he'd returned the chit to Lord Fletcher, McCalpin's father had told him where he could find March.

Now they were alone, and he wanted to brush his lips against hers. Ever since they'd shared their first kiss at Lawson Court, he couldn't get her out of his thoughts. He didn't care that he was responsible for her family. He didn't care they were in a ballroom filled with guests.

He didn't care about anything except her.

Slowly, he lowered his lips to hers. The sweet taste of peppermint and her warm mouth greeted him. She sighed gently. He deepened the kiss until her lips opened, inviting him in.

Not rushing, he tenderly delved into every inch of her mouth with his tongue, exploring what she liked and teaching her in turn. Her moan was a heady sound, and he embraced her tightly to his chest. The softness of the velvet and the crush of her breasts yielding against his chest caused a wildfire of desire to ignite through him. She was as lost as he was if her moans were any indication.

With her fingers threaded through his hair, she urged him closer, almost frantic in her desire for him.

He traced the edge of her bodice with his fingertips as if trying to memorize the dips and swells of her exquisite flesh. With one forefinger he slipped beneath her stays, he explored the gentle curve of her breast and found her nipple. She cried out in pleasure, and he kept up the sweet torment. She pulled him closer, but slowly with infinite care, he pulled away. If they continued, he'd sweep her into his arms and carry her to her bed.

She reached for him as if displeased he broke the kiss. To appease her, he brushed her lips once more, then rested his forehead against hers. Their wayward breathing proved they were both desperate for more.

His lips trailed around the delicate skin of her ear. He closed his body around hers seeking to protect her from any more sadness. Velvet heat coursed through every inch of him. His hard length pulsed against her lower body, electrifying him, and she responded in kind with the tilt of her hips.

He nipped the lobe of her ear to make damn well certain she paid attention.

"Does that feel like a responsibility to you?" he whispered.

# Chapter Twelve

While McCalpin always had a voracious appetite in the morning, today was outside of the ordinary. He generously spread the delicate elderberry jam across his toast and inhaled the sweetness that rose to greet him. He couldn't seem to get enough to eat. Every flavor enhanced, and every bite sweeter, fresher, and better seasoned.

He glanced at William across the table. "Does the food taste any differently to you?"

William sliced another bite of ham. "No."

McCalpin shook his head in wonderment and stared at his empty plate. "For some reason, everything tastes more delectable."

His brother smirked. Before he could reply, their sister, Emma, arrived for their weekly breakfast meeting. The siblings had started this ritual shortly after Emma married Nick. They gathered at McCalpin's townhouse to discuss what was going on in their lives without any interference from parents or spouses. Their cousin Claire always attended as well. More like a sister than a cousin, she grew up beside the three of them. As the sole survivor of the tragic carriage accident that claimed the lives of her parents, the previous Duke and Duchess of Langham, Claire had come to live with them when she was ten. Since she'd just delivered her third child a month ago, she'd chosen to stay away the last several times they'd met.

Dressed to the nines in a light green velvet morning gown with black satin ribbon trim that set off her brilliant-green eyes, Emma gracefully maneuvered her body into the seat beside McCalpin.

One side of Will's mouth twitched up. "Any problems escaping from Somerton?"

With a smile, she arched one eyebrow and leaned close as if divulging a secret. "I always tell him I plan to sleep late on the days of our breakfast morning gatherings. He's been in his study all day."

"Naughty girl, Em." Will resumed eating his ham. "Exactly what I would do."

"Does he mind that you come without him?" McCalpin had always had a soft spot for his high-spirited sister. "I'd hate to cause any disagreement between the two of you."

Emma snorted in that delicate way of hers. "Please. It's all a game between us. He stood by the window and waved good-bye as I entered the carriage. He knows nothing would keep me away from our mornings together."

A footman delivered a plate filled with fresh fruits, cheese, eggs, ham, and toast for Emma. She sipped her tea and addressed a question to Will.

The white of the linen table covering caught McCalpin's attention. His mind drifted to the creamy softness of March's neck. Last night, when he'd nuzzled the delicate skin between her neck and shoulder, it had been heaven—one he wanted to taste again.

She'd bewitched him in that dress, but there had been more. Her scent had him panting like a wild animal desperate for its mate. Her lips had practically caused him to come undone. Soft, sweet, and wet, her mouth was a masterpiece of sensual delights, one he could have studied and tasted for hours.

However, she'd devastated him beyond all reason with the sadness in her eyes when he'd first seen her. Something last night had caused her to shy away until he'd practically begged her for a dance. For the life of him, he had no earthly idea what he'd done. That was what had driven him to take her into the alcove and kiss her until neither of them could remember that the rest of the world existed.

A sheepish smile tickled his lips. It would be his pleasure to beg forgiveness again and again if she'd reward him with her little moans of desire.

"Did you enjoy your supper waltz with March?" Emma asked before popping a slice of apple into her mouth.

"Did I?" Will drawled. He placed his fork and knife on the edge of his plate. "Never has a woman felt so perfect"—he bit one lip and narrowed his eyes in concentration—"and heavenly in my arms."

Emma nodded as if it was nothing out of the ordinary that they were discussing March as if she was William's heart's desire. "Every man there had eyes only for her. Moreover, that dress? It was the perfect statement for her introduction last night. Simple, elegant, but up close that velvet practically begged for a gentleman's touch."

Will wiped his mouth with his serviette and stared at his plate.

Emma buttered another piece of toast. "This morning, Daphne sent me a note. She read in *The Midnight Cryer* that Lord Paul Barstowe had tried to find March for a dance, but she'd disappeared. What if he sets his sights on her? Once he's a duke, she'd make him a perfect duchess."

William's shoulders had started to shake slightly. He could barely choke out, "I might seek her out at Lady Pitman's—"

"Enough," McCalpin roared as he slammed his coffee cup on its saucer. The black brew spilled across the pristine white linen. "You two are absolutely shameless, not to mention obtuse if you don't think I know what's going on here."

William glanced at Emma. "We woke the lion."

Emma nodded, but her gaze grew serious when she regarded McCalpin. "Now that we have your attention, there's something we must discuss."

McCalpin had lived with his sister long enough to know that her tone of voice meant a lecture was in his future. He took another sip of his coffee for fortitude and waited for the inevitable.

By then, Emma had started to twist her fingers together in the telltale sign she was bothered. "Last night, March was the happiest I've ever seen in my life. Radiant, I'd say." She forced her palms flat on the table and stared at McCalpin, then took a deep breath and pursed her lips. "But when she saw you dance with Lady Miranda, it was as if her entire world fell apart. I tried to talk to her about it, but she refused."

McCalpin blinked slowly. That was why she was so upset with him last night. "It meant nothing, Em. You're aware of that, aren't you?"

She nodded gently. "But, McCalpin, she's vulnerable

beneath that hard exterior she likes to show everyone. If you have no interest in her, then I beg you to tell her before she . . . gets hurt." Suddenly, Emma's eyes glistened with tears.

"Please not the waterworks, Em." William inhaled deeply and closed his eyes. "You know I can't stand it when my little sister cries." He released the breath he'd been holding. "Anything but that."

McCalpin reached for her hand. "I won't do anything to harm her, I promise."

As soon as the words slipped from his mouth, it was as if he'd had an epiphany. He'd never hurt March and would never allow another soul to hurt her either. She was vibrant, and to dim that brilliance would be a travesty. She provided him what no other woman had ever given him before. Peace, contentment, and a friendship he'd never thought possible with the fairer sex. Besides, she had experienced enough pain and heartache to last a lifetime. He'd be damned if he'd cause her any additional unhappiness.

One of the first things he'd do today was convince her how beautiful she was and give her some much-needed confidence with men—even if it was to his own detriment.

True, she wasn't what most men appreciated as a typical beauty. Yet her bearing, stature, and intelligence enticed him like no other. Her warm brown eyes and thick luscious hair perfectly complimented her flawless ivory skin. How could any man resist kissing those full lips? Certainly not him. He just needed to ensure she never discovered his deficiencies.

"March is dear to me, and I'll not see her hurt." Emma swallowed and wiped her eyes. "This baby is playing havoc with my emotions." She took a sip of tea. "I only want the best for both of you."

"Thank you, Em. She's my friend also. I'll explain about Lady Miranda."

The longcase clock in the hall chimed the hour.

"Excuse me." Emma stood, and Buxton appeared with her black velvet cloak. "I have a meeting at the bank. March is stopping by this morning to discuss her schedule with Daphne and me." She turned to Will. "I'll see you at Langham Hall later."

Both of them stood and watched her depart. Buxton followed and closed the door, leaving McCalpin alone with William.

"What are your intentions with March?" William's low voice cut through the silence in the room. "I'm all ears."

He cleared his throat in an effort to afford himself more time to come up with the appropriate answer. "Until this morning, I really hadn't given it any thought." It wasn't an outright lie, but perhaps a shading of the truth. "She comes from a well-regarded family. I don't believe anything she's done has been for her own benefit. On the contrary, she's proved herself loyal and determined when it comes to her family."

William nodded in agreement.

"A match with her—"

"My God, you're serious. We were teasing," whispered William incredulously. "You're thinking of marriage?"

"I'd not considered the *bloody* matter until you and Em brought it up." The sharp words shot across the room like an explosion from a pistol. "Besides, it's not your concern."

Will elevated an eyebrow and stared at him. "She's a

forger, and who in hell knows what else. I'm just looking out for your interests."

"What she's done in the past has no bearing on the future." McCalpin was well aware his voice was growing louder the more he defended her.

"McCalpin, I want you to be happy, but"—Will exhaled and then lowered his own voice as if soothing a petulant Arabian stallion—"I also want you to be careful. Emma may not want to see March hurt, but I'll not see you lay to waste either."

There it was—the stark and naked truth. One word of his stupidity with numbers, and he'd become a laughing stock throughout the kingdom. No one would ever take him seriously if he found himself elected to the House of Commons. He'd likely be arguing to an empty chamber.

With March's ability to forge his name and his own lack of ability to run his investments and accounts, he was walking a narrow line. She could easily ruin him without much effort. With one misstep, he and the duchy might topple into an epic disaster, one without any hope of recovery.

He couldn't allow such a disaster to happen. Granted, other peers and their heirs had men of affairs to handle their estates. However, his father had instilled within him a very different set of values. One day he would be responsible for the massive operation of the dukedom. It was a task he wouldn't take lightly, ignore, or pass off to others. He would oversee and protect all of it—including the people who dedicated their lives and service to Falmont, the massive ancestral estate.

He released a tortured breath. This was March, a woman who was loyal to an extreme. She would deny herself happiness if it meant her family would prosper. He had to believe he meant something to her and that he'd have that same loyalty bestowed on him. She'd never hurt him.

"McCalpin, Cavensham men fall in love quickly and decidedly. Our father and late uncle are perfect examples. You're in danger of doing just that with this woman. Please, take your time. That's all I'm saying." William carefully examined him. "You're prickly and short of temper. Don't do anything rash."

"While I appreciate your concern, I'm well aware of what I'm doing." McCalpin threw his napkin to the table, then stood as if issuing a challenge. "I'm going for a morning ride, then I plan to visit Langham Hall."

The steady clip of his heels against the wood floor was the only sound in the room as McCalpin strode purposefully for the exit. For once, he'd rendered his brother speechless.


March descended the stairs of Langham Hall on her way to find Faith and break their fast. She couldn't keep the memory of last night's ball, but more importantly Michael's kiss, out of her thoughts. All night she'd dreamed of his mouth against hers and his body embracing hers. With a small shimmy of her shoulders and a headshake, she tried to ward off her wayward thoughts.

"What are you doing to me?" Faith's whisper dissolved into a soft fit of giggles.

The sound came from the salon to March's left.

"I won't hurt you. I just need to touch you there. How does that feel?" The male voice responded in the same hush tones.

"This is heaven. Please, do it again." Faith's breathless cry rent the stillness of the hallway. "I think I'm going—"

March finally woke from her stupor. Some reprobate was taking advantage of her sister in the Duke's yellow salon. Without breaking stride, she stormed into the room determined to stop the cad from hurting Faith.

"What the *bloody hell* is going on in here?" she snapped.

On the gold settee, Faith reclined against one of the arms. Dr. Mark Kennett had his hands under her dress. The duchess and Dr. Wade Camden jumped from the ivory brocade chairs surrounding the settee.

"March, dearest," the duchess cried. "Dr. Kennett is here to see if his therapy could possibly help Faith."

Faith nodded in agreement. "It's a miracle. The doctor is a certified genius. He knows exactly where to massage my legs and where to apply pressure on my feet and legs. This morning I woke up barely able to walk out of my room let alone tackle any steps. Now, I feel as if I could attend another dance tonight."

March forced her earlier tension to ease. She'd never seen Faith so happy and pain-free in her life. It truly was a miracle if the doctor could actually change Faith's circumstances.

"I apologize for my outburst," she whispered. "I wasn't aware—"

The duchess glided over and clasped March's hands. "No need, dearest. However, it's wonderful news, isn't it? McCalpin approached Dr. Kennett last evening about coming by this morning to see if he could help Faith."

"How thoughtful." He'd arranged it all last night for her sister. March blinked as her traitorous heart fluttered in approval.

"Look," Faith demanded. When she walked without a cane, the usual morning stiffness was absent. "I actually believe I could walk the entire length of Langham

Hall and the adjoining park and still be able to dance this evening."

March cleared the thickness that had roosted in her voice. "Faith, I'm thrilled for you." She turned her attention to Dr. Kennett who had made his way to her side. "Thank you. This is nothing short of amazing."

He dipped his head at her praise, but she could still see that his neck and face had colored into a deep red. "She's barely had thirty minutes of my attention. With regular treatment, your sister will see remarkable improvement. She has a wonderful attitude." His gaze settled on Faith. "Besides a lovely and warm personality."

"That's very kind of you to say," March answered.

Dr. Kennett narrowed his eyes, any embarrassment long forgotten as he once again returned to professional demeanor. "If I might, Miss Lawson, I'd like to continue to treat your sister."

Elated, all March could do was nod. Then she remembered she was no longer responsible for Faith. "While it's my sister's decision, perhaps we should discuss this with Lord McCalpin first before making a final decision. He's her guardian."

A smile tugged at the doctor's lips. The effect transformed him into a handsome man, one who knew how to sway a woman's opinion. "He informed me the decision was yours, and he'd support you."

Surprised at the announcement, she brought her hand to her heart to stop the infernal pounding. Michael had actually considered her wishes to be involved in all of the decisions that affected her family.

"I promise she'll receive the very best care," he added softly. "Now, Miss Lawson, will you allow me to attend to Faith—I mean Miss Faith?"

March nodded. London had certainly been the right place to come. Now Faith would finally receive the care she deserved. Inside, the clump of guilt that March had carried since childhood cracked a little, and a large sliver fell away. Her sister might have a chance to escape from her daily pain. "How much are you asking for the treatment and what are the terms of payment, if I might ask?"

Dr. Kennett shook his head. "Nothing, but if you'll allow, I'd like for Miss Faith to accompany me to the Royal Society of Physicians one day. I'd like to demonstrate the effectiveness of my treatment with someone who has suffered the effects of a severe injury for years. Miss Faith is intelligent and articulate. My fellow members will learn a great deal from her. They'll want to know how her improvement has impacted her life."

"Yes, that's acceptable to me, but only if Faith agrees." She let out a sigh of relief mixed with a huff of consternation at her own attitude. Would she ever escape the haunting need to discover what everything cost? All the years scraping and examining every minute purchase in detail had become a bothersome habit, one she needed to break.

"I think that is a wise decision, Miss Lawson. Both you and Miss Faith will be very pleased with the results. I'm confident," Dr. Camden added.

"I agree," the duchess added softly. Her gaze drifted to Faith. "This lovely girl is radiant."

"Thank you, Your Grace," Faith answered. The sudden blush against her cheeks did make her seem to glow.

"You have my gratitude also, Your Grace," March added. "I appreciate you staying here with her this morning. I'm certain you had better things to do."

"Nonsense, March," she chided. "Your siblings are everything lovely. Both the duke and I were comment-

ing how much we enjoy your family's company. I should
be the one thanking you."

Pitts entered and nodded his head at the duchess.

"If you'll excuse me, I'm needed elsewhere." Without
waiting for a reply, she glided from the room with a solemn Pitts following in her wake.

"Miss Lawson . . ." Dr. Kennett studied his boots as
if finding the sight fascinating. Whatever held his attention apparently lost his interest as he suddenly focused
on her. "Might I call on Miss Faith one day soon? Of
course, with you as chaperone."

She bit her lower lip to keep from jumping for joy. "I
think we'd both like that very much."

March pushed the familiar door open. This time there
wasn't the dread that typically accompanied her when
she entered the bank. Emma had provided money, but
more importantly, friendship when March had needed
it most over the past several months.

At strict attention, a liveried footman nodded as she
entered. Daphne Hallworth, the Marquess of Pembrooke's
sister, and Emma were huddled over something and looked
up when she entered.

"Good morning, March," Emma called out.

"You're just in time for tea. I brought apple tarts."
Daphne scooted another mahogany chair to the table.

March smiled and took her seat. The smell of sweet
fruit and a strong cup of tea wafted toward her. "I didn't
realize how hungry I was until I got a whiff of the tarts."

Emma served the tea, and Daphne handed March a
plate with two tarts. She picked up one and bit into the
delicate pastry crust.

Emma smiled and slid the morning copy of *The Midnight Cryer* in March's direction. "Did you see this?"

March gently placed her cup back on to the saucer and read the headline: THE LUCK OF THE LAWSON SISTERS. She quickly skimmed the article. An unidentified source stated that he saw her and McCalpin steal away to a hidden alcove where they didn't emerge for ten minutes and appeared disheveled.

A scalding heat assaulted her face. She clenched her hands together in a desperate attempt to manage her mortification. The effort failed miserably as she scrambled to find something to say.

"Don't." Daphne reached over and squeezed her hands. "Everyone knows that gossip rag loves to stir up trouble. Just hold your head up high and ignore it. That's the best way to confront this."

Emma didn't say a word but examined her. The emerald green of her eyes shown brighter and more brilliant than any jewel. Finally, she broke her silence. "Oh, my heavens, March. *It's true.* You kissed him."

There was no use trying to deny what had happened, particularly with the two women before her. Repeatedly, they'd extended their hearts and their friendship to her. She relaxed a little in her chair as a sense of calm returned. The paper had gotten the information correct. She was a lucky Lawson sister, one whom Emma and Daphne had accepted countless times without judgment.

March lifted her head. "Actually, he's the one who kissed me."

Emma squealed, and Daphne burst out into laughter.

"I knew it," Emma exclaimed. "When I saw McCalpin this morning, I could tell something was different."

"But there's nothing to it. After you and Lord Somerton left with Bennett, Michael—I mean Lord McCalpin—needed to discuss a few things in private."

"Well, McCalpin allows no hints of impropriety to soil his reputation. So he must think there's something to it or he wouldn't have taken such a risk," Emma announced.

Daphne nodded her head in agreement. The sheen of her blue-black curls caught the light.

The question that begged an answer was whether her two friends would keep the information to themselves or discuss it with their families. She didn't want Michael upset, or more importantly, hurt by his actions, intentional or not. She'd be devastated if their friendship suffered because of a passionate moment that swept them both away.

"I'd hate for this to cause him any embarrassment," she whispered, unsure if the footman could be trusted. She'd probably divulged too much already.

Emma shook her head, sending a couple of loose blond curls cascading around her face as she pulled out several bookkeeping journals. "Nothing ever really affects his demeanor. He's most level-headed." Emma flipped one of the journals open. "I hate bookkeeping. Your turn, Daphne."

Daphne sighed. "I did it last week. It's your turn to go through that torture."

"Let me do it," March offered. They both stared as if she'd grown another head and it was speaking. "I've been doing bookkeeping for years as a way of bartering for goods and services in Leyton. Besides, I love the figures and calculations."

As if the books were poisonous, Emma pushed them toward her with the tip of her index finger. "March, you don't have to do it. Daphne's right. It's my turn, but if you want to take a look at how I prefer to keep the books, please be my guest."

March opened the first book. Neat columns of numbers

with precise totals loomed before her. At the top, the familiar concepts of debits and credits were clearly marked. Listed down the pages were the clients' names. Overall, it would take her perhaps an hour to finish the task. The bank's own bookkeeping for rents, coal, and stationary needs were in the second book. That task would take no more than fifteen minutes.

Without waiting for any encouragement, March took the books to the desk nearby, sharpened the quill, and dipped it in the iron gall ink. She found scratch paper and proceeded to her work. Forty-five minutes later, she stretched. After carefully checking that the ink was dry, she handed the books to Emma.

"I found a couple of mistakes that I corrected. Mrs. Brown had an additional two pounds credited to her account that should have been assigned to Mrs. Havers' account." March pointed to Mrs. Brown's column and Mrs. Havers' column where she'd found the mistake. "Miss Marshall's account shows she has ten pounds, but she's overdrawn. Someone should probably tell the poor lady."

Emma scrutinized March's work with lines across her delicate brow. "I can't believe it took you less than an hour to have accomplished what would have taken me all afternoon." She gazed at March. "Would you be willing to do this every time you're here?"

Her chest swelled with pride. It pleased her to no end that she could help her friend make the bank more successful. With accurate books, Emma would know exactly her reserve funds and how much she'd loaned in total every week, every month, and every year.

"Emma, by the looks of things, you have an additional fifty pounds in reserves that hadn't been recorded correctly. If you'd like, I could spend a day and review the books from the very beginning and catch the discrepancies, if there are any."

"This is brilliant," Emma declared. "If you could do that, then I could deliver this baby without any distractions except Somerton. I was going to ask my father if his auditor could look at the books. I've been concerned the figures weren't correct." She gracefully stood. "Now, let's settle on payment, shall we?"

A flush of heat bludgeoned her cheeks. It was one thing to barter for her services, but another to be paid wages. "I can't take your money. I want to help."

"Nonsense," Daphne added.

March turned to her. "May I ask if you receive payment for your services?"

Daphne's brows drew together as she considered the question. "No. I'm family. Well, practically family," she clarified. "Since Alex is married to Claire."

"I wouldn't feel right if I accepted money from you. Not after everything you and your family have done for mine." March smiled and hoped that it would convince her friend to drop the subject.

Emma cocked her head and stared out the window, completely lost in thought for a second. "You'd be family too if you married—"

"It's growing late. I should return to Langham Hall." March gathered her things. It had been beyond the pale to interrupt her friend, but such nonsense would taint yesterday's wonderful evening. It was her fondest memory, and she wanted it to stay as pure as a newly fallen snow. "The duchess thought Faith and Julia might have some visitors today."

Emma walked to the vault and pulled out a navy velvet bag. She returned to March's side and gently took her hand before placing the bag in her outstretched palm.

"Here's your payment. The loan I made three months ago is forgiven."

"That's too much for the little work I did," March protested.

Emma arched one delicate blond brow. "You'll have to do my books for as long as you're in London." A hint of steel reinforced her normal dulcet voice. "Agreed?"

March felt the familiar weight in the palm of her hand. To have the contents in her possession again was a sign she'd turned the tide in her quest to protect her family. Now, their lives were under their control again.

Daphne had joined them by the vault. "May I see what's in the bag? Emma's described them to me before, but I've never seen them in person."

She gently upended the bag. Two earrings fell into her palm.

Emma's breath caught. "I forgot how beautiful they are."

Daphne's eyes grew round. "Those are the largest sapphires I've ever seen in my life."

A hint of tears clouded the outline of the earrings. Even though it was unladylike, March sniffed. The effort made her errant tears subside. "They were my mother's."

Daphne peered closer. "The pearls surrounding them appear pink in color."

"They are," she answered. "My father had them made for my mother when I was born. He said the sapphires matched my mother's eyes while the tiny pearls matched my complexion."

"There's only one thing to do," Emma announced. "We must go shopping for a dress that will set off these earrings."

Daphne's eyes widened. "Emma! You hate to shop."

"Well, desperate times call for desperate measures.

We all suffer for the greater good. And whatever else generals say before leading the infantry into war." Emma waved her hand as if dismissing the whole affair. "I want my brother to be spellbound when he sees you in those earrings."

"That's very kind." March cleared her throat. "But I don't want to waste my money on another gown."

"Nonsense, March," Emma commanded. "My brother will pay for it. Tell me, when is your next ball?"

# Chapter Thirteen

All the way back to Langham Hall, March considered the shopping excursion with Emma and Daphne tomorrow as they hunted for the perfect gown to match her mother's earrings. Her thoughts drifted to Michael as they usually did whenever she had a free moment. She wondered what his favorite color was. What other types of fabric did he like to caress with his hands? Last night, he stroked and petted her as if he couldn't resist the feel of the soft velvet beneath his fingers.

A footman silently opened the door, and March descended the steps of the Langham carriage that Pitts had insisted she take when she visited Emma's bank.

"Is that you, March?" a male voice called.

Immediately she halted. She didn't have to look as she recognized Rupert Lawson's voice. Somehow, she'd lost her good fortune between the bank and Langham Hall. She glanced at the walk in front of the street and immediately pressed her eyes closed.

Rupert stood ready to approach her, but she hurried toward him. Determined not to let him upset her sisters or force his company on the duke and duchess, she decided to greet him, then send him away.

When she reached his bulky side, she nodded. "Whatever are you doing here?"

His gaze swept the street as if taking notice whether anyone was around. "My my cousin, you've come up in this world. Langham Hall, no less. How did you manage to twist the Marquess of McCalpin to do your bidding?"

"Is there something you need from me? Otherwise, I must go." She tapped her foot in an attempt to quell her nervous energy. Every inch of her skin crawled in a desperate attempt to escape from him. "The duchess is waiting for me."

"Mustn't keep the duchess cooling her heels." His sly smile reminded her of a fox attempting to break into the henhouse. "I stopped by Lawson Court this morning. Everything appears in order. Your Hart is busy with those infernally bleating bags of wool. Filthy loathsome things."

"Thank you for your consideration." She nodded and turned, but his hand shot out and twirled her until she faced him once again.

"Mrs. Oliver said in your rush to leave Leyton, you left the viscount's study a mess. Being the gentleman that I am, I offered to straighten it up for her."

Fear started to bloom like runaway weeds overtaking a garden. "What do you want?" she whispered.

"This little escapade of having the Marquess of McCalpin named your guardian and supervising the estate's money was beyond foolish. I told you that once I married Julia, I'd take care of everything. Now, you've complicated matters."

She stared wordlessly at him.

"I will marry Julia," he warned.

Leaning close, his putrid breath assailed her. She turned her head and inhaled, allowing the cold air to wash away the stench of his breath.

"Don't you dare do anything to jeopardize my plans," he growled. "Otherwise, you'll not like the results, understand?"

She took a step back to escape. Defiantly, she lifted her chin and regarded him. "You'll have to discuss the matter with the marquess. He's Julia's guardian."

"I'm warning—" he commanded.

"Warn away, Rupert." As if preparing to defend herself, she clenched her fists. What she wouldn't give to be able to knock him to his knees. "It's out of my control."

"You leave me no choice, March. I'm sorry it's come to this." His calm voice carried through the cold air as if commenting on the weather.

Shock caused her retort to wedge in her throat. He was threatening her; or worse, he was threatening her sisters.

McCalpin rode Donar to the entrance of Langham Hall and immediately halted. The sight before him sent his blood boiling. Naturally, March would have admirers. She was a lovely young woman, and any man with a lick of intelligence would be calling on her.

It was a bloody inconvenient oversight on his part that he should have anticipated, but didn't. He took a deep breath to quiet the jealously that burned through him. The effort failed completely, so he decided to do the next best thing. He threw the reins to a Langham groomsman and walked toward the couple. He'd do his damnedest to send the fellow on his way. He wanted to spend the afternoon with her. All under the guise that they'd discuss the upcoming events that March and her sisters would attend.

His real purpose was to discuss the kiss and Lady Miranda. If Emma was correct, and that's what had upset March last night, he'd dissuade her from worrying over the chit. Then they could perhaps take a walk through Langham Park. He'd like to show her a tree he'd planted as a boy, then perhaps steal another one of her sweet kisses as a memento of the day.

When he reached her side, he understood this wasn't a caller. Her back was ramrod straight and she was putting distance between herself and the stranger. The tension between the two was obvious.

"Good afternoon, Miss Lawson." In a move designed to allow her to feel safe, he stood close to her side. Why this man frightened her was something he needed to determine before he'd pound the blackguard into the ground. "Would you do the honors and introduce me?"

She inched closer to him. Her slight movement caused his anger to roar as it gnashed and tore through him. When she had faced him in his study that first time, she'd never shown fear like this. Even with her injured hand and blood all over her, she never quivered as she did now.

It took everything in his power not to push her behind him as he dealt with the miscreant before him.

"My lord, this is my cousin, Mr. Rupert Lawson." Her voice was faint, and when she glanced at him, stark, vivid alarm colored her expressive eyes.

He slowly, but with all the haughtiness he possessed, ran his gaze over the corpulent misanthrope before him.

"The Marquess of McCalpin," she offered meekly to her cousin.

The man bowed profusely. "My lord, an honor to meet you."

He nodded, but didn't offer a response.

The man's eyes briefly narrowed. If McCalpin hadn't

been watching him so carefully, he might have missed the brief flash of hatred.

"It's a noble endeavor to accept the responsibility for the viscount and his sisters. As a loyal cousin from March's father's side, I'd be more than willing to handle the guardianship and the estate if you find . . . perhaps it's more work than you'd expected."

The slight grin on his face made McCalpin angrier.

"There's no need, Mr. Lawson. I'm enjoying my new-found role with the Lawson family immensely. They're truly lovely"—McCalpin gestured toward the mansion behind him—"and the duke and duchess are simply captivated by them all. I could never, nor would I want, to shirk my responsibilities." He gently took March's elbow in his hand. "Besides, I understand you're Lord Lawson's heir. Unseemly to put you in such a difficult position. Every transaction you'd approved for the viscount or on his estate's behalf could be questioned." He delivered a composed smile. "No need to thank me. Now, if you'll excuse us, we're expected inside."

"My lord, it's been a pleasure," Lawson said. He turned to March. "Cousin, I shall call upon you again to continue our discussion." He sketched something that looked like a bow, then strode away from them with his cane twirling in the air as if he were the happiest and most carefree man in all of London.

March shivered, and McCalpin's attention immediately switched from Lawson to her. "Are you all right?"

She nodded. "He's despicable, but it's all bluff."

"What did he want?" McCalpin watched Lawson until he disappeared.

"Julia and our money," March sighed. "I told him it was out of my hands, but he kept pressing that something dire would happen."

"Come with me." McCalpin offered his elbow, and she took it immediately. The grasp of her hand around his arm was surprisingly strong, but her gait was weary and hesitant as if she couldn't walk the short distance to the entrance. He wavered between strolling into the mansion like this or picking her up in his arms and carrying her in.

"*Ma belle embezzler*, it's over. He can't hurt you or your family. Now, I need you to stay strong and walk in there of your own accord, or if your preference is something else, I'll pick you up."

"Quit calling me that," she protested.

"What? *Embezzler*?" he teased.

Her eyes widened in confusion. "Beautiful."

Tenderly, he whispered, "I don't like to tell a falsehood. Now, if I had my choice, I'd carry you into the house."

She pressed her lips together and nodded. With an inherent determination, she straightened. "Thank you. I'm ready to *walk* in now."

There was her strong resolve he so admired. "I'm ready to *kiss* you now," he whispered close to her ear.

She bit her lip and glanced away.

God, she was ravishing.

An unbridled need swept through him like a wildfire to protect her from the ugliness that dared harm her or her family. Before he did something foolish like kiss her in the middle of the street, he squeezed her hand and led her to Langham Hall.

Pitts opened the door, and after discarding their wraps and hats, McCalpin took March to the library.

Once inside, he turned the lock to avoid any interruptions from the servants. Once he had her settled in front of the blazing fire, he poured two small glasses of brandy. He settled next to her and gave her the glass of spirits.

"Drink it all." Out of the corner of his eye, he watched her take a small sip. "More," he growled, then took a large swallow of his own. She did as directed. The small act of concession caused a flicker of contentment to take root, pushing aside his remaining discontent over her dismay. She'd be her strong confident self in no time.

He tilted the glass up and finished his own serving. He angled his body close to hers. "Better?"

"Infinitely." The fear had receded from her voice. She even offered him a smile, one that reminded him of last night when he'd held her in his arms.

"I didn't get the opportunity to ask last night, but where did you learn to dance?" An excellent dancer, she'd been warm and supple in his arms as he'd whisked her around the mezzanine. Her height matched his, making it easy to maneuver the steps. He leaned back and regarded her. "You're quite accomplished."

Her cheeks burst into a rosy blush.

*Good lord!* Somehow, such a simple response robbed him of his very breath.

"That's very kind. My mother and father taught me. Then they'd allowed me to practice by attending several small assemblies in Leyton. The wanted me to be ready for my Season." She studied the glass in her hand. Gently, she placed it on the side table without making a sound.

"Have you always been frightened of your cousin?"

She shook her head, then lifted her gaze to his. The fire caught the flecks of gold in her warm eyes, making them flash with light. "Lately, he's become bolder in his demands. He's too old for Julia, and she's too kind for him. I'm afraid he'd crush her spirit if they made a match." Her low voice shook as she returned her gaze to the fire. "His indifference to Faith has turned into something quite cruel."

"How so?"

She grew silent again, and the fire crackled as if encouraging her to continue. She appeared to be lost in her thoughts. He leaned close, and the movement drew her attention back to him.

"March, I can't protect your family if you don't tell me more," he coaxed.

She rose from the chair with an inborn grace that enhanced the lush lines of her body. Her destination was the fireplace where she idly took the poker in hand and jabbed the logs. The flames shot higher. After she was apparently satisfied with her work, she faced him.

"Leyton always has a hunt in early spring. Rupert had planned to present the prize of the foxtail to Faith. It would be unspeakably cruel, and it was a move to hurt not only her, but me."

Her shoulders had dropped as if she'd been defeated. With a sigh, she studied the grounds of Langham Park from the windows that lined the study's far wall.

"Go on," he gently insisted.

"My parents always hosted the hunt for the community. Faith normally trailed after me, but during the hunt one year, she didn't. Caught up in the excitement, I didn't bother looking for her. Yet something niggled my conscience, so I searched for her. She was chasing a pup in training for the hunt. As the dog wandered toward the pack, Faith followed, coaxing it away with a piece of bread. Before I could reach her, the Master of the Hunt had blown the horn, and the horses were off. Faith ran behind the hunters but one man lagged behind. He had difficulty controlling his mount. Faith ran in front of them." Her voice softened until he could barely hear her. "The horse shied and reared up on its hind legs. Faith fell in the commotion, and the horse came down on its front legs."

"So that's how she was hurt," he whispered. He rose and slowly crossed the distance between them. He clasped her hands, ice cold beneath his; he rubbed his thumbs across her palms.

She didn't say anything for a long while, but her stoic face appeared ready to crack under the guilt, the type that tore souls in half. He'd seen and felt it before himself. The pain colored every aspect of one's life. It took every ounce of self-control not to sweep her in his arms and protect her.

"I should have followed her. Because of my lack of regard, Faith suffered a broken leg and severe wounds caused by the horse's shoe. She suffers every day because of my carelessness." Her words were soft, but it didn't hide her pain or the fact her actions haunted her.

"I'm sorry," he said. More than she could ever imagine, he knew her pain and guilt. He lived with it every day also—the gnawing ache of doubting one's own worthiness to exist in this world. Mrs. Ivers' hateful words that he was unfit to be his father's heir were still weapons of torture. The fact he was a simpleton who masqueraded as the heir to a mighty duke, one who loved him dearly, was a heavy burden that sometimes made him numb.

"I'm sorry also." She dipped her head slightly as if she couldn't face him. She drew her hands back and clasped them together. "Rupert wants to publicly present her with the prize of the foxtail as a way to humiliate Faith. He obviously hoped to weaken her chances even further for a match."

"He'll not bother either of you again, I promise." If he could, he'd consume her guilt as his own. It would add little to his overwhelming burden, but it'd release her to live a happy life, one she deserved after all the heartache she'd had to bear.

She raised a dubious eyebrow. "Careful, I may hold you to that promise. He's like a slow toxic poison, but I can't refuse to see him. He's really the only family we have left." She blinked several times as if to clear her thoughts.

"Trust me, March," he said.

She frankly assessed him with a sharp gaze.

"I don't know if I can," she murmured. "I've been on my own for so long. It's difficult to release any of the responsibility. It's like a carefully constructed bridge. If I pull off one plank, I'm afraid the entire structure will fall."

"The guilt and grief you're experiencing can be harmful if you don't try to unburden some of it. We all experience grief in one way or another. It keeps us from reaching our potential if we allow it to become too heavy. Your sister is happy and receiving medical care." He let out his breath.

Her intelligent eyes missed little. "Do you have any experience with such guilt and grief?"

For a moment, he believed she saw every fault he'd tried so hard to hide. "Of course, I'm human. It's part of our being." It was imperative that he turn the conversation to other matters before he confessed how flawed he really was. "Now, I'd like to discuss last night."

She immediately stepped away. "You don't have to explain. The magic of last night caught us both unaware. Let's not mention it again."

Her dismissal burned through him as if someone had

pressed a red-hot anvil against his chest. He'd not allow her to withdraw from him, not after all they'd shared. "Last night was a joy for me, one that doesn't occur that often. I despise society events, even ones my own mother hosts. But nothing would have kept me away from celebrating the night with you and your family." He grasped her chin in his fingers and encouraged her to look at him. He wanted her to see his sincerity. "For selfish reasons, I wanted to see you in that dress. I wanted to dance with *you.*"

With tightly pursed lips, her skepticism slipped once again. "Please, don't. I'm not and never will be fooled by such sayings."

He blinked, not certain he'd heard her correctly. He was giving her a compliment and she was throwing it right back in his face in disbelief. "Why is it so hard to believe that I wanted to spend time in your company?"

"My lord—"

"'My lord' is it?" His nostrils flared as he exhaled in an attempt to keep himself from shaking some sense into her. "Why is it so hard to believe that you're attractive? Sometimes I don't have a clue as to what's going on in that beautiful head of yours."

"I'm not the type of woman you find attractive," she said. By now, that steel determination of hers had taken up residence in her stance. "I'm not Lady Miranda."

He shook his head in an attempt to quiet the need to shout his frustration. "I don't give a damn about Lady Miranda or any of those other chits that parade about town seeking a husband. I danced with her for reasons other than her company."

"Such as laughter and smiles and looks of flirtation and infatuation . . ." Her voice trailed to nothing at the words. Suddenly, a scarlet color blossomed across her cheeks. With that little outburst, she'd disclosed that he did affect her—perhaps a great deal. The idea delighted him and eliminated his remaining consternation at her earlier denial of her attraction.

Not allowing her to turn away from him, he closed the distance between them until they almost touched chest to chest. She had no choice but to look into his eyes. "Perhaps you saw that on *her* face, but I assure you that *I* wasn't feeling *any* of those things."

He drew a deep breath and allowed her lilac scent to fill him. Every inch of his body tightened in readiness as he lowered his lips to hers. The slightest moan escaped her, and her mint breath scented with brandy brushed against his lips. With an ease that warred with his rising desire, he kissed her. The taste of her soft lips threatened to unleash an insatiable need, one only she could satisfy. He forced himself to slow his movements. On a gentle sigh, she opened her mouth, inviting him to take more. For an instant, he slanted his mouth over hers to do just that. Then reason prevailed, and he drew back. He didn't dare take more from her, though he wanted to crush her to him and ravish her mouth as he did last night.

He had other plans for his little embezzler—a long-term strategy that would lead her to trust him and relieve some of her ever-present burden. He'd tease and tempt her until she begged him for more. He'd show her passion and desire until she writhed for more.

He'd make her believe she was beautiful.

Even if it was his complete undoing.

The next morning found March's sisters in high spirits as they broke their fast. Faith leaned close and whispered, "I still cannot fathom why there are four footmen ready to attend us at breakfast every morning. At Lawson Court, we cooked and cleaned for ourselves."

Glee laced the wonderment in her sister's eyes. Their circumstances had catapulted from poverty to great wealth in just a short order. March surveyed the breakfast room that overlooked Langham Hall's beautiful park. The opulent gold and pink baroque decorating didn't diminish the coziness of their morning gatherings. Their acceptance in the Langham home was a true testament of the duke and duchess's generosity.

Julia was a veritable chatterbox this morning. Yesterday afternoon, the Earl of Queensgrace had come to call on her with a small but delightful posy. March and Faith had already heard her thorough monologue regarding the Scottish lord's refined manners and elegance, but the unfortunate Lord William had not. When he happened to sit with them in the breakfast room, Julia had jumped at the opportunity to share her story with someone else.

"The marquess had the posy especially made for me and delivered it himself." As she regaled Lord William with every minute of the previous afternoon's visit with the Scottish lord, Julia buttered her toast. It made little difference that she'd slathered butter on the piece of bread three different times. She was too enthralled with yesterday to pay the poor slice much attention. "He said the violets matched my eyes."

Michael's brother sat patiently sipping his coffee, and occasionally nodded his encouragement. March glanced at Faith, who had bowed her head in embarrassment over Julia's continued onslaught extolling the virtues of the young lord.

"The marquess asked if he could take me for a ride in Hyde Park." Julia finally stopped talking and sighed as she looked at the gloomy gray skies outside. "I don't care if it's a torrential rainstorm. I'm going."

William regarded her and took another sip of coffee while trying to hide his smile. "Julia, it's sleeting outside. You'll freeze to death." He folded the paper in his hands and stared as if it offered a welcomed reprieve from her incessant nattering. "Besides no one of the *ton* will see you with the young lord. They will all be home by a fire staying warm, which is my advice for you. Don't appear too eager, my dear. Men hate that."

"They do?" Julia's brows drew together, and she frowned. "What should I do?" Her beautiful face melted into an unease that lined her brow.

March shook her head. "He's teasing you, dearest."

Julia narrowed her eyes at William, and this time he allowed himself to laugh aloud. "Forgive me, it's just that you reminded me of Emma when she found something passionate to dwell on. She was an expert at holding all of us captive at the dinner table until she had finished her dissertations. I would always tease her unmercifully and couldn't resist with you."

"What types of things did she share about her callers, my lord?" Julia set her cutlery aside and gave him her undivided attention.

He leaned back in his chair and studied the ceiling. "I don't recall her ever discussing any man. She mostly talked about politics and women's roles within society."

"How silly my musings must sound." She shyly dipped her head and bit her lip as if censured. "I apologize for not curbing my tongue."

He briefly regarded March and Faith as if begging for help. "Julia . . . I didn't mean that as a criticism. I was describing my darling sister's personality."

Faith leaned forward and patted Julia's hand. "Dearest, we should probably get ready. Lady Somerton and Lady Daphne will be here shortly to take us shopping."

March wouldn't let her littlest sister suffer either. "Julia, your excitement is perfectly normal for a young woman enjoying her first Season. I dare say if I'd experienced your success, I'd be a prattling fool. No need to feel embarrassed."

Lord William smiled down the table. "Indeed. It's a joy to have you and your sisters here. You bring a vibrancy to Langham Hall that's been missing since Emma married Somerton. I wouldn't have you change a single thing about yourself."

Perhaps it was the words or the way he said it so warmly, but immediately Julia's disquiet lifted. She was back to her happy self again. With a nod and a smile, she took her leave with Faith. March stayed and continued to enjoy her tea and toast in relative silence.

William placed his paper down on the table and studied her. Not with the usual air of interest, but with something that set her on edge, as if slipping on a rocky slope and waiting for the inevitable fall. In response, she straightened her shoulders and stared in challenge.

His gaze pierced hers as if he studied her every mistake and misdeed. After what seemed like an eternity, he spoke. "I was hoping you might share with me your circumstances at Lawson Court before my brother petitioned the court for guardianship."

The question took her by surprise, as she'd assumed Michael told his brother everything. The two were inordinately close. Practically every day they were together. Michael had even shared that when he traveled to McCalpin Manor, William usually joined him.

The attending footmen quietly gathered the used

plates and then left the room. March placed her hands in her lap to quell the sudden nervousness. She despised having to relate how she and her family had lived in abject poverty for so long. Nevertheless, as Michael and his family had been so generous and loving toward hers, she didn't want to keep anything hidden, particularly after the way William had first met her with the fruits of her embezzling spread before him like a proverbial feast.

"I had five pounds left to manage the estate for the next six months. The house had suffered severe damage during a storm along with our one and only tenant who suffered as much, if not more, damage than we did." She gathered enough courage to share the rest. "When your brother came to discover our circumstances, I was at my wits' end. It was horrifying."

"Why? What were you afraid he'd discover?" His voice was pleasant, but there was a hint of skepticism in his drawl.

"How poor we actually are," she murmured, then corrected herself. "How poor we actually *were*. When he found me, I'd been trying to capture some sheep we'd lost, and . . ." She forced herself to meet his gaze. "I was injured in the process. Michael—the marquess—was very kind and helped me back to the house." She took a deep breath for fortitude, but the old familiar humiliation started to rise, much like a dough of bread. The only difference was that the bread could nourish while the humiliation ate her from within. Shameful, burning tears flooded her eyes, but she blinked them away.

"My brother was so delighted there was an actual peer who'd come to 'visit him' that he asked your brother to stay for dinner. Everything we had for the week was served that night."

"Go on." His voice had lowered.

Oh God, was she really going to share the rest? "It's humiliating."

"I won't judge you, March."

"But you want to, don't you?" she whispered. Where had such a spiteful comment come from? He hadn't said anything to warrant such a hateful response.

"No, I want to know what McCalpin has gotten himself into. I need to know what he's facing by helping you."

"Fair enough." She swallowed, but her disgrace had lodged in her throat like a brick. "Bennett's cat brought in a freshly killed rabbit, and my brother joyfully related how it would be our dinner the next night."

His face froze, except for the slight tightening of his jaw muscles.

"Bennett asked if the marquess wanted to eat with us again." This time she laughed in defense of all her failures.

"Did you eat the hare?" he whispered.

Finally, she gathered the courage to face his condemnation. Whether she was twenty-four as McCalpin thought or her true age of twenty-five made little difference. She was unable to keep her family safe and fed. Nothing William could say would make her feel any worse about herself than she already did. "Yes. In a stew the next night."

He didn't have a response, but the shock on his face wasn't something she'd likely forget in her lifetime.

She tried to explain—tried to make him understand that desperate times required desperate measures. "Otherwise, my siblings wouldn't have had anything to eat."

"I apologize that I intruded on your private business." His brow lined as he struggled to find the right words. "You understand I must protect my brother."

"How is asking these questions and discovering my

shame protecting your brother?" Remarkably, she kept her voice from shrieking. Inside, she railed at the way the world had treated her family. Like a building storm, her anger at the injustice of it all grew too big to contain, and she unleashed it. "My father gave tirelessly for this country and for what? All the men he trusted to protect his progeny failed him, and in return, us. The viscountcy is flush with money for the care and upkeep of the estate, but we haven't seen a shilling. My brother is a peer of the realm for goodness' sake. He and his sisters shouldn't have to face poverty. The money I took rightfully belongs to me, but nobody gave a *damn* about us."

Her eyes widened in horror, and she brought her hand to cover her quivering lips. *She'd said the words aloud. She'd let those vile utterings spill and splatter around her like an overturned cup of tea.*

She glanced away in a vain effort to gain some control over the riot of emotions that continued to pound through her. This was her mess, and she'd clean it as she always did—with as much acumen and grace as she possessed. He would most likely condemn her as a common, shrill woman without any class or manners. Perhaps she deserved nothing less for the outburst.

She clenched the fabric of her dress so tightly her hands hurt from the strain. She forced herself to release her grip, then cleared her throat. "I apologize, but I must ask, why are you interested?"

She forced her gaze to his and waited for whatever censure he would serve.

His face softened. "You honestly don't know why I'm asking these questions?"

She didn't answer as she continued to stare at him.

"It's obvious to me, and I'm sure deep down you see it too. My brother has taken quite an interest in your well-being. Not because you've proven to be quite the proficient embezzler. He's taken an interest in your family and specifically *in you*. For heaven's sake, my father has even taken your brother to the House of Lords to hear arguments. Somehow you and your family have bewitched mine." He rubbed his hand down his face as if this exchange was painful for him.

If he wanted to know pain, he should sit in her chair for just an hour. "A proficient embezzler? That's how you see me? Does the reason why I embezzled *my* money mean nothing?"

"But it's not your money until you turn twenty-five, is it? It's the trust's money and McCalpin holds the key."

It was a wasted effort to argue about her age. With her back straight, she refused to be cowered by him. "What would you do if your family literally had to eat what the cat drug in?"

She waited for a response, but he simply watched her—silent but alert. He reminded her of a fox licking its chops as a rabbit cowered in front of him. His silent denial infuriated her even more.

"I'm glad you'll never have to walk in our shoes, William. But I'll share something with you." She leaned close and dropped her voice to a whisper. "If I had to do it all over again, I would, and never think twice." She laughed to conceal her agony. "Frankly, I could care less how you regard me. I'd do anything to protect my sisters and my brother and Victor Hart. They're my family."

"Even steal a man's identity, his name, his good standing?"

"Please," she retorted. "No harm has befallen your brother. What would you do if an immoral man was determined to possess your sister? What if you found Emma receiving the unwanted attentions of a man who valued her for nothing more than her virtue and her fortune? Tell me." Her words echoed through the room when her voice rose in outrage.

She wouldn't stop there until she'd put him on the offensive. "Since we're being so honest, perhaps you'll answer a question for me? Why didn't you join the army or the church like other highborn sons of powerful peers? Why don't you work?"

He laughed, but there was no bitterness in his tone. "A direct wound, my dear. Well done." He matched her movement and leaned close to her. "I work on the estates."

"The duchy?"

He nodded. "And McCalpin Manor."

"Doing what may I ask?"

"Various things." He took a sip of coffee. "But it's really none of your business, is it?"

Once again, his gaze cut through hers as if challenging her to come at him again. She shook her head. Fighting with him served no purpose.

She schooled her features until she hoped she concealed her ire. "The monies I withdrew were mine. I should have had access to them months ago. However, you don't care about that, and I can't say that I blame you. If I were in your position, I'd feel the same way. But you must trust me when I say I'd never hurt your brother."

"We shall see, March." Before he could say another word, Emma and Daphne entered the room. He stood and waited while the two women took their seats beside March.

Emma's gaze shot between the two of them. "Did we interrupt something?"

William sat in his chair and smiled as if nothing untoward had occurred between them. "Emma, you're looking splendid today." His gaze swept to Daphne, and the smile he presented would have lit every ballroom in London that night with its brightness. "Daphne, a vision as always."

Emma studied her brother with narrowed eyes but must have decided not to pursue it. "March, darling, are you ready? I'd like to get this torture over with as quickly as we can."

"Shopping?" William smiled wily. "Emma, you shock me."

She shook her head, and her glorious blond curls bounced as if laughing with her. "March needs a new dress for Lady Carlisle's ball. Daphne and I are helping her."

He narrowed his gaze to March. "Another new dress?"

Emma scoffed. "What do you know about it?"

"Nothing, and that's the problem," he offered.

His sister stared at him with her emerald eyes blazing, but addressed March. "Did William tell you that you couldn't have a new dress?"

"No, of course not." He answered before March could respond. "We were having a lovely discussion before you joined us."

"McCalpin doesn't care if we get her a new wardrobe every week, so I'm perplexed why you should," Emma retorted. Her cheeks had grown bright red.

Daphne watched the exchange between the siblings, then abruptly stood in front of Emma. "William, I don't think Somerton would take kindly that you're deliberately provoking his wife. Nor would McCalpin care for your attitude toward March."

"Always the defender, eh, Daphne?" He stood and gracefully bowed. "My apologies. I have my work patiently waiting for me in the library. If you ladies will excuse me?" He didn't wait for a reply as he strolled out of the room.

Things had gone from pleasant to quite nasty within the last half hour. March didn't even want to go shopping now.

# Chapter Fourteen

The next morning, March rushed into the yellow salon to find a welcome sight. Hart sat in the gold settee surrounded by Faith, Julia, and Bennett.

As soon as he saw her, he stood. Not standing on ceremony, she rushed into his arms. "How we've missed you!"

He held her at arms length for a quick perusal and smiled. "I'd say London agrees with you. You're the proper young woman I always knew existed under that attractive veneer of a sheep farmer."

"Scratch the surface, and you'll see she still exists," March retorted. He always teased her about her abilities on managing the estate and the ever-increasing flock. Her merriment diminished when she stood close to him and noticed the thin lines etched around his eyes and the dark circles under them. "What is it?" she whispered.

"Later, my miss, when we're alone." He softly spoke the words for her ears only.

Bennett demanded his attention as he shared his adventures with the Duke of Langham and the museums that he'd attended since he was in town. Hart listened intently, but he looked tired, as if the weight of the world had settled on his shoulders.

Faith shared her remarkable progress with Dr. Kennett and his daily calls. A pretty flush colored her cheeks as she compared how much they had in common. Hart smiled in sincere pleasure when she swept the length of the room, her limp barely noticeable this morning.

Julia was a little more subdued than usual, but she told Hart all about the handsome Earl of Queensgrace. She left out the posy tale, which was a blessing, but she surprised them all when she shared she wanted to introduce the young earl to Hart.

"I think he's a good man, but I'd like your opinion." She smiled at Hart, and his face softened at her request. "You've always been such a wonderful judge of character."

"Jules"—Hart thinned his lips, a sign he fought for control—"that's lovely. Of course, I want to meet this nonpareil of a man and make certain he's worthy of your affections." He leaned forward to ruffle Bennett's hair. Her brother tried to swat his hand away, but Hart's reach was too long. Soon he had Bennett giggling at their play.

March's heart swooped and buzzed like a swallow at the familiar sight. The busy London Season lent little time for reflection, but with Hart's visit, she discovered she missed their home, missed these exchanges, and missed the contentment she felt at Lawson Court. Even though the family faced incredible circumstances in Leyton, she missed Hart. He was part of their family, and she hated they all couldn't be together.

Always astute, Faith caught March's gaze and nodded.

She urged Julia and Bennett to say their good-byes to Hart. She used the excuse they were late for an excursion to the circulating library.

Hart escorted them to the door. When they left, he closed it and came back to March's side. Worry lined his face and creased his brow. She'd poured tea for them and let the heat of the cup warm her hands.

"Tell me what's happened," she said.

Hart sat next to her. As she waited for him to speak, disquiet vibrated between them like the strings of a pianoforte when someone unexpectedly struck a single key.

"It's Lord Erlington. He's sent for me." He took a deep breath and exhaled, his pain evident. "March, he's dying."

"Oh, no." She pressed her hand over her mouth to subdue the overwhelming stab of grief. "I'm so sorry."

Hart reached with one large hand and grasped hers tightly. Erlington and Hart had been lovers for over thirty years.

When she'd first discovered the truth of their regard for each other, she'd been shocked. She would never have conceived two men could fall in love with each other. Nevertheless, just as her had parents had shared an undying love, so did Hart and Erlington. Somehow, they'd managed to build a life together. Though society ridiculed and punished such relationships, theirs was a thing of beauty, strong and pure.

She'd been in awe whenever she'd seen them together. Once a year, Erlington would come to Lawson Court for a visit. In return, Hart traveled to Erlington's estate in Suffolk at least three times a year to "consult on his Lordship's agricultural experiments." Hart always came back from the visits renewed with a new vigor that was born from the intimacy the two men shared.

"What can I do?" Whatever he needed became her only concern. She'd help him through this grief as he'd done for her when she'd lost her parents. "Shall you and I go visit?"

"No. There's nothing to be done, my miss. The family needs you here. I'm leaving for Suffolk this morning. I'll stay with his Lordship until he passes. Mr. Garwyn will manage the farm with the help of a few others and Mrs. Oliver." Hart rubbed his face with a hand as if he could wipe his grief away, but the strain was still visible. His knee bobbed up and down, and he fidgeted with the teacup handle. "I hate to be so far away from you."

She leaned over and kissed his cheek. "Don't worry for us. London is child's play compared with the estate."

He nodded, and the gesture broke her heart. Lost and alone in his thoughts, he hung his head in defeat. Her eyes burned for the loss he was facing, but she refused to allow any tears to fall in front of him. She had to be strong or he'd never have the peace of mind to leave for Suffolk, where he rightfully belonged.

Hart stood and she followed. She found herself in his embrace as he pulled her tight against him as if trying to take some of her strength with him. She tightened her arms around him and kissed his cheek. "Write and tell me what you find."

He nodded once. The letters would be cryptic as he never divulged Erlington's name in correspondence. Hart would protect his love until the very end. How unfair they couldn't celebrate their lives together in the open.

"One more thing," he whispered. "Lawson came by the other day. I found him in Bennett's study. Nothing was missing, but I'm not certain what he was doing. Mrs. Oliver hadn't even heard him come into the house."

"What could he have been looking for?" If he was

looking for money, the man was a fool. There was no way she'd keep funds at the house without any of them there.

Hart shook his head. "I wish I knew. Be careful, March. I don't trust him."

"Don't worry. We're safe here in London."

"Yes, you are. Lord McCalpin's a good man and takes his responsibility for you and your siblings seriously. It's the only reason I can leave." He kissed her cheek once more. "Good-bye. I don't know when I'll return."

She took a deep breath, hoping the air would help still the reeling emotions inside of her. Everything had changed with the uncertainty of his return, revealing how vulnerable they all were in this world.

"Tell his Lordship . . . I love you both," she managed to choke out as the sorrow threatened to steal her breath.

With his anguish overcoming him, Hart gave her a final hug, then left without a word. The deep unsettling silence of the room felt like a weight holding in her place. How long she stood there alone, she didn't know. Finally, she found herself curled into a tight ball hidden in a curtained window seat.

Maids came to dust and clean the room. Under-footmen prepared the fireplaces for the afternoon. If anyone saw her, they didn't acknowledge her, nor she them. She was too transfixed with the heavy drops of rain that skated down the window. She stared off into the grayness of the day, hoping she'd be lost to the pain.

Her dearest friend was facing the ultimate heartache, and she couldn't share his burden.

Because of that simple fact, London lost its allure and became nothing more than a tarnished and empty waste-land where she didn't belong.

Yet she didn't have any other place to call home.

Lawson Court promised to be just as barren without Hart or her siblings by her side.

Not to mention without the attentions of a certain marquess.

With the note from his brother still fresh in his mind, McCalpin entered Langham Hall. William had informed him of Victor Hart's brief visit and the sudden malaise of the eldest Lawson sister.

As McCalpin handed his black greatcoat and beaver hat to a footman, the steadfast and ubiquitous Pitts waited for him on the other side of the large entry. In several steps, he stood before the loyal butler who volunteered the information without asking.

"Miss Lawson is in the yellow salon." With a gentle smile, he continued, "She's been in the window seat all morning."

McCalpin nodded his thanks and proceeded down the carpeted hallway. His boots sunk into the plush pile as if he were battling against a particularly nasty bog on the Scottish moors. His exploding heart urged him to move faster and reach her.

What had caused Mr. Victor Hart to call upon her, and what had he said to leave her bereft and troubled? If that damn arse Rupert Lawson had anything to do with March's current mood, he'd bloody every inch of his face.

He swung the door open, and silence was all that greeted his entrance. No expected cries of surprise or even sobs of sadness came from the room. Even the normally robust fire had quieted as if it didn't dare intrude on March's private domain while she was in this mood.

There were five window seats on the north wall of the salon. The rain had ceased falling, but the haunting gray of the skies leaked through the windows and cast a grim darkness on the warm gold colors of the furniture. He swept his gaze about the room and found her in the second window seat closest to the corner that bordered the west and north walls.

She slowly slid her feet past the curtain until completely hidden. He let out a sigh of relief at finding her and silently approached her hidden haven.

Four feet separated them, and his body hummed with awareness. This near, her presence behind the curtain seemed to shimmer with an aura he wanted to touch and lose himself in.

He had no idea what she was doing to him, and he was powerless to fight it. Somehow she'd become entwined in his life to such an extent that when he woke in the morning, his first thoughts were of her, not his family or his estate or his responsibilities.

Just her, March Lawson.

"What are you doing there?" He kept his tone low and quiet so not to startle her.

"I'm hiding," she replied. Though muffled by the curtain, the clear, silvery words calmed his frantic worry. "But I failed miserably if you found me so easily. It's hard to tuck such a large body into such a small recess."

"Is that how you see yourself?" he asked, careful of where the conversation could lead. She was sorely conscious of her size, and not in a good way. He waited for her response, but she remained quiet as if ignoring him.

Moving slowly, he sat in the middle of the bench and leaned against the window. Without glancing at her, he surveyed the salon from his vantage point. Keenly aware how near she sat, he simply waited. The tips of her slippers peeked out from under her dress. Embroidered with delicate vines of ivory thread, the dark blue silk begged for his caress. Slowly, as if approaching a wild animal, he rested his hand near her feet. Not touching, but close enough that her heat encouraged him closer. He purposely kept the small distance between them. A saint would be in awe of his mammoth restraint not to take her in his arms. However, he'd not push her until he knew what troubled her.

"Well, since you won't tell me, I'll answer my own question."

The material of her dress rustled as she adjusted her position. When she tried to withdraw farther into the recess of the window seat, the sole of one shoe pushed against his thigh. Her touch burned through the leather of his doeskin breeches.

"When I look at you, I see an important, beautiful, resourceful, and not to mention capable, woman who takes care of the people she loves."

"Thank you," she whispered.

"What's upset you?"

She swallowed and took a troubled breath. "Hart left us. His lo—friend is dying, and Hart's gone to be with him. His friend is a lovely man who always has a kind word or thought for everyone. I offered to travel with Hart, but he refused. He wants me to stay here with you."

"Those are good reasons to be in deep thought." McCalpin turned, expecting to find tears staining her pink cheeks, but March hid her emotions well. Except that her warm, velvet-brown eyes shimmered with pain for her friend's suffering and hers.

She gently waved a hand through the air indicating her surroundings. "I'm surrounded by people and family in this huge mansion, but I felt so alone after he left. He's always been present in our lives."

"Perhaps one of those people who surround you might

take Hart's place?" he asked. The questioning look on her face was so endearing, he smiled. "Would you ever consider me as a replacement for Hart?"

She scoffed. "He's like an uncle, and I don't consider you an uncle."

Her answer caused his pulse to quicken. Just another nudge, and she might admit her true feelings. "Just exactly how do you consider me, March?"

She moved toward him as if involuntarily drawn by the sound of her name on his lips. "The guardian of my siblings."

The words gutted him as no knife could. He drew in a jagged breath, but refused to turn away. The decision proved sound when her shoulders sank in defeat, and she shook her head. Her silky mahogany curls tumbled around her face. "That isn't true. You're my friend, a very dear one."

The vise that had twisted every organ in his chest gradually released its hold. He reached for one of her coffee-colored curls and twisted it around his finger. Her hair was softer than the velvet she'd worn on her luscious body the other night.

"Spend the day with me," he gently commanded. "Your sisters are out with my mother making the obligatory visits, and your brother is busy with his studies. Together let's shove aside your worries for the afternoon."

She chewed the corner of her bottom lip. Full and lush, her mouth demanded attention, and he groaned at the sight. He leaned close, and her scent drew him nearer as if embracing him. He brushed his lips against hers then pulled back. Dazed, she stared into his eyes. Her look made him feel ten feet tall and just as powerful.

"I'd like that very much," she muttered shyly. "But will

it be appropriate? You and me together? What if some-one from *The Midnight Cryer* sees us?"

"No one will question it. Besides, I don't care about the scandal sheets." Even if society might frown, he wanted this time with her alone. They'd be discreet and no one would be the wiser. He stood and held out his hand to her. She hesitated a moment as if unsure what the gesture meant. As far as he was concerned, it could mean whatever she wanted.

For him, the touch of her hand in his meant the world.

After March had changed her slippers for her sturdy half boots and a warm wool pelisse, Michael had escorted her outside for a tour of Langham Park. He'd explained the design of the formal gardens was the forethought of the second Duchess of Langham. Their destination was a grove of trees of various species deep within the park's center.

Every ducal offspring for generations had planted trees on their tenth birthday. Michael had chosen a mighty oak, William had planted a sturdy elm, and Emma's choice was a flashy maple. The trio of trees reigned majestically above them. The slight fog that had developed didn't hide the magnificence of the trees and the lasting impact they had on the park.

The siblings' trees on the grounds were a testament to the strength of the family and their heritage. It re-minded March of her own history and the ties she had. As if Michael sensed the visit to the park would bring her comfort, he continued to share his family's history and encouraged her to do the same.

After the walk, he took her to his townhouse where they had a lovely tea. The respite lifted her spirits, and he charmed her throughout the meal with tales of his childhood and shared the trials and tribulations of being the Langham ducal heir. They discussed Bennett's future education and the possible matches her sisters' might make this year during the official Season. However, since Parliament had been in session since November, many important social events had already taken place.

After they left Michael's home, they had taken his carriage to her family's townhouse. After he'd shared so much of his life, she wanted to do the same with him. She drank in the comfort of his rich voice and his nearness as they discussed everything and nothing during the day. Slowly, her melancholy disappeared, and she found herself laughing and smiling as she led him through the front door.

Once inside, they headed to her father's library. It was her favorite room in the townhouse as they'd spent many a night there as a family. Michael made quick work of lighting a fire, and soon the room was ablaze in comforting warmth.

"Where did your father get this?" He stood beside the desk where an ornate gold inkstand rested. Engraved with the Royal Arms of Great Britain in the center, each side of the base featured the royal arms of four Continental European powers—Austria, Prussia, Russia, and Denmark.

March smiled at the memory of her father's pride as she discussed the piece. "My father was instrumental in creating an alliance with those countries against France. He was present at the signing of the treaties and given the inkstand in appreciation for all his hard work."

Michael's fingers stroked the intricate scrollwork. The gesture caused a tingling to erupt in her stomach, and goose bumps raced across her arms. She fought the overwhelming urge to close the distance between them. She wanted his strong fingers caressing her in the same manner. He strolled to a drum table next to a settee and picked up several etchings. They were from her father's travels to Italy during his grand tour. His gaze captured hers, and her heart flipped as if trained to respond to his every glance.

Suddenly, his face beamed. "How did your father get all these portraits of me?"

The rumble of his deep voice and his teasing tone made her gasp in delightful outrage at such an audacious question. Offering such a handsome smile, she was powerless to resist him and moved to stand beside him. "What portraits?"

"Look for yourself," he offered. In his large hands were three different etchings of *David* by Donatello, Verrocchio, and Michelangelo. Michael studied her with that fiery heat in his gaze that always caused her cheeks to flame. "Didn't you call me David once?" he whispered. "Tell me again which one you think I favor?"

"Did I compare you to *David*? I'd forgotten," she countered.

"Well, I didn't," he smirked. His grin gave her a glimpse of what he must have looked like as a young boy. His expression transformed him from a powerful lord to a playful imp, one who waited to torment her with his pranks.

"Donatello's sculpture is a youth full of himself." As she took the etchings from Michael, their fingers touched, and she immediately felt a shock of electricity. She snatched her hand away from the contact of his warm skin against hers. "As he should be, since he slayed the giant."

"I see that," he murmured. "But there's more, don't

you agree?" He traced the length of David's leg where the decorative wing on Goliath's helmet wrapped around the youth until it touched his genitals. "In his conquest, David appears almost provocative in a sexual sense."

His cadence had slowed, and his voice had grown deeper. She straightened her shoulders and regarded Michael as proof to him, but more importantly to herself, that she would control this conversation. His lips spread into a wider smile as if he recognized his effect on her.

March wrinkled her nose in a weak protest. "Andrea del Verrocchio's sculpture makes *David* appear cocky, sure of himself and his abilities after he slayed his foe. Goliath's head at his feet is proof of his prowess." She hummed low in her throat. "Definitely, you resemble him. The pride and arrogance are unmistakable." She gazed at the last etching, the one by Michelangelo, and her fingers traced the image of the strong line of his body. Immediately, she imagined caressing Michael in the same manner.

As if he could read her traitorous thoughts, his eyes blazed. She was intensely aware of the undeniable force building between them. She couldn't tell what magic he weaved around them, but she didn't want it to stop. Deep inside, she never wanted to leave the townhouse since she had his undivided attention—no one to intrude or interrupt what they shared.

"Michelangelo's *David* is a beautiful young warrior who knows what he's facing. Stoic and prepared for a battle to the death against Goliath, he is sure of his path. This David will not stop until he wins." Her words trailed to nothing. She took a moment, then tilted her head as if examining him as carefully as she studied the etchings in her hand. "David holds a place of honor in the art of

Florence. So many renderings of the youth to choose from, but there is no doubt in my mind now. You remind me of the brazen and overconfident *David* by Verrocchio."

He arched an eyebrow and regarded her with disbelief. Then he tapped a finger against his square jaw as if deeply contemplating her answer.

She wanted to be that finger. Instead of tapping, she'd stroke his skin and memorize every line of his face. He'd be strong like Michelangelo's sculpture, but hot and alive instead of the cool white marble the master had carved from the quarries of Carrara.

"I remember now," Michael whispered. His fingers traced her cheeks, and his touch caused her to catch her breath at the intimate touch. "You told me it was Michelangelo's *David*." His hand fell to her chin, and he held her captive with the intensity of his gaze. "Are you going to deny it?"

Riveted and charmed at the same time, she stared at him. What was he doing to her? As if falling through the air, she knew the inevitable outcome. She'd either crash to the hard ground or soar to the bright heavens. She had to decide if he was a risk worth taking.

She forced herself out of the haze he'd created around her. He wanted to lessen her struggle with life. That was the reason he showered her with attention. "Come. There's something else I'd like to show you."

# Chapter Fifteen

McCalpin tried to concentrate on the rotunda ceiling and the intricate mural painting above, but the woman lying beside him on the plush carpet captured all his interest. March insisted they lay on the floor of the small but airy room on the main floor of the townhouse. Large windows surrounded them and allowed enough light to enter the room without the need for any candlelight.

"Tell me what you see." The brightness in her voice reminded him of winsome wind chimes dancing in a breeze and betrayed her excitement.

He tilted slightly on his side so he could better comprehend what she wanted him to look at. It lent another benefit—he could watch her expressive face. Today after he'd whisked her away from Langham Hall, he'd somehow managed to tease and talk her out of her earlier mood. Her brown eyes reminded him of the deepest copper mixed with bronze. They cast such a glint of pure joy that he lost his breath for a moment. She was so glorious in her passion for life and not afraid of being herself with him. He found everything about her intoxicating.

She pointed to the center of the mural, and he followed the elegant line of her arm, the strong but feminine bones of her wrist, and the long length of her hand. When he'd reached the end of her index finger, he exhaled and gazed at the ceiling.

He'd much rather admire *her* form as the ceiling before him looked like utter chaos. There were roses, angels, and nautilus shells with no clear connection among them. Usually such murals featured some mythical battle between opposing gods or biblical scenes. Here there was no clear story to the artist's work. His eyes darted to the decorative border of the mural. The design featured the Parthenon, much like the wood molding found in Bennett's study at Lawson Court.

"You see? It's the Fibonacci series." The triumph in her voice had to be one of the sweetest and seductive sounds he'd ever heard.

"Fibonacci series," he repeated, not knowing what the bloody hell she was talking about, but hoping he sounded convincing.

"It's a mathematical sequence where each number is the sum of the two preceding numbers: zero, one, one, two, three, five, eight, and so on." She lifted her head and turned toward him. "Some call it the Fibonacci sequence, the golden spiral, or the golden ratio. Some say da Vinci's Divine Proportion is based upon the number sequence."

Obviously, he hadn't succeeded if she felt the need to explain it again. Still he didn't understand, but he was familiar with Luca Pacioli's book that da Vinci illustrated. "Ah, you're referring to *De Divina Proportione*."

Her eyes widened.

Secretly, he sighed in relief. He'd distracted her enough that she'd forgotten what she'd been discussing.

She lay back again and studied the ceiling. "My grandfather loved mathematics. You'll find all sorts of hidden secrets of theorems and geometric patterns throughout Lawson Court and here."

Silently, he groaned. *Not numbers, anything but numbers.* He'd not allow anything to ruin this perfect day. He lay back on the carpet and closed his eyes.

"Michael." The whisper of his name rivaled the ardent calls of a bewitching siren.

Thankfully, he had no defense against her sweetness. As if he were the tide to her moon, he turned to her. Her eyes were like warm, dark pools welcoming him, tempting him to lose himself in their depths.

"Look at the petals of the roses. They represent the sequence, too." She took his hand in hers and tried to point to the center petals of one flower. "See how they spiral outward in a perfect pattern?"

He intertwined their fingers together and kissed her hand. In one movement, he flipped his body until he leaned above her blocking the view of the ceiling.

She gasped and her eyes searched his.

He narrowed the distance between them until her sweet breath brushed his lips. "I've found a pattern, too. In petals," he whispered, then recited his favorite poem.

> *Her closed eyes, like*
> *Weapons sheadth'd,*
> *Were seal'd in soft repose;*
> *Her lip, still as she fragrant*
> *Breath'd,*
> *It richer dyed the rose;*

He gently touched his nose to hers.

" 'On a Bank of Flowers' by Robert Burns," she whispered in awe. "How did you know he's my favorite?"

"I didn't. He's *my* favorite."

That was the irony of it all. He could recite sonnets and poems to her perfect nose ad nauseam in Italian, French, Spanish, Portuguese, and even Greek. Yet, he couldn't share one algebraic formula or geometric series or theorem with her. It was as if she was talking gibberish when she discussed any of this. In order to protect his secret, not to mention his sanity, he had to take matters into his own hands. Literally.

He brushed his lips against hers. "I want to talk about the pattern I've found here. Two soft lips that would make a rose jealous." He kissed her again. Only this time he demanded more. He angled his mouth over hers, and on a soft sigh, she parted her lips in invitation.

Gently, he moved his tongue alongside hers. Tentative at first, she matched his movements. With a growl, he explored every sweet inch of her mouth. Her moan vibrated against his chest and set his pulse pounding. Desperate to get closer, he pulled her tight into his embrace. In response, she twisted her fingers into his hair.

Everything within him combusted into a white-hot flame. He wanted to devour her—every inch of her. He wanted to consume her goodness. He wanted to inhale her passion. She made the most delightful frantic whimpers into his mouth. There was no denying she desired him as much as he wanted her.

He gave her no quarter as he continued to possess everything she was. His cock pulsed with need, and he threw one leg over hers as if capturing her, then ground himself into her hip.

His March didn't shy away in shock. She turned her

luscious curves toward him allowing his cock to nestle close to her center. He could feel her frantic need, one that begged him for relief. "Please," she whispered. "I don't know. . . . Tell me what to do."

God, she was so lovely in her desire to please him. "Shh, sweetheart. Let me," he answered. He trailed his lips up her jaw to the tender skin behind her ear where her scent was faint but still drew him near.

Her skirts had twisted around her legs, and one knee pointed to the ceiling. For a moment, he lost his breath at the sight. The pale lilac of her silk stockings rivaled the flower's loveliness, but the shape of her leg was a masterpiece. She'd taken off her half boots earlier, revealing a high-arched foot that met a delicate ankle. "Feminine" was too bland a word to describe the vision. His gaze moved to her calf, and desire blazed until he thought it a physical burn, one that only she could soothe. Perfectly formed, the lines that defined her leg were as if a master had drawn them just for him.

"How would da Vinci have painted this perfection?" he whispered. With his hand, he caressed her ankle to her calf, the hard muscle a testament to the daily physical work she performed on the farm.

She tried to rise and pushed his hand away. "*Stop.* I look like—"

He silenced her with another kiss, one that possessed her and every negative thought she could summon forth. "Don't you dare," he growled as he pinned her down. "You're beautiful, and I'm going to show you."

Her sharp eyes met his with a bright disbelief.

"Trust me," he whispered against her lips.

After a second, she nodded as if not at all certain. With every fiber of his being, he'd show her how stunning she was to him.

He slid his hand up her thigh, and he wasn't disappointed at the firm flesh beneath his palm inviting to explore further. His heart beat like a drum calling him to battle. A battle where he'd worship every inch of her, claim her, and make her surrender the fear and insecurity that she lacked true beauty.

She moaned and pushed against his cock, hard and unyielding. He swallowed her moan and prepared her for his next onslaught. He caressed her soft skin until his fingers met her springy curls. She gasped, and he grasped her hip and pulled her close. "Please let me," he whispered.

She buried her head against his neck and nodded. Her sweet and simple gesture caused him to shudder. He petted her curls, then slipped his hand lower. Immediately, he stilled. She was drench with an arresting desire that he'd stirred. He wanted to shout to the heavens.

She whispered his name, and her divine lips against his neck almost undid him. He took a deep breath to gain control. An overwhelming need to please her took over all thought. He trailed his fingers over her slick folds until he found her swollen peak. He circled the tender center gently, and she whimpered. With his other hand, he angled her face and kissed her.

She bucked and pushed against him as he continued to please her. His March responded as if perfectly made for him. He slipped one finger inside of her and pushed until he could go no further. She moaned her approval. He slipped a second finger into her wet, tight sheath. He curled his fingers slightly and moved in and out. She squirmed until he found the spot he was looking for. He lifted his head to watch her and found his reward, a most amazing sight. She pressed her eyes closed and canted her hips as if offering herself to him. He'd give everything including his soul to take her gift and lose himself within her.

"How incredible you look," he whispered as his lips traced the fine lines of her cheek. "Desire becomes you. I wish I had a mirror so you could witness the beauty I see beneath me."

With his thumb, he continued to stroke her peak as he slowly continued to pump his fingers. Desperate, she pulled him by the hair and brought his mouth to hers. She thrust her tongue into his mouth as if he were her salvation. It felt perfect. She felt perfect.

*They felt perfect.*

Suddenly, she stilled in his arms with her muscles taunt. Her body clamped down hard on his fingers. Her face transformed, and her innocent amazement melted into pleasure.

Her sounds, the whimpers and the sharp breaths, hit him like bolts of lightning. Her supple body relaxed against him. She was gorgeous in the afterglow of her climax. His thoughts scattered as his cock demanded its own release.

Quickly, he unbuttoned the fall of his breeches and took himself in hand. He lay on his side and clenched his length. He pressed his face against her cheek. Her scent of arousal caused his to strengthen. Hunger for completion took control as his cock pulsed. His climax exploded from him, and he willingly surrendered.

The exquisite pleasure lasted for what seemed like minutes. He found her lips and made love to her mouth again as if possessed. Then as his heartbeat slowed, he kissed her gently, with more tenderness. He wanted all of her. It was madness, but he never wanted to let her go.

He'd just come in his hand like an adolescent. Never

had he been this beguiled and so out of control with a woman. He wanted to see her come again and witness how passion made her flush a brilliant pink. He wanted to take her and make her his in every way.

More importantly, what had she done to him? For God's sake, she was a virgin. He'd made her come as she lay on the floor fully dressed. He hadn't even taken her to bed. It was as if an avalanche had fallen and captured them both in the swirl of their uncontrollable need for each other.

He pulled away and made quick work of finding a handkerchief to clean the evidence of his climax. With a glance, he saw her slight pant, the desperate effort to gather her sanity from the madness they'd created.

He turned on his side and rested his head in his hand. *Magnificent.* There was no other word to describe her. She lay before him like a feast he could spend days devouring.

March blinked away her remaining bemusement, then shifted to meet his gaze. "Why?"

"Why?" he mimicked. It was the only thing that had popped into his muddled brain.

She turned the rest of her body so they lay facing each other. "What we shared. Why did you do it?"

"I wanted to spend the time pleasing you." He released a careful breath as he knew exactly why he had done it. At first, he could attribute his desire as a way to hide his anxiety over her numbers-and-patterns discourse.

However, that was a lie.

When he'd taken her in his arms, the truth had slowly unfurled. She was so beautiful to him and he wanted her—wanted to seduce her and prove how special she was. Only, he didn't realize she could shake his very foundations. Gazing across at her tempting mouth and warm eyes, he wanted her again. "And I'm fond of you. I want more with you."

The utterance should have terrified him. Surprisingly, it didn't. It was the truth.

Her brow crinkled as she considered his answer. "Your brother doesn't care for me. Please don't misunderstand. I enjoyed what we did." She closed her eyes as if to hide, but a perfect blush colored her cheeks betraying her unease.

He leaned closer until a scant inch separated them. "I truly care for you. If I've offended you—"

Her fingers touched his mouth to quiet him. Instinctively, he pressed his lips against her fingers.

Her gaze was fierce. "I wanted this. I know if I would have said no, you'd have stopped. It was amazing."

Some part of him, the hidden primeval beast, made him want to pound his chest and grunt in approval. He reached to embrace her again and prove to her how much she meant to him.

"But . . ." she whispered. A hint of pain shadowed the confusion in her voice.

The word made him stop cold. What they had shared had been beyond his comprehension until he held her in his arms and experienced her affection and desire. There would be no "buts" about the passion storm they'd created between them.

"March—" He took her hand in his and raised it to his mouth. There was no kiss on the top of her hand, but something more intimate. He rubbed his lips against her skin as he spoke and met her gaze as he continued to caress her. "Tell me what William said to you. What did that reprobate do?"

She met his chuckle with a loud sigh. She appeared tired, and sorrow lined her pretty face.

"Nothing that would deserve your wrath." She spoke calmly but her brightness had dimmed. "He doubted my family's circumstances and my reasons for bringing my family to London. I'm surprised he didn't discuss the conversation with you. Emma caught the last tails of the conversation and took him to task."

"William is too skeptical for his own good." McCalpin shook his head. "Those two can fight over what day of the week it is."

She smiled in answer, then asked, "Why does William spend so much time with you?"

His heart jolted to a dead stop, or at least it felt like it. To explain that his brother helped him with the financial aspects of the estate would be akin to admitting his failure. A haunting misery like a familiar jealous lover wrapped itself around him. So acute, he felt as if he were drowning.

Before, when anyone talked of numbers, money—for heaven's sake, even the odds on a particular horse in a race—he could skirt around the issue with some quip or haughty look. But this was March, and she deserved an answer. As the seconds ticked by, he broke into a cold sweat.

"The estates are so vast, he's proven valuable in their management." He cleared his throat and dropped her hand. The silent distance between them grew so great it felt as if an iceberg had wedged itself there. "He's my brother."

The explanation sounded lame even to his own ears, but it was all he could drudge up after the shock of her question.

As he waited for her response, a flash of loneliness tore through him, not only for himself but for March, too. She had borne the responsibility of an estate and raising her siblings at the age of sixteen. She'd never experienced the frivolities of a Season or explored the world of young ladies who were carefully groomed for their introductions to society. While most women her age had been shopping for gowns, March had been shearing sheep and delivering lambs. God, she must have wanted to run away from it all. It was a testament to her character that she shouldered all the responsibility with nary a complaint.

Guilt stole through him. She shared her fears. If he confided his weakness to her, she wouldn't judge him. It might provide a bridge to help them both trust each other better. Could he dare risk it? He'd held everything in perfect balance for so long, he couldn't find the words to start his confession.

She was a remarkable person—intelligent, quick-witted, dedicated, with a common sense that put the majority of the *ton* to shame, and beautiful to boot. He wanted to take her burden from her shoulders and allow her to experience some of life's pleasures, even if they were as dull as society events. "March?"

She sat up and clasped her arms around her knees as if protecting herself. It racked him with guilt that she felt vulnerable and alone. Was it because of this afternoon or her meeting with William?

"How do I get you to trust me?" Earnest, he wanted more from her than this tenuous place they seemed to be stuck in. "You have my word I won't hurt you."

She rested her head against her knees and regarded him. "I could ask the same question. How do I get you to trust me?"

"I think sharing ourselves with each other and spending time alone helps, don't you?" he gently queried. "I'll keep you safe. I promise."

He lost himself in the fire of her eyes. It reminded him of sunshine passing through a glass of brandy. He wanted to drink every drop of her until he quenched his thirst. Inside, he knew he'd never have that particular thirst satisfied, nor was he sure he wanted to.

Like dawn gradually breaking the night's hold on the sky, his mind cleared. He wanted her in his life permanently. He would make himself learn to trust her.

"Have you changed your mind about marriage?" It was a bold question, but he wanted her to know that he wanted more.

She shook her head.

"I could see you married with children tugging on your skirts. Blissfully happy with a husband who adores you." He narrowed his eyes and growled low in his throat. "And I don't like it one bit."

"Is it because you don't want to be burdened with the business of approving the settlements?" Her sparkling laugh showered the room in light. "Don't worry. No one has expressed any interest in me, and I haven't received any gentleman callers."

He could bask in her brightness all day and all night if she'd let him.

"Are you sure about that?" He drew close and whispered in her ear, "I might have somebody in mind for you."

Slowly she pulled away and stared at him. The moment she deduced what he was implying, her eyes widened, the shock evident on her face.

"After tomorrow's night ball, we're going to have a discussion about your future." He stood and extended his hand to hers. As if she expected his touch would burn her, she tentatively took his hand for assistance. With one pull, he had her on her feet.

In an efficient manner, she bent her head, exposing her glorious crown of ebony hair, then briskly brushed her skirts.

He was definitely attracted to her physically. Her attitude regarding family and the Lawson estate perfectly matched his toward his own family and the huge responsibility he felt for the entire duchy.

He caught her gaze. The flush of her cheeks, the remnants of their intimate interlude, brought a lovely vibrancy to her face. Indeed, she was nothing at all like the other society chits. If he'd dabbled with one of those, they'd be screaming for his offer of marriage. As an honorable man, he should marry March for what transpired. However, there was no expectation in her demeanor. She observed him with such candid honesty that her regard humbled him.

"Miss Lawson, it's chilly here, and I think we should return to Langham House. I can't have you catching cold." He wrapped her arm around his and led her out of the numbers room.

If he were truthful, he rather liked the odd, little room. In the future, every time he stepped in here, he'd finally have a happy, if not salacious, memory of numbers—his first time with March as she fell apart in his arms.

In addition, a more important memory—the day he decided they would marry.

Sleep had never been elusive to March until she'd arrived in London. The late nights attending social events, the shopping, the numerous callers who dropped by during the day, not to mention the hectic schedule of events the duchess insisted March and her sisters attend during the day, should have ensured she fell asleep quickly and deeply.

Tonight was no exception, but it differed from her other sleepless nights. Michael had taken control of all her thoughts. She rose from her comfortable bed and slipped on her silk dressing gown. Generous to a fault, the duchess insisted that Mademoiselle Mignon make one for each of the Lawson sisters. Both Faith and Julia had received a delicate pink silk dressing gown. The duchess had chosen a deep-gold silk trimmed with ermine for March.

Decadent but providing little warmth, the wrap was perfect since her room was toasty. She collapsed onto the small sofa that faced the fire and allowed Michael full reign over her thoughts.

Gently, she stroked her fingers over her still-tender lips as she recalled his mouth on hers. Tantalizing and taunting her at the same time, he'd masterfully taught her how to kiss in a way she'd never fathomed. When he'd touched her so intimately *there*, she should have been shocked. Instead, she had begged for more. Her body shivered in response as she recalled the startling release he'd given her. He'd made her feel like an instrument, one he tenderly had tuned then played like a virtuoso.

Then when he'd found his own climax, she'd been enthralled by the act. Unable to look away, she'd stared at his thick and engorged length. All the while, she imagined how gentle he would be when he made love to her.

She closed her eyes and dismissed the thought. At least, she tried to banish such an outrageous thought. Her behavior should bring a mortifying heat to her face. No well-bred young woman should engage in such outrageous and bold behavior prior to marriage. Her parents had raised her to believe such acts would banish her from her society.

Even though she was a viscount's daughter, inside beat the heart of a sheep farmer. After a month, the hard callouses that marred her hands had softened. However, the scars from her work would always remain whether prettily disguised by elegant gloves or not.

There was no marriage in her future, and Michael's teasing when he left her townhome was nothing more than an attempt to bolster her confidence. What rational man, let alone a ducal heir, would be interested in marrying her, especially with the responsibility of caring for three siblings? Perhaps someday, with a little luck, she might find some gentleman farmer or a widower to marry. Her money would certainly convince the poor fellow to overlook her height and size.

Well, she'd discovered something profound about herself over the last several weeks. Whatever attention the Marquess of McCalpin bestowed upon her, she would steal, then preserve the memories for the lonely times she faced in her future. Bennett would likely spend years at school. Her sisters would marry and have families and fulfilling lives—all the usual consequences of being a viscount's daughter.

March wouldn't have such high expectations for herself. She'd accepted her responsibilities. Furthermore, she'd see them finished. It was a promise she intended to keep.

After she settled into bed, the reality she faced tomorrow brought bittersweet thoughts. It was one day closer to her lovely sisters finding their true loves, and one day closer to leaving London and Michael. Life's inevitable passing of time continued its race forward no matter how much she longed for it to slow its progression.

It also brought closure to what her future held. There would be no love or strong arms to hold her at night. Nor would there be that enticing scent of pine and a particular man that she longed for.

Finally, the elusive sleep claimed her, and her dreams took command with her *David* center stage.

# Chapter Sixteen

Tonight, dressed in a mazarine-blue silk and satin gown, March felt a kindred spirit to Cinderella. Emma and Daphne had insisted the elegant dress in a shade between indigo and violet would be the perfect match for her mother's sapphire earrings.

Thank heavens for friends.

As the Earl of Queensgrace whirled her around the dance floor, the dress shimmered and glistened in the reflective light cast by the candles in the chandeliers. Since she and her sisters had arrived at Lady Carlisle's, none of them had missed a dance. Truly, to say her sisters were a success wasn't at all an exaggeration. They seemed to have a following of men and women who craved their attention.

In the earl's arms, she relaxed. Even the Duke and Duchess of Langham had remarked about Faith and Julia's success. Generous as always, they'd congratulated March on her sisters accomplishments. The duchess had even whispered that she fully expected offers of marriage to be forthcoming within the next couple of days.

March exhaled a long sigh of contentment.

"Miss Lawson, might I call upon you tomorrow?" Tall, with a handsome face, the earl peered down. A serious countenance replaced his normal lightheartedness.

"I would enjoy your visit." March waited three steps then pressed him for more details. "Shall I have my sisters with me, or do you wish to speak privately?"

A blinding smile lit his face, and his gray eyes seemed to shimmer in the candlelight. "I should have expected you to be a wonderful tactician." He colored slightly and bent his head close to hers. "There's no sense in keeping the cat in the bag. I'd formally like to discuss my intentions with Miss Julia. I don't want to go into details here, but I'd like to make my case and gain your approval for a match."

March squeezed his hand with hers in approval. "I look forward to your visit. But perhaps afterward we should discuss your intentions with the marquess, since he's Julia's guardian?"

"That won't be necessary, Miss Lawson. I've already spoken to him, and he says the decision should be made by you as the eldest of the family."

She stumbled slightly at the pronouncement. Once again, her heart fluttered as if preparing to take flight. Perhaps it hovered, suspended in her chest with longing, as if encouraging her to find Michael. She wanted to share the news and then discuss how the earl's courtship with Julia should proceed. With an ease March hoped didn't betray her rush, she glanced around the ballroom and found the marquess.

He stood with his father and brother and another man, the Earl of Fletcher, deep in conversation. By Michael's side, Lady Miranda gazed adoringly up at Michael. March's stomach dropped at the familiar uncertainty, the familiar sting of jealously, the familiar thoughts of her own unsuitability.

She turned to Queensgrace. His face softened, and he leaned close. "Miss Lawson, the marquess was highly complimentary of your acumen in matters such as these. I believe he mentioned he held you in 'high regard' when I discussed my intentions with Miss Julia."

A sudden heat rose from her chest to her face, and it had nothing to do with the soft burr of his voice, the one Julia practically melted over every time she talked about him. "I hold the marquess in high regard also. He's taken his responsibilities to our family seriously. We're fortunate he possesses such a keen interest in our welfare."

The earl threw back his head laughing. The deep baritone rang through the ballroom. Several people turned in the midst of their dance and smiled at the happy sound.

"Miss Lawson, there are responsibilities and there are the heart's desires. I'm astute enough not to confuse the two. I believe you are too."

Suddenly, she felt as if the floor had turned into an icy river that was better suited for skating than dancing. One slip, and her heart would be laid out for all to see. This conversation had taken a turn into an unknown area, one she didn't have the faintest clue how to answer.

As the dance came to a slow end, the earl gracefully released her and bent over her hand. "Thank you, Miss Lawson. I enjoyed our dance, *and* I look forward to our visit."

"As do I, my lord." March pushed her anxiety aside. This was a night to celebrate, and she didn't want any of her self-doubts to color her happiness for her sisters' successes.

The earl escorted her back to her sisters where he took Julia's hand for the following set. Faith had promised to dance with Lord Haledrone. Dr. Kennett had worked miracles with Faith and her leg. No one would be surprised if he made an offer for her beautiful sister.

Soon, March stood alone, but she didn't feel lonely. Instead, she gazed about the dance floor with the knowledge that tonight signaled the next phase of the Lawson sisters' lives, one that promised a bright future. A sudden serenity, almost a lightness lifted her spirits higher, one she recognized as pure unadulterated happiness.

Michael was the cause. He'd made their dreams come true. Her mood suddenly buoyant, she had to find him and thank him. When she turned, everything within her stilled. Lady Miranda stood before her.

"Miss Lawson, may I have a word?" Her honeyed voice carried softly without the malice she'd possessed at the dressmaker's shop.

"Of course." It would do no good to refuse the woman, yet that didn't keep March's wariness from sounding the alert. This woman didn't think very highly of her or her sisters as was evidenced by her comments at Mademoiselle Mignon's shop. Whatever she wanted to say, March wouldn't let it ruin her wonderful evening.

Lady Miranda dipped her head with a hint of shyness. "I wanted to apologize for what I said that day at Mademoiselle—"

"Please, my lady, there's no need. Let's not mention it." The night certainly was turning into one filled with surprises.

"That's very gracious," the young woman offered. "Perhaps I might call on you this week."

"It would be my pleasure." March's gaze swept through the ballroom. She found Michael still conversing with his father and Lady Miranda's father. Whether Lady Miranda truly wanted to start anew or it was an effort to bring her into the marquess's good graces made little difference. The young woman would be a part of Julia's social acquaintances, and March didn't want for any ill will between Lady Miranda and her to jeopardize Julia's new life.

As she chatted with Lady Miranda, a commotion arose in the front of the ballroom. There were so many people crowding the front that March didn't pay much attention. The clucking and squawking of discontented voices grew louder until it sounded like a pandemonium of parrots had taken over the ballroom. She chanced another glance. Her cousin Rupert was storming across the ballroom with two men on either side of him. One was the host of the evening, the Earl of Carlisle, and the other was his heir, Lord Radley.

She smothered a cry, and her gaze flew to where Michael had been in conversation. Neither he nor the duke were anywhere in sight.

Her cousin was less than fifty feet from her and making his path quite clear.

He was coming for her.

Desperate to find Michael, she searched the ballroom perimeter. In every corner, she found only strangers and acquaintances. Even her sisters and Lord William were absent. Her heart pounded against her chest with such force she was certain her ribs would crack.

She pivoted on one foot to search behind her, but a gloved hand grabbed her upper arm and swung her around. As if Rupert wanted her to fall, he pushed her away.

"You lied to me," he snarled. "You lied to all of us."

Too consumed with trying to stay upright, she backed away from him.

Lady Miranda gasped and inched away from March

as if to protect herself from the carnage about to spill on the floor. Guests moved closer to the spectacle, their croaking murmurs growing in volume. With their formal wear, the crowd resembled a gathering of carrion-eating ravens ready to feast.

"What are you doing?" March hissed. She had little option but to force him to withdraw before he embarrassed her sisters and Michael. He'd done a fine job of disgracing her, so there was little she could do to save herself.

Rupert ignored her and addressed the crowd that pressed closer. "This woman has been stealing from my cousin, Lord Lawson, and his fine sisters. It's been going on for months, and unfortunately, the Marquess of McCalpin's been a victim too."

She opened her mouth to respond, but her cousin continued his diatribe.

"This woman is a fraud, an embezzler, and is using my poor little cousin, Lord Lawson, as a shield to hide her nefarious purposes." His voice grew louder as the audience kept expanding into a huge circle around them.

By then, Faith and Dr. Kennett had forced their way to the front of the group. Julia and Lord Queensgrace had followed. March had to force herself to breathe as the cold knot inside her chest tightened. Her heart thumped madly as if encouraging her to pick up her skirts and run away.

Rupert closed the distance between them with an unholy gleam in his eyes as he glanced at Julia with Lord Queensgrace. It became readily apparent Rupert would not stop and planned to destroy her before the assembled crowd. Never before had she felt so defenseless as she searched the faces among the throng, praying she'd find Michael.

Her cousin tightly gripped her arm again. With a tug, he forced her closer, and the odor of sweat surrounded her. For a moment, all she could think of was whether her beautiful gown would survive his contamination.

"Ladies and gentleman, this woman is not who she represents herself to be," he boasted.

Julia bravely stepped forward. "Rupert, stop."

Lord Queengrace stood directly behind her in support.

Rupert ignored them all. "She's immoral and a sinner. She's tainted my family with her filth. She represents herself as a Lawson, but her actions prove otherwise. She's allowed a known sodomite to live with her and corrupt my cousins."

She tried to pull herself from his grasp. Desperate, she needed to escape the sea of faces that twisted in contempt and disgust. The seconds turned into hours as her cousin continued to berate her.

*Where was Michael? Surely, someone told him that she was being destroyed in front of the entire room.*

The only sound that rang in her ears was Rupert's continued sermon on her wicked immorality.

"She's a bastard fooling us all. It's a lie she's the eldest of Lord Lawson's proud and noble family." His cool, bug-eyed glare continued to assault her. "And I have the proof."

The words, sharp as an arrow, took perfect aim and pierced every piece of her self-control. The hard pounding of her heart stopped as her entire world exploded into a million pieces.

The ugly rant grew louder and harsher the closer McCalpin came to the altercation taking place center stage in the ballroom. The orchestra still played, but no couples danced.

"Pardon me. Let me through please." Desperate to reach March, McCalpin pushed his way through the densely packed crowd. He managed to bump into quite a few gentlemen, but thankfully didn't step on any ladies' toes. He continued his litany of apologies, but that was the least of his concerns. His only path was to find March and the madman, who continued to hurl his unrelenting chant of ridicule.

The crowd parted slightly, allowing Julia's pale face to come into view. McCalpin continued to press toward the center until he caught sight of March's raven-dark tresses, the soft curls about her head as familiar as his own hands.

With a face white with shock, Faith stood on one side of March. She stepped forward to face the man who was berating her sister, but Queensgrace, next to Julia, put his hand on Faith's shoulder to stop her progress, the act so protective that it caused McCalpin's blood to pound. An unholy demon rose in strength, and the urge to rip the miscreant who insulted March grew stronger. He fisted his hands and shouldered his way to the front.

The sight made him want to roar.

March, *his March*, stood cornered like a fox before the hounds, who were masked as the demigods of society. Except for her sisters, everyone else stood by as she was torn to shreds.

Her eyes narrowed in pain, and she glanced his way not seeming to recognize him. Her crimson cheeks flamed with embarrassment. Frantic, her gaze shifted from face to face as if seeking escape.

Faith and Dr. Kennett shifted so McCalpin could stand beside her. The raw need to take her in his arms overpowered him, but he fought back. He couldn't offer her comfort until he stopped the massacre that was tearing her apart.

He stopped slightly in front of her so Rupert Lawson directed his tirade at him. "What is the meaning of this?" he snarled with his best sneer.

The crowd immediately stepped back at the words. No one wanted to be in the direct path of his anger. He surely resembled a roaring fiend, and he didn't give a farthing.

Lawson's eyes flashed red. Filled with hate and anger, his demeanor bore a striking resemblance to a rabid dog, ready to attack anything or anyone. "My lord, it's most fortunate you've arrived. You above all others have been duped by this woman's immorality."

The crowd murmured again.

Lawson took it as encouragement and continued, "She's a bastard and has been masquerading as the head of the family." His mouth edged up in a mocking smile. "She was born a bastard and has no rightful claim to any of the family's wealth or resources."

"Leave now before I rip you to shreds and carry you out piece by piece." He kept his voice low, but the guttural threat must have reached Lawson's ears since the man leaned back in response. McCalpin leaned forward. The unmistakable smell of depraved determination laced with sweat permeated the area.

Lawson leashed his raging anger. "I have proof, my lord," he offered solemnly. "A vicar from Chelmsford brought the evidence to my attention. The marriage record of the prior viscount and his wife clearly indicates that *this woman* isn't who she claims to be." He sniffed his dismissal at March. "She's duped us all, I'm afraid. She stole from you, from Lord Lawson, and from his sisters. Indeed, by *this woman's* lies, she's injured *my family.*"

The words seemed to have awoken March from her trance. She moved quickly so she stood between McCalpin and Lawson. McCalpin put his hand on her arm to draw her back behind him, but she shook off the effort.

"You are despicable and speak nothing but lies," she hissed. Her voice was soft, but the outrage was loud enough that he and Lawson could hear it. "I'm not surprised you'd say such vile things to me, but you're hurting my sisters, and not to mention Hart."

Lawson licked his lips. "The truth of your sins and Pennington's behavior shall not be hidden."

*Pennington.* Victor Hart was Victor Coeur Pennington. The air collapsed in McCalpin's chest. Years ago, a huge scandal erupted over the close ties Pennington shared with the second son of the previous Marquess of Haviland, Lord Erlington. Now it all made sense what March had let slip in the yellow salon when Hart had left to attend his dying friend.

It made little difference at this point. McCalpin's only concern was to remove Lawson from the premises and calm March and her sisters over the devil's dramatics.

His father and William had managed to break through the crowd and reach their sides.

"McCalpin, I grow weary of this man's presence." His father's gaze pierced their host, Lord Carlisle, who stood by Lawson's side. "Why hasn't *it* been removed?"

"Forgive me, Your Grace," their host offered. With a snap of his fingers, two footmen appeared and grabbed Lawson by the arms to drag him out.

Lawson shook them off and bowed to McCalpin's father. "I'll leave you peaceably to your evening, Your Grace." With a growl he continued, "I'll bring my proof to you, Lord McCalpin. Rest assured, I'll not let this lying woman steal from you any longer."

As the footmen escorted Lawson out, McCalpin turned to March. "Are you all right?"

She nodded, but her face looked brittle as if it had cracked into a thousand lines of grief ready to crumble. The temptation to sweep her into his arms and caress her soft skin became overpowering. However, since they were in a ballroom where every guest had their attention glued to them, McCalpin tamped down the urge to offer such comfort.

His father leaned close to March and smiled. "It would be best if you and McCalpin dance. You need to show these people that nothing is amiss."

Trust his father to provide wise advice.

"Come, March, it's a waltz," he whispered. The orchestra had already started the opening bars.

She let him lead her out to the dance floor, but he wasn't certain she was even cognizant of where they were or what she was supposed to do. Still pinched in pain, her face was frozen, and her movements were stiff as if still in the throes of shock.

He coaxed her into position, and the music swelled in volume. Few couples joined them on the ballroom floor as the crowd seemed to wait with bated breath for another catastrophe to befall her.

She stared off into the distance, not focusing on anything, her limbs rigid in his arms as he twirled her around the floor.

"March, look at me," he demanded.

The low command finally broke through whatever wall she'd erected to protect herself. Her brown eyes brimmed with uncertainty.

"Michael," she whispered as if suddenly aware he was there. The small silvery voice penetrated deep within his chest, and his protective instincts took over.

What he wouldn't give to take her away to a private place and hold her until her fright and shock melted away.

He'd kiss her until she relaxed in his arms and found the comfort she so desperately needed.

He squeezed her hand and smiled.

She answered with one touched by sadness.

He continued to lavish attention on her as they danced by themselves in the center of the ballroom. Time and again, throughout his life, he'd experienced a moment similar to this—a moment where everyone would silently relish his defeat.

"Believe it or not, I know exactly how you feel. You need to show these people that Lawson didn't upset you. Show them you don't care. Otherwise, every paper in London will have a stinging description of what just occurred."

Her anemic grin only made him more resolute. He had to protect her, but the only way he could accomplish that was if she'd play along with him.

"My cousin Claire went through something very similar when her fourth fiancé broke their engagement at the Season's most important ball. She almost collapsed under the embarrassment, but Pembrooke swept in and declared they were engaged." He squeezed her hand in reassurance. "I almost killed him for that, but it was a blessing in disguise for Claire."

As if in reflex, she squeezed his hand in return. A jolt of relief hit him, and for the first time in minutes, he relaxed and took a deep breath. "That's it, sweetheart."

Her eyes searched his at the endearment. He smiled in reassurance as she flushed but remained silent.

"Now Emma was a walking scandal," he whispered.

Lines creased her forehead as if she didn't care for his description of his sister.

He lifted one brow in challenge, and she dipped her head. He'd never seen her so unsure of herself, and he didn't care for this new side of her. Always, her strength was one of her most beautiful traits, and it never ceased to enchant him.

McCalpin leaned close. "She was caught traveling in Portsmouth with Somerton. When they arrived back in town, she faced complete ruin."

With a slight tilt of her head, she regarded him with a questioning look.

"Indeed." He nodded and leaned close as if imparting a state secret. "She survived the endless gossip posted about her wild and wanton ways."

The first real glimmer of hope brightened March's face. He grinned, and she answered him with one of her own, a genuine hint of pleasure that pleased him to no end.

"In fact, because of one scathing article in *The Midnight Cryer*, she ended up marrying the love of her life. To this day, she reads that poor excuse of a daily paper out of loyalty as she credits their reporting for her happy marriage. Sometimes good things come from the most wretched scandals." He brought his mouth close to her ear. Her sweet scent caressed him, and he started to relax in return. "Of course, you'll survive this too. But it's important that you show everyone here tonight that it doesn't matter."

She leaned away slightly with a beautiful grin that didn't meet her eyes. "But it does," she whispered. "Rupert's lies will forever stain my birthright and legacy. He's maligned me and my family."

"It only matters to the ones who feed upon such vicious nonsense," he answered.

"What about you?"

"Sweet March." He shook his head, determined to make her understand. "Not to me. Never to me."

The warmth in her eyes caused his pulse to race in his veins. The sudden whirl of their turn caused the train of her dress to swing in a dramatic movement, drawing their audience's attention to focus on their dance steps. He took the distraction as an opportunity and brushed his lips gently against her head as he turned her in another direction.

His touch precipitated a true smile, one that reminded him of the heavens opening on a cloudy day and sunshine spilling around them.

The sound of his own laughter encircled them as the music slowed to a stop. He tucked her arm around his and escorted her across the ballroom all the while laughing, talking, and ignoring the rest of guests.

He let out a sigh of relief. She'd survived the humiliation.

Proving what he knew all along.

She'd make an excellent marchioness.

# Chapter Seventeen

The following morning, three copies of *The Midnight Cryer* lay upon March's bed along with Faith and Julia. The crisp snap of turning pages broke the eerie quiet. They were all speechless. Except for a couple of articles describing last night's ball, the entire paper was a running exposé on March and her supposed lies she'd used to make her way into the Langham household.

For a moment, she had wanted to laugh at the absurdity of her situation, but one column caught her eye. Riveted, she had to read it three times to ensure she understood what it was saying.

The paper claimed that Rupert had provided a copy of the marriage registry from Chelmsford and a sworn statement from the vicar stating that her parents married nineteen years ago.

How could Rupert have convinced a vicar to support this outrageous fabricated story? It was a complete falsehood. It had to be.

"March, have you read the back page?" Julia was the

first to break the silence. "I must stop for a while as I'm making myself sick with all the lies." Her sister pressed her eyes shut and exhaled. "How could Rupert have done this to us? We are a family," she whispered.

Before March could say anything, there was a knock on the door. Faith rose from the bed to answer. It was a thankful reprieve from the ghastly exposé of March's ne'er-do-well ways.

"These just arrived," Faith offered as she kept one note for herself and gave the other to March. She tore open the seal, and her eyes darted across the page as she read. Slowly, she pressed her eyes shut for a moment. "Dr. Kennett will not be able to attend me this morning as he must spend the day away from London."

Julia reached over and squeezed Faith's arm. "He'll come as soon as he's able."

Faith nodded, but continued to stare at the paper in her hands.

March tore hers open since she recognized the Earl of Queensgrace's seal. Expecting to find the time he would visit today, she stared speechless at the words. He extended his sincerest apology, but he would not be visiting anytime in the near future as he'd returned to Scotland on an unavoidable emergency. He'd simply signed it "Queensgrace."

She stared at the note, desperate to stall for time so she could offer a comforting response to Julia. Her sister would immediately believe he'd left her company for good, and March had no idea how to explain it since she didn't understand itself.

"It's from the earl, isn't it?" Julia asked. She busied her hands with folding a copy of *The Midnight Cryer*. "He's not coming, is he?"

Julia's wispy voice carried an underlying note of disappointment. Her visage didn't belie any upset, but her eyes were bright with pain.

"Sweetheart, he was called out of town," March soothed.

Her youngest sister straightened her shoulders and gracefully moved from the bed to stand beside March. "Did he say when we might expect him?"

March shook her head and leaned close to embrace Julia. "No, he didn't. I'm sorry. But I shall write and ask when he expects to return."

Julia stepped away and walked to the window. She clasped her arms around her waist, either to stave off any more hurt or as a means to keep herself from collapsing on the floor.

"I'd rather you not, March," she whispered. "Whatever friendship we shared is over. He should have written me and explained directly and honestly."

Faith rushed to her side and took her in her arms. "Don't say such words. You need to allow him the chance to explain."

Julia regarded Faith with a seriousness well beyond her eighteen years. "I'm not a child anymore, and I know what his note means. It's easier to leave London and the scandal behind. Within two months, everyone will forget that he had any regard for me. When he returns to town, he'll be able to pursue another without any societal censure."

March's insides twisted at her little sister's painful but truthful assessment. The Earl of Queensgrace's political future promised to be one of great success. He couldn't afford any hint of impropriety or scandal.

The haunted look on both of her sisters' faces nearly brought her to her knees. Rupert had damaged more than he could have imagined by his nefarious accusations. There was only one thing for her to do if she had any chance of repairing her sisters' chances for happiness.

She'd visit the Chelmsford vicar herself and right this wrong.

McCalpin noted wryly that Bennett's tutor had made remarkable progress with the young man's penmanship and spelling. The note from the young viscount was actually legible this time.

However, the contents still caused his blood to boil.

*McCalpin,*

*You've never seen such sadness descend on Langham Hall after last night's despicable actions by Rupert. I loathe calling him my cousin. March isn't the only one who suffers from abject humiliation. Rupert has managed to maim Faith and Julia with his ugly accusations. Neither Kennett or Queensgrace have bothered to visit today after yesterday's uproar. They're all blighters in my humble opinion.*

McCalpin agreed with Bennett's assessment and sneered in disgust for the two men. They'd abandoned the Lawson sisters when they needed them most. He couldn't dwell on it now. He'd decide how to deal with them later. Now, his schedule included only one thing, retrieving March from her hell-bent plan to visit the vicarage in Chelmsford on her own.

*March stole away in mid-morning. I saw her exit the servants' entrance and leave Langham*

*Hall via the alley by the carriage house. I found the note on her pillow that detailed her travel. She plans to catch the mail coach to Chelmsford and will return tomorrow.*

The blasted woman had left three hours before. Bennett apparently had a devil of a time finding an available footman to deliver the note to McCalpin House. The boy stated that he tried to visit McCalpin directly, hoping they both could find her together, but the tutor had immediately quashed the young viscount's plan as he was due for a Latin lesson. He had quickly finished the lesson and penned the last few paragraphs before finding Milton, his favorite footman, and directing him to deliver the missive.

*Man to man, I must beg you to find my sister and bring her home. I can't bear to see her traveling alone. What if trouble finds her? What if she doesn't have enough to eat or money to return home?*

*Respectfully yours,*
*Lawson*

*P.S. I'd find her myself, but Mr. Tatum has insisted we study Latin all day, then we'll visit Gunter's for an ice. The man knows my weakness and preys upon it.*

God, would they ever feel secure in London and at Langham Hall? He released the breath after his lungs had burned in protest.

He pulled the bell and, within seconds, Buxton entered the study. "You rang, my lord?"

McCalpin didn't even bother to look up at the loyal butler. "Have the coach and four prepared along with a basket of food and wine. I'll need a bag. I'm traveling to Chelmsford and plan to stay this evening at McCalpin Manor. I'll return no later than tomorrow."

"Very well, my lord."

McCalpin pulled out a fresh piece of vellum and jotted a few lines to his parents that he was on his way to intercept March. He promised he'd keep them informed of his progress. As he handed the note to Buxton, he met his gaze. "Please ensure the duchess receives this promptly."

Without hesitating, the butler nodded. "My pleasure, my lord." He bowed to leave the study, then halted his exit. "I wish you safe travels and hope you find Miss Lawson before she arrives in Chelmsford."

McCalpin quirked a brow.

"I hope I'm not overstepping, but what if *The Midnight Cryer*'s claims are true?"

His stomach fell as if a barn swallow had taken up residence. March would be devastated, and so would he.

He didn't even want to think about the resulting effects if she was, by chance, illegitimate. Not only would she be devastated, but also the scandal would be a black mark against her sisters. Bennett would be fine until he attended Eton. Then a haranguing consortium of bullies would hound him through the years.

Yet, strategy was his forte. He just hoped it didn't fail him now. This was a challenge he couldn't afford to lose.

It was fortuitous that he had a long carriage ride ahead of him.

March rolled her head in hopes that the ache in her neck would diminish. The cramped quarters in the mail coach necessitated that she keep her shoulders contorted in a slump the entire way from London. However, good fortune, that fickle beast, had shown its favor in March's companions for the trip to Chelmsford.

A kind couple had sat next to her the whole way from London. On the first stop, an older woman had joined them on the bench. She shared that she was returning to her daughter's home after visiting her son.

The young wife who sat next to March had chatted the entire way. Obviously smitten with her new husband, the woman went on relentlessly how lovely it was to be married to such a wonderful man. She'd even shared they were expecting their first child. Her husband had the good manners to redden at his new wife's enthusiastic praise.

When the young woman had inquired about her marital status, March's cheeks had blazed with heat, leaving little doubt that her face had to resemble the young husband's embarrassment. She'd shaken her head slightly. The young woman had bestowed a sympathetic smile and had been blessedly quiet the rest of the trip.

March didn't try to engage the young wife in any other conversation. She only hoped she hadn't appeared rude, but her thoughts had consumed all her attention. Her mind wouldn't let go of how critical it was she find the vicarage quickly and discover the proof that would turn Rupert's claims into lies. Once she accomplished her goal, she'd return to London posthaste and refute the story. She whispered a silent prayer.

*Let it be that easy.*

She'd even bargain her own happiness for her sisters and brother to have the lives they deserved and spare them any more scandal. She tightened her hands into fists. The one holding the valise gripped the leather handles so tight it groaned in protest.

Finally, the coach rolled to a stop, and the sounds of a busy inn surrounded her. The ostler called out a welcome to the newly arrived carriage. Stable-hands changed the livestock on the mail coach, and the innkeeper even made an appearance to greet the mail carriage coachmen as if they were old friends.

With a deep breath for courage, she walked out of the inn's courtyard. She rounded the corner and painfully exhaled. A simple church with a large steeple and a proper garden stood only a short distance away. A small vicarage sat next to the church. The church bell struck the hour, and as if encouraging her forward, the low *bong* vibrated through her tired body.

Soon she found herself in the church vestibule. Windows on both sides provided an abundance of natural light even though it was a winter afternoon. The entry doors to the sanctuary stood open, and a man stood behind the altar arranging items and filling the tall pewter vases with new evergreens.

Rooted to the floor, she waited for him to look up from his work. Eventually, he glanced her way. Without taking his gaze from hers, he wiped his hands on the apron that protected his garments from the menial tasks.

"Good afternoon." His clear tenor voice rang through the sanctuary. He rounded the altar and came toward her.

She pasted a smile on her face and stepped forward. "Good afternoon, Mr.—"

"Noah King." He offered his hand, and for an instant, she hesitated.

This was the man who supposedly swore her parents were married long after her birth? He was little older than she, but his handsome countenance with eyes the color of new spring grass bespoke a wisdom that defied the ages. Not certain what type of man stood before her, she quickly took his hand then released it.

Immediately, she launched into her purpose for disturbing him. "Mr. King, I understand you have a marriage register that I'd be most interested in. My name is Miss March Lawson."

He nodded. "Come with me."

With a graceful turn, he led the way to the vicarage office. He motioned to the two chairs that faced the inviting fire. Without waiting, he poured two cups of tea and placed a plate of biscuits on the small table nestled between the chairs. "My wife is most fastidious that I eat at regular intervals. She always prepares more than necessary in case of visitors."

She let out a breath, hoping it would calm her wayward thoughts. Perhaps it was the hunger in her stomach and not the ache in her heart that made her feel empty. She'd seen so many couples over the last several weeks, ones who cherished each other, and the truth hit her like a blast of wind. If Rupert's lies were true, she'd never have a husband.

A vision of Michael swept into her thoughts, and her heart clenched in panic. She squared her shoulders in a desperate attempt to calm the unease. No matter what she wanted or what she expected for her own life, she shouldn't allow any of it to intrude upon today. Yet, deep inside, she screamed silently. Why did she have to forgo everything? A husband, security, her own family, her own home? Why did she have to forgo even the stark certainty she could spend her life helping Bennett take his rightful place in society while teaching him how to run his estate?

All her life, things she cherished were taken away—fanciful wishes and whimsical wants and eventually, simple needs. Fate had been cruel before, but now it was downright hateful.

After all she'd sacrificed, she could expect abject ruin.

She swallowed the lingering pain. She'd do it all again—subject herself to the sacrifices and the pain and the shame—as long as her family was safe.

"Miss Lawson?" The vicar's brow formed neat lines. "I expect you either are here to rail at me or set the church on fire."

"Neither, Mr. King." She took a sip of the tea for fortitude and released her breath. When she set her cup down, a small amount of liquid spilt into the saucer, betraying her disquiet. "I just want to see the evidence for myself."

His serene expression rivaled one of the paintings that surrounded the four walls in the room. Angels, shepherds, and the church's previous vicars gazed from their frames as if stuck in perpetuity to face a numb purgatory.

Exactly how she felt—numb and stricken.

"I understand," Mr. King offered. His soothing tone indicated he had experience with grief and providing comfort. That talent would serve him well today since she was grieving. He rose, walked to his desk, and unlocked a drawer.

Soon he returned with the register in his hand. A single ribbon marked a page. The large journal dwarfed his hand, and the leather betrayed its age with stains and worn corners on the front cover.

He settled in the chair next to March and flipped open the book to reveal a rainbow of names composed in inks of blacks, indigos, blues, and grays. Silently, he handed her the register. She scanned the sheet bookmarked. The left column on each page listed the date, followed by columns containing the groom's and bride's names and signatures. The last column marked the date of the solemnized wedding vows.

March's gaze slowly swept the page until she found the entry for the eighth of October and the year 1794. Her eyes focused on the names.

On the page was her father's bold signature with her mother's graceful one beside his. Time along with her heartbeat ground to a halt, much like a millstone when it lost its momentum.

She blinked slowly in a poor attempt to clear the burn from her eyes. She couldn't allow herself to fall apart—not in front of the vicar. Otherwise, she'd never be able to pick up the pieces again.

Whether it was a minute or an hour that passed, he finally spoke. "I'm sorry." The whisper floated through the air. "So sorry that my church and I are the cause of such distress in your life. I know this entry is truthful as I was there at your parents' wedding." He continued softly as he turned to face her. "I remember it distinctly."

March jerked her gaze to his.

"It was the first cool day of autumn and my father, the previous vicar, had promised to take me fishing, but . . . when he told me of the ceremony, I bellowed my disapproval. He said if I behaved, I could attend, and we'd leave straight away from the church."

She took a moment to compose her thoughts. She would have been six years old. "Was I there?"

"I don't remember you attending, but your grandparents, Lord and Lady Lawson, were in attendance."

If the service had taken place in October, then her mother had to have been carrying Faith—much too early in her pregnancy to be noticeable.

"I have one vivid memory. Your father was livid at his father. After your parents signed the register, they left without a word."

"Is your father still alive? Perhaps—"

The vicar shook his head. "No. My father died several years ago."

"Why here? My family's estate is in Leyton." She spoke the words to herself, but the vicar nodded as if understanding her confusion.

"I don't have an answer to offer you."

"Did my cousin share why he thought to look for this information here? How would he know?" Her confusion was mounting. None of this made any sense.

"I believe someone advised him to come here and investigate, Miss Lawson."

As if he'd called her a charlatan, she flinched. Her name, the one she'd always answered to, was no longer hers.

Her gaze swept over her pelisse, her valise, her reticule, and her half boots. All familiar but unrecognizable at the same time. Who was she? When she walked into the church, she was one person. Now, when she departed, she'd be another.

There was no denying she was her parents' child. She had inherited her mother's height, and favored her father. For heaven's sake, Bennett favored her. It made little difference as she wasn't born within the confines of a legal marriage. Illegitimate children of peers walked in a no man's land. Being born on the wrong side of respectability was only tolerable if there was money and the parents boldly accepted their bastards. Her parents were gone, so she was already working at a disadvantage.

However, what was worse, she might have to forgo raising Bennett. If society shunned her presence, then by association, Bennett's future could be tainted. If teased by classmates or deemed unacceptable by his peers, his life would be miserable. Her sisters might reject her if their husbands insisted there was to be no further contact or communication with their eldest sister.

She closed her eyes to tamp down the onslaught of nausea. There was no other conclusion she could draw—she was ruined.

"Would you mind if I have a moment or two in the church by myself?" Weakened with pain, she barely recognized her own whisper.

"Take as long as you need." Mr. King stood and escorted her to the sanctuary.

After taking his leave, March studied her clasped hands. Indeed, as long as she stayed inside, her old identity was still hers to possess.

# Chapter Eighteen

The dull gray of day lost its battle against the cold black night. A chill swept through the sanctuary as if seeking refuge, and the wind howled and rattled the windows with a woeful dirge. With her life forever changed, convoluted thoughts and questions preyed upon her.

She *had stolen* from her siblings.

Her parents' signature in the register meant even more destitution. As a bastard, she lost any right she had to her trust funds. The documents stated that those moneys were marked only for the legitimate children of her father.

Her father had specified that for *whatever reason*, if a child couldn't claim their money, then their portion would be divided between the remaining children. He was far too intelligent not to understand that such a statement meant the funds weren't rightfully hers. The only way he could've provided for her was by a special bequeath of money.

Why had her father even bothered with a trust that

provide for her as his legitimate daughter? If she was born out of wedlock, why didn't he provide for her under her mother's maiden name of Featherston?

March Featherston—just thinking in those terms caused her to shrivel inside the shell of her previous life. However, logically, she hadn't changed. She still loved her siblings, Hart, Lawson Court, and everything she'd been fortunate enough to have in her life. *Including Michael.*

The greatest change would be how society would perceive her from this day forward. The illegitimate daughter of a viscount wasn't that much of an oddity, particularly when her mother had married her father. What truly made her unique was the fact that Rupert claimed she had stolen from her siblings' trust funds. As soon as her illegitimacy came to light, she'd lost all rights to her fortune.

The wood floor creaked, sounding the alarm she wasn't alone. She turned in the pew, expecting to find the vicar asking her to leave.

Michael stood at the back of the sanctuary with his feet shoulders-width apart, exactly like Michelangelo's *David* preparing for a mighty conflict. If he expected her to be his opponent, he would soon be disappointed. She didn't have any fight left.

He deposited his black gloves and elegant beaver hat onto the back pew. He resembled a dark panther and never took his eyes from hers as he prowled toward her. Like a trapped animal, her heart pounded at the inevitable surrender and destruction that awaited her. Whether she faced her demise here or outside in the elements made little difference. She didn't care at this point. It would be so easy to give up all hope and stay in this drafty building for eternity, locked in a perpetual purgatory just like the portraits and paintings hanging in the vicar's office.

"Once again, I have to retrieve you like an errant child." The raw sound of his words betrayed his mood. His jaw tightened, and the muscles of his cheeks rippled in consternation. "When will you learn to trust me?" He continued stalking her with his gaze never leaving hers. His eyes roamed over her face as he took inventory of her features. "Enough of your half-cocked travel escapades."

She smiled at the tenderness that escaped through his rough-as-barnwood voice. By the appearance of his pursed lips and narrowed eyes, he was angry. The lines shadowing the corner of his eyes revealed the extent of his worry.

He'd come for her. He must still think she was his responsibility. The only appropriate thing was to tell him that Rupert's hurtful statements were true and release him from any obligation to her. A sudden stabbing pain ricocheted around her chest as she realized that once they walked out the church entrance, she'd truly be alone. "How did you find me?"

"Bennett." He slid next to her in the wooden pew.

His long legs resting against hers resulted in a reassuring, radiant heat. The fresh scent of pine made her relax. He was a real man, and this wasn't her imagination run wild. She leaned closer. He was a magnet and she couldn't resist his pull.

"You've worried the devil out of both of us." Michael pulled one of her loose curls toward him.

It didn't hurt, but the movement caused her to turn toward him. His gaze captured hers. She could drown in the ocean-color of his eyes and never seek any rescue.

She exhaled to break the spell between them. "Bennett is becoming as fretful as Julia. I've tried to instill a sense of security to our . . . home." Was it still her home? She dismissed the thought. No, she wouldn't allow what she'd discovered in Chelmsford to upset her siblings sense of safety and stability. "He must be worried beyond all reason."

"Let's leave this drafty pile of stones and go home," he whispered. "I haven't eaten, and I expect you haven't either."

She shook her head.

One corner of his mouth curved upward, the expression so mischievous and endearing, she was lost for a brief moment.

He laced his fingers with hers. His thumb rubbed her wrist as if trying to offer comfort. He stood and tugged her hand, signaling her to join him. Reluctantly, she followed. Without allowing her to retreat, he pulled her toward the vestibule.

Instinctively, she pulled back, unwilling to leave the cold sanctuary.

"What is it?" He halted his charge to the exit.

She swallowed the words that couldn't possibly explain her new existence. How do you share that, in a short period of time, your whole life or what you thought was your life had completely turned on its head? She took a final glance at the sanctuary before allowing her gaze to rest on the altar. A flash of color caught her eye, and she tilted her head to stare at the vibrant stained glass window above the simple altar. A shepherd tended his flock.

Truly, this proved God possessed a wicked and wry sense of humor since she was a shepherdess—*at least, had been.* Perhaps the glass shepherd represented the promise that some divine entity would protect her family.

She dismissed the thought with a smirk. Only she was capable of such a feat. With a final glance, she left the safety of the chapel and the peacefulness of the vestibule behind her. With a defiant demeanor, she took her first step into the frigid evening air.

The wind bludgeoned her face and body, and the biting cold stole her breath. The tree limbs waved in a twiggy sendoff, almost as if clapping for her stricken state. Tears stung her eyes, but she refused to allow such a weakness. This was her new identity, and the quicker she accepted that fact, the less she'd suffer.

"Come, March." Michael took her arm and situated his body to take the majority of the wind's blast. "Let me get you out of the cold."

She nodded and allowed him to lead her to the carriage.

He held out his hand to assist her. "After you, Miss Lawson."

The wind snapped her cloak about her legs as she stood there and just stared at him. The sound of her former name was once something familiar, particularly when Michael said it. Now, it was achingly caustic to her ears.

"My name is not March Lawson." Her throat closed around the words, but through sheer determination she uttered, "What Rupert said about my birth is true."

He tilted his head and regarded her as if she were an oddity. "We'll see how long that lasts," he muttered.

"Pardon me? The wind must have stolen your words." She threw out the challenge as she narrowed her eyes. Before her stood a typical male, one who thought that all he had to do was wave his hand. The effort automatically setting everything to rights.

Even he couldn't fix this scandal.

"We're not going to stand in the cold and argue." He tipped his head and stared at the sky as if running out of patience. "We have a two-hour ride ahead of us. Get in, March." The growl in his voice was unmistakable.

Without a look back, she climbed into the carriage. Her name on his lips had always caused such a sweet shiver to pass through every inch of her.

Now, his words sounded like a foreign language. One she'd never learn.

The coach rumbled to a halt outside McCalpin Manor. The jangle of the horses' bridles broke the ear-shattering silence within the carriage. For the last two hours, McCalpin had struggled to engage March in any conversation. It had become apparent within minutes that she refused to discuss anything relating to her visit.

With a sigh, he knocked on the roof and immediately one of the footmen opened the door. Anxious to stretch his legs, McCalpin leapt from the coach and held out his hand to assist March. When there was no movement from her, he leaned into the carriage. "Come."

With her own sigh matching his, she followed his command. He made quick work of escorting her inside.

"My lord, welcome home again," greeted Arnsdale, the under-butler who saw to matters at McCalpin Manor when Buxton wasn't available.

"Thank you." McCalpin answered. He handed his coat and hat to the under-butler. "This is Miss March Lawson. We'll stay this evening and leave for town tomorrow."

"A pleasure, madam. I'm Arnsdale. If there's anything you need, please ring." He waited for March to hand him her pelisse.

"It's Miss March Featherston," she murmured.

McCalpin took a deep breath, hoping it would keep his anger from exploding. He didn't want to consider whether the cause was his inability to defuse the situation or because she was so miserable. With a glance around the entry, he thanked his lucky stars the rest of the staff had settled for the evening or were dining downstairs. "We'll dine in my study. Take Miss Lawson's bag to the marchioness's suite."

"Very well, my lord." Arnsdale bowed and took his leave with March's valise in his hands.

McCalpin took her arm in his and proceeded down the hall. The marble floor and thick rugs welcomed him home. Immediately, the tension he'd fought the entire way started to dissipate. In its place, the overwhelming need to change her mood crept over him.

The entire carriage ride to McCalpin Manor had been an icy hell. The miles drifted by like slow meandering storm clouds while March's retreat into silence grew stronger than the north wind. Nothing he'd tried could break her steely recalcitrant mood.

New fires blazed in the twin fireplaces of his study, a luxury some highly practical ancestor had incorporated into the architecture. A simple fare of roasted quail, carrot soup, sliced cheese, and dried figs sat before them on a small round table. March refused to look at anything other than her plate. If he hadn't known her better, he might think she wanted nothing to do with him or their dinner as she rearranged the food around her plate, never taking a bite. Her soup lay discarded by her side.

Her pale face highlighted the evident pain she suffered. The proof of her sadness tore through him until
he couldn't stand her suffering any longer. He turned his
chair and scooted his plate next to hers. His fork gently
pierced a piece of fowl. He brought the meager offering
to her mouth and tempted her to take a bite. She turned
her head as if any morsel of food was poisonous.

"You'll ruin my reputation as a good host if you don't
indulge me." He leaned close, willing her to gaze at him.

She lifted her warm eyes to his. The misery reflected
in their depths hit him like a punch in the gut. He dropped
the fork and completely ignored the clatter of it hitting
the china plate. He was powerless to do anything but take
her in his arms.

"Enough." He pushed his chair away from the table,
picked her up, then deposited her on his lap as if she were
a child who needed comfort after a spill. Without resistance, she allowed him to hold her and burrowed her face
in his neck. Her warmth soothed his own emptiness, and
her touch nourished him like a famished man. "I'll right
this wrong. I promise."

"How can you?" Her lips caressed his neck as a result
of her muffled whisper.

The sensation caused him to pull her tighter against
his chest. She nestled closer. The movement so endearing
he brushed his lips across the tip of her ear. The subtle
lilac scent that was uniquely hers rose to greet him.

"Nothing changed," he whispered.

She didn't respond to his muffled words.

"I promise everything will work out for the best." He
kept soothing her and offering succor. "I promise, March."

Eventually, she drew away. The loss of her heat and
the emptiness of his arms made him want to haul her
back into the safety of his embrace. With a soft gaze, she

studied every feature of his face. With her fingertips, she gently traveled the contours of his skin. The subdued caress caused his groin to tighten, and a heat blazed up his spine. His length started to thicken from his own craving for her continued touch. She was completely oblivious of her effect as she continued to pet and stroke his face.

He straightened in the chair in an attempt to keep his unruly body under control. Her touch, the slow sweep of her fingers, could only be described as exquisite torture. He closed his eyes in an attempt to control his body's reaction to her. She needed comfort—not some randy response from him. She needed security and a sense that she had a safe haven with him.

No matter how much he tried to tame his desire, it became bloody apparent to both of them. She wiggled against his erection, and he grunted.

"Am I hurting you?" she whispered. "I'm too heavy."

For the last four hours, she'd spoken hardly a word. When she decided to speak to him, it was about her own perceived shortcomings.

"Not at all." He rested his forehead against hers. "But you're driving me mad."

From London to Chelmsford, his thoughts had churned. He couldn't keep them quiet any longer. His path and hers were destined to intertwine. He'd known deep in his heart what he wanted to do but had tamped down the urge to say the words aloud until after last night's ball. Then Lawson—that sniveling bastard—had torn her to pieces.

Through the days, he'd courted the idea and had allowed it to roll in his mind—testing the feel and the texture much like a master chef who had created a new confection. Tasting it like a wine steward who would sip a new vintage before serving it to his master.

His earlier concern with her mind for numbers had diminished to nothing. She'd proven herself loyal to her family and her friends repeatedly. Her acumen with running an estate along with her quick intelligence and bookkeeping skills would be a great resource. More importantly, he had no doubt that she desired him as evidenced by her reaction whenever he kissed her. More importantly, their friendship could easily lead to a marriage based upon love and commitment. Of that, he had no doubt.

She stood wearily. "It's been a long day."

"May I take you to your room?" he whispered. Really, he'd much prefer taking her to *his* room and holding her in his arms all night. She nodded but refused to look at him. He took her hand in his and escorted her up the stairs.

March paused at the window at the top and stared out into the darkened night. "Tomorrow, will I have the opportunity to see your estate?" She shyly stole a sideways glance. "Perhaps . . ."

"What do you want?" Not allowing her to escape, he tilted her chin until his gaze met hers. "I'll give it to you."

She shook her head. "It's nothing."

"Nothing" sounded like "something" to him. Once he got her settled, he'd not let her escape until he discovered what she wanted. That was one of the most endearing qualities about her. She never asked for anything for herself. Her first thought was always for her sisters or her brother.

They continued down the hall until he opened the door to the green and gold sitting room of the matching suite next to his. A set of double doors led to the bedroom.

Gold and ivory satins and brocades decorated the marchioness's bedroom suite, while his was green and ivory. A joint dressing room connected the bedrooms, making access to each other discreet but easily attainable. It was another ingenious design from a previous Marquess of McCalpin, and he was thankful for such foresight, particularly this evening.

"This is my room?" The incredulity in her voice was utterly charming. "Where's the bed?"

"In here." He took her hand and led her to the room left of the sitting room. A massive gold pedestal bed stood in the center against the far wall, as if holding court with all the other furniture.

March's gaze swept the room until it landed on the bed. "These rooms are larger than the entire family wing at Lawson Court. Is that bed even in the same county as the sitting room?"

He couldn't help but laugh. Slowly, her darkness faded. Still holding her hand, he drew her until she faced him. He smiled at the flash of brilliance from her eyes.

"What were you going to say on the stairs? Perhaps what?" he cajoled. Without letting go of her hand, he pulled her close and pressed a kiss against her lips. "Answer now, or I'll use more of this type of torture until you reveal all your secrets."

"I wouldn't think that the mighty Marquess of McCalpin would stoop to such atrocities just for an answer to a silly thought."

He pressed his lips against hers again and whispered, "You would be shocked at my level of depravity. Now tell me."

She stood on tiptoes and pressed her mouth to his ear. The warmth of her breath caused his skin to tingle in response. "Perhaps someday you'll show me your estate. I would love to see how *you* raise sheep."

When she pulled away, her eyes blazed with laughter. He leaned close as her mirth transformed her into the most gorgeous creature he'd ever had the pleasure to behold. "I'll do more than that. I'll *give* you my sheep."

She wrinkled her nose. "That's too generous."

"Not for my marchioness." McCalpin held his breath as her playfulness fell into shock, then tumbled into disbelief. The silence of the room gave way to the swish of her muslin gown as she stepped away. He took a step forward so as not to give her any quarter. "Marry me."

"I don't understand," she whispered.

"Will you, March, take me, Michael, as your husband?" he teased as he squeezed her hands. "It's simple. I want you as my marchioness and as the mother of my children. I can't imagine my life any other way. Marry me."

She blinked twice, and her brows drew together as she contemplated his words. Her eyes filled with hope, as if he'd given her the world on a gold platter. "Truly?"

"Unequivocally," he answered. The moment, and her reaction, were perfect. He'd made her happy. "I want you to say yes."

She bit her lower lip, but he already knew her answer by the fire in her eyes.

"Yes, yes, yes." She rushed into his arms. "If that's not enough, let me repeat it a million times."

He took possession of her mouth, and she took possession of his happiness. Never had anything in his life felt so perfect and untainted by any of his failings. He hadn't planned to propose tonight. He wanted to wait until they reached London, but seeing her suffer and distressed made him want to cure her melancholy. Perhaps it wasn't the perfect time, but he was satisfied. It'd been the right thing to do.

Perhaps with March by his side, he could make his mark on the Langham duchy without destroying it into the ground.

# Chapter Nineteen

Before Michael had retired for the evening, he'd shown March the connecting door to his suite and insisted she come to him if she had any worries or concerns. The euphoria over his marriage proposal had pushed aside her gnawing emptiness that had resulted from the truth of her birth. But as sure as the sun surrenders to the night, so did her elation. The minutes ticked by, and an ill sense of doom clouded her senses much like the smoke from a green wood fire.

After she'd soaked in a rose-scented bath, March had collapsed in a yellow-and-ivory striped brocade chair and studied the fire. Her illegitimacy once again consumed her thoughts. How could she share a life with someone as wonderful as Michael when her own identity would always be a whispered rumor behind her back? Ghosts of innuendos and slights by the elite members of the *ton* would haunt her. She couldn't bear it if her past compromised Michael's political career or damaged his standing in society. Rupert would inflict more damage if he continued in his accusations that she was a forger and an embezzler. She should wait to discuss the matter thoroughly with Michael on the morrow, but it was too important to wait.

She had to reassure herself that he understood what it would mean if he married her. The honorable thing was to allow him to withdraw his proposal, even though she'd be heartbroken if he agreed.

The more March tried to settle her thoughts, the wilder they swirled. When she started to pace, her heartbeat raced in an attempt to keep up with her frantic steps. Soon she found herself walking across the shared dressing room. When she reached Michael's door, she tentatively knocked.

"Come in." Even through the thick wood door, his deep voice carried.

Quickly, so she wouldn't lose her courage, she entered his private domain.

Instead of darkness, soft light bathed the room from a well-tended fire before her. Two candles flickered in welcome on a table to her right. Next to the table stood a massive four-poster bed covered with elegant emerald-green satin and brocade hangings with a faint tartan pattern of blue and red. A velvet spread covered the bed in the color of hunter green. Every piece of fabric, artwork, and furniture in the room signified power and opulence. However, the most amazing sight lay in the bed.

In repose and shirtless, Michael reclined holding a book, his other arm stretched across an ivory bolster. The muscular contours and valleys of his body emphasized his strength, reminding her once again that he was a virile, masculine creature who could break her without much effort.

As she struggled with her thoughts, another crossroad

lay before her. Whether she chose the right path and offered to release him from his marriage proposal or selfishly clung to the life he promised was a deadly battle, one her mind and heart fought with vigor. To free Michael from his promise could very well result in her heart not surviving the night, but it was the right decision. Slowly, her labored breath grew less frantic while her heartbeat skipped in fits and starts, urging her to join him.

He smiled briefly, the one he used when he was about to tease her. The sight so familiar and comforting it reminded her of home and the sun on a summer day. When she caught his gaze, his eyes glimmered with a sensual magnetism that compelled her forward, but riveted to the spot, she lacked the ability to move toward him.

"Sweetheart, what is it?" His brows drew together in a line.

"I can't"—she struggled for the right phrase, for the correct words, for anything—"marry unless you understand all the ramifications of what I discovered today in Chelmsford—"

"You can." Michael threw aside the velvet spread and rose from the opposite side of the bed. He turned toward the wall with his backside facing her, leaving March with a clear view of his *naked* body. The muscles in his back rippled with his movements. Unable to tear her gaze away, she studied every line of his form as her heart hammered against her ribs. Wide shoulders narrowed into strong hips. His perfectly formed buttocks tensed as he reached for his banyan.

The air around her grew heavy and locked her into place. There was no need for the forced captivity. She could watch him all day. With wide eyes, she consumed him with her gaze. Michael was perfect.

She shook her head to clear the spell that held her enthralled. With a turn, she faced the ebony door and rested her forehead against it. The smooth wood comforted the fever that had swept through her. She wore only the dressing gown the duchess had given her. When she'd finished her bath, she'd searched for her nightgown, but it was missing. The maid must have snatched it up along with the rest of the laundry. Servants acting as lady's maids were still a foreign concept to her. Now because she'd carelessly left her nightgown next to the clothes she'd worn today, she was practically as naked as he was.

"I apologize for interrupting you." As if it were perfectly normal she'd be addressing the door, she continued, "It can wait until morning."

Mortified, she wanted to melt into the woodwork. She'd ogled him as if he were a sweet treat especially prepared for her. Eyes closed, she fumbled to find the door handle.

Suddenly, warm fingers laced with hers. Like a phantom, he'd reached her side without making a sound.

"You can interrupt me anytime." His warm breath tickled her ear, while he pressed his hot body against hers. "Anywhere."

Caught between the cool wood and Michael, she should escape.

Thank goodness "shoulds" carried less weight than "wants."

As if demanding her to stay, his scent of evergreen mixed with pure male, covered her—no, marked her. She inhaled deeply.

He nudged her ear with his nose. "If you're planning on breaking our betrothal after only two hours, I'll kiss you senseless until you renege," he whispered.

With their fingers still clasped, he wrapped their arms around her waist and pulled her tight against him. She was helpless when a slow throb pulsed in her belly. With no hesitation, she leaned her head against his shoulder. In a rare feat, he made her feel small and feminine.

Cherished.

"What shall I do to convince you that our marriage is a wise decision?" he murmured. He turned her to face him and their eyes met. Never breaking their gaze, he leaned close, rested his elbow against the door, and framed her with his body.

He tenderly touched his lips against hers. He demanded nothing. When she tried to deepen the kiss, he pulled away slightly.

"I want this marriage. Let me try to persuade you that I'm the perfect man for you," he hummed.

She could only nod in response.

"I'm very effective with my arguments." He kissed her again and gathered her in his arms. Chest to chest and leg to leg, their bodies fit together perfectly. His untied banyan had fallen open, and his hot chest burned through her dressing gown. Her breasts grew heavy and her nipples tightened into peaks as he finally, and thankfully, deepened the kiss.

She wrapped her arms around him, and a slight sigh escaped her when his hands caressed a path down her back, the touch mesmerizingly slow. Somehow, her dressing gown had come untied. She gasped at the shock of his smooth skin against hers. In response, he growled. His tongue tangled with hers in an erotic dance, one he was teaching her.

One hand grazed her breast in the barest of teasing

touches. She moaned in protest, and he chuckled. He traced the taunt nipple with one finger, then stepped away. Holding her hand in front of him, Michael allowed his gaze to sweep down the length of her body.

After an eternity, his gaze caressed her. Finally, he lifted his eyes to hers. His dilated pupils were huge, but it was the sight of his erection that caused her breath to hitch. Its hard length mesmerized her. A drop of his essence leaked, and in the candlelight, it glistened.

She chanced a glance at his face. His nostrils flared as he watched her. "I've wanted to do this since the first time I saw you dance in the attic with your court dress."

He kissed her cheek, then trailed his lips across her neck, then lower. Her breath caught at his touch. Tenderly, he sucked one nipple into his mouth while he gently kneaded the other. The feel of his lips and hot tongue, alluring and tormenting at the same time, churned her desire. Like a puppet on a string, she reacted to his every touch, and her center tightened in response. The room faded from view. She was only aware of his mouth and the bristles of his evening beard brushing against the sensitive skin of her breasts, bewitching her more with his magic.

He glanced up. The lazy smile he delivered was spellbinding. There was no need for words. He wanted her as much as she wanted him.

As if worshipping her body, he knelt before her, then trailed his mouth down her abdomen. Framing her hips with his hands, he kissed her in the most secret of places. With his mouth on her, he licked through her folds until he found her sensitive nub. Her eyes fluttered when his tongue circled her clitoris.

Her body was embarrassingly wet from her desire.

Thinking he would be horrified, she shifted to escape. He gently pulled her back, then captured her gaze.

"Don't you like this?" He pressed a slight kiss in the valley where her hip meet her leg, then studied her.

"I do, but . . ." God, how could she even discuss this? "I'm . . ."

He cocked his head, and the uncertainty in his eyes tugged at her heart. "You're what?"

She closed her eyes, and heat bludgeoned her cheeks. "I'm wet," she whispered.

"I know. Look at me," he commanded, his voice gentle but unyielding.

She did as directed.

His eyes flashed, and a devilish grin suddenly appeared. "I'm wild about it." He grasped her hand and laced their fingers together. "Don't be embarrassed. You excite me. Here's the proof." He waved his other hand at the hard length of his erection. "Let me take care of you?"

Without letting go, he rested their entwined hands on her hip and proceeded to pleasure her. The splendid slow sweep of his tongue against her center teased and taunted her unmercifully. Sparks of pleasure burned through her. The sensation increased and built to a point she didn't know if she'd survive. Uncertain whether she could stand of her own volition, she grabbed his hair with her other hand to keep from falling. As if pleased, he squeezed her hand, the one he held.

He continued the sweet caresses and kisses, sweeping her into a wonderfully mindless world. His touch, his mouth on her body, and his gentle strength overwhelmed her. At this point, she wanted more. The pleasure he gave was not only relentless, but also addictive.

Soon, every nerve stood on edge ready to explode. She

labored for breath and tried to rein in the effect he had on her, but soft mewling sounds escaped. She'd never experienced anything this fantastic before. Like a feral animal, her response bucked to be set free. When her body reached its peak, she let go and fell completely into the passion he'd created.

Slowly, she awoke from the sensual dream. Without realizing it, she was gently running her fingers through his hair. When he pulled away from her to stand, he took her hand and kissed it.

"You're even more beautiful when you come," he whispered. His lips touched hers, and she could taste herself. No dream and desire she'd ever experienced could compare with the giving lover before her.

Like a gust of wind clearing the winter leaves, his enchantment eliminated her concerns. She would marry him.

"Let's go to bed," she whispered.

As if the tethers holding her in place suddenly released, she allowed her decision to take charge. Whether her heart had completely defeated all doubt in her mind made little difference. It was all so perfectly clear. Everything she needed and wanted was with Michael.

She grasped his hand and led him to bed. The warmth of his fingers against hers encouraged her to face the chill of the linen bedding. They both shed their robes and climbed onto the master platform bed. Instinctively, she moved closer to him when he lay beside her.

As he pulled her tight against him, the soft sound of his chuckle swept across her. "You're a determined thing when you make a decision."

"Yes," she whispered. It was difficult to keep the wonderment out of her voice when a bare chest was right in front of her eyes for her viewing pleasure.

Michael trailed his fingers through her hair, combing it while soothing her. "Your soft tresses belie your hair's underlying strength. Just like you." He pulled a thick curl to his face and brushed it across his cheek. The movement brought her mouth close to his, and he brushed his lips across hers.

She released a ragged sigh. She was in deep and wanted to go to the bottom.

"Kiss me," he whispered. Almost a plea, his words caused her to shiver.

She ducked her head against his neck. His scent enticed her closer. God, she wanted it to cover her like the heat from his body. She trailed her lips across the sharp angle of his jaw until she found his square chin.

"Kiss me," he growled in response, but he didn't attempt to take her mouth with his.

She ignored his command and gently placed her lips on the dimple of his chin, the one that had fascinated her since she first met him.

"Why won't you kiss me?" His eyes blazed. With a swift turn, he twisted with her in his arms until he loomed over her, forcing her onto her back with her head against his pillow.

"Why won't you kiss *me*?" she softly demanded in return.

He rested on one elbow and with his other hand played with her hair. His piercing gaze made her believe he saw every crevice of hope and longing in her being. "I've always kissed you. Now, your turn." With that last statement, he lifted one perfect eyebrow in challenge. "We are to be married if you remember."

His encouragement was the sweetest seduction. She dipped her gaze to the smooth skin of his chest. The perfect flow of muscles, sinew, and chiseled planes would have kept any artist spellbound. As a simple sheep farmer, what chance did she have to resist? None. So she reached for his broad shoulders. His skin twitched beneath her hands in response.

"Kiss me, I'm begging you." His deep gravel tone reminded her of a smoke-infused whisky—sharp but mellow at the same time. Yet, there was a hint of vulnerability, a longing. One that made her believe she was the only woman who could soothe and love him the way he deserved.

She pressed her lips against his in a gentle touch of yearning. He rewarded her with a groan that vibrated through every part of her. In answer, her pulse pounded, and her body throbbed once again. She'd happily surrender all her reservations to this night and to him.

He deepened the kiss, and she sighed in response. His tongue coaxed and petted hers, then withdrew. She whimpered at the loss. Without preamble, her lips played with his and her tongue slid across his full lips. Pulling her tighter as if never wanting to let go, he groaned again and let her inside. Her tongue swept and explored until both were out of breath.

With his chest heaving, Michael pulled away and stared down at her. She would give him everything if he'd just keep kissing her. The tenderness in his expression was like a caress, one that made her aware of his every breath and every inch of skin where they touched. The beauty of it was almost incomprehensible. Even the air surrounding them seemed to shimmer with unspoken words of tenderness and love.

Such emotion could easily replace the need for actual nourishment. She could live off his attentions and kindness and never crave anything else in her life. No wonder these feelings held such power over a person.

He cupped her face gently, and the splay of his fingers against her cheeks made her breath catch. Gently, he trailed those same fingers down her neck, causing her nipples to harden in anticipation. "Are you sure?"

"Yes. I'll die if you don't touch me." He made her believe she was truly precious.

"We can't have any of that, can we?" he whispered as he slid his knuckles across her nipples.

Wanting more, she arched her back. The slide of his fingers against her bare skin made heat flash outward from her body as if struck by an uncontrollable force of nature.

He rose above her, and his breath caught. A look of awe crossed his face. "Oh, darling, look how beautiful you are." He cupped one breast, then nestled the underside with his mouth. She closed her eyes and allowed the sensation to take control.

Each kiss, each stroke, each graze of his teeth caused a new restlessness within her. She'd experienced desire before, but this was different. This was hunger, one only he could satisfy. She stroked his back as if playing an instrument. The slide of her fingers down his skin made each muscle contract. His response to her touch made her want him more. As if he knew what she wanted, he slid his body over hers.

She spread her legs, and he settled his hips against hers. Hot, hard, and unbelievably large, his erection slid through her folds. She cried out, then stilled. It took every piece of willpower she possessed not to angle herself to take him. He quit attending to her sensitive breasts and gazed into her eyes.

"*My God*," he whispered. "You're ready to come again."

The shock was evident on his face, but he recovered quickly. His fingers lightly danced over her abdomen and slid through her nether curls until he touched her sensitive nub. She bucked in response.

*Yes, that was what she needed.* Instead of saying the words, she moaned and lifted her hips as if offering him anything and everything if he'd just continue to touch her there.

"Darl—" He broke off and closed his eyes. He inhaled and held his breath. Slowly, he released it. He took possession of her mouth with his tongue mating hers. Her taste still lingered, and she reveled in it.

He continued to kiss her until he took her hand and placed it on his erection. "Feel me. I want you so much I'm in agony."

The hot, hard length throbbed in her hand as his pulse pounded through the thick vein that twined around the underside. She traced the silken head in her hand. On instinct, she gently squeezed, and he hissed. Her gaze shot to his, and he smiled as if encouraging her to continue. She released a ragged breath as the sensation of different textures of touch, scents, and sights curled into smoky clouds in her head.

He laced their fingers together and raised her hands over her head where he rested his elbows next to hers. He nudged her nose with his. "We don't have—"

"Yes, we do," she whispered. She took possession of his mouth just as he'd done to her earlier. He shifted slightly, and his cock barely entered her.

Inside, she could feel her muscles clenching for more—more of him. She moaned his name as her body prepared for release. With infinite care, his mouth brushed hers and, inch by inch, he moved inside her.

With his girth, she had expected to be uncomfortable.

Instead, her body hungered for more of the exquisite fullness that he was giving her.

"Put your legs around my hips," he whispered, never taking his lips from hers.

She did as instructed and lifted her hips. Swiftly, he seated himself fully. She felt a pinch and jerked in reaction.

"All right?" His gaze locked with hers. A longing gleamed from the blue depths of his own that made her feel revered like a divine and rare creature in his safekeeping.

She nodded and hoped he could see the trust and love she felt for him. Such an exquisite being, and she was going to marry him. He kissed her again and started to move slowly away. She groaned in protest, but he entered her again.

The pleasure built into a force that fed itself. It became stronger and faster until all she could do was hold him close. His hands gripped the sides of her head as he studied her. Slight trickles of sweat streamed down both sides of his face, so she brushed them away. Each time, he kissed her hand or her fingers—whatever was in his reach.

What they'd created continued to gather strength. Every touch and move became a force she could no longer harness. Finally, her pleasure took control of all of her senses. Stars exploded behind her closed eyes, and she whispered his name. Inside, her body clenched his as if never letting him go. With a final thrust, he groaned as his seed filled her.

Their joint release continued in waves. He buried his head in her neck and repeated her name over and over as if in prayer. She'd never felt closer to another being in her entire life. Slowly, their breathing calmed as she stroked his neck, down his muscular back to his taut buttocks, and then reversed the pattern while the sound of his heartbeat echoed in her ear.

If she never had to leave his arms, it would be too soon.

He pressed his lips against her cheek. As if luck was against her, he rose from the bed, then crossed the room to a small pitcher and basin where he dunked a linen towel in water. Suddenly shy and unsure, she quietly stood and donned her dressing gown.

He walked back to her with a surprising frown replacing his easy smile. "Is something amiss?"

She shook her head and chanced a glance his way. "I'm not certain what I should do."

In a move even the most experienced dancer would appreciate, he dropped to his knees once again. She knew him well enough to know he'd never be a humble supplicant. Before she could protest, he unbelted her gown and pressed his lips one the slight curve of her abdomen. "Stay with me."

Her mind stilled at his words, but her heart beat frantically, trying to reach the spot where he kissed her. With hooded eyes, he gazed at her, then turned his attention to her body. With utter tenderness, he cleaned her, stroking the linen against her inner thighs. Stains of red marred the perfect white of the cloth. For once, such a sight didn't bother her. When he finished his ministrations, he kissed her leg again before proceeding to the other side. At his touch, her breasts tightened as if he were making love to her once more.

Slowly, he stood and tended to himself before he washed the cloth again to remove any evidence that they'd been together. When he returned to her side, he pulled her into his arms. "Will you sleep with me?"

She nodded and relaxed into his embrace.

"Did I hurt you?" He pressed a kiss against the top of her head.

"Never." She tilted her head back so she could meet his gaze. "It was everything I dreamed it would be."

A true genuine smile broke across his face, lending him an exceedingly happy but very satisfied expression. "Come to bed."

She pressed a kiss against his heart. Soon, they were nestled next to each other with his hand stroking her hip. They whispered things to each other about everything and anything.

Eventually, his rhythmic breathing told her he'd fallen asleep. Instead of joining him in slumber, her mind refused to quiet, and her earlier worry and tension returned. How could she marry him with all the upheaval in her life?

The fire snapped and blazed in answer. Instead of worrying, she should determine the extent of the damage and see if she could rectify it herself. She'd make an accounting of every pound she'd embezzled and the same for her expenditures, then she'd divide it into estate management, household, and personal expenditures.

At least her mind could concentrate on something besides worries that she had no answers to.

When McCalpin stepped into his study in the wee hours of the morning, he found March huddled over his desk, sound asleep. With a single candle flickering beside her, she appeared so alone that his heart lurched. Biting cold, the kind that reached inside you and took hold like a rabid dog, permeated the room. She'd wrapped herself with a fur cover from one of two sofas that framed the fireplaces.

He stoked the fire and fed several logs until the room, or at least the area surrounding the sofas, was toasty warm. It'd make the perfect place to hold her while she slept. He might suffer from the heat, but he wanted her comfortable and safely ensconced within his arms.

He approached to pick her up, then suddenly stopped. Not only were the McCalpin Manor books open, but also the McCalpin House books he'd brought with him when he traveled to find her. They surrounded March as if she were holding court.

Pieces of vellum where she'd written columns and tables of numbers were stuck between the pages. Scrap sheets where she had added amounts lay partially hidden beneath her arms. She'd remembered to cap the ink-stand but her quill lay beside her as if waiting for her to resume whatever she'd been doing.

She stirred then blinked her eyes several times at the fire. Slowly, she turned. When she recognized him, her mouth twisted into a sleepy smile, the effect so powerful he wondered if she'd drugged him. All he could do was reach for her.

He stopped, suddenly frozen, but his blood burned like fire. The one book that held all his secrets lay under her hands.

"Michael." The remnants of sleep colored her words.

"What are you doing at my desk?" She flinched as if he'd hurt her, and immediately, he regretted the curt words.

"I couldn't sleep. All I could see in my mind were numbers regarding the purchases and withdrawals I'd made over the last several months. I—I needed to determine how much money I'd taken." She shrugged her shoulders as if defeated. "I wanted a list of each expenditure along with its purpose."

"Why are my estate books open?"

"I needed a distraction and thought I could help with the bookkeeping."

He reached for the book that would expose his deepest shame, then stopped stock-still when her hand covered his.

"I know," she whispered.

"Exactly what?" Much like that fateful day when Will's hand covered his, time screeched to a halt. He almost sneered, but thankfully, with the slimmest of willpower he held himself in check. It was the natural reaction whenever anyone came close to discovering his problem, but it was completely inappropriate for March. For God's sake, she would be his marchioness soon.

"Your difficulty with numbers." Her face glowed in the candlelight, but her eyes made his heart tumble in his chest. Tender without any judgment or condemnation, they melted into his.

He plowed a hand through his hair and exhaled. Never before had he ever laid every weakness he possessed at someone's feet. God, the ability to share this failure, this defect, would be so freeing. To explain how frustrated it made him would lift the heavy burden he'd carried all his life. She would listen. He only prayed she wouldn't condemn him.

He took a deep breath and relaxed. Nay, she wouldn't judge him.

"Let's sit by the fire." He tugged her from the chair and swept her into his arms. She uttered an endearing feminine yelp that was perfectly charming. When he settled her on his lap, she rested her head against his shoulder.

"I'll try not to make the story boring."

"Nothing you could ever say to me would be the least bit boring." She leaned and captured his gaze. "I want to know everything."

He escaped her stare only to study the fire. It made it easier. "It became apparent to me that I was an idiot with numbers early on. My old governess had railed at my lack of abilities. She even told me that I should be relieved of my responsibilities as the heir to my father."

Her eyes narrowed in pain as she she gently squeezed his hand in comfort. "How horrible. I hope she was dismissed."

"She was . . . because of William. But by then, Will and Emma had surpassed me in their mathematical prowess. Thankfully, my parents replaced her with a kind tutor who didn't punish or rail at me when I struggled with assignments."

"You're one of the most intelligent and empathetic men I've ever known. But it must have been difficult to see your siblings surpass you." With her hand, March turned his face until she held his gaze once again. "Go on."

The nurturing gentleness in her tone encouraged him to exhale his trepidation. "I am the mighty Langham ducal heir, and I couldn't add a column of numbers together successfully." He rested his forehead against hers and closed his eyes at the painful memories. "I was so ashamed. My tutor tried everything, but nothing worked. Every time I had a problem or equation to solve, I was off by one. If the answer were five, I'd find it as six. If it was subtraction and the answer was thirty-six, I'd solve it as thirty-five. If it was a fraction, heaven help me. It was as if my brain played nasty tricks on me."

His throat tightened as the familiar panic gripped him, as if he was struggling with calculations now. He shook his head to banish such wicked thoughts and glanced at her.

She stroked her fingers along his cheeks, the touch soft and reassuring. "How did you hide it at school?"

"It was Eton." He grunted with a sound that belied his disgust with himself. "Not much is expected of ducal heirs. I either canceled the exam or went home. Sometimes I wrote a note informing them I was ill and refused to take the exam."

March nodded as she continued to offer comfort. "Did your parents ever address it with you?"

"They never raised it, and neither did I. I thought if I didn't admit it, then I wasn't a failure." He exhaled with difficulty as a vise of shame tightened around his chest. "I exceeded all their expectations in my other subjects. In logic, literature, history, even languages, I received top marks. No one ever questioned my ability in mathematics. I believe they just assumed I excelled in that subject also." He cleared his throat of its thickness again.

"Michael." The soft whisper was as soothing as a caress. "You've never been a failure. You're as brilliant as the sun."

"I disagree, my beauty." He pressed a kiss against her cheek. "That's why you always see William with me. He plays the role as advisor to me, but really he's reviewing the accounts and investments." He chanced a glance her way. "That's why he was so pointed in his questions to you. He's protective of me."

"Even though he's skeptical and quite annoying at times, I'm finding he's one of my favorite people in your family." She reached out and brushed away an errant lock of hair that had fallen onto his brow. "But if you ever tell him such, I'll deny it."

The simple touch caused something to melt inside of him, a piece he'd kept frozen deep inside, one he believed he'd never share with anyone.

He bit his lip as he fought to find the right words. As an honorable man, he had to ask if she still wanted to marry him. What a lark that was. How honorable had he been last night? He'd taken her virginity, thus leaving her stranded with him. He'd never let her go now. She was his completely.

"I should have confessed before I made love to you." Holding her gaze, he waited for the disgust to cross her beautiful face. "I'm afraid you don't have any choice now. You'll have to marry me."

March shook her head and bit her lower lip. "Have I ever told you how crazed you make me sometimes?" She pressed her hands against his cheeks. "You glorious foolish man. I love you. This changes nothing for me. I want to marry you."

Her dark copper eyes never looked away from his as she waited. She'd just confessed her love, and he stared, unable to repeat them back. What was wrong with him? She meant more to him than words could even express. He'd never shared so much of himself with another person, not even the members of his own family, yet he couldn't say those three words back to her.

"I didn't say that so you'd repeat it in return." She brushed her lips against his, then regarded him. "Thank you for sharing so much of yourself with me."

He blinked, not knowing what to say. She was all things lovely and beautiful. His instincts had been spot-on. "You'll make a marvelous marchioness. Someday, you'll make a devastating duchess."

"I hope in the distant future. I owe your parents so

much." She released a ragged sigh. "May I tell you what I discovered in your account books and investment records?"

"With what I've just shared, you'll have to go slow."

She nodded briskly. "Every book and record has been meticulously managed except for one."

"It's my practice account," he interrupted. "I try to improve my skills with the household account book. There are two. One for me and one for the housekeeper. It's the simplest account to try to balance."

Her brilliant smile broke through her pursed lips. "Your threes look like reversed *E*'s and your fours look like upside-down *h*'s. Your handwriting is distinctive. That's how I learned . . ."

"That I'm an id—"

"Please, don't. I'll not listen." March attempted to get off his lap, but he was faster and grabbed her hips.

He secured her to his lap once again. "Please, go on, sweetheart."

"After I finished with your account, I started on the others. I've been through every one."

"Every one?" He drew his brows together. She couldn't have accomplished that. It took William two days to review every account and investment attached to McCalpin Manor and McCalpin House. Many of them were complicated investment portfolios tied to the Langham Duchy.

She tilted her head in challenge. "Every single one."

It was a pleasure to surrender to her. She could teach him things about managing an estate and, in return, he could teach her all the things they could do in bed.

And out of it.

Completely oblivious to his thoughts, she continued,

"Someone has deliberately understated the returns on your personal investments. When you compare Lord Somerton's correspondence on investment returns, they aren't the same numbers in the accounting books. In addition, the estate books have entries for expenditures that have either been increased by adding a zero or marked out completely with an increased amount written above."

Keenly interested in understanding her explanation, he nodded for her to proceed.

"For instance, last month, you acquired a draught horse. The expenditure was initially marked as twenty-five pounds, then a zero was added. Two sheep were purchased for seventy-two pence. The amount was crossed out and seven pounds, two pence replaced it. No one would likely notice these changes on a daily basis, but if you look at it over the last several months, there's a pattern."

He exhaled his frustration. Not just at the numbers floating in the air, but more importantly, someone was stealing from him, and he'd had no idea. He never checked the books himself. Even William didn't catch the errors.

"Plus, the entries in your household account don't match the housekeeper's account. Someone has manipulated the numbers there too." She narrowed her eyes. "Thank heavens you had the foresight to maintain another book. Otherwise, I'm not certain anyone would have caught the modifications. By my calculations, there's at least a five-thousand-pound discrepancy."

She walked to his desk, then returned with one of the account books. She opened it to a marked page and pointed at one account entry. "See the sevens and ones?

They're distinctive. Dashes or serifs slash the middle of the sevens. The ones have serifs at the top. Whoever is manipulating the books has a unique writing style."

Even he could understand what she was stating, but it was difficult to believe someone would deliberately try to steal from him.

"Are you suggesting William or a member of my staff is stealing from me?" The fire hissed as if it found his question unbelievable.

Such an incredulous thought made his insides twist in a knot that he doubted would ever untangle. These people had been with him, if not for all, then for the majority of his life. The staff at McCalpin House had served him and his uncle faithfully for years. William's dishonesty was not something worth considering.

"Of course not," she answered with assurance, then wrinkled her nose in the adorable way that always reminded him of how they first met in his study.

"Wouldn't the annual audit find the discrepancies?"

"I can't answer that as I don't know how your staff manages such a task," she answered. "I could certainly ask William what he suggests."

"Excellent idea." He nodded in agreement and tugged her tighter to him.

With a yawn, she didn't resist and leaned her head against his shoulder.

"We'll finish our discussion tomorrow. Let's go to bed," he whispered. He took the book from her hands and placed it on the sofa.

She stood. Together hand in hand, they made their way back to his bedchamber where he made love to her again. In the dawn, he lay with her warm lush body nestled next to his. He realized he'd never have enough of her in his days, his nights, his bed, and most importantly, his life.

Luck had a strange way of turning an obstacle into good fortune. Who would have thought that his beautiful embezzler would be such a wonderful ally and a strong partner for him? Someday he'd thank her for forging his signature.

# Chapter Twenty

In record time, the coach made it back to London. As soon as Michael saw her safely inside, he returned to McCalpin House. They'd agreed that tonight they'd share their plans to marry first with his parents, then with her siblings. Afterward, they'd privately discuss their findings in the account books with William. March headed for the upstairs living quarters. No doubt, her sisters and brother were beside themselves with worry.

As soon as she walked into her bedroom, all three siblings descended.

"March! Thank heavens you're home." Julia rushed into her arms.

March squeezed in return and kissed her sister on her cheek.

Faith was the next to join in the hug, followed by Bennett. All four clutching one another as if the missing pieces of their hearts were once again reunited.

March was the first to break away. "Come and sit on the bed with me. I have much to tell."

All her siblings were solemn as they joined her on the

massive bed. She said a quick prayer that she'd get through the story without falling apart.

"I met with the vicar in Chelmsford." She glanced at her sibling's dear faces. The pain and worry presented itself so differently on each precious face. Julia's eyes told of her torment, while Faith appeared ready to cry out in pain, her mouth pinched. However, it was Bennett's face that almost brought her to her knees. Stoic and proud, he fought to keep the glistening tears from trailing down his face.

She loved them and wanted to make this right so they didn't suffer her humiliation. They did nothing wrong and shouldn't have to pay for her new circumstance in life.

She forced herself to continue. "What Rupert said was true. I saw the register with my own eyes."

"Oh, March," Faith whispered.

Julia's hand flew to her lips as if to keep her shock inside. Bennett turned away and discreetly brushed his fingers under his eye. That small movement burned through her chest like hot iron. Her own tears started to gather, but she drew in a deep breath and held it until she could finish.

"What shall we do?" Julia whispered.

Indeed, that thought had consumed her on the way back from McCalpin Manor. She wouldn't tell her siblings about marrying until she and Michael could tell them together.

"I think it best if you and Faith continue to have Lord McCalpin escort you to social events. The duke and duchess will ensure that your reputations are protected." She turned to Bennett who had learned quickly how to master his emotions. "You should stay and continue your studies with Mr. Tatum. I'm very happy with the progress you've made in all your subjects. I think it best that for the time being I return to Lawson Court."

Bennett vehemently shook his head. "Not without me, you aren't."

The defiance in his words was something she hadn't expected. "Bennett—"

"No, March. I'm head of the family. You're my sister. I'll not allow you to go back there alone." His emerald eyes flashed in warning.

Bennett stood before her almost unrecognizable. A boy, but a boy whose behavior over the short time he'd stayed at Langham Hall hinted at the man he would become. His staunch proclamation he would protect her caused a slew of errant tears to make an unwanted appearance again. Her baby brother, the one she raised from infancy, would soon be an adult. It had to be Michael and his family's influence. The unguarded love and affection they showered on her and her siblings were nothing short of a miracle.

"Bennett, perhaps you and I should talk with Lord McCalpin. Would you be agreeable to that?" Their father would be so proud if he could see his son today.

"Agreed," Bennett said.

She released the pent-up breath and turned to her sisters. "So, tell me what's occurred since I've gone."

Faith and Julia stole furtive glances at each other. Julia swiftly scooted off the bed. "Nothing. Lord Queensgrace hasn't sent word. If I see him at an event, I'll cut him if he doesn't cut me first."

Faith stood and put her arm around Julia's waist and drew her close. "Darling, don't make any rash judgments. Give him a chance."

Julia whirled swiftly and escaped Faith's arms. "Will you give Dr. Kennett the same courtesy?"

Faith shook her head. "I haven't heard from him either, so I take your point." With an uneasy sigh, she turned to March. "The duchess is taking us shopping at Grigby's in an hour. Then tonight, we're to attend Lord Sinclair's soiree musicale. Will you come with us?"

"No, I'll spend the day at Lawson Court, then come back this evening for dinner."

Both Faith and Julia tried to argue and change her mind, but much to March's relief, they easily capitulated to her decision. Neither sister could afford another mark on their reputation if they wanted to make successful matches. If March were present, a scandal would erupt. No doubt, she was still the favorite topic of gossip for *The Midnight Cryer*. It made little difference whether the powerful Duchess of Langham was by her side or not.

"Bennett has a history lesson with Mr. Tatum soon. Julia and I should get ready for our outing with the duchess." Faith reached over and kissed March on the cheek. "We're so happy you're home."

Julia kissed March's other cheek, and Bennett took her hand and bent over it like a perfect gentleman.

At the click of the door, the terror of the unknown from last night rose in a wave. What if she was always a pariah? Truly, what if she was always a constant embarrassment to her family and to Michael and his family? Her gaze skimmed the opulent gowns that the duchess had generously provided for the balls. Silks, satins, and lace would never hide her true self.

She was a sheep farmer, and a bastard one at that. March bit her lip and stared out the window. She quickly changed her gown and slippers for one of her old muslin frocks and sturdy half boots she wore when tending sheep. She'd spend the rest of the day at Lawson Court working.

Perhaps she'd find some peace there, or if she was lucky, a little piece of her old self, the one she'd lost two days ago.

Being in London for the past weeks had turned March into someone she didn't recognize. She loathed admitting it to anyone else, but the pampering she experienced at Langham Hall had turned her tender. After a full afternoon of cleaning the sheep pens and the barn, and walking the fields of Lawson Court, the wind had burned her cheeks and her legs ached from all the walking. Her arms and hands throbbed in protest from all the physical work required to muck the barn and the sheep enclosures.

There'd been little else to do as Michael had sent Mr. Severin, his land steward, to oversee the estate's operation. Like a tightly wound precision timepiece, the farm didn't need her help anymore. Mr. Severin had hired staff to perform the daily work. Walking through the fields had allowed her time to gather all the emotions that she'd stuffed inside her heart and mind. It had taken hours, but she managed to make some sense of the chaotic events of her life since she'd arrived in London. When she'd made love to Michael last night, she'd found a comfort she hadn't experienced since her parents' death. To lie in his arms had made her feel that she had a place in the world. That someone actually admired and held her dear.

This had nothing to do with her family loving her, but everything to do with being perceived as a woman and revered. Michael saw her grief and struggles, then helped her because she meant something to him.

She'd not waste this opportunity. She'd seen too many women in her small town of Leyton live their entire lives alone without ever experiencing what she'd had last night.

A man, who with infinite care and grace, had made love to her as if she was his greatest treasure to protect and nurture. She'd put everything behind her and concentrate on Michael and their upcoming marriage.

March took one final look at the rolling fields of her youth and remembered her parents. They'd be pleased with not only Bennett, but with the fine women Julia and Faith were today. Indeed, they'd be pleased with her choice of husband. There was no use wondering if they'd be pleased with her. They'd be ecstatic to discover their embezzling bastard had even found happiness and true love.

A kernel of unease flared deep inside. She had every right to be angry with her parents. She could easily let such feeling ferment and grow, but she extinguished such thoughts. She couldn't change the past—only protect her and her family's future.

Perhaps Michael didn't love her now, but she'd make it her life's work to show him what he meant to her. If she were lucky, maybe someday, he'd love her in return.

Whatever fate had in store for her, she wasn't afraid of it.

Not anymore.

She walked into Lawson Court to say good-bye to Mrs. Oliver. When the housekeeper wasn't in the kitchen, March ventured toward the dining room. She passed the study, then stopped. She'd never delivered Michael's fraudulent seal, the one she'd had made to secure funds from her family's trust. She opened the desk drawer, then opened the others in rapid succession.

There was nothing—no sheets of velum, no sealing wax, no extra quills or ink. Just empty drawers.

However, most horrifying of all, Michael's seal was gone.

"Are you missing something?"

Her lips curled at the taunt. Immediately, she knew who stole the items without looking up from the desk. She should have come home sooner after Hart told her that Mrs. Devin had caught Rupert in the study.

She lifted her gaze to his and narrowed her eyes. "Come to see if you left anything?" She'd not let a bully come into her home after the havoc he'd created for her and her sisters.

"Actually, no. I saw you roaming the fields and thought I'd make certain you don't steal anything else that doesn't belong to you." Rupert sniffed then scrunched up his nose. "You smell as if you've slept with those wooly fur balls."

"What did you do with my things? The ones you stole?" Remarkably, she kept her tone even and calm. Inside was another story. She was seething. Once she found out some answers to her questions, she'd throw the bastard out of her home and out of her life.

"Where they belong. I gave everything to the Marquess of McCalpin." His nose rose another inch as if the air were more rarified in his area of the study. "His solicitor offered to pay me if I retrieved the items you were using to steal from my family and the marquess."

"What solicitor?" She didn't bother to hide the curtness in her tone. Michael hadn't mentioned a peep about sending a solicitor to the estate. Something that important, he'd have discussed with her. Rupert was lying.

He waved a hand in the air as if tired of her questions. "Someone from Russell & Sons. I don't recall their name. They paid me a finder's fee, which I was happy to collect. Made up for the aggravation of smelling sheep manure." He whipped out a handkerchief and held it to his nose. "What you've done to this family is disgraceful!"

She ignored his theatrics. "Tell me his name, Rupert."

"Jameson." His unchecked vehemence caused a downpour of spittle showers. Luckily, their distance apart kept her from a soaking. "Mr. Jameson. He's the one who informed me you stole from the family's trusts."

Even she had her limits. "Leave, Rupert. This is still my home, and I say who's welcome and who's not. You're on the *not* list."

"It'll soon be my home. Mr. Jameson said they're going to have you arrested for impersonating a noble and stealing charges. Once you're on your way to Australia or Timbuktu, I'm seeking Julia's hand." He turned to leave.

"Wait." She ran forward to stop him.

He turned and lifted a haughty brow. "I don't answer to you as you're no longer part of this family. I will be the man in charge once I get the marquess's permission to marry Julia."

She schooled her features and clasped her hands in front of her. "How did you know to go to Chelmsford?"

With a smirk, he regarded her as if she were a pile of manure. "Mr. Jameson. He told me he had good information that your parents were married there years after your birth. He needed me as a member of the family to come forward. And I was only too happy to help," he sneered.

This morning on their way back to London, she'd told Michael what the Chelmsford vicar had shared about Rupert and a Marquess of McCalpin representative visiting and examining the marriage registry. Michael had been adamant that he hadn't sent anyone to the church.

"Of course, when I discovered the truth, I couldn't let your deception continue." With a final smug smile, he turned and left her alone.

Her heart started to pound and a trickle of sweat slowly slid down her back. Someone was out to destroy her.

A lighthearted smile pulled at McCalpin's lips as he walked up the steps of Langham Hall. He'd chosen well. March would be an excellent partner as they traversed through all of life's joys and perils. Miraculously, confiding his secret, that black mark he carried with him every hour, lightened his burden. It only reaffirmed his decision.

Last night when she'd come to him, she'd been frantic for comfort. Holding her in his arms and making love to her had been perfect. He'd never let her suffer the taunts or the ridicule that society loved to bestow on people, women in particular, who found themselves lambs at the slaughter.

He'd protected himself for so long, it was second nature to protect her.

William approached with a deliberate step and a stern countenance. His brother could be a menacing sight when riled. "McCalpin, I need you to come to the study. There are some disturbing things that demand your attention at once."

McCalpin followed William into their father's study and closed the door. At the burl maple table in the center of the room sat their sister, Emma, with her husband, Somerton, who handled McCalpin's personal investments.

Unease pushed aside all of his good humor when he saw the look of fury on his sister's face. Her straight shoulders and the haughty tilt of her head foretold something truly serious was afoot. The fact that his solicitor Russell and the bookkeeper, Jameson, were present didn't help matters.

He sat at the head of the table, and William took the seat to the right of him. The tension in the room was palatable. Somerton clenched a document in his fist.

"Did someone die?" A stony silence met McCalpin's attempt at humor.

William took a deep breath, picked up a document, then set it before him. "This is a letter sent to Mr. Rupert Lawson from you demanding he stay off Lord Lawson's property during the annual Leyton hunt. Note that the date is after the first time you met with March."

His brother had his attention now. He'd never sent any correspondence to March's poor excuse of a cousin. "Go on," he demanded.

William placed another document in front of him. "This is a directive from you to have three thousand pounds withdrawn from McCalpin Manor's household account and deposited directly into an account under March's name at Fleming's Bank. It was delivered to Emma's bank by mistake."

His heart pounded with a force strong enough to break through his ribs—and lay the carnage before everyone in the room. He examined the document. Perfectly centered on the bottom of the page was March's signature of his name.

Somerton cleared his throat, then slid another document to him. "This is a request from you to withdraw twenty-five thousand pounds from your investments and deposit it into March's account also."

The regret on his brother-in-law's face pierced him like a stab of a stiletto. McCalpin held his body taut as the pain coursed through every inch of his body. This was worse than a stab—a more apt description was a gutting. He wouldn't believe she'd betray him—not like that. If true, then his carefully crafted persona of an intelligent lord who handled his estate matters with aplomb would crash to the ground.

"I didn't proceed with the transaction." The empathy in Somerton's voice was unmistakable. "I told Emma of it last night. That's why we're here."

Emma's cheeks were crimson. "I don't believe any of this. I know this woman. She wouldn't steal. She corrected discrepancies in my own books."

William pursed his lips. "Could that have been a ploy to gain your allegiance so these transactions wouldn't be questioned?"

Emma snorted. "Don't be ridiculous."

"I'm not, Emma," William answered. "But I'm also not blind." He turned to McCalpin and lowered his voice. "There's more."

"There must be an explanation." *God, was that his voice?* The weak protest barely escaped.

"My lord, Jameson was the one who discovered all these shenanigans." Russell pointed at his bookkeeper. "He offered a reward to Rupert Lawson if he could find your seal. It was in her desk with the stationary she used to embezzle from you. Jameson went through the previous viscount's legal papers and letters. That's where he found the marriage certificate. Lawson offered to verify its accuracy by traveling to Chelmsford."

He fought through the fog that had descended into his brain. How could March have done this? His shook his head to clear the miasma that was slowly choking him.

Russell turned his attention to Emma. "Lady Somerton, we believe it's all part of her plan. She's done these things to gain Lord McCalpin's trust—"

"You're wrong," Emma bit out as she stood and faced McCalpin. The flash of her green eyes demanded his full attention. "Do you hear what they're saying?"

The anguish in her plea caused her husband to stand abruptly. "Enough! You're either going to have to calm down or we're leaving." Somerton captured her gaze. "This isn't good for you or the baby," he whispered.

The tenderness in his voice and the way Somerton searched Emma's face bespoke a love true and strong, unbreakable in their troth together. The image seared McCalpin's heart. This morning, he was so certain he shared that same fidelity with March.

After all the revelations, how could he? He didn't want to believe the evidence, but in black and white it lay before him. He clenched his fists underneath the table to keep from roaring at the pain.

Jameson approached with an open account book. "Sir, these are the accounts at McCalpin Manor. I've a detailed description of each suspect transaction." He placed the book in front of him and pointed at a page. "See here—"

McCalpin held up his hand to stop the bookkeeper. He'd enough torture in the last few minutes to last his entire lifetime. "I'm aware of it. Mr. Russell and Mr. Jameson, thank you for your efforts. Mr. Russell, try to find the funds. Hire a private investigator. I prefer Mr. Macalester. He's discreet and works fast."

"Should we tell the duke?" Russell asked.

"Not yet," Michael said.

Russell nodded and gathered his belongings.

How would he ever be able to explain it while keeping up the façade that he was in control of the estates? With an angry swipe, he brushed away a trickle of sweat that trailed down the side of his face. The day Mrs. Ivers had predicated long ago had finally come to fruition. His father might reevaluate his confidence in his heir's abilities. A suffocating weight of shame smothered him.

Jameson slipped a piece of paper in front of him.

"My lord, these are the funds Miss Lawson has taken from the trust fund. It totals one thousand one hundred and twenty-three pounds and seventeen shillings. Since she's illegitimate, her fortune is to be split between her siblings."

McCalpin lifted his lip in a sneer. "I've no need for the dissertation, Mr. Jameson. I'm aware of Miss Lawson's changed circumstances."

"Very well, my lord." Jameson apologetically nodded.

He didn't spare a glance at Russell or Jameson as they left. He picked up the tally of March's embezzlement and put it aside. How could she have duped him in such a manner? Yet, he couldn't believe—couldn't fathom such a betrayal.

William quirked an eyebrow. "How do you know about the books? I just became aware of them today."

He held William's gaze while schooling his features into a proper haughty ducal heir expression. He was ready for whatever lectures or scathing comments his brother might share. "March showed them to me. She went through the books."

"All of them?" Incredulous, William voice trailed to a whisper.

"All of them," he replied.

Emma released a sigh. "That proves my point."

Somerton placed his hand over hers. "Macalester's a good man. He'll discover where the funds are." He released a breath. "McCalpin, it's possible the monies will leave England. Miss Lawson's Mr. Hart is traveling to the States and may settle there. Bennett told us earlier this morning. While you were out yesterday, Hart came to visit the Lawson siblings." Somerton stole a glance at Emma. "How are you?"

She nodded. "I'm fine. Go ahead and tell them the rest of it."

Somerton placed his arm around her shoulders and drew her close. "The fellow inherited the majority of Erlington's wool mills in the States. He's getting ready to set sail later this week. If it was March, she may have given him the missing funds to hide over there."

Emma gently batted Somerton in the chest. "Nick, that's beyond ridiculous. Why would she do that? Her family is here."

"My love, I'm just trying to follow the money," Somerton offered.

"That's the point, Emma," William whispered. "To protect her family from bearing any of the guilt or shame when it's discovered what she's done. It makes perfect sense."

"Let's not convict her without at least hearing from her directly," Emma pleaded.

McCalpin's mind raced while his gut twisted. March couldn't have done this, but the facts were staring him in the face. Now nothing made sense.

Her constant worry over money and the way she took the opportunity to get close to him at every turn were clear warning signs. She'd never even looked at another gentleman at all those balls she'd attended. Had her wayward trip to Chelmsford been part of her plan? When she'd come to his room, he'd seduced her ensuring he'd have no recourse but to marry her, thus absolving her of all wrongdoing.

His heart clenched and demanded he look deeper. She'd been so loving and vulnerable last night when he took her in his arms. All along, she'd never asked for anything for herself. It was always for her brother and sisters.

His old familiar enemy, humiliation, crowded his thoughts and took command. He had no idea how to rectify the damage. Hell, he didn't even know who to blame or what to think.

Emma broke away from Somerton's embrace and stood before him. She placed her hand on his arm. "Mc-Calpin, she'd never do anything to hurt you. She loves you. Can't you see it?"

His conscience demanded he focus on his duty. He could only see the wiles March had used to gain his trust, and he'd freely given it to her.

William cleared his throat. "You need to think this through, McCalpin."

"Will, what are you doing?" Emma's voice trembled with barely held outrage. "Since she and McCalpin started spending time together, you've never cared for her."

William narrowed his gaze to hers. "Are you suggesting I'm jealous of her?"

"Not jealous." Emma sighed. "That you're not needed anymore. Perhaps ignored."

"Must I spell it out for everyone? Think of everything that's happened since that family has come into our lives." William's outrage grew in volume. "Embezzling from trust funds, household accounts, and investments funds? Think of the scandal when Lawson announced March was a bast—"

The Langham butler, Pitts, entered without knocking. "Lord McCalpin, Miss Lawson has arrived."

March rushed in like a fierce wind of her namesake. "Michael, I have news—" She came to an abrupt halt and glanced around the room. "Hello, everyone. What's wrong?"

McCalpin took a deep breath and prepared for the worst. He had to know the truth. Slowly, he stood and faced her. "I need you to answer a question for me." Without betraying any of the anguish that tore up his insides, he continued, "Have you used my seal for anything after I told you not to?"

She tilted her head and regarded him. "No."

"Think carefully," he cautioned. He prayed she had the answers to prove her innocence to William and truthfully to him.

"I said no. Why do you ask?"

He exhaled his last bit of hope. He picked up the letter to Lawson. "Did you write this?"

March's brow drew together. She approached silently and took the letter from his grasp. She lifted her gaze from the paper. "Yes, but I can explain—"

He whipped out the withdrawal demands from the household account and his investments, then handed it to her. "Are those your signatures of my name?"

The color leeched from her face.

"It's an easy question to answer. Did you sign these? Yes or no?" he clipped.

"Michael, you're scaring me," she whispered as she searched his face. She turned her attention to the documents and swallowed.

The slight movement in her long elegant neck told him everything.

She'd done it.

He failed to brace himself as a chain reaction exploded inside. His lungs quit working, and he couldn't move—couldn't process a thought. As if in a free fall when the ground finally greets you in one crashing blow, his heart shattered. For an eternity, he couldn't catch his breath.

Finally, his body protested, and he inhaled. The effort did little to suppress the need to pound his fist through the wall.

"These are my practice sheets, but I didn't write the directives to have those funds withdrawn." Her gaze captured his, and her eyes implored him to believe her lies. "I can explain. Rupert stole these sheets and the seal from my desk—"

"How convenient," Michael whispered to her. In a louder voice, he announced to the others, "I'd appreciate the courtesy if you'd allow me a private conversation with Miss Lawson." His eyes never left hers as his siblings and Somerton exited.

What a fool. He'd allowed a beautiful but beguiling wolf under the guise of a simple farmer to devour his heart and soul all the while pretending to guard the proverbial sheep. The startling truth almost knocked his knees out from underneath him.

He'd given her the pistol and the powder to blow his entire world asunder. One word from her about his failings, and he was ruined.

# Chapter Twenty-One

M arch's pulse pounded in a frantic rhythm as Michael's whisper accosted her. When the door clicked, he pivoted and stalked to a small buffet table. He poured two fingers of brandy in a glass and downed it one swallow. As if an afterthought, he turned and lifted the glass in the air as if offering her one. She shook her head once. Without a word, he returned his attention to refilling his glass.

Wary, she never once took her gaze from his backside. This was a side of Michael she'd never seen—a man brimming with loathing and ready to explode in an anger she didn't quite understand.

"What's happened? Why are you so angry?" Her muffled voice sounded hollow to her ears. She hadn't felt this terrified since her parents had died, and she alone had carried the responsibility for her siblings.

Gently, he placed his glass on the table and slowly turned to her. "I've been given information that leads me to believe that the woman I asked to share my life is *stealing* from me." With his broad shoulders and dark visage, he slowly stalked toward her like a panther ready to annihilate her with a single bite.

"Wouldn't you agree that makes an excellent reason to be angry?" His subdued voice held a wrath that was terrifying.

"Only if it were true," she whispered. "What makes you think I've done that?"

"Your own words." He stood before her and his blue eyes seemed to radiate fire.

"You didn't let me finish," she protested.

"How Lawson is the one behind all of this?" He took a step closer, and she took a step back in retreat. "Come now, I wasn't born last night."

"Today I was working at Lawson Court hoping it'd clear my mind. When I passed by Bennett's desk, I realized I hadn't given you back your seal. When I opened it, everything was gone." She wouldn't let him get a word in edgewise as she had to make him see reason. "Rupert was there and informed me someone from your solicitor's office asked him to clean out the desk and bring it to him. That same person, a Mr. Jameson, told Rupert to go to Chelmsford and look at the marriage register."

"Jameson informed me of those facts today." He lifted one eyebrow and regarded her. "After our first meeting, you used my seal after I told you to bring it back to me."

She started to pace in an effort to escape the cold desperation that had invaded her body. "I was desperate to keep Rupert from humiliating Faith with the foxtail. I just acted." She forced herself to stop. "I'm sorry. I shouldn't have done it, but I didn't steal from you. Please, you have to believe me."

"Why didn't you bring the seal to me?" Like a vise, the slow cadence of his baritone voice wrapped itself around her heart and squeezed.

She drew a painful breath frantic for some relief from this paralyzing unease. "I didn't think of the ramifications. I'm sorry."

"March, every withdrawal instructed the funds be deposited into your new account at Fleming's Bank." He rubbed his hand down his face. "By coincidence, you find a culprit who's stealing five thousand pounds from my accounts. Moreover, it just happened to be last night. Now, I have to ask—how did you know what accounts had errors? There's no conceivable way you could have examined every account book at McCalpin Manor."

"Fleming's? I've never stepped foot in that establishment. I don't bank anywhere else but at Emma's." Her pulse raced, and she grew lightheaded. "I told you last night. I'm quick with numbers."

"Undoubtedly, a trait that served you well in dealing with an idiot like me," he whispered.

"Don't you dare say that about yourself." She took a step toward him to offer comfort and reassurance that the horrible things he repeated weren't true. He didn't give her the chance as he turned abruptly and walked to the fire.

He bent his head and clasped his hands behind his back.

"I've only taken money from the trust account I thought was mine. The exact amount is one thousand one hundred and twenty-seven pounds—"

"And seventeen shillings," he finished for her. "But that's just a small part of it, isn't it?"

"Michael?" Her whisper turned into a plea, and she didn't care. She'd get down on her hands and knees and beg him to listen to her. She had to make him understand that she would never do such vile things—not to him or anyone else for that matter.

"Why, March?" He didn't turn from his study of the fire. "You could have had jewels, gowns, carriages, a generous allowance, not to mention a rare position in society that women around the continent would die for. You would have been the Duchess of Langham someday."

His solemn words cut her in two. He actually believed she'd stolen from him. "Do you think I care for any of that except being your wife?"

"Last night, I didn't. But today?" He shook his head. "Today, I don't know what to believe." He finally turned and stared at her. "Did none of this"—he waved his hand between them—"mean anything to you? Did last night mean nothing but a way to force me to marry you so you wouldn't get caught?"

"What are you saying?" She could barely speak. His words were so demeaning she wondered if she could withstand the assault. "Did you look in your household account book to see what I'd written?"

"Why? Will I find more of the same stealing and embezzling that we didn't cover last night?"

"You should read it," she whispered.

"I'm finished with that nonsense," he murmured.

He turned away, and her heart sank as if tied to an anchor seeking the ocean's bottom. She closed her eyes and hoped she wouldn't fall into a heap. This morning, she'd written him a note, a very personal note, one that described her complete commitment and love for him.

The door swept open, and the Duke of Langham appeared. While most men simply entered a room, he commanded it. The duke locked the door behind him.

"What is going on?" The duke's gaze darted from Michael's to hers.

Immediately, March executed a proper curtsy. "Your Grace."

Michael acknowledged his father with a dip of his head but didn't say a word. Immediately, his face turned into a haughty mask, one she'd seen repeatedly worn by the nobility that had to deal with undesirables like herself.

Without pause, the duke walked to his desk and settled into the massive chair. How a man so large could move so quietly and gracefully had to be inborn. Once he settled and straightened the documents on his desk, he directed his attention to Michael. "Explain to me how this happened."

Michael lifted a brow and regarded March. His unwavering gaze full of disdain penetrated hers. "Perhaps Miss Lawson might be able shed some light on the errors."

"Errors?" The duke's voice was even, but the lethal sharpness of a steel sword underscored the word. "These aren't simple errors, McCalpin. This is an uncontrollable bleeding from the estates, one you should have caught immediately. Not only is there damage to McCalpin Manor, but Falmont is impacted. Severin and Merritt met me after my last appointment and are in the library with every account book. As we speak, they're combing through every account and every entry trying to find out exactly what happened. The auditor, Mr. Wilburton, is on his way to join them. No one will rest until we determine the actual amounts stolen and who did it."

The duke waited for a response. When none was forthcoming, he started to drum the fingers of one hand on his desk. The rhythm began slowly, but as the silence grew between the three of them, the movement quickened until finally, the duke slapped his hand on the desk.

"Is there something I'm missing?" The duke stared at Michael, whose attention was devoted to the fireplace.

Lost in another world, he didn't answer his father. The duke exhaled and directed his attention to her. "March, you've reviewed the books. Can you shed any light on this?"

She stole a glance at Michael. The comfort and affection she'd experienced in his arms last night was a distant dream. A trickle of sweat meandered down the side of his face. His olive-toned skin had faded into a pasty pallor that marked his handsome face with irrefutable pain. He clenched his fists so tightly that the white of his knuckles was visible across the room. He was completely unraveling before her into someone she didn't recognize.

What she'd remember for the rest of her life was how motionless he stood. Without taking a breath, he appeared frozen, ready to crack into a thousand pieces.

Not only was she being destroyed, but the man she loved and had thought she'd spend her life with suffered from her annihilation, too. Second by second, the ugliness of her previous embezzlement actions and the accusations of today were eradicating the strong, resolute man she had come to know during her stay in London.

Michael might not love her, but she loved him and she loved her family. Her love had to be strong enough for all of them. She was utterly ruined. Yet, Michael would preserve her family's reputation and protect them from the taint of her illegitimacy and her embezzlement of her family's money. He would ensure that none of her filth soiled her siblings. She had to believe that simple truth. Otherwise, there was nothing.

In that singular moment, she only had one choice. She had to release him from his promise to marry her. She had to preserve the integrity of her family, while protecting her sisters' chances for finding a suitable match for marriage. As important, she had to protect Michael's chance for happiness.

She straightened her shoulders and tilted her chin. She had to let him go. Otherwise, society would mock him if they believed she'd used him. His greatest fear he'd disappoint his father would come to fruition.

With what little armor of self-preservation she possessed, she captured the duke's gaze. His blue eyes had darkened to the color of the sky during a pounding thunderstorm.

"The solicitor and bookkeeper have evidence that I'm the guilty party," she announced. Surprisingly, she didn't tremble when she uttered the words, even though it was as if she'd announced her own death sentence.

"And are you?" the duke asked.

Michael's gaze flew to hers. The poignant flash of betrayal in the depth of his lovely blue eyes nearly leveled her. Soon, it blazed into a fire of hatred. She locked her knees so she wouldn't fall into a pile of ashes.

To escape the inferno that threatened, she turned her attention to the duke.

"Tell me. Are you the one who stole those monies?" The duke's eerily quiet voice permeated the room. The soft words hit her with the force of a cannon, and she immediately started to shake.

Michael straightened his shoulders and walked to the side of his father's desk. Together, side by side, the power emanating from both could have blown London Tower into a rock rubble. If she had any chance to withstand such a force, she could focus only on the duke. One glance at Michael would render her heart and her very soul in two.

"I'm guilty of many things, Your Grace." *For one, loving your son. Two, stealing money from an account I believed was mine. Three, for being a bastard.* "But I didn't steal anything from Lord McCalpin or the duchy."

"How did you even know where the records were?" The duke fired the question to her.

"I went through them last night at McCalpin Manor." Her voice didn't waiver at the admission. They all knew last night that she'd stayed with Michael at his estate without a suitable chaperone.

"I thought to do a little work while at McCalpin Manor. I brought them from London when I went to Chelmsford to retrieve March," Michael answered, his voice distant. "She's also been to McCalpin House with me. Alone," he added.

It was another stab to her heart. Like Cesar, she was suffering through her own ides of March. *How appropriate.*

The look of astonishment on the duke's face pierced her confidence.

Tears welled in her eyes, but she refused to let them fall. Not now. She would collapse into nothing later.

The duke furrowed his brow in disbelief. For a moment, she wanted to cry out and deny everything again. She finally found the courage to chance a glance at Michael, but thankfully, he had bowed his head.

The duke exhaled. "March, do you know where the monies are?

"There's eight hundred and fifty-eight pounds in my account at E. Cavensham Commerce. I'll have the amount sent to Lord McCalpin immediately."

"And the rest?" the duke asked.

"I have no idea, Your Grace." It was the only truth she

possessed. She wasn't the one stealing from McCalpin, nor did she know where the missing money was.

A grim silence took possession of the room, broken only by the intermittent crumple of logs under the blazing flames. Fitting, since her life had just collapsed into the fires of Hell.

"March, with what was discovered in Chelmsford and at Lawson Court, your cousin's claims have standing." The duke's voice softened. "Is there anything else you can share that will help clear up this matter?"

The duke thumbed through Michael's household account book. She held her breath. Inside, her love note contained the promise she'd never hurt or divulge Michael's secret.

In a subtle movement, Michael stiffened as if preparing for an onslaught of questions. Thankfully, the duke pushed the journal away from his reach.

The duke cleared his throat. "McCalpin, you make the decision as to what shall happen next."

She couldn't breathe or swallow as she waited for Michael to refute her denial.

The silence stretched into years as she waited for his next words.

"Under the circumstances, I think it best for all if Miss Lawson returns to Lawson Court until we have more information." The ice in McCalpin's veins melted enough that he could return his gaze to March. The sharpness of his words seemed to have impaled her. She stumbled backward with her eyes wide.

There was little else he could do. His father had his household account book in front of him. At this point, he couldn't think or barely breathe with her so close. It would be so easy to accept her word, but he had to find the truth for himself. He was responsible for the marquessate, and one day he'd be responsible for the duchy and all the people who worked for the Duke of Langham.

For his own sanity, it became paramount that he remove March from the library. He took her by the elbow and ushered her to the door.

When they reached it, she gracefully turned to face him. The movement forced him to release her arm.

"Why are you doing this to me?" The agony in her whisper nearly brought him to his knees. "Why are you sending me away? I can help you."

"It's the best solution for now. You can't be involved in the investigation." Every second that she stared at him made his mind more muddled. "You need distance from this house and London. My solicitor, his bookkeeper, and my brother believe you're the guilty party."

"You also believe me guilty." Her honeyed alto voice normally soothed, but not now.

"March, I don't want to believe it." He stepped closer to ensure his father couldn't overhear them. "I don't know how to prove your innocence."

"I can help you." Her shallow breath indicated her stress.

*Was it a lie?* She'd lied to him before. She'd used his seal and sent a letter under his signature after he'd instructed her not to.

He closed his eyes in a silent prayer that this was all a bad dream. "It's best if you go now. I must have time to resolve this. You above all others know I have a duty to the title, duty to my family, and a duty to the estates and all the people whose livelihoods depend upon the Langham duchy. Because of those responsibilities, sometimes hard decisions are required."

When his gaze returned to hers, he was the one to stumble backward. The revulsion in her normally warm eyes stunned him.

"You're choosing duty over me." Her words were a bitter accusation. "My lord, I've *told* you how to find the thief."

Suddenly, guilt fell upon him as if he'd been the one to steal and lie. Perhaps he had by holding everyone's high regard under false pretenses. The simple truth? He'd stolen March's newfound security.

Nausea threatened to overtake him. He had no idea how to untangle them from this mess.

Before March left Michael and her shattered heart in London forever, she had to secure one more promise. "Please, my family can't suffer because of this," she whispered with as much dignity as she could muster. "Allow me to tell them."

He stared at the floor.

"Promise me they'll not suffer," she repeated more forcefully than before. She'd not leave without his agreement.

Without looking at her, he nodded.

"I'll be gone within the hour." Without a glance back, she left the study and the life she'd dreamed of as she toiled for years on the estate. Why did she think she deserved any happiness?

Just as the Leyton vicar had warned, it made little difference whether it was an apple or a necklace. She was as soiled and dirty as if she'd actually taken the missing five thousand pounds from the Langham and McCalpin estates. She'd stolen property from her family through a trust that wasn't hers, and it was within the Langham family domain.

When she'd taken those funds by fraudulently signing Michael's name, she'd taken the first step into her own damnation. Now she had to find her siblings and tell them of her exile and the reasons why. Only afterward, when she walked the grounds of Lawson Court, could she silently descend the rest of the way to meet the devil. Perhaps then, she'd be able to shed the cold that had invaded her veins.

Acting as if nothing were amiss, she walked down the hall with her head held high. Inside, gossamer-thin pieces of her heart broke apart and floated away—lost forever.

After March had silently left his father's study, McCalpin spoke with him about hiring Macalester to find the remaining stolen monies. Both agreed such an independent party was necessary. After taking his leave, he roamed Langham Hall, hoping that March would find him and privately explain her actions. She'd explained quite a bit earlier, but still a biting nag wouldn't quiet and relentlessly pounded his head. Why would she use his seal to steal his money? He'd taken care of her family without exception. Why did she need the money?

When she'd left the room, he'd retrieved his household accounts journal and his relief had surged in waves. The land stewards and the auditor would not discover the true extent of his idiocy—at least not today. More importantly, his father, the invincible Duke of Langham, wouldn't have to decide whether his heir was unworthy to bear the title of Marquess of McCalpin and all its responsibilities.

That was only part of his burden. Today his heart had crashed as if hurled from the heavens to the cold ground. Two hours had passed when Pitts informed him that, as he had demanded, March had left the premises after she'd spoken to her siblings.

Numb, he found himself back at McCalpin House with a glass of brandy, trying to soothe the pain drumming through his head. If he had any luck, the spirit would take control of his senses and tamp down the continual ache in his chest.

"My lord?" Buxton had silently entered the study. "Lord Lawson is here to see you."

McCalpin stood quickly. Since March had left London, the first hint of relief swelled within his chest. Bennett would share his sister's conversation and her current mood.

The young viscount stood resolutely in the doorway. His big green eyes and piercing gaze belied a wisdom that not many adult men possessed.

"Come in, Lawson," McCalpin coaxed. He approached the young lord and extended his hand. Bennett tentatively reached for it, and after a firm shake, dropped it as if it were scalding hot.

"McCalpin—" The boy immediately turned red as his voice broke into a squeak that foretold his coming passage to adulthood. He swallowed, then started again. "I'd like to discuss my sisters."

McCalpin didn't blink. Bennett's request for such a conversation about all three Lawson sisters was unexpected. He'd fully anticipated that the boy would launch into a one-sided conversation about March. "Of course. Come sit by the fire."

Bennett nodded and proceeded to take a seat in the chair next to McCalpin's. With a deep breath, the young lordling stoically commenced, "After my eldest sister left Langham Hall, I discussed our living arrangements with Faith and Julia. We believe it best for all that we take up residence at our family townhouse as soon as possible. Perhaps you would hire an appropriate chaperone for my sisters. Under the circumstances, it's best I return to Lawson Court with my eldest sister. I plan on leaving tomorrow."

McCalpin choked on the last swallow of brandy as the shock of what Bennett was asking sunk in. Finally, he recovered the ability to talk. "I thought you were comfortable at Langham Hall. Have you discussed this with March?"

"She really has no standing in this discussion, does she? When she was forced to leave Langham Hall, I took over the role as head of the family." Bennett raised one eyebrow and regarded him. "I can't leave her alone." The boy swallowed, and fear flashed briefly in his eyes. It was the first sign of weakness since he entered.

"Bennett, there's no cause to worry. I won't allow anything or anyone to harm her." McCalpin leaned close to the boy. "She'd want you to stay here and continue your studies."

"With all due respect, my lord, I'm the only man she can rely on now." The boy stared into his eyes, but the fear was still present. "She told Faith and Julia that Rupert said you were going to charge her with stealing." The boy sniffed as he was close to tears. "I'll not allow her to suffer any further humiliation. You can have my money to pay for the missing funds. Nor will I allow her to suffer the constant threat of Rupert's taunts or live by herself. She needs someone with her."

"I have no plans to charge your sister with theft or harm her in anyway." She'd done enough harm to both of them to last their lives. His gaze drifted to the window. How had something so perfect turned into a lie, one that cut him to the very bone. He exhaled, but the pain refused to leave him. "Your sister can handle herself."

"She won't have enough to eat. She has no money. She

told us that she's repaying all the missing money including the amount she borrowed from the trust fund. She plans to find full-time employment in Leyton." By now, the boy was practically frantic. "Julia is beside herself in grief. She can't stop pacing the length of her bedroom. She keeps asking Faith who will take care of March. Poor Faith doesn't have an answer, but I do." He stood defiantly and declared, "I will."

He gripped the boy by one shoulder and looked directly in his eyes. Bennett's love for his sister reminded him of his love for Emma. The boy's fear that something evil would befall March was very real. McCalpin's own doubts and worry started to break free in his chest.

"I know it's hard to believe now, but I care for your sister and would never allow her to suffer or be hurt. You and your family are under my protection and that includes March. Understand?" He squeezed the boy's shoulder once more. "If it'll ease your worry, I'll go see her tomorrow."

Bennett swallowed, and his Adam's apple bobbed into prominence. The boy nodded and stood. "Thank you, but you should know that I don't approve of what you've done. She'd never steal, and she's never cheated anyone. I've known her my entire life. She's the most honorable person I've ever met." He wiped his check to hide the evidence of his emotion. "Please see about employing a chaperone. If you don't, I'll find a solicitor to help me. Imagine the headline in *The Midnight Cryer* the next day. 'The young Lord Lawson must seek his own legal counsel to break free from the tyranny of the Marquess of McCalpin, who seeks retribution at all costs.'"

Stunned, he simply stared.

"The duke has taught me strategy in our chess matches," Bennett offered with one brow lifted. "I've discovered tactics required to play the game can be used to pursue other interests."

His father was having marvelous success with the little rogue. Even though his threat was unorthodox, it proved the boy accepted his family as a responsibility and would protect them by all means necessary.

"I'll consider your request for the chaperone." There was no way in hell he'd let the Lawson family out of his sight. Not after what had happened over the last several days. The vultures of the *ton* would slaughter Bennett's sisters with their cuts and sharp retorts if not accompanied by either his mother or himself personally.

"Thank you. I mustn't tarry any longer. I have a mathematics lesson in a half-hour." Without a customary handshake, Bennett quietly exited McCalpin's study. His disappointment in his guardian readily apparent for both of them to see as his eyes clouded with worry.

At the word "mathematics," McCalpin's heart had clenched tight as a fist. What if she didn't steal the money, but he couldn't prove it? It would ruin her life. The thought spiraled him into a near panic. How would he ever discover the truth? He couldn't even add a column of numbers together, let alone discover an embezzler within his own employ.

Whatever moral high ground he stood upon was fast eroding in a storm of doubts.

# Chapter Twenty-Two

The Langham footman quickly deposited March's trunks and bags inside Lawson Court. Soon thereafter, the carriage, emblazoned with the Duke of Langham's crest, exited the drive. Its quick speed was a sore reminder of her banishment from Michael and her family. The heaviness she'd fought on the way home descended with a fervor that even Hercules couldn't lift. The life she'd dreamed of as she'd toiled the fields evaporated before her eyes.

Inside the familiar entry, she leaned against the door of the home she'd known all her life and closed her eyes. One tear escaped, followed by another, then another. She'd never realized how alone she was until she came home. She had no one.

"My miss, what's happened?" A masculine voice followed by a sure step greeted her. Her heart fluttered at the welcome sound. She opened her eyes to find her darling Hart before her. He reached out with a gentle hand and brushed away one renegade tear.

"I'd heard you were in London yesterday." She pushed away from the door and straightened her shoulders.

"He's gone." Hart's voice cracked, but he presented a small smile. "Erlington's not suffering anymore."

"I'm so sorry," she whispered. Hart opened his arms and, without hesitation, she flew into his embrace, intending to give comfort, but like the thief she truly was, she took every morsel offered.

"Thank you." He pulled away and tucked an unruly lock of hair behind her ear. "Have you eaten?"

She shook her head.

Without hesitating, he escorted her to the modest but comfortable sitting room decorated in bold burgundy and navy, the favored colors of the viscountcy. Mrs. Oliver stood guard and welcomed her with her own hug before leaving and returning with a tray.

Everything March tasted reminded her of paste, so she concentrated on her tea. Soon Hart had her on the sofa in front of a blazing fire.

"Should we be wasting firewood like this? Just for the two of us?" God, she despised the constant worry over funds for the estate. Now with her new status as a social outcast and displaced from her old life, it became all the more critical to worry over money. She didn't have the security her father had set aside for her, nor did she have access to the estate funds. What little food she ate twisted into a ball and bounced in her stomach. She didn't own one shilling to her name. The only thing of value she possessed was her mother's earrings.

"Tonight, let's not worry about such trivial matters," Hart coaxed. "Tell me what happened in London."

Hart's face was so earnest in his wish to share her troubles, she couldn't refuse him. Perhaps if she told him the horror Rupert had inflicted when he confronted her at the ball, her old friend might have some insight why her father hadn't provided any money for her.

"What didn't happen in London?" She bent her head until her chin rested on her chest. "Several days ago, we were attending a ball, and Julia's suitor asked if he could visit and discuss his intentions to marry her."

He smiled. "You mean the perfectly estimable Lord Queensgrace?"

She nodded. "Perfect" wasn't the description she'd use, but she continued with her tale. "Rupert confronted me in a ballroom full of people and announced I was a bastard. He said he found proof in Chelmsford." The horror of that night still gave her nightmares. She'd never forget the guests watching, almost thirsting for her annihilation. "I went to Chelmsford the next day, and what he said was true. I saw it with my own eyes. My parents were married five years after I was born."

Hart's look of horror quickly transformed into doubt. "That's preposterous. Your parents were married when I went to work for your father."

"How do you know?" The humiliating pain had never left her side since she found out the truth at the vicarage—except when she was with Michael. "I saw the marriage registry myself."

He opened his mouth to refute her charge, but she wouldn't let him.

"I am a bastard." He shook his head, but she raised her hand to stop the denial. "But what I don't understand is why would my father leave me money as his legal heir? I can't fathom why he'd purposely hurt me."

"Oh, sweetheart." Hart took her in his arms and squeezed. "Your mother and father were married. She always wore her ring. It was even a cause of conversation when we were over in the States. Women had never seen the color of gold your mother wore. Remember the red tint? Copper had been mixed with the gold?"

She nodded in his arms. "Perhaps it served as a ruse to hide their true relationship. She wore it to protect father's career."

"I doubt that," he whispered. "Your mother had the kindest heart and loved your father. However, she would have never jeopardized your future happiness by having you out of wedlock. Neither would your father."

Hart's warmth and embrace was a temporary haven from the ugliness she'd experienced over the last three days. He'd surely be disgusted when he heard the rest.

"There's more." She tried to swallow the pain that was choking her. "I've done the unthinkable." She pulled away from the security he offered and walked to the fireplace. By rote, she stirred the embers as she waited for the hiss of the fire to grow. "I started to embezzle from my trust account about three months ago. I had Mr. Garwyn copy the Marquess of McCalpin seal. Then I studied the first letter McCalpin sent me. I practiced until I had mastered his penmanship and his signature. I started to direct funds to be deposited into my account at E. Cavensham Commerce."

Hart shook his head. "I don't understand."

"Since I'm illegitimate, the funds I've taken from my trust aren't mine. I've stolen from my siblings, and Michael and the duke think I've stolen from them."

She didn't know how to explain it. How her life of struggle had turned into something magical, then without any warning, she'd lost everything.

"Father entrusted the estate monies to Lord Burns, who in his old age completely forgot about his responsibilities to us. His solicitors didn't care enough to check on our welfare. The amounts he sent dwindled to nothing.

When he died, I contacted Lord McCalpin, but I didn't hear from him. Therefore, I took matters into my hands. I was careful. The requests started out small. But it wasn't enough after the massive damage we suffered this winter, so I directed one thousand pounds be deposited."

"Oh, March." His whisper lashed at every speck of her self-control.

She tipped her chin as she regarded him. "I was desperate. Besides, it's my money." She mockingly corrected herself. "At least, I thought it was my money. Once the marquess discovered my deception, that's when he became involved and sought guardianship over the estate and the family. He told me I never had to worry again. He'd take care of things."

"He didn't shy away from the responsibility. He was the reason I could leave you and take my place with Erlington. What happened next?" Hart coaxed.

Until she tried to utter the words, she hadn't truly grasped how difficult it would be. She tilted her head at the ceiling in an effort to harness the strength to confide the rest. "When I went to Chelmsford, Michael followed and took me back to his estate at McCalpin Manor. It was late and I was distraught . . ."

When her gaze met his, she could see fire in his eyes. "What happened?"

She swallowed and forced herself to continue, though her throat protested as if it'd been skinned raw. Heat rose until her cheeks felt ablaze and her eyes burned. "He asked me to marry him, and at first I agreed." Hot tears streamed down her inflamed cheeks. The debilitating pain mimicked a hot poker piercing her chest. She gasped, but made herself continue. "I went to his room"— she closed her eyes to gather what little strength she could muster to finish—"to make certain he understood who I really was. I wanted him to realize that as a bastard and with the horrible accusations that Rupert had announced in public, I'd bring shame to him and my siblings. I couldn't live with that."

"Sweetheart, if anyone can withstand that type of scandal, it's a ducal heir. No one second-guesses them."

"No, Hart. You see, it's worse than that. Rupert proclaimed in front of everyone that I was not only a bastard, but a thief." Her voice weakened as the next words would wound her friend. "He said I harbored a known sodomite at Bennett's estate."

With a loud exhalation, Hart ran his hand through his hair. "My God, you suffered because of me—"

"*No.*" She held up her hand to stop him from speaking. "Don't you dare say that. If it hadn't been for you, we'd have been dead or worse—in a poor house or begging on the street. No one wanted or cared for us, but you did. You stayed with us. You allowed us to be a family."

Hart came to her and took both of her hands in his. "Go on."

"I thought about how Rupert's accusations would hurt you and my family. He'd hurt Michael." She smoothed her gown to keep her hands from shaking. "I love him too much to see him damaged by Rupert's action." She curled her shoulders toward her chest. "So I went to Michael hoping to discuss what he'd have to look forward to if he married me. I—I was in his bedroom."

He squeezed her hands encouraging her to continue.

"Hart—" She swallowed her humiliation in an attempt to force it to leave her be—at least until she finished. "I . . . we made love."

"That happens, sweetheart. It's not uncommon for

couples who are betrothed." His voice didn't carry any censure.

"The next morning I woke up." She searched his eyes hoping he'd understand. "I was so happy. For the first time in my life, I thought I might have a different life, the one I dreamed about when I was girl before we left for Brighton."

He smiled, but it didn't reach his eyes. He surely realized her tale would turn ugly.

"When we arrived in London the next day, I came here to Lawson Court and did some menial chores to clear my thoughts. Rupert was here crowing about how he'd found the seal and taken it to Michael's solicitors. When I returned to Langham Hall, everything had changed. Michael had met with his solicitor and bookkeeper. A lot of money is missing from the accounts, and my seal and my practice papers were the instruments of the theft. It was my signature on the documents, but I hadn't filled out the pages. Whoever did this had mastered the marquess's handwriting, too."

"Did you explain?"

She nodded and bit her lip to keep from crying out in agony. "I don't think he believed me." She took a deep breath and exhaled. "I really can't say I blame him. I'd done it before, and I confessed it was my signature. What else could he believe?"

She wiped a lone tear from her eyes. In seconds, Hart had her sitting in the sofa beside him.

"I'm banished to Lawson Court until he decides what to do to me."

"Let me go talk to him," he offered.

"No. I don't want you to be involved. It's finished. Whatever happens, I deserve. I stole from him. It just wasn't the amount that the bookkeeper insists is missing."

He embraced her. "Let me make this right. You need to be by your siblings' sides."

Adamant in her refusal, she stood and shook her head. She wouldn't divulge Michael's secrets. Nevertheless, her actions prevented her from ever taking her place beside her siblings again. "My presence will ruin Faith and Julia. Michael will take care of them. After they marry, Bennett will come home."

He turned away, but not fast enough. Crimson colored his cheeks.

"What is it?" Immediately, she dreaded asking the question.

"You—" His voice softened in sympathy. "You have several notes from the merchants in Leyton. They no longer need your assistance in keeping their books."

Stunned, she couldn't say a word. The rancid rumors had reached Leyton before she did. Her plans to rebuild her life were destroyed. She'd thought to start a full-time bookkeeping business in Leyton and use those wages as a way to pay the money back from the trust she'd borrowed.

"Oh." That's all she could manage when the truth assailed her.

She wasn't simply ruined.

She was a pariah.

Earlier, when she disembarked the Langham carriage, the laborers close to the house didn't acknowledge her or even look her way in greeting. People she'd known all her life looked through her as if she were invisible. She'd been cut before, but never from the kinsfolk she'd been raised to respect and taught to be kind to.

"Let me pay it back," he offered.

Confused, she searched his face. "How could you?"

Hart dipped his head and studied his entwined hands. "Erlington left me his holdings in the United States. He has a collection of wool mills in Massachusetts worth over two hundred thousand pounds. I had no idea he had that type of fortune."

She shook her head at the heady sum. Hart's wealth exceeded most of the nobles in the aristocracy. "That's yours?"

"Not all of it. Erlington gave you twenty-five percent."

"What?" Her pulse raced at such an unimaginable figure. "Fifty thousand pounds?"

"Indeed." Sadness dulled his smile. They both would have preferred if Hart's lover was still alive and in possession of his own fortune. "He wanted you to have it. He shared he'd never forget your kindness and how loving you were to us. His brother, the Marquess of Haviland, will not fight Erlington's wishes." He took one of her hands and squeezed. "Haviland was there, and I'm relieved to say we both appreciated each other's company during Erlington's final days."

"I'm sure you both brought each other comfort during the most difficult of times," she whispered.

"Come to Boston with me," he offered.

"What?" she asked incredulously. "Why?"

"You could be my bookkeeper and help manage the mills. You know wool and have experience negotiating prices. We can run them together."

"I don't think—"

"What if you're carrying his child?" Hart asked softly. He didn't mean to wound her, but the words stole her breath.

"No, it can't be." She shook her head in denial. Her luck couldn't be that bad. She moaned at the unfairness of it all. Yes, luck had always been a fickle friend.

"Either way, it would allow you a new life, a new opportunity to find happiness. You could come live with me."

His offer was sincere and proof that March had one friend she could rely on. Yet, she couldn't fathom leaving Faith, Julia, and Bennett to face the wreckage she had caused.

As if hearing her thoughts, Hart added, "It might give some much needed distance between your siblings and the scandal. You could return to Lawson Court in a year or so."

"You think it wise?" she whispered.

"Yes. McCalpin promised he'd take care of them for you." He kissed her cheek and stood. "I'm leaving in two days. Consider it. We'll talk tomorrow."

Once again, her gaze drew to the fire as if Hell called for her. What choice did she have? She had no place here in England—no safe sanctuary and no one to help her except for Hart.

Suddenly, Maximus jumped and settled on her lap. With a soft purr, he gently kneaded her legs as if offering comfort.

She closed her eyes to stop the onslaught of tears as she stroked his soft fur. She'd have to leave her family with Michael.

She'd already left her heart with him.

And he didn't want it.

# Chapter Twenty-Three

After Bennett's visit, McCalpin had spent the rest of the night in his study mulling over the events of the day. March disavowed any guilt except the trust fund thefts and the use of his seal to keep Rupert off the Lawson lands. However, when she'd turned to him and demanded his promise to care for her family, it hadn't set right with him. Almost as if she was leaving him.

He'd hurt her when he'd sent her away, but it was best for both of them. It protected her and her family somewhat from the critics. For him, he'd hoped he could clear his thoughts. After last night, his mind was still swimming with all the revelations.

When morning came, he rang the bell and ordered a bath, then directed Donar saddled. He promised Bennett he'd visit March and see how she was faring. He'd do more than that. He'd press her until he discovered what thoughts were rolling around in that beautiful head of hers. Chocolate waves of curls twined about his fingers crowded into his thoughts. His body tightened in response to the image.

He closed his eyes and forced himself to relax as he remembered holding her sweet body next to his. He'd taken her virginity. No matter what, he was an honorable man. He'd still marry her.

Within an hour, he found March standing guard on the crest of a hill overlooking the valley that bordered Lawson Court and the next farm. Decorating the landscape, white sheep with black faces dotted the slopping hill's dormant grass. He brought Donar to a halt. The wind howled in concert with the cold winter day as he gazed his fill at the sight of her.

Without delay, he urged his horse forward. Before he could dismount, the sound of Donar shaking his bridle caused her to turn. Tears streamed down her face. The look of anguish so acute he tasted her bitter torment.

In that moment, a part of him withered as pain wracked through him in waves. Deep inside his chest where his heart resided, he knew the truth.

He'd destroyed a part of her.

At the sound of a jangle of a bridle, March turned, fully expecting Hart. He wanted her decision whether she'd come to Boston with him.

Instead, Michael stood before her more beautiful than ever. She catalogued his features carefully so she could remember them perfectly during the lonely days ahead. The task proved difficult as her recalcitrant tears refused to obey.

With grace and quickness, he dismounted and moved toward her, his eyes never leaving hers. She didn't know how it happened, but she was in his arms with her head buried against his chest. His arms tightened as her tears turned into sobs.

"Oh, sweetheart, don't," he whispered.

It was pure bliss in his arms, as if everything would return to the way it was before yesterday. She stole one more moment of comfort before she forced herself from his embrace. "Why are you here?"

The startling blue of his eyes contrasted perfectly with the gray winter day. An omen he could steal the cold and loneliness that had captured her heart. She blinked to clear such silly nonsense. Her fate had been cast when everyone believed she'd stolen from him.

"I promised Bennett I would see how you're faring," he whispered as he framed her cheeks in his hands.

"I'm fine." With all her practice, the lie slipped easily from her lips.

He gently traced the angles of her cheeks with his thumbs. The leather of his gloves teased her skin, reminding her how safe she felt in his arms. "You don't appear fine."

"It's hard to say good-bye." She took a step back. Her gaze skimmed the muddy hem of her cloak. Walking the fields for hours, she'd tried to memorize each hill and valley of the estate. Always, her thoughts circled back to Michael. "I'm leaving for Boston with Hart tomorrow." She lifted her head and waved a hand behind her at the hill. "I wanted one final walk—"

"Boston?" His eyes widened, making the blue even more striking. "What about Bennett and your sisters? What about me?"

All she could offer was a shrug and hoped it hid the depths of her desolation. "I'm ruined. I'm a bastard, and it's clear you think I've stolen from you and my family."

"I want to believe you, March."

The plea in his voice was unmistakable, but she had no answers for him.

"But you don't believe me, and *neither* does anyone

else. When I arrived home yesterday, it became clear that even the people of Leyton don't trust me. I'd hope to work as a bookkeeper for the merchants around town to reimburse you, but they want nothing to do with me. . . ." She let the words drift to nothing. "I want to right this wrong, but I can't do it here."

Michael clasped her elbow, forcing her to look at him. His stern countenance baffled her. "You can't accomplish anything halfway around the world. People will think you're guilty if you leave. No, you stay here." He pulled her close. "You needn't worry. No matter what has happened, I *will* marry you. We shared a bed. You could be carrying my child as we speak."

She broke from his hold. With him this near, her senses would stage a revolt, demanding she seek comfort in his arms again. She had to keep her mind sharp if she wanted to survive this. The haunting memory of a future with him had died a slow death after the wounds from last night.

He started to say something, but faltered in the enveloping silence that had descended between them. He ran his gloved fingers through his hair. "I don't understand yesterday, but deep down, I want to trust you. *I need to trust you.*" He smiled, but the effort lacked his natural warmth. "We can mend this breech between us. Your fears made you act in ways that went against our interests. Even if you thought you had good reason to do what you did, we both realize that wasn't the case."

"What are you saying?" Caustic, his words burned her ears. Another roll of emotion swept through her. Like water on the verge of boiling, her irritation started to simmer into little pops of anger.

He lifted one brow in that provoking manner like

every other arrogant English lord. "I'm not here to argue. As I said before—"

A searing pain twisted around her heart smothering some of her anger. He actually believed she'd been disloyal to him. What else could he think? At Langham Hall, all the circumstances had baked into a concoction of proof that made all his nightmares come true.

She drew in a gasp to quell the misery. "I didn't betray your trust," she whispered fervently, hoping he'd believe her. "I guarded it. Don't you see that?"

It was the only thing she wanted from him. His belief she wouldn't hurt him. She could never forsake him— not for any amount of money.

"I don't know what I see." He turned and studied the hill. In profile, the clench of his jaw was evidence of his own pain and anger. He cleared his throat and returned his attention to her. "I'm still responsible for your siblings. We'll have to discuss their welfare from time to time. Let us make this right between us." He was practically shouting at her with an indignation that matched hers. Perhaps it was agony she heard vibrate in his voice. "We shall still marry."

"Why would you want to?" She knew the answer, but wanted to hear it from his lips. He didn't love her, but his honor demanded he take her as his wife.

"It's the honorable thing to do."

She sighed and the wind captured her despair and threw it into the air. "Don't worry. If there's a child, I'll take care of it. A bastard having a bastard isn't uncommon. No one will know in the States."

"*Bloody hell,*" he roared. "You've cut me deep enough. What else do you want from me? Every spec of blood?"

"I could say the same to you," she shot back. *I want*

*you to love me*. Though she thought it, she didn't dare utter it. Whatever chances she had for love, she lost yesterday. She closed her eyes, desperate for equilibrium. "Please don't do this."

"What have I done to you? You're the one who appears to have taken advantage of my family and me. Can't you see how difficult this is for me?" He clasped her arms and shook as if gently trying to dislodge the truth. "Do you know what would make this right? If you were in my bed and in my arms, I'd kiss you senseless while we made love." He shook his head in disgust and let her go. "That's the only logical thing I've understood in the last two days. Perhaps we'd find our way out of this nightmare."

For a moment, her heart pounded, encouraging her to forget everything and take what he offered. The comfort she needed would be so easy to take. However, she'd only fool herself. The next morning, she'd find him questioning her again. Examining her. In her heart, the harsh truth wouldn't quiet. Inevitably, the doubt in his eyes would tear her apart piece by piece until there was nothing left. His lack of trust would whittle away what remained of her self-respect.

Even though her heart might not survive, she'd made the best decision for them both.

She'd done this to herself—undermined her own happiness. If she stayed at Lawson Court, her taint would ruin her family. Boston was the only option. She'd find a new life until she could return. Once her sisters married, she'd come back for Bennett.

His pointed stare captured hers as he closed the distance between them. It'd take little for him to vanquish the scant resistance she clung to as a lifeline. He grabbed her without apology and crushed her to him as his lips met hers in a blinding kiss full of anger and passion. Her knees buckled under the assault of his possession, but he wouldn't let her go. He devoured her and what little resistance she had left. His tongue fought with hers. Yearning for more, she moaned, all her fight withering. The sound seemed to increase his hunger for her. Holding her tightly, he dominated every inch of her until his kiss softened almost as if pleading with her.

Suddenly, he drew back and fought for air as he regarded her. "If you go to Boston, it's admitting your guilt."

She scoffed her denial and fought to get her traitorous body under control. His kisses had robbed her of the ability to think. "Don't manipulate me. I don't want you like this."

"You may not want me, but your kiss and your body tell me differently." His hoarse whisper slashed through her resolve. "When you started your embezzling perhaps you thought you could manipulate me. Perhaps you saw how easy it would be to gain my fortune. Tell me, did I mistake genuine affection for subterfuge?"

Reeling from his kiss, her disloyal body leaned into his as if recognizing that he was hers. She straightened to her full height and found the words to challenge his hateful question. "Don't you know? Look at your household accounting book."

"The account book." His guttural laugh sliced through her. The contempt clear in the cold air. "Thank you for reminding me of my failures. I don't need it, nor shall I waste any more time on that tripe."

His vitriol made her recoil. There it was. The push she needed—the knowledge that her heart hadn't wanted to accept. She'd made the right choice to go with Hart. He didn't care what she'd said about loving him and keeping his secrets safe. He only cared about his honor and duty. "Yesterday you said sometimes hard decisions must be made. I understand what you mean." She lowered her voice. "I've made the hardest decision I've ever made in my life. Go back to London, Michael."

She turned and faced the valley in an effort to shield herself from the pain. In seconds, Donar's pounding hooves broke across the meadow, creating the much-needed distance.

It would be the last thing Michael ever gave her—the eviscerating sound of him leaving her behind.

After McCalpin had returned from Leyton and his disastrous meeting with March, he'd sought refuge in his study. He stared out the window and saw nothing. He'd found no peace. Just an emptying pain.

A lone tear escaped.

His mind and his heart were engaged in a fierce battle with the winner taking all. Whatever the inevitable spoils of war, he knew he would be the loser. All his life he'd just assumed love would find him. He'd always considered it his due much like his duty was his birthright.

What he felt for March consumed him and made him want to disavow every responsibility he'd been groomed to accept and manage. Never in his wildest imagination did he think he'd face something this brutally unfair—choosing between duty and a woman he thought would be the perfect wife—even if she stole from him. If forced to choose between the two, he wasn't certain of the outcome. That was the extent of his so-called honor. However, he'd never face that decision.

March had made the choice for him. Her true regard had been as clear as the country air he'd breathed today. His throat tightened as the pain rose in surges like angry waves in a storm. She'd cast him aside and ripped his heart to pieces in the process.

He suddenly realized both of his cheeks were wet. How appropriate. He hadn't shed any tears since that fateful day with Mrs. Ivers. He brushed a hand down his face in a feeble attempt to clear his misery. It did little to subdue the gut-wrenching despair.

How could he have been so mistaken to think she was different from any other woman he took great means to distance himself from?

Thankfully, Buxton interrupted his pitiful musings with a summons that the duchess needed an escort home from Hailey's Hope, the charity for homeless soldiers that she managed along with Claire. His mother never asked for his assistance, so without delay, he headed her way. It would keep his thoughts from March.

Within minutes, he was escorting her into his black-lacquered carriage. As soon as they settled opposite each other, the vehicle moved like a well-oiled machine through the streets of London heading toward Langham Hall.

He said little since he wasn't interested in conversation. His only desire was to return home to the solitude of his study. He was poor company and didn't try to hide it.

His mother tapped the roof once, and the carriage slowed to a halt at the Hyde Park entrance closest to the Serpentine.

"Madame, are we *stopping* because you're interested in some exercise?" he drawled.

His mother sat in the forward-facing bench and scooted over to the window. She patted the seat beside her, indicating she wanted him to sit next to her. "I want to show you something."

McCalpin did as requested. His mother pulled her own curtain back and pointed to a group of three women and one boy standing off to the side of the main walkway.

"Look there," she commanded. Her melodic voice held the unmistakable hint of steel.

His attention was riveted to the sight of March with Bennett, Julia, and Faith.

"At this very moment, March is telling them she's leaving for Boston. This is her farewell," she whispered.

"How do you know? Why isn't she at Langham Hall saying her good-byes?" From this distance, he could easily make out the distress on Julia's face. Faith had her back to him. Bennett had his hands clasped behind his back, studying the ground.

"She believes she isn't welcome." His mother's voice cracked, but he couldn't see her expression as she held a vigilant watch with her face turned toward the group. "She sent notes to all of them to meet her here. She also left one for your father."

Immediately, his guard went up, but he slowly released his breath. She'd never divulge his ineptitude with numbers to his father in such a manner. It wasn't in her character. She'd be the type to cut him in pieces in person so she could enjoy the carnage. That talent was in evidence today when she'd desecrated him at Lawson Court. "Madame, how are you aware of all this?"

His mother turned her gaze to his. "The footman Milton is Bennett's favorite. Bennett told him his plans, and Milton is loyal to me. I know what is occurring in my own household."

"Remind me never to attempt a coup when you're home," he chuckled. It was the only way to mask his unease. He'd tried to convince himself March wouldn't leave her family, which meant she'd still be in his life, but the proof was before him.

His mother ignored the quip and studied the sight before her. Finally, after a few minutes, Julia's hands flew to her mouth and her shoulders shook. Faith tried to pull her close, but Julia shrugged her sister off and launched herself into March's arms. Even though he couldn't hear the conversation, his heart wrenched in two as Julia's grief became poignantly bare to all.

A knot rose in his throat when Faith pulled Bennett to her side as if needing his strength. The boy succumbed to his sister's wishes, but his face bore the torment he suffered. March released Julia and hugged Faith. The two sisters exchanged words and nodded to each other, then Faith bowed her head.

"I can't perceive how agonizing this must be for her." His mother's soft whisper slashed straight through his resolve not to care. "She's struggled for over eight years to take care of that family, a responsibility foisted upon her because of ill luck."

He refused to glance her way. With one look, he'd be on his knees—leveled from the pain.

"Can you imagine a girl turning into a woman overnight? Everything she expected for her future turned upside down because she was responsible for three children when she was still a child herself?" His mother exhaled loudly. "She knows it's in their best interests if she leaves them since she can't protect them anymore. She believes her presence puts their social standing in jeopardy. Envision the love and trust she must possess to give them up to you. A family she's loved her entire life."

"Perhaps it's justice," he whispered.

Her brow crinkled in perfect lines as a fierce scowl marred her face. "No. It's a woman who loves deeply. A woman who loves her family, but more importantly, a woman who loves the man sitting beside me."

"You see things that aren't there, Mother."

March held Bennett's full attention. The light caught the glistening tears on her cheeks as she talked with him. The boy's face was near colorless. March was saying something, and the boy nodded with a bowed head. Gently, March tugged his chin until she held his gaze. The sight so raw and crushing in its pain, he turned away.

His mother blew a stray piece of hair out of her eyes. "She raised that boy. She taught him everything she knew. He's a wonderful, loving, and an extremely talented human being. And your March shaped him into a person who will grow into a fine man who will do great things in his lifetime." She took a shuddered breath, then released it. "I can't help but wonder what she would do with her own child now that she's matured into the woman before you." His mother placed her hand over his. "And she's entrusted Bennett's care to you. If that's not love, I don't know what is, son."

He squeezed her hand, hoping she'd stop. However, his mother possessed a strength that could defeat Napoléon and his forces with one stare.

"We Cavenshams pride ourselves on doing the right thing. We try hard to help others. But your March"—she bent her head and stared at their clasped hands—"is in a category all by herself." His mother smiled, but tears threatened. "When I picked her up that day from Mademoiselle Mignon's, she'd been embarrassed by several women in the shop. On the way home, I made a comment that you should have told her we would pay for everything. I was really quite upset with you."

His heart grew heavy at his mother's affectionate smile.

"Her defense of you was blinding in its warmth and respect. It was then that I knew she loved you."

Through the pain, he returned the smile, then shook his head. "Madame, are you telling me that I've made a mistake?"

"I'm telling you that no matter your doubts, you must discover the truth for yourself." Much like March with Bennett, she captured his gaze as she continued. "You'll not be able to live with yourself otherwise. I don't want to see you or March hurt."

He clenched his eyes shut. Never did he think he'd share his shame so honestly with his mother, but with his heart and soul bleeding, he had no choice. The woman he loved was leaving him and her family. He had never allowed himself to consider the truth of his feelings, but today they couldn't be denied. Nor would they stay quiet. He loved March so completely he doubted he'd ever recover if he lost her. However, he had no idea how to right this wrong. With his heart ready to fly apart in anarchy, he nodded.

He swallowed the thickness in his throat. "Mother, I don't know how I can discover the truth. Even if I had years, I can't do it. I only have this evening, and the task is too great for me." He covered his hands with his face, then forced himself to face her. "I can't add more than three numbers together."

Tears streamed down his mother's face. "I know, my love."

"It's an impossible task. I shouldn't even be allowed near the duchy's accounts."

She raised her hand for him to stop. "My heart broke countless times when I saw how you struggled, but you learned to compensate." Her eyes searched his as if encouraging him to listen. "But don't ever doubt your ability or right to run the duchy. You have an undeniable strength that masters your weakness. You look beyond someone's mistakes and see their worth. Can't you try to do that for your March?"

McCalpin chanced another glance outside. The Lawson family were gone. A hole caved in his heart. He didn't get the chance to see March leave. She was his. God, how could he stop her?

"Examine her conduct and judgment as you wrestle with her motivations. If you don't think she deserves that courtesy, then that's your decision." His mother's eyes glistened with more tears. "But I would hate for the opportunity of a lifetime to be missed because you doubt your own worth and ability. We all have weaknesses. A brave man knows how to work around his." His mother tapped lightly on the roof, and the carriage lurched forward to return them to Langham Hall.

How in God's teeth could he discover the truth about who was embezzling from the estates? The weight on his shoulders grew by a hundred stone.

Then the truth hit him square between the eyes. He was going to lose March and couldn't prevent it from happening. A blinding pain cascaded through him.

Before the carriage slowed to a halt beside the Langham Hall mews, his father jumped into the carriage and joined them. Without a glance at McCalpin, he drew his wife into his arms. "Ginny, I would have come for you."

The tremble of her lips betrayed the sincerity of her smile. "I needed Michael today," she whispered.

His father pressed a kiss against her forehead, then brushed his index finger across her cheek in a tender caress. "My lovely, lovely duchess," he soothed as he rocked her in his arms.

In that intimate moment, McCalpin realized what he'd

miss in his life if he couldn't find a way to keep March from leaving. A partner and a wife who would love unconditionally and protect his interests with everything she possessed.

His father's gaze swept to his as he settled his wife into the crook of his arm. "I received a letter from March today. Erlington bequeathed part of his woolen mill fortune to her. It's worth roughly fifty thousand pounds. She's signed it over to you. She says it's to pay for the monies that are missing. She didn't apologize or seek forgiveness. Just the directive that any remaining amounts are to be equally split between her siblings."

"Fifty thousand pounds?" he whispered. It was inconceivable.

"She could've had any man in London with that fortune." His father pulled his mother closer.

Inside McCalpin's chest, a demon warrior rose, one ready to defeat any man who wanted her. She was his.

"But she wanted you to have it," his mother whispered. "For you and for her sisters and her brother."

He released the breath he'd been holding. Soon an ocean would separate them, and this rift between them would never heal.

His father narrowed his eyes, oblivious to the unease running amok through McCalpin. With his free hand, he held up three fingers. "How many fingers?"

He exhaled. He may be in turmoil, but he still possessed all of his senses. "Three."

His father nodded, then pulled the familiar red accounting book from his pocket. "What is this?"

He snarled by reflex. If his father had examined the entries, he had discovered the extent of McCalpin's debilitating failure with numbers. "My bookkeeping."

"Excellent. I was afraid you couldn't see what was right before your eyes," his father taunted. "You left it in the entry hall, and Pitts found it. Turn to the last page of entries."

McCalpin reached to take it from his father's out-stretched hand, then hesitated. As if today and tomorrow weren't enough punishment, now he had to withstand the disappointment he'd surely find in his father's eyes once he realized what a simpleton he had for a son. "You are aware that I suffer from an inability to do even the simplest calculations?"

"Do it," his father demanded.

Wary, he opened the red-leather journal and flipped to the last page of entries. His gaze skimmed the last column of numbers until his eyes fixated upon the writing so similar to his but with a distinct feminine slant and curls to the letters.

*My dearest love,*

*Last night in your arms and your bed, you gave me a gift I never thought to receive or experience in my life. Your tenderness and care proved that I could have the happiness in my life that I thought I'd lost. My thoughts are in a jumble as my lips still crave your kisses, but you must know that you own my heart and all my soul. I want to shout it to the world, that I, March Lawson, love you, Michael Cavensham, without reserve or caution. With complete and total abandon, I freely give you my heart. Whatever you choose to do with it is your prerogative, but I will not deny my love. Ever.*

    *However, the greatest present you've ever*

*given me—besides asking me to be your wife—is
the trust you've shown when you shared yourself
and what you perceive as your failings. Know I
cherish your trust, and I will proudly stand by
your side everyday as you work. I promise I'll do
everything and anything in my power to help you
with the financial aspects of the estate, your
political work, and every glorious moment in
your life.*

*I'll keep your every secret and guard your
trust fiercely. It's my greatest gift to you as I love
you more than life itself.*

*Yours forever,*
*M*

He closed his eyes in a desperate attempt not to cry
out as he leaned against the carriage bench squab. At
Lawson Court, she'd asked him if he'd read the journal.
He called it tripe. What had he done? She must think he
didn't care what she'd written. His beautiful, giving
March had been loving and protecting him just as fiercely
as she did her siblings. "How stupid could I have been?"

"That's only true if you don't try to win her back," his
father said without a hint of mockery or disdain.

"How can I? I'm an idiot when it comes to numbers."
He was so lost he didn't think he'd be able to find his way
out of the carriage. He didn't even care that he was speaking so freely about his shortcomings with his parents.

His father grinned with an understanding that gave
him hope. "My father suffered from something similar,
but his duchess was gifted with figures. No one ever knew
how much he relied on her for financial help. Together,
they made the Langham duchy one of the most powerful
and profitable titles in all of England." His father kissed

his mother tenderly on her cheek before he turned his attention to McCalpin. "You and March could have the same impact."

"If we have even a fraction of the impact you and mother have, I'll consider both the duchy and myself most fortunate." McCalpin felt the heaviness in his chest slowly release. "Do you think you might be able to help me?"

His father nodded. "It would be my pleasure."

They couldn't waste any additional time. He had to find out who was embezzling from them. As McCalpin reached to open the carriage door a piece of paper stuck in the household bookkeeping journal floated to the ground. He picked it up and examined the numbers. Jameson's note listed the entries for the amounts that March had embezzled from the trust. The handwriting was of little distinction except the dashes decorating the sevens and the decorative serifs atop the ones screamed for his attention.

As if the night turned into the day, the answer became crystal clear.

"I need to see Macalester. I know who's stolen from us."

# Chapter Twenty-Four

A fter McCalpin finished his evening visit to Mr. Russell's office, he met his investigator, Macalester, at the designated address. The clean but modest home had several rooms for let. It had only taken a couple of coins, and the owner, a kind elderly man, had directed McCalpin and Macalester to the second floor.

Without a word spoken between the two, McCalpin and Macalester exchanged a glance outside the designated door. Without a knock, McCalpin lifted the latch and swept inside with his investigator following in his wake.

In his shirt and waistcoat, Jameson sat behind a writing table and immediately stood with such force he knocked over his simple oak chair. Wide-eyed, he glanced between the two men. Immediately, he schooled his features. "My lord." His gaze swung to the investigator. "Mr. Macalester, you must have news pertaining to Miss Lawson's theft."

"Indeed," McCalpin answered with a single nod. "I've

discovered who's behind the thefts, and it's not Miss Lawson."

"Step away from the desk." With pistol drawn, Macalester approached Jameson.

With shoulders slumped, the bookkeeper did as directed. With little fanfare, he took his coat hanging from a hook on the wall and slipped it on. Behind him, Macalester opened the single drawer of the table and pulled out a sheath of papers. He held up March's seal for McCalpin's view.

"Why did you do it?" He studied Jameson as the bookkeeper's cheeks flamed.

"It was an opportunity I couldn't dismiss. When I discovered Miss Lawson was embezzling from the trust without repercussions, I decided to use her as my shield. I'd planned to stop once you discovered the missing funds." The man sighed in resignation. "I had no other options. I needed money."

"For what purpose?" It took every ounce of patience McCalpin possessed not to punch the man in the throat. Likely a deathblow, but Jameson deserved it.

"My invalid son lives with my elderly mother in Lancashire. She can't care for him anymore. I needed to hire someone who would live with them. My wife died a year ago." Jameson's arms hung limp at his sides as if utterly defeated. "I tried to work two jobs, but there still wasn't enough money for his care."

McCalpin released a heavy breath. Not the villain he'd expected, but still a man who deserved punishment. "How old is your son?"

"Ten, my lord." Jameson's anguished whisper hung heavy in the air.

The boy was slightly older than Bennett. What would

March do if she faced such a circumstance? He knew the answer—anything and everything to protect the boy.

"Lord McCalpin, you should look at this." While still aiming the pistol at the bookkeeper, Macalester handed two sheets of paper to him.

The first was a copy of a marriage certificate. McCalpin quickly skimmed the contents. March's parents had been married at Gretna Green in an "anvil marriage" two years prior to her birth. The second was a letter from March's father to her grandfather, railing at the viscount for insisting her parents marry again in a "proper" Church of England ceremony. Since March's parents had recently returned from Italy, Chelmsford was the most convenient place to meet and have the second ceremony.

"This proves she's not a bastard." His blood was boiling with the discovery. Jameson's actions had ensured March's destruction in front of the gossip-loving *ton* for no reason. "I should kill you for hurting my betrothed."

"I never wanted to ruin Miss Lawson." Jameson's voice weakened. "Her cousin was easy to manipulate into believing the tale. I thought it would be a quiet matter handled by our firm. I never dreamed Lawson would confront her at a ball. I just needed to prove she'd embezzled funds that weren't rightly hers. I opened the account at Fleming's Bank under her name. That gave me the opportunity to"—he stared at the floor—"steal from you without anyone looking beyond Miss Lawson."

"Why did you try to have the withdrawal from my investment funds deposited into her accounts?" he asked.

"More evidence of her guilt. Lord Somerton wouldn't authorize such a transaction without coming to you first. In turn, you would think she was embezzling from you.

It was a way to end it. I didn't have the stomach to steal from you anymore." Jameson shook his head then raised his gaze to McCalpin. "You should know the exact amount I've taken is roughly five thousand pounds. All but one hundred is here." He pointed to the desk, and Macalester brought out a leather pouch. "I didn't have any other options. My son can't walk and can barely communicate with anyone, but"—tears welled in his eyes—"I love him, and my wife loved him dearly. I wanted to give him the very best."

"Well, since your crimes are not only against me and the duchy, but also harm Miss Lawson, she should have a say in what becomes of you." McCalpin's chest tightened. He rubbed the middle of his forehead and closed his eyes to consider this development. He'd fully expected to find a selfish, self-centered criminal who'd preyed upon March and his family. Instead, he found a man desperate to care for his son. Still, it didn't excuse the havoc the bookkeeper had created in McCalpin's and, more importantly, March's life.

"Macalester, will you stay with Jameson until Miss Lawson and I decide how we wish to proceed with this matter?" He didn't spare a glance at Jameson. "Perhaps, it'd be beneficial to determine if he's telling the truth about his son."

McCalpin had never seen anything but a cool demeanor from the Scotsman. With a face made of stone, the investigator nodded. Did the man even have a heart? Probably not a useful tool in his bag of investigative tricks.

"I'll send someone to visit the family," said Macalester.

"I need to see Miss Lawson straightaway with the news we've discovered tonight."

"Go ahead, my lord. I'll handle everything from this end," the investigator added.

Without delay, he set off to find March and share his discovery. His mother had sent word March was spending the night at the Lawson townhome before setting sail in the morning.

If he had any luck, he hoped tonight's discovery would be enough to keep her here in London and win back her good graces. Whatever it took, he'd convince her to stay and become his wife.

Once again, Michael haunted March's dreams. Only this time, his fresh pine fragrance became vivid when he kissed her on the cheek. When had her dreams become a sensual feast of scents?

"March, my love, wake up," the dream Michael whispered.

She sat up with a start. It wasn't a dream, but the flesh-and-blood man. Michael sat on the edge of the bed with his hip resting against hers. He leaned close, touching his lips to hers with the gentlest of kisses.

*Sweet heavens, how she'd miss—*

"Are Faith, Julia, and Bennett all right?" The words tumbled from her before all her senses fully awoke. She blinked at the candle lit beside her. Michael must have seen to it.

"They're fine, my love." He dipped his head again for another kiss, this one longer with a hint of passion mixed with the taste of mint and fresh air.

"How did you get in here?" Still a little groggy, she pushed the mass of tangles away from her face. Instantly, he cupped her face, and his thumbs caressed her cheeks.

"There you are," he whispered. "Hart let me enter. I

have to share what I discovered tonight. It couldn't wait until tomorrow."

She leaned into his hand as if famished for his touch. Before she got on that ship, at least she'd be able to give him a proper good-bye without the anger and anguish of their last meeting.

"I found the person stealing from me." His eyes were so tender in their gaze, a quiver started in her chest and radiated throughout her body.

"Tell me."

"The bookkeeper, Jameson." With his other hand, he'd taken hers and laced their fingers together as if he couldn't get enough of her. He studied their entwined hands. "It's a sad story of why he did it, dearest. We'll save it for later. We have much more important things to discuss."

He drew a breath and kissed her slowly as if savoring something precious, then gently pulled away.

"Jameson prepared a list of all your withdrawals from your trust account and gave it to me. All the ones and sevens were marked with dashes and unique serifs. That's how I discovered he was the thief. You solved it, sweetheart." He stopped abruptly and held her gaze. "Will you forgive me?"

She could only nod as she battled not to get her hopes up.

"Thank you." He closed his eyes and exhaled a shuttering breath, then reached into the pocket of his evening coat. "I found these in Jameson's home. They're the original documents that belonged in your family's files along with the trusts. He'd stolen them from the solicitor's office."

He handed the papers to her. The first was a marriage certificate. She quickly gazed at the date and the names, then captured his gaze. He smiled, and she looked at the other, the angry letter from her father to her grandfather for not recognizing her parents' Gretna Green marriage. Her hand flew to her mouth as tears of joy came from nowhere. "Does that mean . . . ?"

Did she dare hope this nightmare might be over for her and Michael and her family? When he nodded, she leaned against his chest. His arms immediately surrounded her.

"Sweetheart, look at the last one."

She leaned away and studied the letter from her father to her grandfather announcing her birth—after her parents' marriage and proving she was twenty-five. Finally, she had every piece to the puzzle—the reason they married in Chelmsford and proof of her legitimacy.

"Thank you," she whispered.

"No. I'm the one who should thank you." Michael's voice soothed her with its huskiness. He cradled her head and coaxed her to lean into his strong chest, his scent and strength overpowering in his embrace. "After I left you at Lawson Court, I didn't know where to turn or what to do. I was beside myself with grief and misgiving. I didn't know how to repair the damage between us. Believe it or not, it was my mother who helped me."

"The duchess?" The mortification still stung that his lovely mother knew about her ghastly confession.

Michael kissed the top of her head as if he revered her. "Yes. She had me escort her home from her charity and made me watch your good-bye to your siblings."

She tensed in his arms. The earlier devastation on Julia's face and the emptiness in Faith's eyes still brought her pain. When Bennett's stalwart demeanor broke into tears, it ripped her heart out of her chest and left it laying in Hyde Park. She loved them, and their agony almost made her stay.

"I'm so sorry you went through that," he whispered into her hair. "I can't imagine letting my sister or brother go."

"It was horrible." She couldn't say anymore as her gaze clouded with hot tears again.

"My father met us with my account book when we arrived home. In no uncertain terms, he told me to find out what happened and bring you back." A chuckle escaped. "I believe my parents were almost as devastated as I was at your pending departure."

She pulled away to gauge his reaction. "Really?"

He nodded, then kissed her nose. His endearing attention caused her pulse to quicken.

"My father told me that my grandfather suffered a similar affliction." He cupped her cheeks once again. "My grandmother, his duchess, had a head for numbers, and the duchy grew and prospered under their direction."

For the first time in days, hope started to trickle through her anguish, washing it away bit by bit.

"Sweetheart, I read my account book." He wouldn't let her look away. "As soon as I read it, everything made sense." He traced one cheek with his thumb. "The sacrifices you made for your family throughout the years are nothing short of awe-inspiring. I should have never doubted you or your belief in me. You make me believe in myself. Make me believe that I could conquer this weakness by understanding it and accepting it. You make me believe I'm worth loving."

She closed her eyes, fighting to find the right thing to say. What use was it? She still loved him. "I will always love you," she whispered.

"With your trust monies and Erlington's bequest of your portion of the woolen mills, you're an heiress worth close to seventy-five thousand pounds. You can choose any husband you want." The ocean-blue of his eyes flashed. "Choose me. Let me prove I'm worthy of your love. Let me prove how much I love you every day. I'll take care of you and your family. Be my wife, March. I'm begging you. Stay with me and raise our family."

Her heart burst free—free from the chains she'd feared would drown her in a life of misery forever. Her *David*, the consummate warrior, had delivered her from a purgatory she'd had no way to escape. How could she deny him? She'd loved him from the first time she'd ever laid eyes on him.

If she spoke, her tears would fall in a never-ending stream. Therefore, she did the next best thing. She nodded, then kissed him with a passion that rivaled the force of a meteor striking Earth and exploding. It was exactly the way she felt. All the grief and heartache had shattered, and a blinding lightness filled her heart. Finally, she could answer, "Yes, I'll marry you."

"Thank you." He rested his forehead against hers. "Forgive me for not seeing your trust and faith earlier—"

"Let's not dwell on the past, but look to our future." She put her fingers to his lips. "Come to bed."

The fire in his eyes lit a heat within her that quickly spread to her heart. He was so dear to her. He quickly disrobed, then stood before her, his desire for her apparent. Without any hesitation, she rid herself of her nightgown.

Though the room was quiet except for the occasional crack of the fire, the sweet yearning between them charged the air as they stared into each other's eyes. Michael came to her, never taking his gaze from hers, and with a natural athletic grace, he joined her in bed. He covered her with his body and consumed her with his kisses.

She touched him everywhere. Ensuring he was real flesh and blood. Ensuring the moment was heartfelt.

Ensuring her dream was genuine. She didn't try to contain her outcry of delight. Their passion and love was a force that neither wanted to control.

They found their shuddering ecstasy together, and slowly their passion melted into heartfelt murmurs and kisses.

As she lay in his arms, she couldn't deny the truth. The ugly path her life had taken had brought her here, a turn that had led to a future filled with happiness and joy. Michael had given her everything—her family's happiness, his family's love and support, and if they were truly blessed, a family of their own.

Whether she possessed the devil's own luck or she'd created her own with her embezzling made little difference. She'd give the devil his due.

She was the luckiest bride in the world.

# Epilogue

*The Next Afternoon*
*Langham Hall*

March stood before the vicar with Michael by her side. He inclined his head toward her as he repeated his vows. The rugged strength in his voice made her tremble.

The reflected light in the room glimmered as it kissed his handsome face. Yes, heaven did favor him. The marvelous ocean-blue color of his eyes stole her breath. So magnetic, his gaze held hers, and she was powerless. She leaned near so as not to miss a word.

She squeezed his hand, then repeated her vows. She tilted her head to the ceiling and said a silent prayer. She missed her parents every day but knew they would be pleased for her.

Before the vicar pronounced them husband and wife, she stole a glance at her family. The duke and duchess stood with clasped hands. The duchess smiled with shimmering tears of joy. Even the duke's eyes glimmered with emotion.

Faith and Julia stood side by side, their blinding smiles brighter than a summer's midday sun. Beside them, Hart stood with his hands clasped in front of him. Without hesitating, he had postponed his trip to Boston so he could witness their vows. He'd promised to return within a year.

Next to Hart, William caught her glance and smiled. Before the ceremony, he'd apologized for his doubts, then had been the first to congratulate Michael. Without warning, William had picked her up and twirled her in a circle, all the while proclaiming *he* should have married her. Michael had laughed, but then quickly brought her to his side with his arm wrapped around her waist. The strength in his grip reminded her their love was a bond that even when tested would be unbreakable.

Claire and Alex were present with their three children who were quite well behaved. When the couple looked at each other, their obvious love was breathtaking.

Emma and Nick were there, too. Nick's arm was around Emma's thickened waist. March had glanced their way several times and caught Nick kissing the top of his wife's head as if she was the most precious creature in the world.

Finally, March allowed her gaze to settle on Bennett standing beside the duke. The boy must have grown an inch since yesterday. He'd brought her a copy of this morning's *The Midnight Cryer*. Surprisingly, the paper had discovered that Dr. Kennett and Lord Queensgrace truly did have emergencies that had called them both out of town. The article went on to advise that the Lawson sisters should expect a roomful of flowers soon from their respective beaus.

Rupert didn't attend the ceremony. When he approached the duke to offer glad tidings for March's innocence and felicitations for her and Michael's wedding, the duke had cut him directly by ignoring him—

causing Rupert to be ruined socially. This morning, the duke's barrister brought charges against Rupert for perpetrating a fraud against the Marquess of McCalpin and the Duchy of Langham.

However, Rupert wasn't getting off that easy. With the duke's help, Bennett had hatched a plan to eliminate Rupert as his heir. Yesterday, with the Prince Regent's blessing, a special session of Parliament amended the original letters patent of the viscountcy. If Bennett died before providing an heir, then the title would go to March's second-born son, making all future viscounts descended from the House of Langham. If the title failed to pass, then the peerage became extinct.

Earlier, she and Michael had decided not to punish Jameson. Though the man had committed the crime, he'd readily admitted it. Macalester had been so impressed with Jameson's embezzling talent, he decided to hire him to help investigate other suspected financial ne'er-do-well dealings. She and Michael had settled a large enough sum on Jameson that he could move his son to London and afford full-time care.

She'd made the front page of the paper again. Only this time, the article retracted all their earlier posts. It declared she'd been a victim of a huge scandal and the handsome Marquess of McCalpin had used his clever mind to defend her honor in words and actions. Of course, always ready to start a scandal, the publisher lamented the fact that not a single drop of blood had tinted the ground.

"My lovely wife," he whispered.

"I adore you," she answered.

"Have I ever told you thank you for embezzling from your dowry?"

"Hush, David."

His blinding smile stole her breath, but that wasn't what caused her heart to explode in an effort to reach his.

His eyes spoke with love.

An endearing perfect love.

As the vicar pronounced them husband and wife, she gladly relented her earlier title of the luckiest bride.

She was now the luckiest wife.

Don't miss the next sparkling novel
in the Cavensham Heiresses series

# THE GOOD, THE BAD,
# AND THE DUKE

Coming December 2018
from St. Martin's Paperbacks